Time traveler

She darted back across the redwood grove and dove
headlong into the Ancient One's hollow. Biting her lip,
she lifted the walking stick and struck it hard against the
wooden wall. Once, twice, three times.

Nothing happened.

She held the owl's head in front of her face, but no
illumination glowed within the yellow eyes. It was merely
a shaft of lifeless wood. "Take me back," she pleaded, her
voice trembling. "I don't belong here."

After waiting for an endless moment, she lowered the
stick reluctantly. Outside, Monga gave two sharp barks.
Kate leaned toward the light. Through the shifting mist
she saw the dog sitting, as before, next to Laioni, a living
member of the Halami tribe.

And she knew that she had traveled back in time.

THE
ancient one

T. A. BARRON

PUFFIN BOOKS

To my mother,
GLORIA BARRON

With special appreciation to
DENALI,
age three, for the name Kandeldandel

PUFFIN BOOKS
An imprint of Penguin Random House LLC
375 Hudson Street
New York, New York 10014

First published in the United States of America by Philomel Books,
a division of The Putnam & Grosset Book Group, 1992
Published by Ace Books, a division of Penguin Group (USA) Inc., 2004
Published by Puffin Books, an imprint of Penguin Young Readers Group, 2014
This edition published by Puffin Books, an imprint of Penguin Random House LLC, 2016

Text copyright © 1992 by Thomas A. Barron
Illustration copyright © 1992 by Anthony Bacon Venti

THE LIBRARY OF CONGRESS HAS CATALOGED THE PHILOMEL BOOKS EDITION AS FOLLOWS:
Barron, T. A.
The Ancient One / by T. A. Barron
p. cm.
Companion vol. to: Heartlight.
Summary: While helping her Great Aunt Melanie try to protect an Oregon redwood
forest from loggers, thirteen-year-old Kate goes back five centuries through a time
tunnel and faces the evil creature Gashra, who is bent on destroying the same forest.
ISBN 978-0-399-21899-6
[1. Time travel—Fiction. 2. Conservation of natural resources—Fiction. 3. Fantasy.]
I. Title.
PZ7.B27567An 1992 [Fic]—dc20 91-45862 CIP AC

Puffin Books ISBN 978-1-101-99702-4

Printed in the United States of America

1 3 5 7 9 10 8 6 4 2

The Halamis, the Native American people who figure prominently in this book, are completely fictional. All aspects of their life, including their beliefs and their mysterious disappearance several centuries ago, were created exclusively for this book. For authenticity, certain aspects of their culture are drawn from the author's research into the history of actual residents of the region, including the Tolowa, Takelma, Coos, Yurok, Wiyot, Hupa, Karok, Coquille, and Tututni peoples.

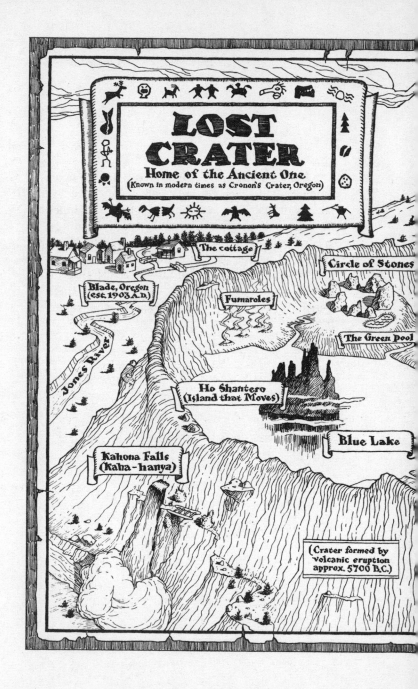

Brimstone Peak

Sanbu's camp

Dark Valley

Pacific Ocean

Atlantic Ocean

N
W E
S

Hidden Forest
(little people?)

New road entrance

Tinnani tunnel?

Swamp

Halami camp

True of heart and straight of spear
Find the forest walled in fear
Through the Gate of Death unknown
Past the Circle of the Stones
To the trees that touch the sky
Blessed by spirits ever nigh
Enter at the start of day
Dawn's first light will show the way
~Halami legend

A.B. Venti

INTRODUCTION
to the 2016 edition

Twenty-five years ago, I finished a new novel called *The Ancient One*. Unlike most of my books, whose titles have remained a mystery to me for much of the writing process, the title for this one announced itself loud and clear at the very start.

I knew that this book simply had to be named for the great redwood tree who was a towering presence (in every sense) in the story. For the Ancient One was more than a mighty creature, the oldest and grandest tree of the hidden forest in Lost Crater. It was, as well, a central character in the book, a sentient being, and a magical time tunnel.

What few people know is that *The Ancient One* was inspired by a hike in California when I encountered the most magnificent tree I'd ever seen—a redwood of such grandeur that I nearly fell over backward trying to see its highest boughs. As I came closer, the smell of its resins enveloped me. When I ran my hand across the deep creases of its bark, it was almost like touching the face of an old friend. My other plans for that day suddenly evaporated; I wanted to stay right there with the tree.

I lingered in that grove for the rest of the day. But at sunset, I still wasn't ready to leave. Though I hadn't expected to camp out, and hadn't brought a sleeping bag or food, I decided to stay for the night.

Snuggled against the ancient tree's gnarled trunk, I opened myself to the sounds, shapes, textures, and aromas around me. All through that night, I listened to the great tree's swaying, creaking, and—I felt sure—breathing. Just as I was breathing. Sharing the same air, the same moments, breath for breath.

Whether or not I slept that night, I don't remember. But I do remember feeling an extraordinary sense of peace. And I also remember wondering, all through the dark hours, what amazing stories this two-thousand-year-old tree could tell, what rich wisdom it could share. If only I could hear its authentic voice.

By the time the rosy rays of dawn touched the tree's uppermost branches, I knew I wanted to open myself to that voice. To hear those stories. And to travel through time with this awesome companion.

That campout began the journey that concluded—after two years, lots of research, nine drafts, and a whole lot of ink (since I write the first drafts of my books by hand)—with the novel you are about to read. My highest hope is that, amidst the adventure of Kate's journey back in time to the Native American tribe who had vanished so mysteriously, you will feel a hint of the majesty of that tree. I hope you'll catch a whiff of its sweet resins, feel its deeply rutted bark, and perhaps even hear its resonant voice.

For that voice is very, very old. Not as old as the mountains or the oceans—as the tree itself reminds Kate in the chapter "Deep Roots"—but far more ancient than any human being. That is why, even centuries ago in the time of the Native Americans, they reverently called that tree the Ancient One.

In the quarter century since its publication, *The Ancient One* has reached a wide audience. I recently received, for example, a long letter from a German woman whose passion for the book has led her to plan a trip to see the California redwoods. And I also just received a photo of the book (appropriately tattered and torn) from a family who took it hiking with them in Patagonia. Never would I have guessed the wide-ranging travels of this story, crafted in my attic with my writing pen.

That's the remarkable magic of stories. They do travel—reaching people in distant places as well as distant times. And they also reach deep into our hearts and minds.

Having now written more than thirty books, I am still surprised by how much more a story contains than its plot and characters. For stories are, in truth, vessels—boats that sail to faraway shores, carrying something far more valuable than physical treasures.

Ideas.

Stories enable us all, writers and readers alike, to consider large, complex ideas about life—but to do so indirectly, through the bent mirror of imagination. Those ideas often come in the form of questions: What difference does one life really make? Where do we find meaning? What, if anything, has lasting value?

To illustrate this point, consider the immense array of ideas carried in one well-known story: Noah's Ark. Ever since that story was first told many centuries ago, it has been shared and celebrated as a tale about faith, perseverance, and powers greater than ourselves. And it is also, I think, a parable about the responsibility of humanity to be wise stewards of nature and our fellow creatures—a parable that is more important than ever today. After all, if God asked Noah to go through so much trouble to protect two of every species—how can we do any less?

You will, of course, discover your own ideas in *The Ancient One*. For what it's worth, I would suggest that this story's questions might include: How are we all connected? Are there invisible bridges that link us to other people, other cultures, other times, and other species? What does it take to find those bridges—and cross them?

Now, before you begin this story, be warned: You may, like Kate, find yourself breathing not like a human being—but like a towering tree. If that happens . . . you may also discover what it's like to sink your roots deeply into the soil. To reach your boughs higher than you ever imagined, stretching toward the stars. And to experience the enduring peace of the most ancient tree of all.

— T. A. BARRON

contents

PART ONE: INTO THE CRATER

1 The Brown Envelope   3
2 Fennel Seeds and Scottish Roots   12
3 Visitors   22
4 Lost from Time   26
5 The Forgotten Trail   36
6 The Legend of Kahona Falls   45
7 Deadly Water   56
8 The Hidden Forest   68
9 The Walking Stick   75

PART TWO: INTO THE ISLAND

10 Maidenhair   87
11 Ebony Eyes   97
12 The Time Tunnel   107
13 The Circle of Stones   112
14 Fallen Brethren   124
15 The Blue Lake   133
16 Thika the Guardian   137

17 The Black Island of Ho Shantero   145
18 The Tale of the Broken Touchstone   157
19 Airborne   169
20 Call of the Owl   173
21 The Crossing   181
22 The Burial   191

PART THREE: INTO THE TREE

23 Night Vision   205
24 Attack   216
25 The Sacrifice   227
26 Dying Flames   232
27 Alone   238
28 In the Lair of the Wicked One   243
29 Torrent of Fire   256
30 Torchlight   263
31 The Fire of Love   268
32 Laioni's Promise   281
33 Deep Roots   287
34 New Light in the Forest   292

    Afterword   299

PART ONE

Into the Crater

1

the brown envelope

FIRST, God created Rain. Then Drizzle. Then Mist, then Fog. And then: More Rain.

Kate smiled soggily at her own adaptation of the story of creation, Oregon style. Her sneakers were wet enough that they squelched like sponges as she walked. She could feel the warmish water sloshing between her toes. No use even trying to stay dry anymore.

She stepped deliberately into a muddy puddle that nearly filled the heavily rutted street. The splash of water slapped against her lower leg, pressing jeans against shin, as brown circles spread outward from her submerged sneaker. Only Aunt Melanie's bright green shoelaces, reluctantly accepted by Kate when her own ones broke, remained visible in the muddy water.

Water everywhere. At this very moment, she could be curled up by the fireplace, stroking the shaggy gray cat Atha. But Aunt Melanie, usually delighted to spend a rainy afternoon warmed by fire coals, quilts, and homemade spice tea, was in no mood for such things just now. Something was troubling her, something serious. So serious she didn't want to talk about it, even to Kate.

She had thought about calling her parents. They'd know what to do, what to make of all this. But they were on that ship, with only a radio telephone on board. Her mother had given her the number in case of an emergency, but Kate did not want to use it. She knew better than anyone how much they needed a few days together without telephone calls, faculty meetings, or research projects that kept them working until all hours. Besides, this was not an emergency, not yet anyway. She had to work this thing out on her own, without any help from Mom and Dad. And, she thought with a sigh, without any help from Grandfather.

A lone hound, squatting beneath a dripping wooden bench, shook himself vigorously. As Kate turned toward him, the dog ceased shaking and gazed back at her, watching her pass with expressionless eyes.

Just a few minutes ago, when Aunt Melanie had checked her watch and realized it was nearly five o'clock, she had beseeched Kate to run to the post office before it closed. Never mind the downpour, or the fact that Kate was warm and dry for the first time since arriving at the cottage five days ago. Muttering something about an important telephone call she had been waiting for all day, Aunt Melanie said she could not go herself. With an edge of urgency, she described the envelope she was expecting: long and brown, pretty thick, the kind lawyers like to use.

Why lawyers? Kate had asked, but her great-aunt didn't answer. She merely ran a hand through her curls of white hair and glanced out the window toward the dark reaches of forest beyond, where the whine of distant chain saws mingled with the sound of swishing branches. Then she had handed Kate her rain jacket and pulled open the cottage door.

Kate leaped across a small stream flowing through a rut, only to land with a splash in another puddle. Without the slightest pause, she continued walking. Her many visits to

Aunt Melanie over the years had developed in her a grudging appreciation for the gentle rains of this land. There was something she had come to expect and even, at rare moments, enjoy about the sound of soft rain on the old cottage roof, the awareness of lush greenery all around, the mist against her cheeks. So much rain back home would have depressed her thoroughly, especially if it meant canceling an after-school softball game. But here in the forest country of southwestern Oregon, the rain felt no worse than a nuisance. It was part of the landscape, just as much as the trees.

Trudging onward, Kate surveyed the scene on Main Street even as her mind played over and over again Aunt Melanie's words. *Long and brown, pretty thick, the kind lawyers like to use.* Although Blade, Oregon, didn't pretend to be a booming metropolis, it could claim most of life's necessities. Blurred by mud and mist, the storefronts seemed to run together like an oversized watercolor painting. She passed the local Laundromat, right next to the Texaco station, where townspeople often gathered for good conversation. This afternoon, though, it was deserted. The street itself was strangely empty, nothing but a string of connected puddles.

As she turned the corner, the scene swiftly changed. A jumble of cars, Jeeps, and mud-splattered pickups lined the street outside of Cary's Tavern. There was even a logging truck, bearing emblems of snarling tigers on its mud flaps, double parked near the entrance. Of course, thought Kate. It's Saturday afternoon. She had seen Cary's Tavern once before on a Saturday—packed to the rafters with loggers, fifty percent sober and one hundred percent boisterous, celebrating the end of another hard week's work. Or, as Aunt Melanie had told her was the case more and more, mourning the end of another week without work.

As she approached the tavern, she could tell today's mood was not one of celebration. She heard several angry voices rising above the downpour. Several loggers, wearing gray and yellow rain jackets, milled around outside in the parking lot despite the wetness. One pair sat behind slashing windshield wipers, engaged in heated conversation. But she had no time to investigate. It was five minutes to five.

Breaking into a jog, she splashed down the remaining block to the old brick building sporting a white cardboard sign in the window with the words *Post Office*. She scampered up the moss-coated wooden steps, slowing only to reach for the rusted door handle. At that instant, the door flung wide open and a lean, red-haired boy not much older than Kate's thirteen years darted out, clutching a parcel of some sort under his arm.

They plowed straight into each other. Kate tumbled backward down the slippery steps, landing on her back in the muddy street. The boy cried out in surprise, almost landing on top of her.

"Hey, watch where you're going," he said accusingly, wiping some mud from his cheek with the sleeve of his yellow rain jacket.

"Watch yourself," Kate retorted. Suddenly her eyes fell upon the parcel the boy had been carrying, now resting on the street only an arm's length away. It was an envelope, brown and shaped like a long rectangle. She caught her breath as she read the name clearly typed on the mailing label: *Melanie Prancer.*

The boy snatched up the brown envelope, rose quickly, and started running down the street in the direction of Cary's Tavern.

"Hey, come back," Kate shouted. She leaped to her feet and flew after him with the speed of a shortstop dashing to snag a line drive. They raced past the buildings of the town, their feet pounding through the puddles. Kate gained on him, but slowly. Just before the parking lot outside the tavern, the boy swerved toward the assembled vehicles.

Kate stretched out an arm and barely caught him by the collar of his rain jacket. She pulled, and the boy lurched backward, his feet sliding out from under him. Before he had even hit the ground, she was on top of him.

"Give me that," she demanded, pulling at the brown envelope.

"No way," answered the boy, struggling to hang on. He kicked at her savagely, spraying mud into the air.

Finally, Kate loosened his grip enough to yank the envelope away. Just then the boy rolled to his knees and butted against her with such force that she fell back into a deep puddle. The brown envelope skidded across the muddy street, coming to rest at the edge of a rut just outside the tavern. Kate crawled madly after it.

As her fingers started to close on the edge of the envelope, a heavy boot slammed down on top of it. At once, Kate knew it was the boot of a logger—beat-up brown leather, without steel toes because if a tree trunk falls on a logger's foot he prefers to have his toes crushed rather than sliced off by the steel lining. She raised her head, seeing the heavy denim pants, the burly chest wearing a yellow slicker over a white T-shirt saying *I love spotted owls—for dinner,* and the grinning face looking down on her from under a weather-beaten hard hat.

She tugged on the brown envelope. "It's mine," she said.

The boot did not budge. For a moment, nothing seemed to move but the grin, which widened slightly.

"Mine," repeated Kate, tugging unsuccessfully. "The envelope's mine."

The man, whose brown eyes watched the girl at his feet with amusement, spoke gruffly. "What envelope?"

Kate furrowed her brow. "This one, here. You're standing on it."

"I don't see any envelope," he answered. He turned toward an older boy standing nearby, as burly as himself but not as tall. "Sly, do you see any envelope?"

"No," the older boy answered, himself grinning. "All I see is my brother Billy, and some girl who likes to crawl around in mud puddles."

At that moment, the red-haired boy, his yellow slicker splattered with mud, moved to Billy's side. "Well," he said, eyeing Kate hatefully. "I brought you the envelope."

"Yeah," answered Sly, stepping closer to them. "But you brought her too."

"I couldn't help it," protested the red-haired boy, bending his lean frame to retrieve the brown envelope. Billy lifted his boot just enough to let him slide it out. "She chased me here from the post office."

The big logger gave him a teasing shove on the shoulder. "That's a new experience for you, getting chased by a girl." He winked at Sly. "He's so excited, he's still puffing like a bay steer."

Even in the rain, the boy's blush was clearly visible. "Look," he said, waving the envelope. "You asked me to get it, and I did. It wasn't so easy, either."

"You're a thief," declared Kate.

Billy's grin disappeared as he concentrated his gaze on her. "Go home now and there won't be any trouble."

Kate pushed herself to her feet. Her heart pounded, but she made herself look the broad-shouldered man directly in the eye. "That's not your envelope. It's not. It's addressed to my Aunt Melanie."

"Aunt Melanie?" asked Billy, his eyebrows lifting. "So you're related to the old schoolteacher?"

"Yes. And that envelope belongs to her."

Billy scowled at the red-haired boy. "You really botched this one, Jody." He stepped toward Kate, so that his ample chest almost touched her chin. "You've got five seconds to disappear, kid. Are you gonna go all by yourself, or do I have to chase you from here to hell's half acre?"

Before Kate could reply, a heavily laden logging truck rumbled down the street. The noise drowned out the voices from Cary's Tavern as it splashed past. Just as Billy, Sly, and Jody turned toward the sound, Kate lunged at the brown envelope, tearing it from Jody's hand. She darted behind the logging truck and ran as fast as she could down an alley behind the tavern.

Leaping over a broken crate, Kate could hear the slapping sound of heavy boots behind her. She grasped the brown envelope as tightly as she could, determined not to lose it again. Not even when she stole home plate in the league softball tournament in May had she run so fast. Yet the heavy boots drew closer by the second, smacking against the mud.

She didn't dare turn around. All her energy was focused on one thing and one thing only: running. For her life. Now she could hear someone's breathing drawing nearer. Seeing a corner just ahead, she didn't slow down even to make the turn.

As she rounded the corner, her foot suddenly slid out from under her. She lost her balance, flipping onto her back in a spray of brown water. Lifting her head, she saw Billy, followed by his brother and the red-haired boy, bearing down on her. Billy's eyes glared angrily as he ran right at her, barreling ahead like a fully loaded logging truck.

Kate rolled to her hands and knees in the deep puddle, still clutching the envelope. She wanted to scream, but her throat released no sound. Water dripped down her back and across her abdomen. She stiffened, preparing to be caught.

Then, unaccountably, Billy and the others ran straight past her, as if she weren't even there. The heavy boots slapped into the puddle, only inches from her submerged fingers, splashing muddy water in her eyes.

As she wiped her face with the inner collar of her jacket, she slowly lifted herself to her feet, panting heavily. Her pursuers turned a corner onto the next street, their pounding boots punctuating the steady sound of the rain. *How?* she asked in disbelief. *How did they miss me?*

At that instant, she heard a rustling sound behind her. Out from the shadows of the windowless building on the corner stepped a diminutive figure, whose curly white hair was visible at the edges of a tightly drawn hood. Holding in one hand a slender walking stick, the figure regarded her intently.

"Aunt Melanie," cried Kate, stumbling toward her. "Did you see that? They—they were chasing me. But when— when I fell, they—"

"Easy, dear, easy," said the woman in a soothing voice.

"Ran right on like—like they didn't, didn't even see me," panted Kate. "I don't get it. They were chasing me, I know it."

Aunt Melanie merely nodded, her dark eyes glinting. She tapped her walking stick sharply against the side of her boot, as if trying to knock some mud off it.

Kate started to speak again, when her attention was caught by the walking stick. For a brief instant, the yellow eyes of the carved owl's head on the handle seemed to glow strangely. Then, swiftly, the brightness faded.

Puzzled, Kate looked over her shoulder to see the sun trying to make a late-afternoon appearance through the slackening rain. Of course, she realized. It's just catching the sunlight. She turned again to the stick, now looking like an ordinary piece of wood, its color and grain dulled by wetness. The owl's head handle had no more life than the handle of an old umbrella.

She shook her head and focused once more on Aunt Melanie. "How could they have missed me?"

Blowing a drop of water from the tip of her nose, the woman examined Kate thoughtfully. Her white curls, studded with raindrops, framed her face like a fluffy cloud. "Heaven only knows. I daresay they were going awfully fast. Why were they chasing you?"

Proudly, Kate raised the brown envelope. Mud streaked its crumpled surface, obscuring the address label. But Aunt Melanie recognized it immediately, and her eyes opened wide.

"Good grief. You mean they tried to steal my mail?"

Kate nodded. "Came pretty close, too."

Aunt Melanie took the brown envelope and stuffed it into the pocket of her blue rain jacket. "Never thought they'd stoop to such a thing, or I wouldn't have sent you. Something told me I shouldn't have let you go by yourself. I'm glad the phone call finally came, so I could come after you." She pursed her lips. "This whole town is coming apart at the seams."

"What do you mean by that?"

"Oh, nothing, nothing. You're all right, though?"

Refusing to let her change the subject, Kate asked, "Aren't you going to see what's in it? Must be pretty important."

"It can wait till I get home." With a tilt of her head, Aunt Melanie beckoned Kate to follow and started walking down the deserted street. "Let's get moving before they decide to come back this way. Billy's got a nasty temper."

Kate frowned, reluctantly giving up for the moment. She trotted to her great-aunt's side, musing, "Sure would be nice if we could make ourselves invisible any time we wanted."

Aunt Melanie made no response. She merely hesitated slightly in her step, as if she had caught her foot on something, then resumed her normal pace. The walking stick continued to poke its way rhythmically through mud puddle after mud puddle.

2

fennel seeds and scottish roots

THEY turned down a side street, soon leaving behind the last moss-covered buildings of Blade. As they passed a junkyard piled high with used tires and rusting auto parts, the rain ceased, at least temporarily. Kate threw back her hood, unsnapped her jacket. The thought of her pursuers began to fade, like water evaporating in the sun's rays.

Before long they reached the bridge across Jones River, so murky from erosion that it supported no more than a few struggling fish. Kate leaned over the railing to watch the dark water flowing under the bridge. Someone had tied an old tire to a worn length of rope and dangled it from the branch of a sturdy cedar across the bank, making a simple swing.

Instinctively, she stooped to pick up a small rock, hefted it for a moment in her right hand, then hurled it at the tire. The rock whooshed straight through the hole in the middle, striking the trunk of the cedar with a smack.

"Not bad," said Aunt Melanie, laughing. "I can see why you're so good at baseball."

"Softball," corrected Kate. "Someday I'll have to teach

you how to throw. Who knows? You might end up a better shortstop than me."

"Don't count on it. Remember what happened when you tried to explain baseball cards to me?"

Kate shook her head. "I couldn't even get into hall-of-famers and batting averages. I spent the whole time convincing you that a baseball club and a baseball bat are two different things."

The elder woman grinned at the younger. "Consider that an accomplishment, dear."

They continued walking, soon reaching a lane lined with Norway spruce, whose upturned boughs never failed to make Kate wonder whether they had happy, uplifted spirits. Of course, trees didn't really have individual personalities, but it was fun to imagine such things nonetheless.

Not far up the road she spied a rusted green mailbox with hand-painted black letters reading *Melanie Prancer.* Parked next to the mailbox, leaning precariously in a deep rut, was an equally rusted red Jeep. Trusty, Aunt Melanie called it. A soggy daisy hung twisted around the top of the antenna.

Kate leaped across the permanent puddle beneath the mailbox and stood facing the cottage. It was a cramped, box-shaped structure, thought to be the first house built in the settlement of Blade almost a hundred years ago. The old squared-off logs, hewn with a broad ax so that diagonal chop marks were still visible, were warped to the point where the chinking in some places was as wide as the logs themselves. Permanently musty, the house felt cold in the summer and still colder in the winter. Aunt Melanie's heating system consisted of a large fireplace, a small electric space heater (reserved for overnight guests), and a huge cedar chest filled with bulky sweaters of all colors, styles, and patterns.

Tiny though the cottage was, it was roomy enough for Aunt Melanie. As long as she had space for a few garden tools, her favorite Native American artifacts, and a jar or two of peppermint candies, she could practically live inside the trunk of a tree. At times she even reminded Kate of some spritely gnome, standing amidst the sword ferns and flowering rhododendrons that surrounded the little house, smelling like spice tea and wet moss, scratching the top of her white head with a look of both wonder and mischief. Also like a gnome, she had the annoying habit of appearing and disappearing suddenly, usually when Kate least expected it.

Rain started falling again, and Kate pulled up her hood. At that moment, two mud-splattered ducks waddled onto the driveway, side by side, quacking noisily. Like a pair of old men trading boastful tales, they jabbered constantly, oblivious to anyone else. She recognized them as Chuck and Chuckles, the ducks Aunt Melanie had adopted, or more accurately, who had adopted Aunt Melanie, last spring. They waddled over to the puddle by the mailbox and began to glide around, quacking continually.

From the moment Aunt Melanie had invited her to spend the first week of summer vacation with her here at the cottage, Kate had known that this visit would be different from the others. Not just because her parents would be on the ship and unreachable the whole time. Though she would not allow herself to say so out loud, she hoped in her heart that being here would help her get over Grandfather's death.

I still miss him, she told herself, brushing away from her nostrils the river of drizzle that started at the crook in her hood and ran all the way down the bridge of her nose. She remembered Grandfather saying once that the creation of the universe wasn't just a onetime event, that it was going on all the time, right now even—that the briefest afternoon shower helped continue the process. Given that, she thought wryly, this rain-soaked land must be the most creative place on earth. Grandfather hated foul weather. It depressed him. Made him, as he said, think like a duck instead of a man. He never could understand why his younger sister had chosen to teach school in rural Oregon, where any creatures who lacked webbed feet were at a big disadvantage.

Visiting Aunt Melanie was more than an escape, though it was a relief for Kate not to look out her window every day and see the garden where she and Grandfather had so often picnicked, where not even the relentlessly playful golden retriever Cumberland felt like playing anymore. More important was the simple fact of Aunt Melanie's quiet company. No words needed. Whether they were baking bread together, or husking corn before supper, or walking in the woods, Kate felt accepted with all her flaws, in a way that could heal even the deepest wounds.

She watched as her great-aunt mounted the cottage's stone step and fiddled with her keys. She seemed very small, even delicate, the sort of person one could easily pass on the street without noticing. It was Aunt Melanie's eyes that were impossible to forget: dark, almost black, resonant as ebony, with a few flecks of hazel green around the edges of the pupils. Eyes like hers seemed to reveal Native American, rather than Scottish, ancestry. Her high cheekbones and wide face also contributed to the impression. Only yesterday, Kate had found an old photograph of her as a youngster (with jet black hair instead of the current creamy white) playing with Grandfather on the Isle of Skye, and it was impossible to tell they were related to each other.

As Kate herself ascended the step, she paused to read the crudely carved wooden plaque leaning against the porch railing:

> There is a pleasure in the pathless woods,
> There is a rapture on the lonely shore,
> There is society, where none intrudes,
> By the deep sea, and music in its roar:
> I love not man the less, but Nature more.

She recalled that Lord Byron's words had once hung on the front door, but the plaque was torn off and broken by some rowdy high school students last year. Aunt Melanie had put the pieces back together, with some help from a carpenter friend, but had not gotten around to hanging it again.

A few moments later, having deposited her foul weather gear in the mud room and her wet sneakers by the hearth, Kate was cuddled beneath a soft blue-gray quilt in front of the fireplace. She knew her damp jeans would dry quickly. Aunt Melanie rested beneath her own quilt, a green and lavender check, in the rocking chair opposite, sipping spice tea.

Pulling her quilt higher so that it wrapped around the back of her neck, Kate blew across the rim of her stoneware mug and took a swallow. "We had this kind this morning. What's in it? Tastes so different from other teas. Sweeter somehow."

"Crushed fennel seeds," came the reply. "Good thing you like it, since it's the only kind I have right now. It's good for afternoon chills." The white-haired woman paused reflectively. "And other things too."

Kate blew again, sipped again. "Like what?"

Aunt Melanie grinned imperceptibly. "Like making youngsters ask lots of questions."

Crinkling her nose, Kate protested, "Come on, tell me."

"Well, if you really want to know . . ." she began, before her voice trailed off. She loosened her quilt and slid forward in her chair. Casting her eyes around the room in mock suspicion, she whispered, "Drinking fennel seeds can make you invisible."

Kate giggled, dribbling some tea down her chin. "So that's why Billy missed me?"

Aunt Melanie savored the question, then replied, "Yes, but it only works on people as big as tugboats."

They both burst out laughing. Aunt Melanie shook so hard that some of her tea sloshed onto her quilt. "Of course," she added, "the bigger they are the more fennel seeds it takes." She dabbed at the spilled tea with a tattered kerchief from her pocket.

"I thought maybe those neon green shoelaces you gave me scared them off," teased Kate.

"Really, now," answered Aunt Melanie, pretending to

be insulted. "Those laces have nothing to do with neon. They're bright, that's all. Like new green leaves on the first day of spring."

"More like the sign in front of Cary's Tavern, if you ask me."

Aunt Melanie shook her head. "No taste in your generation, none at all." She winked at Kate. "Of course, there was no taste in my generation either. We're the ones who invented supermarkets and eight-lane highways." Then all at once, her mirth evaporated. "All the same," she muttered, "it's hard to believe they'd try something like that."

Kate studied her closely. Her thickly woven Cowichan sweater, milky white and decorated with rows of tiny black eagles with wings spread wide, bunched up against her chin so that she looked almost like an owl peering out from a small snowdrift. From each of her ears dangled a string of silvery shells that clinked together gently whenever she turned her head.

No other person in Kate's experience was quite like Aunt Melanie, certainly no other schoolteacher. She could be playful as a kitten or solemn as a tree stump. Something about her just didn't seem to belong here in the middle of rural Oregon. Yet that wasn't it, exactly. Aunt Melanie didn't seem so much out of place as she seemed, inexplicably, out of *time*. There was something mysteriously ageless about her, both younger and older than her years, almost as if she belonged in some other century.

Kate especially enjoyed the times when Aunt Melanie— usually crunching on a peppermint—shared some of her knowledge of Native American lore. She knew as much as anyone alive about the Halamis, a people who vanished so long ago from this area that their lives were almost completely veiled in mystery. Sometimes Kate would return to the cottage to find a Native American friend sitting by the fire with Aunt Melanie, trading speculations about why the Halamis disappeared so suddenly, almost without a trace. And Aunt Melanie's library on Halami life and culture was so good that professors, researchers, and archaeologists from all over the region often stopped by just to borrow a book or check a reference.

Yet it was less the lore than the telling itself that Kate so loved. There was an air of elemental peacefulness in Aunt Melanie when she told some of those nearly forgotten stories, customs, and recipes, an air she seemed to inhale and exhale in deep drafts. More than once Kate had wished that some of that peaceful quality might enter her own being and choose to stay, at least for a while.

This week, however, there had been no time for Halami lore. Whatever was on Aunt Melanie's mind, it crowded out almost everything else. She was more relaxed right now than she had been since Kate's arrival. Maybe whatever was in the brown envelope had solved the problem, or at least made it better.

"So tell me, what was in the envelope?" she ventured, trying her best to sound casual.

Aunt Melanie, who was looking at the fire, started. "Oh, just some papers—legal papers." She worked her jaw for a moment. "I really don't want to talk about it, dear. Maybe another time."

Sensing it would be fruitless to push, Kate forced herself to rein in her curiosity for the time being. She took one of the still-warm oatmeal cookies piled on the plate on the knotted spruce table in front of the fire, dunked it deep into her mug, let it drip into the tea for a few seconds, then took a hearty bite. "I love dunking," she said through a mouthful.

"You definitely have Scottish roots," observed Aunt Melanie, her expression more relaxed again. She reached for one of the peppermint candies resting in an abalone shell next to the cookies. Pulling off the plastic wrapping, she popped the red-and-white striped sweet into her mouth. "No doubt about it."

Placing her mug on the table, Kate gazed across the room to the rickety bookshelf behind Aunt Melanie. In addition to notebooks, articles, and unpublished treatises about the Halamis, it was stacked haphazardly with books on trees, edible plants, and forest ecology. Her eyes followed the lines of the warped living-room window, its sill crowded with a small painted drum, a slab of bark from a Douglas fir, a bag of twisted roots, and a delicate miniature basket that conjured up the image of a Halami woman skillfully weaving it long ago. The room seemed more like the local natural history museum than part of someone's house.

Next to the fireplace rested the walking stick, the deeply carved markings on its shaft reflecting the shifting light of the fire. For the first time, Kate noticed that the face of the owl's head looked oddly human from a distance. The beak could almost pass for a jutting nose; the mouth was more like a man's than a bird's. Only the enormous eyes, yellow and unblinking, were unmistakably those of an owl. They seemed to be watching her closely, observing her every movement.

Just then, a gray cat with white paws padded into the room. Athabasca (called Atha for short) had lived with Aunt Melanie for nearly a decade and was still limber enough to catch an unsuspecting bird on a low-hanging branch. As she passed the fireplace, the cat made a wide detour around the walking stick, as if sensing some secret danger. In two bounds, she leaped to the piano bench and then to the top of the old upright that had never been in tune as long as Kate could remember.

Kate turned in her high-back chair so that the crackling fire could warm her other side. She could almost see steam rising from her damp jeans under the quilt.

"How do you do it?" she asked suddenly.

"Do what, dear?"

"You always seem so, I don't know, so comfortable being in lots of different places, or really times, at once. In this house things that are centuries apart feel so natural together. It makes me feel—well, amazed."

Aunt Melanie crunched down on her peppermint and eyed her pensively. "Is that all you feel?"

Shifting her position under the quilt, Kate said slowly,

"I guess . . . I guess it also bugs me a little. Maybe because there's part of me that would like to be that way too. Connected. Part of something. I mean, I don't even really feel at home in my own town, in my own time. About the only time I feel like I belong there is when I'm shagging balls to somebody behind the house for a few hours. Pretty weird, huh?"

Aunt Melanie stroked her chin, considering the question. "No," she said finally. "It's not weird. Maybe your hometown just isn't big enough to hold you. The world is a big place, you know, full of all kinds of connections. You might find that you're one of those people meant to touch many different times and places. That requires certain gifts, you know."

Kate shook her head. "Whatever they are, I'm sure I don't have them."

"Don't be so certain." A slight grin formed at the corners of her mouth. "Maybe what you need is a vision quest."

"A what?"

"A vision quest. The Halamis, when they got to be your age—aren't you thirteen or so already?—would go off to some remote place in the mountains, sleep alone, fend for themselves for a while. They'd come back with a new understanding of themselves, of their own power." Observing Kate's glum expression, she added, "Forget that. All you really need is a little more humor about yourself."

Again Kate shifted, drawing the quilt closer. "I suppose I have a lot to laugh about."

"We all do." Aunt Melanie leaned back in her rocking chair, which creaked loudly. "I hope you at least appreciate how much it's meant to me to have you here this week. I'm afraid I've been rather distracted." Her expression clouded. "But there never was a time when I needed good company like I do right now."

Kate lowered the quilt and leaned forward, her long braid coiled upon the tabletop. "Aunt Melanie, why is some lawyer sending you mail? And why did they want to steal it? Seems like something pretty strange is going on."

Aunt Melanie's already wrinkled brow wrinkled even more. "You're right about that, dear. Stranger than you know." She sighed, and her dark eyes concentrated on Kate. "But I don't want to get you involved. The kind of help I need is more than any human being can give, I'm afraid."

"But—" protested Kate.

"No buts. That's all I have to say." A sudden idea came to her. "I'll let you help with one thing, though." She found Kate's knee beneath her quilt and squeezed it gently before reaching for her walking stick. "How would you like to come give me a hand in the kitchen? I've got all the makings of a good salad set out. You do that while I do the salmon. It's getting on toward supper time." She set her mug on the table with a thump of finality.

Pouting, Kate protested: "Are you sure there's nothing else I can do?"

Aunt Melanie started to say something, then caught herself. "You can peel the avocado."

Kate shook her head. In a beaten tone, she muttered, "You share another thing with Grandfather. Total, complete, absolute stubbornness."

Feigning a frown, the woman asked, "What's the matter? Don't you like avocados?"

"Sure I do. I just—"

"Enough," said Aunt Melanie, raising a weathered hand. "I know you'd like to help, dear, but you can't." She rose from the rocking chair, leaving her quilt crumpled on the seat. Then, forcing a smile, she added, "I'm glad you like avocados. Me, I can't get enough of them."

Kate stared at her blankly.

Her brow again deeply furrowed, Aunt Melanie whispered, "Don't worry about me, dear. I'll be fine." She pivoted on the walking stick and started toward the kitchen.

Just then they heard a loud banging on the front door.

visitors

Two sodden figures faced them on the porch. Closest to the door was an older man, tall and gaunt, whose torn gray jacket hung on his body like a loose sack. His crystal blue eyes, though strangely sorrowful, looked as if they belonged to a much younger man. Behind him stood the red-haired boy who had tried to steal the brown envelope. He shifted nervously, peering down at his shoes.

Aunt Melanie regarded them solemnly. Finally she said, "Good day, Frank."

"Wish it was," the man replied, his voice joyless. "Hasn't been a good day in this town for near on eight years."

Kate moved closer, so that her arm was lightly touching Aunt Melanie's. Several seconds passed with no one willing to speak. Then Frank broke the silence.

"Look, Melanie," he began. "We've been friends a long time, you and me. Helped each other out a few times. More than a few, in fact. I didn't come over here today expecting to change your thinking, but I wanted to warn you. The

temperature in town is getting hot. Real hot. People are
bound to do almost anything to keep the sawmill running."

Aunt Melanie studied him without emotion. "Including
stealing other people's mail?"

The red-haired boy lifted his head. As his eyes met
Kate's, they narrowed with anger. She returned the favor,
staring back icily.

"I'm not excusing that," said Frank earnestly. "But you've
got to remember what it's like for all the folks who work
like hell beating tan bark just to get through the day. When
you start bringing in some fancy lawyers, they get mad.
And for good reason."

"They were my last resort, Frank. I hate lawyers as much
as you do, and you know it. You and the others wouldn't listen to reason, no matter what I tried. You were about to
destroy the whole crater, before we even know what's up
there. The injunction gives us all a little time, that's all."

"People don't need time, they need jobs." His face reddened. "For heaven's sake, Melanie! Sometimes I think all
you care about is owls and trees. Not people."

Aunt Melanie stiffened. "Of course I care about people.
Why else do I spend all my days laboring with youngsters?"
She shot a glance at the red-haired boy, who avoided her
gaze. "But you can't just keep on destroying the forest without giving something back. Look around, will you? Clear-
cuts everyplace. If we're having tough times, the fault
belongs to all of us—me, you, and everybody else who let
the forest get cut faster than it could grow back—not the
folks who want to save the few remaining scraps."

"I'm not disputing that," retorted Frank. "But people
have to eat somehow."

Aunt Melanie's voice dropped to a hoarse whisper.
"Those old trees were God's first temple, and now they're
almost gone."

At that, Jody spoke, though without looking at Aunt
Melanie. "The preacher says trees weren't made in God's
image. But men were."

The white-haired woman looked at him sadly. "I wish, Jody, you'd use your own good head instead of just repeating whatever Reverend Natello says. Then maybe you could decide for yourself what's right."

Jody continued to stare at his shoes.

"You might try to ask the reverend a few questions," added Aunt Melanie in a gentle voice. "Ask him whether God made all the creatures of the earth, including the ones we're wiping out. Or you could remind him of the Psalm that says *the righteous shall flourish . . . like a cedar in Lebanon,* and then ask him why there aren't any cedars left in Lebanon now. Ask him why the people cut them down so fast they never grew back."

"I wouldn't waste his time," snorted the boy.

"That's enough, Jody," snapped Frank. "I didn't bring you along to act rude."

"Then why did you bring him along?" demanded Aunt Melanie. "To hear you spout the same old wisdom that got us into this holy mess in the first place?"

A pained look crossed the logger's careworn face. His shoulders sagged from his drenched clothes and something still more weighty. "Understand me, Melanie. I'm only trying to do what I can to keep this place from becoming a ghost town."

For an instant, she regarded him with unmistakable tenderness. Puzzled, Kate pondered this. Then Aunt Melanie's jaw tightened and she asked, "But why steal my mail, Frank? What good does that do?"

"Some of the boys thought, well . . . They thought it might put things off. I tried to talk them out of it, but they wouldn't listen."

"Whatever are they thinking, Frank? The injunction starts on Monday whether I get my mail or not. The crater's off limits. There's no way to change that now."

Jody raised his head and started to say something, when Frank suddenly cut him off. "That's right," he agreed. "No way to change that now."

Aunt Melanie eyed him suspiciously. "What aren't you telling me?"

The crystal blue eyes peered at her. "Nothing, nothing at all. I just wanted to warn you that you're best off staying at home for the next few days, until this whole thing blows over."

At that moment, Chuck and Chuckles came waddling up the driveway, quacking proudly in duet. They hopped up the stone step and walked single file between Jody's legs. While Chuck continued on his way across the porch, Chuckles chose to linger momentarily by the boy's left boot. Jody, watching Frank's face, paid no attention until, with a loud quack of satisfaction, the duck made an unceremonious deposit of greenish-brown matter on his toe.

"Hey!" the boy exclaimed, kicking the duck down the step. Quacking and fluttering in protest, Chuckles quickly collected himself and started to waddle back toward the mailbox. Hearing Kate's snickering, Jody glared at her. Then he turned back to Frank and declared, "I'm leaving." Thrusting his hands in his pockets, he wheeled around and walked off.

Frank lingered on the porch, studying Aunt Melanie closely. He started to speak, hesitated, then shook his head, spraying some water from his rubberized hat. He turned away, moving off into the rain. Soon he was nothing more than a misty shadow.

Slowly Aunt Melanie closed the door, leaning heavily on the handle of her stick. The normal ruddiness had drained from her cheeks. Facing Kate, she said simply, "Something's wrong."

4

lost from time

NOT until supper had been prepared, eaten, and completely cleared did Aunt Melanie choose to speak again. Kate had been waiting, it seemed endlessly, for the silence to break. She had hardly tasted her salmon.

Laying her thin hands firmly on the dining table, a wide slab of richly grained fir resting against the kitchen wall, Aunt Melanie drew in a deep breath. "You're about to get your wish."

Before Kate could respond, Aunt Melanie reached for a weather-beaten roll of paper resting on the row of teacups above the table. With the mud-stained paper in one hand and her walking stick in the other, she started down the hall toward the living room. "Come," she said distractedly. "We'll light the fire first. Bring the pie and the plates."

Soon the fireplace was crackling and orange-tinted shadows flickered across the walls. The room seemed very different to Kate now that the sun had gone down. Firelight now played upon its contents, coaxing out textures and colors less visible in the harsher light of day. Facing Aunt Melanie, she asked, "What's wrong?"

Aunt Melanie didn't answer, but began to unfurl the roll of paper. Using her walking stick to hold down one end and two plates to anchor the other, she flattened it across the knotted spruce table.

It was a map of southwestern Oregon. Amidst the many shades of green that indicated national, state, or private forest lands, Kate could see dozens of winding river canyons flowing westward to the Pacific Ocean. Between the coast and the rugged chain of mountains that ran forty or fifty miles inland, there were several small towns. Kate found herself searching for the name Blade.

"There," said Aunt Melanie, pointing to one black dot, about ten miles inland from the coast, surrounded by a wide swath of green. "That's us." Moving her finger in a wide circle around the spot, she added, "Most of this area's been logged at least once."

"What's this?" asked Kate, pointing to a place a few miles east of town marked Cronon's Crater. A large blue lake sat in the middle, ringed by densely packed contour lines that were broken only by a single high waterfall spilling into a rugged river canyon.

"That's the crater Frank and I were talking about. It's called Cronon's Crater by the mapmakers." Aunt Melanie paused, weighing her words carefully. "But I call it Lost Crater." She swung her eyes toward the fire. "Why it had to appear just now, I'll never know."

"I don't understand," Kate said. "That crater must have been there for ages."

Aunt Melanie turned from the fire, light from the coals still playing on her face. "Not so long, really. In geologic terms, I mean. It's what's left of an ancient volcano that appeared, oh, maybe eight or nine million years ago. Then, about seven thousand years ago, it exploded so violently that the summit collapsed completely, leaving nothing but the huge crater—technically, a caldera—that you see there on the map."

She reached toward the abalone shell of peppermint candies that had been pushed to the edge of the table and then, thinking the better of it, withdrew her hand. "Got to cut back on those," she muttered. "Such a bad habit." Her gaze fell to a cozy gingerbread house that had rested on the bookshelf behind her rocking chair since Christmas, and her eyebrows suddenly lifted. Pinching one of the striped peppermints from the row upon its roof, she said somewhat sheepishly to Kate, "But first I have to finish these or they'll go stale." She popped it into her mouth. "Now, where were we?"

"The crater. You were starting to say why it's such a big deal."

"Oh, yes," said Aunt Melanie, biting into the peppermint with a hearty crunch. "You've got to understand something first. Lost Crater is so steep it's literally unclimbable. It rises a good three thousand feet from the forest floor, much of that straight up. The only way anyone's even known there's a lake inside is from aerial photographs. But since the crater is almost always filled with fog, even those are rare."

"What's all this got to do with the loggers?" pressed Kate, increasingly exasperated. "I still don't get it."

"You will, dear. You see, everyone assumed the lake filled the crater completely. And who'd be foolish enough to try to scale those slippery walls to find out? For most people, it's been just a blank spot on the map, not even worth a second thought. The kind of place Scotsmen call *the Back of Beyond.*"

She pointed to the map. "See this big waterfall coming out of the crater? The mapmakers didn't even bother to name it, even though it's one of the biggest around. A few of us call it Kahona Falls, after the old Halami name, but for most people it doesn't even exist."

Her finger traced the crater's steep contours. "Nobody even takes a hike up there. There's never been a road, not even a trail, that goes the whole way." She smiled almost imperceptibly. "At least none that anyone knows about."

Aunt Melanie's eyes, dark as the bark of rain-washed

cedar, concentrated on the girl by her side. "It's a forgotten place, Kate. Lost. Lost from time." She sighed, running her left hand along the shaft of her stick. "Until now."

Kate leaned forward. "Why until now?"

The earrings clinked gently as Aunt Melanie shook her head at the thought. "Just two weeks ago," she began, "a Forest Service technician happened to be flying over this part of the forest, doing an aerial survey. On the spur of the moment, he decided to fly over the top of the crater, hoping to see the lake. Turned out, he was in luck. The fog in there was a lot thinner than usual, and he had a good view inside. What he saw was—well, amazing."

"What did he see?"

Aunt Melanie's eyes moved to the pie dish. "How about some huckleberry pie, before it gets cold?"

"No thanks, I . . ." Kate's words trailed off as she saw Aunt Melanie reaching for the dish. "Okay, sure. I can't say no to that. So what did he see?"

"These huckleberries I found right out back. Two kinds, in fact. One red, the other purple. Got to learn their names someday." She slid a hefty slice over to Kate, allowing the corner of the map that had been held down by the plate to curl inward. As she took a heaping forkful from the pie dish for herself, the old woman's face crinkled in a smile. "Still as tart as the day I picked them."

"Aunt Melanie! What did he see?"

"Well," began the white-haired woman, pointing at the map with her fork, "there was, in fact, a lake. But to his surprise, it filled only half of the crater. The rest of it was very dense, very old forest. A hidden forest. As he circled closer, he could see some true giants, the kind of trees that make foresters salivate, lots of them bigger than twenty-five feet around. Took pictures of everything, he did, or nobody would have believed him. There were Douglas firs, spruces, cedars, and—most precious of all—a large grove of ancient redwoods."

Suddenly Kate understood. "And the loggers want to cut them all down?"

Aunt Melanie nodded gravely.

"But I thought the crater's impassable. You said yourself there's no road up there."

"Only because there wasn't any reason to build one. That's all changed now. Just before you arrived, a few of them—led by your friend Billy—put a Jeep road up there. Not all the way to the top of the rim, but high enough to get inside if they blasted a hole through the rock."

Kate dropped her fork onto her pie plate. "They're really going to blast their way in?"

"They already did," declared Aunt Melanie. "Yesterday." She rose and moved around to the window. "The only thing left for me to do was get a lawyer in Portland to file for an injunction."

"A what?"

"A court order, one that stops them from entering the crater or cutting anything in there until it's determined whether to make the place into a park."

Kate nodded. "So that's what was in the envelope."

"That's right. Copies of the injunction filing. And we got it. The call came right after you left for the post office. It takes effect Monday morning, first thing." The fire surged brightly as a pocket of resin exploded, shooting glowing embers into the air and over the hearth. Aunt Melanie kicked one back toward the fireplace and returned to her rocker. "I can't believe they thought that stealing my mail would change anything."

"They must be pretty desperate."

"So desperate they might try anything," said Aunt Melanie, tilting her head pensively. "The way Frank was so quick to agree with me out there, did you see? He wants me to think there's no problem. He's probably trying to protect me, the old fool. Afraid I'll get hurt. But I can see right through him. They're up to something, I'm sure of it."

"But what?"

Aunt Melanie shook her head in frustration. "I wish I knew. All I know is this discovery is like manna from heaven for the loggers. Most of them are out of work. The last mill in town is ready to close. The trees from the crater would keep them employed for another year or so, delaying the inevitable at least a little while longer."

She glanced toward the fire. "It's a natural human instinct, Kate, to try to keep your old way of life from changing. I really feel for them. They're proud, independent people, the kind you can depend on. Even Billy. It's hard not to like folks like that."

"Including Frank?"

Caught off guard, Aunt Melanie blinked, her eyes moist. "Yes," she said quietly, "including Frank." She cleared her throat. "And to answer your next question, we were friends once. Special friends. He's—we were—well, that was a long time ago."

"And the red-haired kid?" asked Kate. "He doesn't seem so likable to me."

"Oh, Jody. He's not so bad, really. He's had a hard time since his parents died last year. Worst crash in years, out on Highway 26. Before that happened, he was one of my best students—smart, sensitive, curious—though you'd never know it now. Frank's his grandfather, and agreed to take him in after the accident."

"Frank's a brave man," said Kate under her breath.

Aunt Melanie pushed a hand through her untamed white curls. "That he is. He's one rare human being. One of the few in this town willing to stand up and say that the old ways have to change, that there are no simple answers. Not everyone may agree with him, but they all respect him enough to listen."

She continued rocking, the repeated creaking of the chair punctuating the steady sound of rain drumming on the roof. "Everybody knows that those big trees are good for the air, the water, the soil—and even for fighting disease. But not many people know that the trees in the crater could be the oldest untouched forest in the world. And the northernmost stand of redwoods ever found." Her eyes seemed to shine with a faraway light. "And something more."

"More?"

"Yes," continued Aunt Melanie, leaning forward in the chair. "The Hidden Forest—the whole crater, really—was well known to the Halamis five hundred years ago. It was their most sacred place of all. Since they left, it's been totally undisturbed."

"Lost from time," said Kate, remembering the phrase.

"That's right," agreed her great-aunt. "There's no map anywhere that tells what you might find up there." Her face half lit by the dancing flames, she hesitated, then said in a voice so low it was barely audible: "Except one."

As Kate watched wide-eyed, Aunt Melanie reached across to the spruce table, pressed firmly on the center of one of the knots, then pulled out a small secret drawer. Within it lay a single square of white paper, tattered around the edges, labeled *Lost Crater.* Kate recognized the handwriting at once.

"You made that?"

Aunt Melanie made no answer. Slowly, carefully, she took the paper and laid it on top of the larger map. "Yes," she said at last. "I made it."

"But how? I thought you said no one's ever been up there."

The dark eyes gleamed. "Except the Halamis."

"But they disappeared centuries ago."

"That's right. They left something behind, though. Songs and stories about their way of life, their beliefs, their prophecies. Whatever disaster wiped them out—no one knows for sure what it was—a few of them survived somehow. They blended in with some of the other native peoples who settled this area later. But still they managed to keep their wisdom alive. For hundreds of years, every child with some Halami blood has learned the sacred chants word for word, then passed them on faithfully to the next generation."

"Whew," said Kate. "That's no small feat. It's hard enough for me to remember something for even a day or two, let alone a whole lifetime."

"I used to be the same way," Aunt Melanie replied. "Something happened, though, the first time I heard a Halami song. It stuck in my head, as if it had been there all along, and I couldn't put it out of my mind." Her face crinkled into a grin. "Maybe there's some truth to the rumor I've got some Halami blood in me."

Kate leaned over the hand-drawn map. The words *Lost Crater* were ringed by several small characters that she recognized as symbols from Halami rock carvings. A few names, like Kahona Falls, she also recognized. But others, like Circle of Stones, were completely new. Near the Hidden Forest, she spotted a question: *little people?* Then she noticed some strange words printed at the bottom of the page, but got only as far as *True of heart and straight of spear, Find the forest walled in fear* before Aunt Melanie lifted the map off the table.

"This is my biggest accomplishment," said Aunt Melanie, her white hair aglow with firelight. She brought the map closer and examined it, as one studies the face of an old friend. "It's taken me more than a decade to put it together, piece by piece, from talking with everyone I could find who knows something about the Halamis."

"How did they vanish?" asked Kate. "I know you must have a theory."

Lowering her map, Aunt Melanie pointed to a jagged mountain drawn north of Lost Crater. "Brimstone Peak," she said with certainty. "It had something to do with Brimstone Peak."

Kate turned a puzzled face toward her. "Meaning what?"

The elder sat back in the rocker and gazed into the fire for a moment. "There is a legend," she said, "but it's awfully vague and incomplete. No one, including me, knows quite what to make of it."

"Tell me anyway."

Aunt Melanie gathered her thoughts before speaking. "Well, it seems that Brimstone Peak—we don't know the Halami name for it—was an evil place for the Halamis. They believed that a wicked being called Gashra lived deep inside it. He wanted to control all the lands around him, but apparently the Halamis resisted him. So out of anger and revenge, Gashra decided to destroy both them and their home. He made the mountain erupt and fill the valleys with lava, hoping to wipe them out completely." She glanced again at the hand-drawn map. "Whether he succeeded or not, no one knows. And almost nobody takes the legend very seriously. But it's interesting to note that the last eruption of Brimstone Peak was just about five hundred years ago."

"The same time the Halamis disappeared," said Kate. "Makes you wonder."

"Oh yes," added Aunt Melanie. "There's one more piece to it, though it's the vaguest part of all. Some versions of the legend say an important role was played by a mysterious tree spirit."

"Tree spirit?"

"Don't ask me what it means. Could be just a mistake that crept into the story after so many repetitions. Could be a tree that becomes a person somehow, or the reverse, or something even stranger. I have no idea."

Placing her map back in the secret drawer, Aunt Melanie closed it tight, then faced Kate. "Lost Crater is like no other place on the planet, you see. It holds the Hidden Forest, that much we know. But it holds other things too. Strange things, stranger than you can imagine." A log collapsed in the fireplace, sending up a shower of sparks. "The Ancient One lives there."

"The what?"

"Never mind. My point is that it's a place no one really understands. It ought to be left alone."

"I wish we knew what the loggers are planning to do."

"So do I, dear. So do I."

"What can they do now, though?" wondered Kate. "Tomorrow's Sunday, and then the injunction starts."

She caught her breath, staring at Aunt Melanie, as the same thought flashed across both of their minds at once. "Sunday!" they exclaimed simultaneously.

"That's it," announced the elder. "That must be it. It's just the sort of thing Billy would think of. He was always trying to skirt the rules back when I had him in school, and he's still the same—except now he's angrier. And hungrier too. Frank told me he and Sly existed on nothing but potatoes all last winter." She shook her head slowly. "I'm sure he's planning to go up there tomorrow, before the injunction, and cut down as many redwoods as he can. That way there can't be any more talk about a park."

"You think he'd really do that?"

Frowning, Aunt Melanie replied, "I'm sure."

"But that's terrible! If only—if only there were some way to hold them off, just for one more day." Kate looked into her aunt's eyes, but found no comfort there. "Who's going to stop them?"

Aunt Melanie reached across the table and laid her small hand upon Kate's. "We will."

5

the forgotten trail

THE earth shook with a deep, volcanic rumbling. Force enough to fling incandescent lava into the darkened sky like a pyrotechnic fountain. Masses of thick lava oozed from crevasses along the ridge of the cone-shaped summit, triggering avalanches of superheated stone and mud that roared down river drainages and glacial valleys with enough speed to obliterate whole swaths of forest. Hissing vents and fumaroles blasted columns of super-heated steam high into the sky.

Kate was running from the eruption, dashing through the dense forest, her heart pounding. There was no chance of escape. Drenched from the heat of the inferno behind her, she couldn't even avoid the oncoming lava by climbing a tree, since every tree in its path was instantly incinerated. Rivers of fire, bubbling violently, rushed steadily toward her from the seething summit.

Then the ground shook again. The sky flashed with a brilliant light. Kate screamed.

And she awoke. Aunt Melanie, who had stopped shaking

her bed in order to turn on the overhead light, stood over her, wearing a dark blue nightgown.

"That was quite a dream you were having."

Kate sat up in bed, wet with perspiration. She wiped her face with the edge of the sheet. "You mean—you mean there's no . . . volcano? It was so real, I even felt the heat."

Aunt Melanie laid a gentle hand on her forehead. "The only volcano still active around here is Brimstone Peak, and it hasn't erupted for centuries. I'm the last person to take any dream lightly, mind you, but the only reality to this one is the temperature in here. How did this room get so hot?"

"I did it," confessed Kate. "I was still cold from getting soaked yesterday so I turned on the space heater full blast before I went to bed." She looked sheepishly at Aunt Melanie. "Guess I cooked my own goose, huh?"

"That you did," replied the white-haired woman. "But you did us both a favor. It's only two-fifteen, but since we're both awake, we're going to go now. The earlier we get started, the earlier we'll get there. And we must get up there by dawn."

Kate threw back the sheet. "You think they'll be up there that early?"

Aunt Melanie shook her head. "No, they'll take their new road. It's very long and steep, so it should take them at least until mid-morning."

"Then why do we need to get there so early?"

"Because, dear, we're going by a different way. A better way."

"I thought you said their new road was the only way into the crater."

"It's the only *road*. The way we're going is—well, not a road." Aunt Melanie brushed a moth off the shoulder of her nightgown, then turned to go. "Now hurry. I'll meet you in the kitchen."

The next half hour saw the little cottage in a whirl of activity. Kate quickly braided her hair, threw cold water on her face, and pulled on her green Bulldogs Softball sweatshirt

and jeans. Aunt Melanie set out food for Atha and prepared
hot chocolate. "There are times when no spice tea can com-
pare to this," she said as she poured the steaming brown liquid into an old thermos and screwed tight the cover.

At last, they left the cottage. Though the rain had
stopped, fog had settled so densely on the ground that Kate
felt a fine mist on her face as she followed Aunt Melanie
onto the porch. There was no light, only gradations of darkness, since there was no moon and the flashlight was not
working. Even the neon green shoelaces weren't visible
now.

I hate walking at night, she muttered. Although she
didn't like to admit it to anyone, including herself, she never
felt very comfortable in the dark. Especially outdoors.

Kate stayed as close as she could behind Aunt Melanie,
even though it meant slopping straight through a frigid
puddle. Ahead she sensed the vague shape that she knew to
be the Jeep but that in the gloom could just as easily have
been a sleeping stegosaurus. Then, from some faraway
place, she heard the distant *hooo-hooo* of an owl.

Aunt Melanie stopped suddenly, causing Kate to walk
into her. They listened for a moment, hearing only the
sound of their own breathing and the gentle rustling of
evergreen branches in the pre-dawn breeze. Kate wondered
whether the owl was sailing through the vaporous darkness
in search of some small animal to eat, or was even now following their movements from some broken-topped tree.

At last, the call came again, closer this time. *Hooo-
hooo, hooo-hooo.* The voice seemed to hover in the moist
night air.

As if responding to the signal, Aunt Melanie began
walking again. Soon she reached the Jeep, which she
announced by tapping its fender with her walking stick.
Pulling open the door, whose window consisted of a thin
square of plastic wired to the frame, she wiped the puddle
off the seat and climbed in. By the time Kate had clambered
in the other side (without remembering first to wipe the
seat, to her chagrin), the old Jeep was sputtering noisily.

"Hang on, now," Aunt Melanie shouted above the roar as she turned on the headlights. "The road is lousy in any weather, but especially when it's this muddy." She patted the red metal dashboard affectionately, then released the clutch. Trusty lurched forward and off they drove into the night.

Soon after crossing the bridge over Jones River, Aunt Melanie turned onto a heavily rutted road ascending a steep hill. Before long the jostling beams of the headlights revealed forest all around them. Curls of mist wove around small trees, snags, and stumps on both sides of the dirt road. A rivulet running along the left side sometimes curled into the middle of the track, causing Aunt Melanie to swerve sharply to avoid losing a wheel in its channel.

The road was filled with rocks, roots, potholes, and ruts half as high as Trusty's tires. As her stomach tightened from repeated bouncing on the rock-hard seat, Kate began to wonder what the two of them could possibly do to stop a whole team of loggers. She glanced toward Aunt Melanie, hoping she at least had some kind of plan.

At that moment, the Jeep slowed markedly and the driver shifted into low gear. Kate heard the sound of rushing water below as they drove onto a creaking wooden bridge, so flimsy it seemed to tilt sideways under their weight. Slowly, they crept across, bouncing over every crosspiece. Then, with a jolt, they reached solid ground again.

Aunt Melanie rammed the stick shift into a new gear with a grinding crunch and gunned the engine. Keeping her eyes on the potholes ahead, she reached into her sweater pocket and pulled out a peppermint. Handing it to Kate, she said, "Here, dear, eat this. It ought to help."

It was nearly another hour of wrenching jolts, deep gullies, and sharp turns before Aunt Melanie pulled into a ditch on the right side of the road, shifted the stick into neutral, and yanked on the parking brake. She turned off the ignition and the lights and sat back in her seat with a sigh. "We made it."

Kate, who had managed somehow to doze during the

last part of the agonizing journey, woke up with a start. "Did we crash?"

"No, although I guess that would have put you out of your misery." She patted Kate's thigh. "The only good thing about this road is how rotten it is. Like most roads around here, it doesn't get much traffic. Until they built that new road last week, this was the nearest you could drive to the crater." With a sigh, she added, "There's nothing like the combination of bad weather and bad roads to keep a beautiful place beautiful."

Kate opened her door carefully, given the steep pitch of the Jeep. All four wheels were caked with mud, and Aunt Melanie's daisy, more tired than ever, still hugged the antenna. Gingerly, Kate placed her wobbly feet on the ground. To her surprise, it was not muddy but covered with a layer of soft evergreen needles several inches thick. She could almost bounce on the padded surface, but her stomach told her to resist the urge. The sky seemed a touch lighter than when they had started out, but she still wished she had a flashlight.

As she slipped Aunt Melanie's small blue day pack over her shoulders, she was struck by the rich smells surrounding her. She drank in the fragrant air like someone encountering her first rose garden, and her nose tingled with fresh, vibrant aromas.

"Wondrous air, isn't it?" spoke the familiar voice by her side.

"I can't believe how good it smells."

"A friend of mine who plays the cello calls it 'a symphony of scents.' Isn't that so?" Aunt Melanie pointed to the trees on her left with her walking stick. "Over there, if aromas were sounds, would be the violins, dancing brightly. On the other side we have the French horns."

"And the trumpets?"

"Right," she replied. "And sometimes we get jolted by some new spring flower that's like crashing cymbals." She grinned at Kate. "How about a quick cup of hot chocolate?"

Kate smiled, took the thermos and two cups from the

day pack, and poured some in each. After taking her first swallow, she asked, "What did you mean last night about strange things happening up there in the crater?"

Aunt Melanie shifted her weight from one leg to the other. "It's hard to explain, dear."

"Can't you give me an example? Just one?"

"Almost anything is possible in a place that's been undisturbed for so long."

"Like what?"

"Well, for starters, you could assume pretty safely there are plants and animals up there no one's ever seen before."

"Like the Abominable Snowman?" joked Kate.

Her companion did not laugh. Instead, she took a sip of hot chocolate. "There could be things beyond anyone's imagination," she said quietly. Then, rather incongruously, she added, "I read an interesting article recently. By a physicist. He proposed a new theory, about something he called *time tunnels*—places that open up ways to travel to the past or the future."

"Are you serious?" asked Kate.

"This fellow certainly was. He thinks time tunnels are most likely to occur where things have lived without interruption for long periods, so their energies can multiply and magnify enough to distort the flow of time." She fidgeted again, then added, "Pretty farfetched, I admit. But your grandfather would have said that farfetched theories are the ones to take most seriously."

The mention of Grandfather made Kate's stomach clench again. She stared into her cup.

The white-haired woman reached out a hand and stroked her cheek. "I'm so glad you were with him at the end."

Kate's eyes filled with mist. She swallowed, then said mournfully, "I still miss him. So much."

Aunt Melanie nodded, her shell earrings clinking softly. Then her brow wrinkled. "Drat," she said. "In all the rush, I forgot to pack some matches."

"Why would we need matches?"

"You never know when they might come in handy." She checked her watch. "Come. If we hurry, we can still get to Kahona Falls by dawn."

"To the falls?" asked Kate, replacing the cups and thermos in the day pack. "I thought we were going—"

"Into the crater," finished Aunt Melanie. "But we're going by the old Halami trail, the one they used centuries ago and then abandoned. Until I found it again last week, it had been completely forgotten."

Stepping over a gnarled cedar limb by the side of the road, the woman waved her hand toward the forest. In the dim light, Kate could barely discern a shadowy path, overgrown with low-hanging branches, snaking into the trees.

"But," protested Kate, "if the walls are unclimbable, how can there be a trail into the crater?"

"You'll see," declared Aunt Melanie.

Kate scanned the subtle indentation on the forest floor. "If the Halamis haven't been here to walk on it for five hundred years, then how come the trail is still visible?"

Aunt Melanie grinned. "Someone else has been walking on it." She started down the path, her waterproof boots crunching across the bed of needles.

Full of doubt, Kate followed behind. The trail dove straight into the thick forest, climbing gradually uphill. Whenever Aunt Melanie came to one of the many overhanging boughs, she lifted her stick and pushed it aside, holding it just long enough for Kate to pass. When she let go, the bough would spring back into place, showering them both with a spray of dewdrops.

As they moved deeper into this realm of green and brown, the sky, barely visible through the thick canopy of branches above their heads, grew lighter by degrees. Subtle sounds came more and more frequently: Shadowy wings fluttered, twigs snapped, branches creaked, small creatures squealed. It was impossible to tell whether forest beings, alarmed by intruders, were scattering to escape, or whether they were simply stirring in anticipation of the sunrise.

Kate felt the give of the needle-strewn trail under her

feet. As the sky lightened, the trail did as well, until it seemed like a radiant pathway into the woods. She felt for a moment that she was one of the long-vanished Halamis, padding softly along a route that her people had traveled for generations.

Before long, she detected a new openness in the trees ahead of them. The misty light showed a clearing about fifty yards up the trail. Seeing it, Aunt Melanie broke into a run. Kate jogged along behind her, imagining the crashing splendor of the waterfall that would greet them.

At the edge of the clearing, they halted, panting. Together they surveyed the scene before them.

It was not Kahona Falls. Nor was it like anything Kate had ever seen before, except in some old photographs of trenched battlefields in World War One. An entire section of the forest, a square about a quarter mile on each side, had literally vanished. Nothing remained but a wasteland of torn limbs, uprooted trunks, slashed bark, and mangled branches strewn across the pockmarked terrain.

Kate turned to the rear, in disbelief, to see again the rich forest they had just passed through. She could still smell its intertwining fragrances, but a new odor hung over the clearing, an odd mixture of wet sawdust and discarded gasoline cans. She turned back to the clear-cut. No birds sang, no animals stirred, no branches clicked and swished in the breeze. If this had once been a forest, it was no longer. The land lay naked and exposed to the cold mists of morning.

"I had no idea," said Aunt Melanie, trying to contain her anger. "Just a week ago this was all still forested. Last time I was here a family of deer ran across the trail right over there."

"How did the loggers get in here?" asked Kate.

"They must have used their new road."

Without another word, she strode forward. As best she could, she worked her way across the trampled terrain, using her stick to help her step over ripped-up roots and muddy trenches. Kate followed in silence, feeling at times like she was walking on the face of an open wound.

At last, with a sense of relief, they reached the edge of the clear-cut and entered a new section of forest. The trail picked up again, and Aunt Melanie did not linger. Who could blame her? Kate, too, wanted to get far away, deep into the woods, before looking back.

Gradually, amidst the growing light, the forest began to work its healing powers. Subtle aromas comforted her, sounds of the living woods encircled her again. The clearcut moved farther and farther into the distance, until it was difficult even to remember in the presence of such lush greenery.

Soon the terrain grew rockier and the trail sharply steeper. For an instant, Kate worried that Aunt Melanie might have trouble making it up the slope, but one glance ahead told her otherwise. The small woman moved steadily along, pausing only to lean briefly on her walking stick after climbing the steepest sections.

The trail wound back and forth in an endless series of switchbacks, gaining elevation at every turn. At one point, panting from the ascent, Aunt Melanie halted. Kate, who was huffing as well, used the opportunity to bend over to touch her toes. It felt good to hang there, stretching her thighs; she hadn't had much exercise this week.

As she straightened up, she detected a new sound, one she could not immediately recognize. It was continuous, like the rustle of wind, but deeper, like faraway thunder. As they returned to working their way up the switchbacks, the mysterious sound grew gradually louder. At first, she wondered whether it could be a distant storm. Then, with a pang, she feared it was the sound of a logging crew at work up ahead. Were they already too late?

Finally, as the forest gave way to yet another clearing, she knew what lay ahead. The sound had swelled to such a roar that it could be only one thing.

They had reached the waterfall.

6

the legend of kahona falls

SPRAY soaring in every direction, Kahona Falls leaped out of the side of the steep wall of rock fifty feet above them. It sprung straight out of the mountainside, as if it were a geyser laid on its side, then arched earthward, plunging down the slope into a deep canyon hundreds of feet below. Behind it, the cloudy sky was lit with a pale wash of peach and pink. Dawn.

Kate turned to Aunt Melanie, who was herself capti-vated by the waterfall. Looking beyond her great-aunt to the landscape stretching far to the north and west, she saw they had ascended to a rocky ledge nearly fifteen hundred feet above the forest floor. To one side, the sheer face of the volcanic cone rose precipitously into the clouds. To the other side, gently rolling ridges reached as far as she could see.

At the edge of the horizon, probably twenty miles away, another volcanic peak loomed high and jagged. A thin trail of steam spiraled skyward from its summit. Even the peaceful glow of sunrise could not disguise the violence and torment of its past. This was not a gentle or strength-giving mountain, but a fang-shaped pinnacle that seemed somehow sinister. In a flash, she realized this peak must have been the legendary home of the Halamis' evil spirit. *Brim* something-or-other, though the name really didn't matter.

Focusing on the nearer ridges, Kate noticed that they looked like a vast checkerboard. Squares of dingy brown alternated with squares of vibrant green. Suddenly she understood that most of them had been clear-cut. So much of the original forest had been removed that she could see clearly the route of Jones River's rugged canyon from its source at the base of Kahona Falls, twisting and turning into the misty distance.

She moved nearer to Aunt Melanie on the ledge, joining her at the edge of the falls. All about them, trees and shrubs had adapted to the constant spray by rounding themselves, bending low toward the ground, anchoring their roots for the duration of their stormy days. Not far above their heads, the forest vegetation grew quite sparse and then ceased entirely. The black volcanic slopes became too steep for anything larger than the occasional tuft of grass or clump of moss to cling to them. The trail did not end here by accident: One could go no farther.

"If this is the way into the crater," said Kate, "then I'm a stewed prune."

"Better start stewing," replied Aunt Melanie, glancing toward the sunrise.

"How can you be so sure?"

The dark eyes concentrated on Kate. "Because," she said slowly, "I've gone this way before."

Staring up at the sheer cliffs, Kate shook her head. "I don't see how." Probing her great-aunt's face, she asked, "How did you find this so-called trail, anyway?"

Aunt Melanie glanced down at her walking stick, its wood warming to the colors of dawn. "When Billy and the others started building their road, I was desperate to get inside the crater before they did, since there's no telling what damage they could do. I had to see it, to record what's in there, before they messed everything up. I knew there would be Halami artifacts like no one's ever dreamed of finding, and lots more besides. Then I remembered the old legend about Kahona Falls."

"What legend?"

The elder ran a weathered hand through her curls. "It goes like this," she said, and she started to chant:

> True of heart and straight of spear
> Find the forest walled in fear
> Through the Gate of Death unknown
> Past the Circle of the Stones
> To the trees that touch the sky
> Blessed by spirits ever nigh
> Enter at the start of day
> Dawn's first light will show the way.

"My own translation," she said proudly. "Everyone has a hobby, you know. For some, it's baseball cards." She paused, watching the waterfall. "For me, it's the Halamis."

"But what does it mean? *Through the Gate of Death unknown.* That doesn't sound too promising."

Aunt Melanie moved closer to the edge of the precipice, where water from the falls drenched the rocks continually. "There's another piece to the puzzle. A long time ago, I did some research into the origins of the name Kahona. Turns out it's an Anglicization of an old Halami word, pronounced *kaha-hanya.* That's all I could find out. There wasn't a decent translation anyplace. So I put aside the problem and forgot about it." Her white curls caught the light of dawn. "Then, the night after they started making the new road, I couldn't get to sleep. I started reading an old Halami song sent to me by a friend, and I saw it used the word *kaha-hanya.* The meaning was crystal clear, and suddenly the legend made sense."

"What does it mean?" asked Kate, creeping closer to the edge herself.

Aunt Melanie's ebony eyes glinted strangely. "It means passage, or doorway. Another word would be—"

"Gate," completed Kate, in a flash of understanding. *Through the Gate* . . . She peered over the edge into the churning cataract below, and her bewilderment returned. "But how could a waterfall like this be a gate leading anywhere? This thing's two or three hundred feet high. It's a lot more likely to kill somebody than to take them anywhere."

"Through the Gate of Death unknown," repeated Aunt Melanie, swinging her head toward the waterfall. Feeling more exasperated than enlightened, Kate followed her line of vision.

Aunt Melanie was looking neither up at the waterfall's source nor down into its crashing cascade, but straight across its churning surface. There, Kate could see the pale light of dawn glistening in the spray of droplets. Slowly, the effect of the light began to change. The gleaming droplets seemed to melt into each other, to merge into a single beam of light that stretched across the middle of the waterfall. As the shining droplets merged, they began to scatter the sun's rays into a broad spectrum of colors, until at last the glowing beam transformed itself into a shimmering, shifting rainbow.

As Kate watched, the swath of colors grew bolder and brighter. She thought of the way prisms had always fascinated her, so much so that when her father gave her a pair one Christmas, she took to walking around the house holding one in front of each eye in an effort to see the world's true colors. She had never seen any rainbow as intense as this. But a gate it was not.

"I still don't get it," she declared.

"Look more closely," replied the white-haired woman. *"Behind* the rainbow."

As Kate searched the roaring curtain of water to find Aunt Melanie's meaning, she suddenly saw something strange. Whether it was an optical illusion or whether there was really something there, newly revealed by the first light of day, she wasn't certain. She studied the waterfall closely.

Running along the same path as the rainbow, but deeper—
as if it were actually behind the waterfall—was a luminous
line of some kind. It appeared to be a long rock ledge, protruding from the cliff at about the same elevation as the
place where they now stood.

Then Kate realized that the ledge behind the waterfall
could once have been connected to the ledge under their
feet. There was a small crevasse dividing the two, about six
feet wide, which dropped two hundred feet straight into the
churning waters of the canyon. But for that gap, the two
ledges seemed to be the continuation of a single outcropping
that ran like a belt around the outside of the crater cone. She
noted also that if the sun were even a little higher in the sky,
the ledge behind the falls would probably not be visible,
for the angle of sunlight would make it blend in with the
background.

Then, the words of the legend came floating back:

> *Enter at the start of day*
> *Dawn's first light will show the way.*

"Yes," said Aunt Melanie, reading her thoughts. "That is
the Gate into Lost Crater. Until I found it again last week, it
hadn't been used by anyone for over five hundred years."

Kate was awestruck. "You're not serious," she protested.
"Who would be crazy enough—even five hundred years
ago—to try to walk on that ledge?"

Aunt Melanie patted her chest. "I am. You can watch me
do it, before you follow."

She then stepped closer to the crevasse. Reaching beneath
a dense tangle of shrubbery on the side of the ledge, she
pulled out a wooden ladder only slightly longer than the
width of the crevasse. It was difficult for her to lift, especially
given the treacherous footing, but at length she succeeded.
Then, as Kate watched in dismay, she crawled closer to the
crevasse, planted the base of the ladder on the edge, and let
the ladder fall across the gap. The ladder crashed to the rock
ledge on the other side, making a primitive bridge.

"But Aunt Melanie," Kate protested, listening anew to the crashing roar of the waterfall as it poured countless thousands of gallons into the canyon below. "One little slip and you'll die! Are you sure you want to go this way?"

The white head nodded.

"But," tried Kate again, "even if you can get in this way, do you really think you can convince a whole team of loggers to go back home? What if they refuse?"

Aunt Melanie crawled back from the slippery edge, lifted herself to her feet, took again her walking stick. She stood erect, but she seemed small and frail against the backdrop of the falls. "I don't know," she answered. "All I know is I've got to try."

She approached Kate, turned her around, and unzipped the blue day pack, removing a small painted drum. Kate recognized it as the one she had seen so often resting on the living-room windowsill, and her heart longed to be there right now, curled up safely with Aunt Melanie by the fire. The drum's tan-colored hide was decorated with images of boldly drawn animal faces, all in black. Seating herself on a rounded rock, she motioned for Kate to come sit beside her.

Reluctantly, Kate obeyed. Her head was spinning with doubt about the whole idea of entering the crater, especially this way.

Then, apart from the din of tumbling water, Kate heard another sound. Using only the tips of her fingers, her face angled toward the luminous ledge behind the falls, Aunt Melanie had started tapping the drum. Striking with a light but firm touch, in no particular rhythm, she seemed to be listening to something far away—a special beat, perhaps, or a melody Kate could not hear.

Aunt Melanie's fingers searched for the hidden rhythm, until finally a regular pattern took hold, one that coincided with the splashing and crashing of the great waterfall. Slowly the drumming swelled into a complex sculpting of sounds. Deftly swishing and sliding across the hide, her hands danced eerily on the drum. At last she raised her voice, chanting some mysterious words that made no sense to Kate. Of these words, one that sounded like *halma-dru* was repeated many times.

When finally the hands came to rest, Kate could still hear the echo of drumbeats in the moist air around them. Her concerns, for the moment, had dissipated. She looked up at Aunt Melanie and said, "That was beautiful."

Aunt Melanie's lips curled into a half smile. "The Halami way of asking for good luck."

"What does that word *halma-dru* mean?"

"That's hard to explain. It's a kind of blessing, and it means something like *May your spirit be one with the spirits around you.*"

"Wasn't there a line in the legend about spirits?"

Nodding, Aunt Melanie said, "And the Halamis meant more than just human spirits. They included animals, trees, air, water, and soil as well."

She replaced the drum in the day pack and zipped it closed. Ignoring Kate's worried expression, she regained her feet and slid the walking stick under her belt. Gingerly, she moved to the very edge of the crevasse. She positioned herself at the spot where the ladder met the rock outcropping, overlapping by only a few inches, her hands gripping the ends of the poles. With a brief glance behind her, she started to crawl slowly across the ladder, placing her knees and palms on the crosspieces. The ladder bent visibly beneath her weight.

Kate, her fears reawakened, approached the crevasse. She grasped the ladder in her hands, steadying it against the rock, so that the repeated crawling motion didn't work it over the edge—taking Aunt Melanie with it. Against her will, she looked down. All she could see was a billowing cloud of spray from the falls exploding against the rocks far below.

"I'm over," called a voice. Kate raised her head to see Aunt Melanie standing on the opposite ledge, pulling the walking stick from her belt. She beckoned, saying, "Your turn now."

Remembering how the ladder had sagged, Kate shivered at the thought of what her own weight might do to

those creaky wooden poles. She glanced from the ladder to
Aunt Melanie and back again.

"Come, Kate," shouted Aunt Melanie. "I'm going to need
you." Then she added, "Don't look down. Just keep looking
at me."

Clenching the poles with all the strength her hands
could muster, her neck craned to keep her eyes on Aunt
Melanie, Kate moved cautiously onto the ladder. The deafening roar of the falls shook the very marrow of her bones.
She placed one knee on the first rung, then slid the opposite hand forward, then moved her other knee, then the
other hand, again and again and again.

A sudden plume of vapor slapped her face. Without
warning, one knee slid sideways off the ladder. Kate's
heart pounded rapidly and she froze, grabbing the ladder
so tightly she drove splinters into her palms. She was looking down, deep into the crashing depths. Her ears buzzed.
The words *through the Gate of Death unknown, Death
unknown, Death unknown* echoed inside her head.

This is it, she thought, even as she slowly raised her
knee and planted it back on the ladder. *I'm going to die.
Right here, right now.* The buzzing in her ears grew louder,
obscuring even the roar of the falls, as she forced herself to
push one knee forward, then a hand, then the other knee.
Slowly, haltingly, she crawled, her heart banging against
her chest until she thought she would burst.

Finally, another hand clasped her own. Aunt Melanie,
kneeling on the ledge, pulled her by the wrists from the ladder onto water-blackened rock. Kate fell forward into her
arms.

"First time's always the hardest," said the elder.

Kate, however, saw no humor. "First time's going to be
my last."

Standing up, Aunt Melanie moved closer to the edge.
With a grunt, she hauled the ladder across the crevasse.

Kate, her head still buzzing, merely watched. Slowly,
she rose to her feet, in time to help her great-aunt stash the
ladder behind a thick knot of wet roots and branches. As

they finished, Aunt Melanie touched Kate's nose with her finger and said simply, *"True of heart."*

Kate merely shook her head. She observed silently as Aunt Melanie turned to face the dark cavern behind the falls.

Mist billowed about the shadowed entrance. The line of the ledge, now barely visible beneath the tumbling water, seemed to disappear in a jumble of foam and spray. After a moment of deliberation, Kate began to follow Aunt Melanie along the ledge, placing her feet carefully on the wet rock. The ledge narrowed severely as they came nearer to the falls.

Turning sideways, their backs pressed against the wall of vertical rock, the pair moved cautiously into the gap under the waterfall. Kate's toes extended past the lip of the ledge, feeling the vibration of water pummeling the rocks below. Water splashed at her from all directions, drenching her completely, and the constant crashing grew steadily louder. If she could have turned back, she would have. But she wasn't about to desert Aunt Melanie now.

Slowly, she made her way along the outcropping, inching to the right with small sideways steps. Before her she could see nothing but the great waterfall, arching over the ledge like a giant curtain, thundering endlessly. Behind her, the sheer face of the crater rose precipitously, and she tried in vain to find handholds for her fingers to grasp. Spray was everywhere, but she dared not raise her hands to wipe her eyes lest the motion throw her off balance. Light filtered through the watery curtain only dimly, shifting and glinting on the black wall of rock.

Despite the peril, she found herself appreciating the smoothly cut surface of the ledge. So perfect was it that it almost seemed to have been carved by intelligent hands. Perhaps the Halamis had maintained this as a secret trail so many centuries ago. But how could anyone have hammered this ledge out of the rock? Unless, of course, they knew how to fly. No, she concluded, this had to be the chance product of endless amounts of water and endless amounts of time. Nothing more complicated than that.

At that moment, her right shoulder bumped into a vertical wall. She looked down at her feet. The ledge had come to an abrupt end. It met the new wall in a clean, impassable corner. Worst of all, Aunt Melanie was nowhere to be seen.

"Aunt Melanie!" she cried, hoping against hope that her great-aunt had not tumbled to her death in the cataract below. But where else could she be?

Frantically, Kate scanned the black wall of rock above and below her, spray splashing in her eyes. There was no way out, except the way they came—or over the edge into the falls.

Angrily, she kicked the back of her left heel into the rock wall. To her surprise, no solid rock met her foot. Angling herself slightly, she bent very carefully, feeling down the flat rock wall behind her with both hands as she dropped lower.

The fingers of her left hand suddenly curled over the lip of a large hole. It was as high as her waist, quite rounded, its base aligned with the surface of the ledge. A tunnel.

Bending lower, she squeezed into the entrance. Then she discovered something strange: Rising from the rock was a row of perfectly carved miniature steps, half the size of normal steps. They ascended gradually into the tunnel from the narrow ledge.

As she crawled into the tunnel, she encountered a tiny but persistent stream of water flowing out of its upper reaches. The stream splashed down the steps, then plunged over the ledge, a dwarf version of Kahona Falls. She puzzled again at the miniature steps; they were far too small to be of any use, even to a diminutive person like Aunt Melanie.

Yet she must have gone this way, Kate assured herself. She must. Peering ahead, she could see a single pinpoint of light at the far end of the tunnel. A prickle of doubt ran through her. Aunt Melanie could never have climbed through to the other side so quickly. Perhaps the falls took her first, before she could even cry out in warning.

Then in the shifting light, she spied a small object resting on the uppermost step. Reaching for it, she recognized the round shape, the clear plastic wrapping. It was a piece of peppermint candy.

Kate clutched it and pushed it into her jeans pocket. She crawled deeper into the tunnel, climbing upward toward the light. As she placed hands and knees on either side of the streaming water, she wondered whether water had made this tunnel. Or perhaps it was made by something—or someone—else, someone who required small steps.

Upward she crawled, not knowing what lay ahead. She knew only that this was indeed the Gate of Death unknown.

7

deadly water

CLAMBERING out of the tunnel, Kate stepped into a world of pervasive whiteness.

Fog was everywhere, licking at her face and the back of her neck. She held out her arm and could barely see her own hand. The mist felt strangely warm, like steam rising from a hot bath.

"Aunt Melanie," she called, surprised to hear her own voice magnified by the fog. "I'm here."

No answer came. Kate stepped forward, her feet crunching on a surface of small stones. She reached down to pick one of them up and found it as light as a handful of popcorn. Bringing it close to her face, she saw hundreds of little holes dotting its buff-colored surface, making it seem more like sponge than stone.

"Aunt Melanie," she called again, fighting back the growing fear that something was wrong. Maybe she had taken false comfort from the peppermint on the step. Maybe it was merely left behind from an earlier trip. Or Aunt Melanie might have emerged from the tunnel only to

meet some unexpected danger. She squinted, trying in vain
to see through the omnipresent shroud of fog.

"Where are you?" she cried, an edge of panic in her voice.

Listening for a response, she heard nothing but the
faint trickle of water entering the tunnel and a distant clap-
clapping, like waves beating against some faraway shore.
Then she heard another sound, a rushing, moving sound.
Could it be the wind swirling about the crater? Yet she felt
no wind. Sniffing the air, she sensed a slight smell of sulfur
mixing with the mist.

"Welcome," said a voice, so close it made Kate jump.

A shadowy shape emerged from the fog, stepping toward
her. It was not very large, and one hand grasped some kind
of shaft or stick.

"It's you!" she exclaimed. "I thought you'd disappeared."

"I'm sorry, dear," replied Aunt Melanie, her tone somewhat distant. "I didn't mean to vanish on you."

"It's all right," said Kate. "I should be used to it by now.
Where did you go, anyway?"

"Oh, just got ahead of myself. I was hoping to see
some . . . friends."

Kate looked at her quizzically. "Are the loggers in the
crater yet?"

"No. We could hear them if they were."

"Then who is here for you to talk to?"

The woman gazed at her intently, as the fog dissipated
slightly. "Friends. Sometime, when we have more time, I'll
introduce you. But for now, what do you think of Lost
Crater?"

Kate wiped the droplets of warm mist off her brow with
the sleeve of her sweatshirt. "There's something weird
about it. Like it's, I don't know, dangerous somehow."

Aunt Melanie's hand, brushing some dirt off her
sweater, paused for a split second at her words, then continued. "There is danger, yes, as in any dormant volcano. I
see you've discovered pumice."

"You mean this rock? It's amazingly light. What was
that about a volcano?"

"Just another name for the crater," explained Aunt Melanie. "Don't worry, it probably won't erupt again in your lifetime."

Kate tossed the rock into the mist, hearing it clatter as it fell. "That doesn't sound too good to me."

"You're still feeling your nightmare, poor child. Anyway, this volcano hasn't been active recently."

"What does 'recently' mean?" probed Kate.

"Oh, in the last seven thousand years." She grinned impishly. "Geologic time always makes me feel so young."

The fog swirled again, pressing closer, turning Aunt Melanie into a mere shadow in the mist. "I still don't like this place," said Kate. "How come it feels so warm?"

"Here," answered her great-aunt, taking her by the sleeve. "I'll show you."

Aunt Melanie led Kate down the sloping rock-strewn terrain for eight or ten paces. Halting suddenly, she bent down for a piece of pumice, then tossed it underhanded into the fog. To Kate's surprise, she heard an unmistakable splash.

"I had no idea the lake was so close."

"Understandable, since you couldn't see it," her great-aunt replied. "The volcanic plumbing under the lake keeps it warm, you see, so steam is rising all the time. The geologists tell me it's had cold spells and warm spells, alternating over the ages. We're in one of the warm ones now. That's why the crater is usually fogged in."

Kate picked up a fist-sized rock and threw it into the fog with the force of a first-string shortstop. The splash soon followed. "Why did the Halamis come all the way up here, if they couldn't see anything when they got here?"

"There are many ways to see," replied Aunt Melanie, her voice seeming to swell in the fog so that it sounded quite close to Kate's ears.

"How many times have you come up here, since you found the way?"

"Twice before. I'd have come more often if this whole business with the new road hadn't kept me tied down all week. There's plenty to explore; the crater's almost a mile across, you know. But even just two visits were enough to find plenty. For instance, there's an old Halami camp on the other side of the lake, right where the old songs said it would be. I found some beautiful tools there. Stone bowls, knives and spoons, a sewing awl, two—"

A sudden movement in the mist distracted her, and she halted. Instinctively, Kate moved closer to her side.

All at once, the fog started to shift. The clouds of mist grew rapidly thinner, like fabric of filigree whose ornamental tracery was pulling apart before their eyes. First to unveil itself was the lake, deep turquoise in color, so utterly blue that Kate felt if she put her hand into the water, it would come out blue.

Across the water and through the mist, Kate could now make out the dark rock of the crater rim, rising straight up another thousand feet or more. She glanced behind to look at the entrance to the tunnel, but she could not find it amidst the jumble of gray and buff-colored pumice. A pang of fear shot through her: If the tunnel was invisible when it was this close and the air was this clear, how could they ever hope to find it again in the fog?

Before she could voice her concern, however, she discovered the source of the rushing sound that she had earlier mistaken for wind. At the edge of the lake, no more than twenty yards to her right, a river of water cascaded briskly down a channel, then disappeared into the rocks. Here was the origin of Kahona Falls.

"Look there," announced Aunt Melanie, pointing toward the middle of the lake.

Kate's attention turned to a shadowy mass that seemed to be rising out of the water. Her skin prickled. The mass, dark and foreboding, seemed like something from another planet. At first it appeared to move, and then she realized that it was only the effect of the swirling mist. It was jagged, covered with spires, and blacker than the blackest thing she had ever seen.

It was an island.

"What—is that?" Kate sputtered.

"That's what the Halamis called Ho Shantero. It means Island That Moves."

"It does seem to move, doesn't it? Of course, it's only a trick of the fog."

Aunt Melanie said nothing.

"I remember now," Kate continued. "It was there on the map, the one you made. But there wasn't any island at all on the big map."

"That's because the mapmakers didn't know it existed until that Forest Service man flew over the crater. I suspect he didn't pay much attention to it, though, since it doesn't have any trees."

Kate furrowed her brow. "I can't imagine flying low over that thing and not paying attention."

Aunt Melanie cocked her head thoughtfully. "I did hear from Frank that he said something curious about it later, in Cary's Tavern after he had a few beers in him."

"What?"

Aunt Melanie looked at her watch, and her face turned grim. "It's later than I thought. Let's get going or they're going to get to the redwoods before we do." She started walking parallel to the shore, away from the bubbling cascade.

Kate jogged to her side. "What did he say about the island?"

The woman shrugged. "Something about the surface of the island seeming to move. Like it was crawling or something."

Kate glanced at the dark mass warily.

Aunt Melanie sped up her pace a bit. "Right after he saw the island, he said the plane was shaken by a sudden updraft—so hard it nearly knocked him off his seat. Made him concentrate on flying for a few seconds, and by the time he was past the turbulence, the island was well behind. Then he saw the forest, and he never looked back."

"Did his pictures show anything weird? You said he took lots."

"None of the pictures he took of the island came out, for some reason."

"Fog," suggested Kate hopefully.

"Or maybe it was the work of Tinnanis," said Aunt Melanie.

"Tinnanis?" Kate wasn't sure she really wanted to know what the word meant.

"Just pulling your leg," answered Aunt Melanie, hopping across a small rivulet that drained into the lake. "They're part of Halami mythology, a magical little people who lived in the most ancient part of the forest. The Halamis believed that they kept the forest healthy, through some secret power of their own. Don't worry, though. I doubt we'll be meeting any."

Kate tugged on her sweater. "It makes me wonder who made those tiny little steps back at the entrance to the tunnel."

"Most people would tell you it was the Halamis. After all, they made all sorts of things in honor of the Tinnanis. Tiny tools, things like that."

"And what would *you* tell me?" asked Kate.

Her great-aunt smiled curiously. "I'd say nobody knows for sure."

"What did these, um, Tinnanis supposedly look like, aside from being small?" Kate rather liked the idea of little people who lived among the trees. Perhaps they could even make themselves invisible at will, or change themselves into animal shapes.

Aunt Melanie slowed her step, peering for a few seconds into the mist swirling about the black island. "Once again, nobody knows." She turned and winked at her companion. "But if you should see one, be sure to tell me, won't you?"

Kate gave no answer. Then she spied an odd protrusion rising from the pumice stones just ahead. Standing about two feet tall, the powdery yellow outcropping looked like an upside-down funnel.

"What's that thing?" she asked, pointing.

"A fumarole," said Aunt Melanie, pausing to bend over it. "Once there was a geyser here, maybe a hundred feet high. Can't you imagine a big plume of steam and sulfur gushing out of this thing?"

"Sure," Kate replied. "Too easily."

Aunt Melanie again checked her watch. "Let's keep moving, Kate." She nodded toward the thick line of trees not far ahead. "That's where we're going."

She resumed her pace, and Kate fell in behind. Over her right shoulder, Kate could see the island, partially obscured by shreds of fog from the ceaselessly steaming lake. It resembled a phantom ship, hovering between darkness and invisibility. Then she noticed that the deep blue water around it permitted no reflection. She pondered whether that was because of the water or the island itself.

Kate turned to the other side, hoping to crowd the haunting thoughts of the island from her mind. Not far above them, resting on the jumble of broken pumice just in front of the dark cliff wall, she noticed a collection of six or seven enormous boulders. They appeared to be arranged in a ragged circle, like rocks around a giant's campfire. Some of the boulders looked bigger than Aunt Melanie's cottage, and none were smaller than Trusty.

She recalled the Circle of Stones she had seen on Aunt Melanie's map. Vaguely, she remembered seeing the word *Beware* written nearby in small letters. But beware of what?

Something about these strange shapes tugged at her, made her curious. *I'll just have a quick look,* she told herself. No need even to tell Aunt Melanie, who had strode off ahead. Better just to dash up there and back before she even notices.

Turning her back to the blue lake, Kate started to scramble up the rock-strewn terrain. At once she discovered how steeply it sloped from the shoreline to the base of the vertical cliffs. The angle was close to forty-five degrees, forcing her to use her hands frequently. The rocks, dampened by fog, were slick and slippery, slowing her progress even more. But as the circle of giant stones drew nearer, their inexplicable attraction grew stronger.

Stopping at one point to catch her breath, she turned and took in the full expanse of the crater. Seen without its normal filling of fog, it was impressive indeed. High cliffs rose along the far rim, some pointed like giant teeth, others curved into monumental domes. New morning light streamed across the undulating wall of rock, staining it deep red. Below, the white sweater of Aunt Melanie moved steadily along the edge of the lake, approaching the forest. Meanwhile, spiraling columns of mist swirled slowly around the cinder-black island.

Kate caught a whiff of an enticing aroma from somewhere above her. Curious, she continued upward. Moving like a spider, she scurried up the slope. At length, the incline leveled off somewhat. She raised her head to see that she had arrived at the circle of boulders.

She stood there, huffing. The stones, she realized, were ribbed with deep cracks that covered their entire surface with a net of dark lines. Whether they had been shattered by an explosion or baked by a burst of volcanic heat, she did not know. They had clearly withstood some sort of violence, powerful beyond imagining. For an instant she wondered whether these giant stones actually were pieces of a puzzle, remains of a single, enormous rock that had been blasted to bits long ago.

Then she perceived again the aroma, unlike anything she had ever smelled before. It was sweet, almost like Aunt Melanie's spice tea, but with an alluring quality no tea could possibly possess. To her surprise, cloves, cinnamon, ginger, and even the essence of lilac—all her most favorite smells—wove themselves through the perfume. It was almost as if this aroma had been created exclusively for her. Underneath, she detected the barest breath of sulfur, strong enough to give added zest, yet not so strong as to detract from the enchanting sweetness.

Searching for the source, she quickly found it: a pool of dark green liquid bubbling beneath the smallest of the huge stones. She stepped closer, immersing herself in the fragrant smell. The pool was lined with some sort of soft green algae whose undulating hairs danced gracefully, making the rocks lining the sides seem gentle and inviting.

What could this lovely liquid be? She wanted to touch it, to taste it, to bathe in it. Heedless of any danger, she kneeled by the side of the frothing pool and reached her hand toward it.

"Kate!"

She jolted at the distant voice. It was Aunt Melanie, calling her. A wave of resentment raced through her, something she had never felt before toward her great-aunt. She called back angrily, "Don't bother me now. I'll be there in a minute."

Again, she cupped her hand, eager to take a drink. She leaned forward, reaching toward the bubbling green pool.

"Kate!" came the cry again, closer this time, as Aunt Melanie toiled her way up the steep slope behind her.

Kate froze, as an inner voice told her to be careful. Perhaps she would wait a moment longer. Then, in a flash, her anger surged anew. Aunt Melanie only wanted to spoil her fun. She wanted the whole crater to herself, wouldn't let her discover anything. But she had. She had discovered this beautiful pool. *I'll show her,* Kate thought. *I can make some discoveries too.*

The pool seemed to reach out with fragrant, comforting arms to embrace her. Kate smiled, leaning still closer to the frothing green liquid. Slowly, she stretched out her hand.

Just as the back of her cupped hand touched the surface, she heard a shrill whistle and looked up. Some sort of bird, looking like a red streak, hurtled at her from the top of the giant stone behind the pool. It smacked full force into her shoulder, knocking her backward onto the rocks, then flew off.

"Ehhhh!" she shrieked, landing on her back with a thud.

Before she could roll back to her knees, someone clasped the arm of her sweatshirt. Aunt Melanie stood above her, breathing heavily. Suddenly, Kate felt a sharp pain on the back of her left hand. Turning it to her face, she saw a mass of green wormlike creatures writhing on her skin. They seemed to be burrowing into the back of her hand.

She screamed again, shaking her hand wildly. Aunt Melanie grabbed Kate's wrist, thrust her hand into a rivulet of water flowing into the pool, and started scrubbing intensely. Kate squealed in pain and tried to pull away.

"I know it hurts," said Aunt Melanie with a scowl, "but it's necessary. Hold steady." She continued the scouring despite Kate's squirms and cries of anguish.

At last, she relented, releasing her grip. Kate looked at the back of her hand to see red and blistered skin below her knuckles. It was bleeding, and ached as if it had been scalded, but the writhing worms were gone.

Aunt Melanie pulled a faded purple kerchief from her pocket. She wrapped it carefully around Kate's hand, securing it with a knot. Holding Kate firmly by the shoulders, she scrutinized her. "Are you feeling all right now?"

"I guess so," muttered Kate, sheepishly avoiding her gaze. "My hand hurts like crazy."

"It will for a while, I'm afraid. It's going to sting for a couple of days, and then you'll probably have a scar."

"What—what happened to me?" Kate stammered. "All I wanted was to get closer to—"

"The green pool," completed her great-aunt grimly. "You were caught in its spell."

"Spell?" repeated Kate, incredulous. She looked over at the pool, frothing energetically. The fragrant perfume had vanished, and so had her desire to touch it. "But how could it? Spells aren't real."

"This one is."

Kate pursed her lips. "And that bird . . . the red one that flew into me. Was it part of the spell too?"

Aunt Melanie stroked her chin. "No, I don't think so." She paused, thinking. "It looked like an owl. Maybe a flammulated owl. It's a rusty color—and small, about the right size. They can be downright feisty. But I've never heard of one flying right into somebody like that. And in broad daylight, too, when it should be sleeping."

"I still can't believe there's some kind of spell."

Shaking her head, Aunt Melanie declared, "Then watch this."

She thrust the end of her walking stick into the pool. Suddenly, it ceased bubbling. The green liquid seemed to evaporate, and in its place Kate saw thousands upon thousands of the same venomous worms that had been on her hand, writhing over and under each other in one massive heap. They filled the depression that had once been the pool, slithering across rocks that had once been its sides. Then, to her shock, she saw several knobs of white mixed in with the gray rocks, and she recognized them at once.

"Bones," she said in horror, drawing her left hand close to her chest. "There are bones in there."

Aunt Melanie pulled out the walking stick, and immediately the bubbling pool returned. The green worms, if still there, disappeared in the froth.

"How does it do that? The stick, I mean."

"This stick is, well—unusual," answered Aunt Melanie, cocking her head to one side. "I've only begun to discover what it can do. It's full of puzzles, like why this owl's face on the handle looks almost human. I found it on my first trip through the tunnel behind the falls. It was just lying there, as if it were waiting for me. Somehow, it has the power to show what the pool really looks like. Don't ask me how."

She hefted the stick in her hand. "It's the only thing that saved me when the spell first drew me up here. I forgot all about the Halami chant about *deadly green water,* though it was one of the first I ever heard:

> *Beware of the deadly green water*
> *That swallows whatever it sees*
> *You shall not escape from the Stones*
> *You shall not encounter the Trees.*

I was about to fall in just like you, when the end of the stick happened to slip into the pool. Suddenly, the spell was broken, and I saw everything. Even that wonderful aroma of juniper berries and peppermint—my favorite smells—vanished instantly. Did I ever feel stupid."

"You and me both," said Kate, regaining her feet.

Aunt Melanie faced the green pool. "Apparently, once the spell's been broken, it doesn't affect you again. That's why it isn't pulling on us now."

Cautiously, Kate stepped nearer to the edge of the boiling liquid. She could not help but wonder how many creatures had been drawn to their death there. "I wonder how it got here," she said, holding her left hand protectively. "It isn't natural. No way. And the stream there, where you washed those—those *things* off my hand, it's clear as anything. But, look, when the water gets to the pool it turns that horrible green color."

Her gaze moved to the assembled boulders. She counted them: There were seven, all deeply cracked. Behind them, a colonnade of eroded lava columns lined the cliff wall, resembling the ribs of a decomposing skeleton. "Something's weird about these boulders too. They feel—I don't know, strange."

"They should," replied Aunt Melanie, as she started down the slope toward the lake. "They are the Circle of Stones."

"The ones in the legend," recalled Kate, hustling to catch up to her. "What else do you know about them?"

"Later," came the response. "Right now we have to get into the Hidden Forest. Before anyone else does."

Kate glanced over her shoulder at the great boulders. "All I know is they make me nervous."

"That," answered Aunt Melanie with a mysterious gleam in her eye, "is because they're watching you."

8

the hidden forest

AUNT Melanie's pace quickened as they rounded the last inlet on the lake before the deep woods. Whether she was worried that they would arrive after the loggers, or simply excited to be nearing the Hidden Forest, Kate could not tell. Probably some of both. They stepped rapidly over the buff-colored rocks lining the shore of the steaming lake.

At last, they approached the deep woods. The jumble of rocks underfoot turned to sand, then soil, then a curvaceous carpet of grass. Several streams of bright water flowed from the forest across the grass to empty into the lake. Mosses, vibrant green, clung to the broken branches that lay on the ground, while small birds chirped in the branches overhead.

Kate had never seen a meadow so verdant. Her left hand continued to ache, but she gradually grew less aware of it. Flowers—white, yellow, violet—draped the sides of the rivulets. Looking at them instead of where she was going, she thrust her foot into a deep well of mud. She had to lift it out carefully, toes high, to avoid losing her sneaker.

At the border between the meadow and the forest, she looked back once more at the blue, blue lake. The fog was swiftly returning, making the island seem to glide ghost-like over its surface. How deep this lake must be, she could not even guess. She wondered what strange beings might live within its waters.

In a few seconds, fog had completely obscured the island, as well as the Circle of Stones some distance above the shore. Billowing clouds now blocked the sun. It would not be long before the day's first rain would fall, filling the lake and fueling Kahona Falls.

Stepping across a moss-covered log, she entered the Hidden Forest. At once, she was greeted by the familiar fragrance of resins, needles, berries, cones, leaves, bark, and soil, mixing together in a powerful perfume. Yet this time something was different. These woods smelled older, deeper, and something more, something she could not quite identify. She saw Aunt Melanie, looking smaller than usual against the backdrop of tall trees, disappear behind a double-trunked cedar.

A thrill ran through Kate. She and Aunt Melanie were the only human beings ever to walk in these woods since the time of the Halamis. As she strode quickly to catch up, her feet practically sprang across the forest floor. She understood that this buoyancy came from the thousands of years of living and dying that had occurred beneath her feet. A delicate ring of pink sorrel caught her attention, and next to it she saw an enormous snail slithering across a toppled fir. A cluster of sword ferns shone in the dim light ahead; the fronds, three or four feet long, glowed with a soft radiance.

Aunt Melanie, while working her way through the trees, pointed out some of the herbs and flowers springing up from the soil, from between roots, or sometimes straight from the ragged bark of the trees. Eschewing their tongue-twisting Latin names as "more for show than anything else," she used only the more expressive common names. Kate liked especially the ones called bleeding heart, sugar scoop, fairy lantern, scarlet paintbrush, and glade anemone.

Like the crater filling with fog, Kate's heart began to fill with a sense of unaccustomed peace. Everything here seemed to fit somehow, to belong just where it was. She turned slowly around, discovering new seedlings sprouting from almost every surface. Sinuous vines of purple and brown wound around trunks, making little rope ladders for small animals to climb. One tree, long dead, was covered completely with a leotard of light green lichen. Across fallen logs marched dozens of colorful mushrooms, some no bigger than ants, some shaped like luscious red lips, some round and wrinkled like exposed brains. From virtually every cavity in the trees something surprising appeared. Ferns and fungi, conifers and broadleafs, each one unique in dress and design, each one part of the common community. Life of all kinds was here wholly at home.

Despite the accumulating clouds above, sometimes a stray shaft of light would penetrate the intricate mesh of branches to reach the forest floor far below. One of these, stretching like a fiery filament, fell upon a moss-covered rock by Kate's feet. She leaned closer to study it.

To her amazement, the rock had some lines deeply etched on its surface. Many of the lines had been filled with moss, and she had to trace their pattern with her finger to feel where they ran. When she found one line encircling the others, she realized they were too deep and regular to be accidental. There could be no doubt. They had been carved.

She stepped back a pace to get a better perspective. Then she saw the unmistakable design of the lines. It was a face. A human face. With wide, deep-set eyes, the face glared at her, across time beyond memory. Its open mouth seemed to be shouting something, a warning perhaps, in a tongue Kate could not comprehend.

"Hey, look at this," she said, pointing.

No answer. She whipped around to see where Aunt Melanie had gone. But she was nowhere to be found. Kate ran a few steps ahead, suddenly finding herself at the edge of a clearing. Not again, she thought. Where could she have gone this time? A pang of fear shot through her, and she noticed her aching hand. For the first time, the forest began to feel somehow perilous.

"Aunt Melanie!" she called.

No sound but the swishing of branches.

Kate ran deeper into the forest. Again she shouted.

No answer.

Then she saw them. Arrayed before her were the most awesome trees she had ever seen. As solemn as a group of pilgrims gathered to pray, they stood together in silence. Drawing in a deep breath, Kate gazed at the uplifted boughs arching three hundred feet above her head, their lacy branches permeated with light. At the base of the trees, heavy burls hung like jowls, bordered by fibrous bark as delicate as strands of hair. Powerful roots clenched the soil firmly, as they had for centuries upon centuries.

Redwoods.

Then, in the center of the grove, she saw the most majestic tree of all. It stood taller and broader than the rest, older than anything else in the forest. It rose straight out of the earth with all the strength and grace of a monarch.

Kate moved closer, laying her hand respectfully on the tree's gnarled trunk. So thick was its base that she guessed it would take five or six grown men holding hands to encircle it but once. She craned her neck backward, following the narrowing girth higher and higher, through successive canopies of mossy boughs.

Lowering her eyes, she discovered a hollow cavern within the folds of the massive trunk. Although it was only as high as her waist, it seemed to be quite deep. Something about its dark interior frightened her, yet tugged at her as well, so she approached it cautiously. Stooping to peer inside, she suddenly froze. Staring at her from the blackness of the cavern were two gleaming eyes.

The eyes regarded her intently. Then, in a flash, she recognized them.

"It's you," sighed Kate. "I called and called and when you didn't answer I got scared."

"No need to be scared, dear." A hand reached out from the cavern and, taking Kate's arm, drew her inside. "I didn't hear you calling. As it happens, I was listening to something else."

"Aunt Melanie, you're impossible."

Her heart still beating with excitement, Kate slipped the day pack off her shoulders and sat beside her great-aunt within the hollow of the tree. Slowly, her eyes adjusted to the dark, and she perceived the subtle gradations of colors around them. Rising from the earthen floor, the ribbed wooden walls of the inner trunk were streaked with black, charred by some forest fire perhaps a thousand years before. She looked at the wood bordering the cavern's entrance and saw that it was only four or five inches thick, yet she knew it must be supporting considerable weight.

As she leaned back against the wood, her body relaxed. She felt safe. As if this tree would hold her, protect her against anything that could possibly happen. She looked through the entrance to the grove outside. The scattered shafts of light and wispy streaks of mist made the scene look more like an impressionist painting than a real stand of redwoods. It was cooler here amidst the trees than it had been near the lake, and she folded her arms against her chest to stay warm.

"We beat the loggers here," said Aunt Melanie. "Let's be glad of that. I wanted you to feel the power of this place, when everything's quiet, at least for a minute or two. Before we head up to where their road comes into the crater, how about a quick taste of hot chocolate?"

Kate nodded at the suggestion. Swiftly, she unzipped the pack and poured out two cups of the steaming liquid. The smell was as delicious as the taste, and she held the cup close to her nose. Stretching out her legs, she realized that she had not sat down since emerging from the Jeep before dawn.

"I saw a face back there," she said, her voice echoing dully within the hollow. "A face carved in a rock."

"You mean a petroglyph," corrected Aunt Melanie. "You must have found one of the Halami warning stones."

Kate took another sip of hot chocolate, warming her hands against the cup. "Warning stones? What were they warning about?"

Aunt Melanie answered in a near whisper. "This redwood grove was the most sacred of all places for the Halamis. They believed that spirits would gather here, among the redwoods, sometimes even coming and going through the trees themselves. Anyone who enters this grove does so at his own risk."

Kate fidgeted on the earthen floor of the hollow. "Spirits who live with these redwoods couldn't be evil," she said. "This feels like a place for good spirits."

The elder nodded. *"To the trees that touch the sky, Blessed by spirits ever nigh.* I feel that way too. But even good spirits can do strange and frightening things sometimes." She tilted her head in her usual way. "This grove is in the heart of the oldest forest you or I will ever see."

"And this tree is in the heart of the grove."

"Yes," replied Aunt Melanie. "I call this tree the Ancient One."

The Ancient One, repeated Kate to herself. Older than old. The very center of the Hidden Forest. As she reached to touch the inner wall of the tree, her thoughts drifted from the hollow to the grove to the great woods itself. From the first moment she stepped across its green border, she had been struck by the diversity of life around her. Yet now she sensed something else, something even more remarkable. This forest not only had diversity, it had unity. Just as the branches overhead intertwined in a complex pattern, so did the living beings of the ancient forest intertwine in a way she could scarcely begin to comprehend. Perhaps that was what made her feel so peaceful here. Connected, part of this place, in a way she had never felt before.

Lightly touching Aunt Melanie's thigh, she said, "I'm

so glad to be here, with you. I could never be here alone, though. It wouldn't be the same."

"Even if I weren't here," replied the elder, "you wouldn't be alone."

Kate nodded, absently reaching for the delicate frond of a fern that had sprouted near the entrance.

"Maidenhair fern," said Aunt Melanie reflectively. "See how black the stems are? The Halamis used it for making their baskets. Down lower, the color isn't so strong, so they used to get it from the highest places they could find. And when it grows near redwoods, the tops are good for making tea that helps to ease a fever. That may be what first tempted them to find a way into the crater, looking for plants like maidenhair."

Stirring, Kate bumped her bandaged hand against the wall of the hollow. It throbbed, aching. She thought of the bubbling green pool, and the ghastly wormlike creatures it harbored. "Do evil spirits live by the Circle of Stones?"

"Not spirits," replied Aunt Melanie. "Not exactly." She cleared her throat.

Kate looked at her uncomfortably, remembering her uneasy feeling about the stones. "What then?"

"It's best we discuss it later, dear," she said, her voice again almost a whisper. She scanned the shaft of her walking stick, leaning against the wall of the hollow. The yellow eyes of the carved owl's head seemed to be observing them. "Some other time."

"Can't you tell me just a little?"

Aunt Melanie's tongue pushed against her cheek. She seemed to be on the edge of answering, searching for the right words. *"Azanna,"* she said at last. "The Halamis called the Circle of Stones *Azanna.* What it means is—"

Just then they heard something new. Distant, yet still jarring. Kate, like Aunt Melanie, held her breath, straining to hear. The sound grew steadily louder, until there could be no mistaking its source.

"Loggers," said Kate. "They're in the crater."

9

the walking stick

"COME on," replied Aunt Melanie, already on her way out of the hollow. "I want to meet them before they reach the redwoods."

"But what will you do then?"

"I'm going to confront them. Face to face. I'm going to count on the fact they all know me. Heavens, I taught most of them how to read and write! And if Frank's with them, I know he'll listen to reason. He knows that cutting down these trees won't do anything to solve our real problem. Not really. It just postpones things." She halted, hearing the distant revving of a chain saw. "They're up by the road cut, trying out their saws. Let's go."

"What about Billy?" asked Kate. "He's not going to listen to reason."

The dark eyes hardened. "He'll have to hurt me before he hurts this tree."

Aunt Melanie strode across the redwood grove, heading the opposite direction from the way they had entered. Grabbing the day pack, Kate followed, her moment of peace now shattered. The noise of the chain saw buzzed through the forest like an angry hornet, searing her ears. She wished they could go faster, wished they could fly over the forest and descend on the intruders like a pair of eagles.

Soon the great trees grew thinner, and they sloshed through a swampy section where the air was alive with mosquitoes. Sometimes they could keep their feet on small stones sprouting from the water, but more often they had to trudge straight through the muck. At last, brushing away a cloud of insects, Kate could see the misty cliffs ahead.

Higher they scrambled, until finally they left the woods and were moving across the rock-strewn rim of the crater. Aunt Melanie turned to the right, traversing just above the trees. The fog grew thicker, covering the cliffs and flowing over the forest. Kate could hear the distant lapping of lake water on the shore below, but saw only a vaguely blue shadow beneath the clouds. Once she caught a glimpse of the dark island through the gathering mist; it seemed closer to the shore than she remembered.

Aunt Melanie stopped suddenly. More chain saws revved from somewhere nearby. "Their road cut is just above us," she said, breathing heavily. "Thirty yards, maybe. But since the road stops at the hole they blasted in the cliff wall, they'll have to carry their gear down inside, and that will take some time. A few of them may already be down in the forest, I'm afraid. With this fog, they could have passed us without our knowing it. But judging from the sounds, I think most of them are still up there. And they'll have to pass by here if they want to—"

She stiffened, her eyes widening in sudden dread. "My stick!" she exclaimed. "I left it in the redwood grove—in the tree."

The distraught woman started back across the rocks when Kate caught her by the arm. "What are you doing?" she asked in disbelief. "You can't go back for it now."

"I must," panted Aunt Melanie. "It mustn't fall into their hands. It mustn't."

Kate studied her in consternation. "But we can't leave

here now. Not if you want to stop them before they're all in the forest."

Aunt Melanie shook loose from her grip. "I don't know what else to do."

"Wait," said Kate. "Let me run back for the stick. I can run a whole lot faster than you can. With any luck I'll be back here before you have to face any of them."

For a few seconds, Aunt Melanie's eyes searched hers. "All right," she said at last. "But be careful. As important as the walking stick is, you are more important to me."

"I'll be careful," Kate promised.

Nervously, the white-haired woman squeezed Kate's unbandaged hand. "Then run like the wind. And stay as quiet as a Halami, in case some loggers are already down there. *Halma-dru*, my child."

Throwing her braid over her shoulder, Kate turned and ran back across the crumbled pumice they had just traversed. She could not see more than a few feet ahead in the fog, so she had to judge distance solely by instinct. After a few moments, she left the rocky rim and veered into the forest.

Before long the rocks were swathed in ferns and mosses. She found herself in the swampy place again, but without any landmarks it was difficult to know where to cross. She felt a twinge of fear that she could easily get lost in this dark forest, full of strange places and, she suspected, still stranger beings. A mosquito stung the back of her neck and she slapped herself.

She plunged forward, stepping through the thick mud, avoiding the deeper parts by staying near the shoots of bright green grasses that sprouted on all sides like miniature bamboo forests. Squelching rapidly through the marsh, she tripped on a branch and landed with a splash on her hands, immersed up to her elbows in cold, murky water. Regaining her feet, she sloshed ahead, not bothering to brush the mud from her legs, arms, and chin.

Finally she reached more solid ground, a grassy meadow much like the one they had met when first they entered the forest. Leaping across a rippling rivulet, she scanned the trees ahead for any signs that might guide her to the redwood grove, but saw none. She entered the mist-filled woods, padding across the springy terrain in the hope of seeing something familiar. But for her own breathing and the crunching of needles underfoot, she heard no sounds. The forest was eerily silent.

Then she heard voices. She ducked behind a moss-covered boulder. There were two people not ten feet from her when she again raised her head from a spray of ferns. To her surprise, they were not loggers, but boys. She recognized them immediately: Jody, who had stolen Aunt Melanie's envelope, and Sly, Billy's younger brother. She scowled at the very sight of them. Sly wore a .22-caliber rifle over his shoulder. He was poking Jody with his finger, goading him about something. Kate pushed apart the ferns, straining to hear what they were saying.

"C'mon, Jody," urged the older boy with the rifle. "This is your big chance."

"My chance for what?" replied the other, taking an awkward step backward.

"To prove you're not a chicken heart."

"I don't have to prove anything," Jody replied. "I just don't like killing things when there's no reason. C'mon, Sly, let's go find the others."

"Chicken heart."

"I am not," protested Jody, pushing a lock of red hair back from his forehead. "Killing them is bad luck, and besides, it's just too easy."

"Show me," demanded Sly, taking the rifle off his shoulder and inserting a bullet. "Show me how easy it is, or I'll make sure everybody knows what a chicken heart you really are. They already know how you botched getting the envelope."

Jody said nothing, but glanced over his shoulder at a low branch of a broken-topped Douglas fir towering above them. Following his line of vision, Kate saw nothing but a brownish hump rising vertically from the branch. Then, astonishingly, the hump rotated its head, revealing two perfectly round brown eyes. They studied the scene below with unmistakable curiosity, unaware of any danger.

It was an owl. Not twenty feet above the ground, the bird rested regally on its perch, its chocolate-colored plumage dotted with white spots. Kate sucked in her breath. She knew she should not take any more time here than she had already. But she could not bear to leave now.

"Jody Chicken Heart O'Leary," recited the barrel-chested boy. "That's gonna be your name for the rest of your days."

Jody gave him a sharp look. "Gimme that gun," he said, reaching out for the rifle.

With a smirk, Sly handed it to him. "Good. Now let's see you blast that owl over hell's half acre."

He won't do it, thought Kate. It's just sitting there, innocently sitting there. Though it was larger and lacked the same red color, it reminded her of the owl who had saved her life at the green pool.

Her mind raced to find some way to stop the shooting without giving herself away. Then she spied a small rock by her feet, tangled in the roots of a fallen sapling.

Jody stood still, rifle by his side. Slowly, he raised it, planting the butt of the gun against his shoulder. Motionless, he held that position for several seconds. Perspiration glistened on his cheek.

At the same time, Kate reached for the rock. She took careful aim at the branch supporting the owl, then wound her arm like a shortstop about to fire the ball at home plate. Meanwhile, the proud bird did not move so much as a feather. It simply stared at the people below, watching them with huge round eyes.

"Chicken heart, chicken heart," taunted Sly.

"Back off," Jody retorted.

"Chicken heart!"

Kate released the rock just as the boy squeezed the trigger. The gun exploded, shattering the stillness of the forest. The rock whizzed past the owl's perch, but it was too late. As she watched helplessly, the bird tumbled backward off the branch and fell with a thud to the forest floor. It landed in a craggy bed of downed branches and dead needles.

"Took you long enough," said Sly roughly as he took back his rifle. He strapped it over his shoulder. "I'll try to find another one so you can get some more practice." Grinning at his own joke, he started off into the forest.

Jody didn't answer. His eyes were fixed on the place where the owl had fallen. As Kate watched from her hiding place, he slowly approached the spot, pushing aside the stiff branches that hid the bird's body from view.

Bending down, he looked at the creature, whose enormous eyes were now closed. Absently, he stroked the bird's round chest. Then, as if he were performing a small act of repentance, he lifted a large slab of moss from the wet soil at the base of the fir and started to lay it over the body of the owl when a soft hooting sound echoed out of the forest mist. *Hooo-hooo. Hooo-hooo.*

Jody straightened himself, his expression grim. Then his face seemed to tighten. "Aw, who cares, anyway?" he said. "It's just a stupid old bird." Without looking at the owl again, he walked off in the direction of a whining chain saw.

Taking care to avoid Jody, Kate sprang into the forest. Swerving around massive trees and leaping over fallen logs, she moved as fast as she could. The sound of the chain saw drew nearer, leading her, she knew, to the redwood grove. Some of the loggers must have passed them in the fog, as Aunt Melanie had feared. *There's no way to stop them now,* she lamented. *All I can possibly do is get the walking stick.*

Concentrating on following the sound, Kate did not notice the steady darkening of the forest. The fog itself grew thicker, while less light fell from the sky above the trees. Nor did she feel the forceful sweep of the wind that leaned ever more heavily against the trunks and boughs around her.

Suddenly, she burst into the redwood grove. Just to her left was a logger sitting on a downed limb, struggling to repair his chain saw. "Mother-killing saw blade," he grumbled, removing his hard hat and wiping his brow with the sleeve of his red plaid shirt. "I didn't carry you all this way just so you could break down on me."

Kate then focused on another logger, tall and wiry, who had buried his chain saw deep into the trunk of one of the redwoods. He was sliding it up and down, back and forth, gunning the engine as sawdust sprayed in all directions. Then he pulled out the saw, set it idling on the ground, and reached his arms upward to stretch his back.

"Hey, Dick," he called to the man working on his saw. "Sure beats having a desk job, doesn't it?"

"Uh-huh," grunted the other. "And sure beats unemployment checks."

"You can say that again," agreed the first, picking up his saw once more.

Standing deeper in the grove was Billy, wearing a red T-shirt with the Blade fire department emblem. Kate froze as she saw him yank the starter rope of his chain saw, then lift it into the air, preparing to slice into the Ancient One itself, home of the hollow where she and Aunt Melanie had quietly rested only minutes before. The chain saw screamed as he lowered it to rip into the tree's midsection.

At that instant, the sky flashed with an explosion of lightning. Kate looked up to see black clouds condensing above the branches. She realized the forest had grown much darker, as the tall trees started to sway under gale-like winds.

One by one, the chain saws went silent, as lightning flashes grew more frequent. The howling wind brought an enormous limb crashing to the ground near Kate, and one man cried out in pain as another falling branch clipped his leg.

"Make a run for it," shouted one logger.

"Let's dust this place," called another. "Get back to the trucks and we'll wait out the storm."

Lightning sizzled across the sky, punctuated by earsplitting blasts of thunder. Branches waved wildly, and some splintered off and came tearing down from the higher canopies. Hail the size of golf balls pounded the trees and the forest floor. The great redwoods swayed back and forth in the wind, creaking and groaning like wrathful beasts.

For a moment, Kate stood paralyzed. Then she dashed toward the Ancient One and threw herself into the shelter of its hollow. Hailstones pounded the trunk, and some rolled harmlessly through the entrance. She sighed, knowing she was safe, as were the trees, at least for the moment. She spotted Aunt Melanie's walking stick, leaning against the inner wall of the hollow.

A person moving outside the entrance caught her attention. It was Jody, loping past in an effort to escape the raging storm. Just then, a branch as broad as an anvil came crashing down directly on his shoulder. He was flattened by the weight, his jacket torn open. He lay motionless on the ground outside the hollow.

Without thinking, Kate bolted out and rushed to his side. With a heave, she managed to pry the heavy limb off of him. Hailstones bounced off her head, arms, and back as she worked to lift him to his feet. He was semiconscious, but too limp to stand. Pummeled by hail, she grabbed him under his armpits and dragged him over the ground and into the hollow of the great tree.

She propped him up against the wall, trying her best to make him comfortable. His shoulder was bloody, but there was no way to tell if any bones had been broken. He leaned his head back against the cavern wall and moaned painfully.

Jody then opened his eyes. A look of confusion and fear filled his face as he saw Kate bending over him in the dark cavern. He rolled to the side and tried to wriggle away from her. Before she could restrain him, he was already halfway out of the hollow. Hailstones pounded him, but still he tried to crawl away.

"Let me go," he cried, half delirious. He kicked his legs wildly to break free of her grip.

"I'm just trying to help you," protested Kate, struggling to pull him back inside.

"Let me go," he shouted. At that instant, he caught sight

of two loggers running past the tree. "Harry," he called to one of them. "Harry!"

Kate's mind raced. If the loggers found him they would find her as well. And if they found her, they would also find the walking stick. With great effort, she caught hold of his leg and dragged him back into the hollow.

Desperately, she tried to pin him to the earthen floor. Yet despite his wounded shoulder, he was too strong for her and soon wriggled free. She jumped him again, trying to clasp both her arms around his waist. Jody grabbed her left arm above the elbow and rolled over, throwing her to the ground. He crawled madly toward the entrance, but before he reached it Kate reared back with both feet and kicked him as hard as she could in the ribs.

He flipped over, smacking his head full force against the wall of the hollow. With a groan, he slumped into unconsciousness and lay limp on the earthen floor.

Meanwhile the logger, hearing Jody call his name, stopped in his tracks and wheeled around. He seized the other man by the sleeve and gestured toward the tree. "It's the orphan kid," he declared, raising his voice to be heard over the clattering hailstones and crashing thunder. "He's in some kind of trouble."

"Let's get him before this mother-killing storm kills us all," shouted his companion.

The two loggers approached the redwood. Her sore hand throbbing, Kate pulled Jody's body back into the far extreme of the hollow. She cowered there in the darkness, trying desperately to breathe quietly. She could see the leather boots of one of the men planted just inches away from the entrance.

"Where the hell is he?" demanded a husky voice. "I know I heard him calling."

"Maybe you just thought you heard him," answered the other man. "He ain't here now, that's for sure."

A bright flash of lightning illuminated the grove, and for an instant, the inside of the hollow. The first logger laid his hand against the entrance, wrapping his callused fingers around the edge.

"Just let's check out this little cave," he called as he bent lower to look inside.

Kate scanned the hollow cavern for something—anything—she could use as a weapon. Her eyes fell upon the walking stick. The intricately carved markings on the shaft seemed to be glowing dimly, apparently reflecting the lightning outside. Strangely, the stick was vibrating, twitching, as it leaned against the wall.

Must be the vibration from the storm, thought Kate, as she reached to grasp it. Just then the face of the logger came into view. He searched the interior, his eyes adjusting to the dark.

Suddenly, a powerful energy flowed into Kate's hand holding the walking stick. It coursed through her whole body, a rising river of electricity. Without willing herself to do so, she struck the head of the stick hard against the wall of the cavern. The sound reverberated as though she were inside a bass drum. Then she struck it a second time, and a third.

A burst of white light filled the hollow. Pulsing bands of electricity leaped outward from the trunk, encircling it with fire, as if the tree had been struck by lightning. The logger fell back, stunned.

When the afterglow had faded away, both Kate and Jody had vanished. No sign of them remained, but for a small stain of blood mixing with the soil and hailstones at the base of the Ancient One.

PART TWO

Into the Island

10

maidenhair

KATE awoke in darkness. Was it all just a dream, a terrible dream? Had she never left the comfortable bed in the cottage?

She rolled to one side and felt a piercing pain in her left hand. Pulling the hand to her chest, she could see the dark ribbing of the hollow trunk surrounding her. Opposite, still unconscious, lay the boy Jody, blood smeared over the shoulder of his jacket. He looked more pitiful than hateful right now, but still Kate detested him. Then she felt the shaft of the walking stick resting against her thigh.

It was no dream. She struggled to kneel, grabbing the stick. At least it's safe, she congratulated herself. Aunt Melanie will be relieved. Then she noticed something curious about the cavern. It seemed smaller, more cramped somehow than she remembered.

In a flash, she thought of the logger who had almost found her—and the stick as well. Thank heaven lightning had struck the tree at just that moment. She chuckled at the memory of the big man, wide-eyed and fearful at the sudden flash of light. Peering out the entrance, she could see no sign of him or his companions. Scared off by the storm, probably. Her grin evaporated as she realized they would soon be coming back.

She looked again at Jody, slumped against the cavern wall. He'll survive, she told herself. That shoulder will be plenty sore, but he deserves it, every bit. He didn't really want to shoot that poor owl, that was clear. So why did he do it? A stupid dare, that's why. Probably stole the envelope on a dare too.

Dutifully, she reached over and wrapped the torn edge of his jacket over his injured shoulder, arranging his arm in the most comfortable position. Then she crawled out of the hollow.

She was surprised to see no hailstones on the ground. It seemed very odd, until she realized that she must have been unconscious for quite a while. Maybe the loggers had given up and gone back to town. In that case, Aunt Melanie might be somewhere near.

She called Aunt Melanie's name, but heard no answer. She must be back at the loggers' new road. It might take some time to find her again in the fog, but now that Kate had the stick it didn't really matter. She stretched stiffly, reaching first to the sky and then to her feet, then headed for the far side of the redwood grove. As she walked, she couldn't banish the feeling that something about the grove felt different than before. What exactly had changed, she didn't know, but the strange feeling nagged at her nonetheless. She stepped across a fallen branch and into the thick forest beyond the grove.

Soon her worries disappeared, as the Hidden Forest felt as dense and alive as ever. Nothing here had changed. In fact, it hadn't changed for thousands and thousands of years. It must have been her imagination, or the shock of the lightning bolt.

Hopping over a tangle of ferns growing from a long, cylindrical mound of earth that she guessed was the remains of a decomposed trunk, she tried to recall how Aunt Melanie had led her out to the rim. Fog shrouded everything as before, even obscuring the lower branches of the mammoth firs and cedars and hemlocks that surrounded her.

For the moment, she put the loggers out of her mind and moved silently through the misty woods. *Stay as quiet as a Halami,* Aunt Melanie had said. Kate began to pretend she was a young Halami, padding across the soft forest floor, stalking an elk or a deer. The walking stick became a spear, her sneakers disappeared, and she was barefoot. The land around her felt full of life, awesome, mystical, sacred.

Then she heard a voice, a small, lilting voice. Someone was singing, not far ahead. She knew at once it was Aunt Melanie, singing to guide her through the fog. All must be well, or she would not be making such lovely music.

Still the Halami, Kate resisted the urge to cry out and run to her. No, she would steal even closer, silent as the flowing fog. She would surprise her, leaping out from behind a tree at the last possible instant.

Stealthily, Kate approached. The singing grew clearer, stronger. She recognized it as one of the old Halami chants that Aunt Melanie often sang while working in her garden. A woodpecker battered against the trunk above, almost in time to the rhythm.

The music was now just a few feet away, behind a curtain of fog. Kate moved slowly, placing her feet with great care so as not to make any sound. Then her arm brushed against a protruding branch and a twig snapped sharply. The singing stopped.

Kate strode forward, holding the walking stick high. A diminutive figure, bending over a clump of maidenhair fern, stood up to greet her. Two dark eyes opened wide when she stepped into view.

Kate's eyes, too, opened wide. She was standing face to face not with Aunt Melanie, but with a girl dressed like no one she had ever met before.

The girl, high cheeked and round faced, looked at Kate fearfully, as if she were confronting a ghost. Three vertical black lines marked her chin. Upon her head rested

a bowl-shaped hat, woven from reeds like a basket, decorated with a geometric design. Her black hair, tied in two
ropes with simple strands of cedar bark wrapped around
the ends, fell over her shoulders and almost to her waist.
One hand clutched a small, straight-sided basket without a
handle that was filled with fronds and stems of maidenhair.
A square leather bib hung over her chest, dangling above
the loose skirt made from strips of reddish-brown bark.
She wore nothing on her feet.

With a shriek, the girl dropped her basket of ferns and
ran like a frightened deer into the forest. Kate hesitated for
a moment, then ran after her.

"Hey, come back!" she shouted, leaping over fallen limbs
and dodging trees. "I won't hurt you. Come back."

But the girl didn't stop. She tore through the forest, leaving Kate farther and farther behind. Soon the gap was great
enough that she could no longer be seen or heard through
the fog, and Kate slowed her pace. Giving up the chase at
last, she was preparing to halt when, without warning, the
ground gave way beneath her.

She screamed, plunging downward, until she landed with
a thud on a floor of packed dirt. Her hand throbbed painfully,
and the back of her neck stung when she lifted her head.
Clambering to her feet, she brushed a chunk of mud off her
jeans and anxiously surveyed her surroundings.

A pit, she realized in disbelief. *I've fallen into a pit.*
Despite the pain in her neck, she craned her head upward.
The pit was about ten feet deep, vertically walled, with a
steep overhang near the top to prevent anyone who was
trapped from climbing out. Above, she saw the fog filtering
through canopies of branches. Escape was impossible
without help.

"Aunt Melanie," she cried, mortified. "I'm in this pit. Can
you hear me? Aunt Melanie, please hear me!"

No answer came but the gentle swishing of branches in
a light wind. Again she tried calling, again without success. Dejectedly, she sat down on the dirt floor of the pit,

arms around her knees, her head bowed. She kicked the walking stick away from her foot.

Then she heard a snarling sound above her. Looking up with a start, she saw the face of what looked like a coyote, brown ears erect, peering down on her. Teeth bared, the animal growled viciously as though getting ready to spring.

Kate's heart pounded. She scuttled to the far side of the pit, but the snarling beast could still see her. Leaping to her feet, she grabbed the walking stick and held it like a baseball bat.

"Stay away from me, you," she said fiercely. "Or I'll make a home run out of you."

At the sight of the stick, the animal ceased growling, dropped back its ears, then retreated out of sight. An instant later, another face appeared in the same place. It belonged to the girl. She studied Kate apprehensively, her brow beneath the basketry hat wrinkled in fear.

There was a bark, then the girl turned and said something unintelligible. Another bark, this time softer. The girl again stared into the pit. At once, Kate realized that the coyote-like creature must be her pet, a scruffy sort of dog.

"Help me out," said Kate. "Please. I won't hurt you, I promise."

Consternation showed in the girl's dark eyes. She drew back from the edge of the pit.

"Please," Kate called after her. "Please help me out." Then, on a sudden intuition, she shouted, "*Halma-dru.*"

Tentatively, the girl's face reappeared.

"*Halma-dru,*" repeated Kate in a quieter voice.

At that, the girl clenched her jaw and pulled back out of sight again, leaving Kate shaking her head despondently. It was no use. She could be stuck in this pit until the end of her days.

Suddenly the end of a large branch appeared at the edge of the pit. With a groan, the girl heaved it over the lip. It crashed onto the earthen floor by Kate's feet, showering her with broken twigs and strands of moss.

The girl pointed to the branch, saying, *"Ai-ya, ai-ya."* The dog's face appeared by hers, and it barked excitedly.

Without hesitating, Kate started to ascend the makeshift ladder. Placing her feet in the notches where smaller branches protruded, she climbed higher, holding the walking stick between her teeth. Occasionally the notches would break, sending her sliding backward again. Gradually, however, she made progress. When she had climbed as far as she dared without breaking the branch, she raised her arms skyward. Her hands reached barely above the opening.

The girl clasped Kate's wrists and heaved, pulling her upward. For a moment she hung there, suspended, her legs kicking freely. A clod of dirt from the edge of the pit dropped onto her head, stinging her eyes. Then the girl pulled again, this time hard enough to lift Kate's head and shoulders above the hole. Swinging her legs to the side, she caught the edge with one foot and hauled herself out of the pit.

She lay on her back on the bed of needles, exhausted. Rolling to her side, she found herself eyeball to eyeball with the carved owl's head of the walking stick. The yellow eyes gleamed at her, and she rolled back quickly.

She heard the girl also panting heavily, and sat up just as she did. Seated on the verdant forest floor, they observed each other warily. Kate dared not move, lest she frighten her again.

Cautiously, the brown dog approached Kate, fluffy tail curled up high over his back. Forcing herself to remain still, she nevertheless glanced at the walking stick on the ground by her side. The dog nudged her shoulder roughly, then sniffed her sweatshirt with a thin, pointed nose. Suddenly, he licked her on the side of the neck.

"Monga," said the girl sharply, but the laughter in her eyes betrayed her true feelings. *"Monga ha-lei shluntah."*

The dog padded to her side, nuzzling her cheek. The girl giggled, grinning bashfully at Kate.

"Halma-dru," said Kate slowly, her brain refusing to accept what her heart told her must be true. "Do you speak English?"

The girl's face went blank. Tentatively, she said, *"Yiteh neh chi wiltu."* She studied Kate searchingly, as if expecting an answer.

Kate could only shake her head. Looking from the girl to the walking stick and back again, she patted herself on the chest and said softly, "Kate."

A light of understanding kindled in the strange girl's eyes and she patted her own chest. *"Laioni."*

"Lai-oni," repeated Kate.

The girl smiled again. Indicating the dog, she said, *"Monga."* In response, it pawed her playfully.

Keeping her gaze locked on Laioni's, Kate reached up and touched her own head. "Nice hat," she said, pointing toward the basketry cap.

Laioni didn't seem to register the compliment. Instead, her attention focused on the long blond braid drooping over Kate's shoulder. Seeing this, Kate lifted the braid. "You like this?" she asked, somewhat puzzled. "It's just plain old hair, like yours."

As Kate lifted her braid, Laioni lifted her own two ropes and giggled again. *"Hunneh,"* she said carefully.

"Hunneh," repeated Kate, knowing she had just learned another word for *hair.*

Laioni, however, was not yet finished. She pointed at the braid and said something Kate couldn't catch. Sensing she hadn't communicated, the girl looked around for something to help her express the new thought. At last she noticed the walking stick. Taking care not to touch it directly with her hand, she indicated the owl's head handle.

"The stick?" muttered Kate. "What does that have to do with—" Then suddenly she understood. Laioni did not mean the handle itself, but rather the eyes. The yellow eyes. "Yellow," declared Kate. "You mean my hair is yellow." She paused, then lifted her braid again. *"Hunneh* yellow."

Laioni's eyes glittered. *"Hunneh* yell-ow," she replied, laughing.

Guess she doesn't see too much yellow hair where she

comes from, thought Kate, laughing herself. Then she
wondered: Where does she come from, anyway?

At that moment, Laioni rose to her feet with effortless
grace. Pointing at Kate, she said, "Ka-teh." Then she beckoned, apparently asking her to come. She walked backward a few steps, Monga dancing about her feet, before
turning into the forest.

Full of uncertainty, Kate took the walking stick, stood
up, and started to follow. There was something distinctly
familiar about this utterly unfamiliar girl. Yet what could it
be? Where was Aunt Melanie when she needed her? She
would know where this girl came from, maybe even speak
some of her language. Perhaps she was one of those modern descendants of the Halami who lived somewhere in the
region, keeping the old ways alive. But was it possible that
included not learning to speak English? In any case, she
knew enough of the old ways to have figured out how to
get into the crater.

Kate shrugged, deciding to save her questions for later.
As they strode through the forest, she spotted a moss-
covered boulder she had seen near the place where she had
first met the girl. Sure enough, a few steps later Laioni
picked up her basket of ferns, hardly slackening her pace.
She continued to lead Kate into the forest, Monga at her
heels, moving confidently despite the heavy mist. It was
clear she knew these woods well.

Some distance farther, Laioni stopped. Kate came up to
her side and saw, to her surprise, that they had arrived at
the redwood grove. Laioni lowered her head briefly, indicating Kate should go forward.

Hesitantly, Kate stepped into the clearing. Once again
she felt the indefinable difference in the great trees. Her gaze
fell to the Ancient One, and with a start she realized that it
looked smaller than before. Or were the other trees in the
grove larger?

She glanced at Laioni, standing at the edge of the clearing. Kate motioned for her to come, but she remained

there, both wonderment and fear written on her round face.
Monga sat expectantly by her side, tail wagging.

What does she think I am, some kind of tree spirit? Kate
grinned morbidly at her own humor, trying to dispel the
queasiness in her stomach. Something about this place was
just not right. She turned again to the Ancient One and
approached it gingerly, her sneakers crunching on the needles.

Placing her left palm on the gnarled trunk, she lowered
her head to look inside. She realized that she had not
thought about Jody since leaving the tree. It took a few seconds for her eyes to adjust to the dark, but when they did,
the scene stunned her.

Jody was gone.

Whirling around, she scanned the grove for any tracks,
any signs. There were none to be seen. He couldn't have
gone far, she reasoned. He wasn't even in shape to walk.

Uneasiness swelling steadily inside her, Kate walked
back across the grove toward Laioni. As she came near, she
spied a small, rounded boulder at the edge of the clearing.
Her spine tingled. It was the same warning stone she had
seen before, or one just like it. Yet something had changed.
Not the expression on the face, still screaming some silent
admonition. Not the depth of the lines carved into the surface. Not the position of the stone, warning anyone who
might dare to pass too near.

Then in a flash she knew. The stone bore no moss. The
lines seemed freshly cut, as if carved only yesterday.

Catching her breath, she looked to Laioni. Who was this
girl dressed in Native American clothing who spoke no English and watched her with eyes as alert as an eagle's? At
once, the answer came clear. She did not want to believe it,
but the trees and the warning stone and the girl herself told
her she must.

She darted back across the redwood grove and dove
headlong into the Ancient One's hollow. Biting her lip,
she lifted the walking stick and struck it hard against the
wooden wall. Once, twice, three times.

Nothing happened.

She held the owl's head in front of her face, but no illumination glowed within the yellow eyes. It was merely a shaft of lifeless wood. "Take me back," she pleaded, her voice trembling. "I don't belong here."

After waiting for an endless moment, she lowered the stick reluctantly. Outside, Monga gave two sharp barks. Kate leaned toward the light. Through the shifting mist she saw the dog sitting, as before, next to Laioni, a living member of the Halami tribe.

And she knew that she had traveled back in time.

11

ebony eyes

NOT knowing what else to do, Kate rejoined Laioni and Monga, whose foxlike tail wagged energetically as she approached. For her part, Laioni seemed surprised at first that Kate had not simply vanished altogether into the redwood grove. After a few seconds, however, she beckoned shyly for Kate to follow her into the forest, apparently concluding that this visiting spirit had decided to stay with her for a while. Reading her expressions, Kate solemnly trudged after her.

Laioni led her purposefully through the woods, without any visible signs of a trail to guide her. Monga, meanwhile, ran around them in wide circles, returning occasionally to brush Laioni's leg with his tail before darting off again. The fog seemed to be lifting, and soon Kate could see shreds of deep blue through the branches ahead. The trees soon thinned and they passed into a verdant meadow, much like the one where Kate had almost lost her sneaker with Aunt Melanie . . . was it just this morning? Or several centuries in the future? Kate noticed little of her surroundings this time, stepping mechanically over fragrant flowers and brightly flowing rivulets. All she could think of was the white-haired woman who was anxiously waiting for her to return with the walking stick. She hoped Aunt Melanie was all right.

As they neared the shore of the blue lake, Kate's lingering doubts that she had indeed traveled back in time disappeared. For there by the lake she saw what could only be an encampment of Halamis. Seated beside a fire pit were two women, one much older than the other. They seemed to be preparing food, singing softly as they worked. They were dressed much the same as Laioni, wearing woven hats, loose leather tops, shredded bark skirts, and three lines on their chins.

Near the younger of the two, a shallow cradle made from woven willow shoots held a sleeping infant, laced into the cradle with a long strip of deer hide. A few paces farther from the lapping waters of the lake stood a brush hut, appearing rather temporary, conical in shape with a dense covering of grasses and tree limbs. Tools of all descriptions lay scattered on the ground: a pouch made from some kind of bladder, a scraping implement carved from an antler, a gouging tool that had what looked like a beaver's tooth for the blade, a comb and a sewing awl that gleamed like polished bone, a gray stone dish holding some oily substance, a spoon sculpted from a seashell, and other implements.

When Laioni and Kate came within ten feet, the two women halted their singing. Seeing Kate, they dropped their work and leaped to their feet, fear clearly visible on their faces. The younger woman, probably Laioni's mother, barked some stern words at the girl that caused her to frown. Laioni then stepped nearer and engaged in an animated exchange during which she pantomimed Kate's rescue from the pit. Grimly, her mother took Laioni by the wrist and placed herself between Kate and the girl. She faced Kate, scowling, and spoke sharply, motioning with her hands for Kate to go away and leave them alone.

"Believe me, I'd go if I could," muttered Kate. "Do you have any bus tickets to the twentieth century?"

Suddenly, the woman's eyes focused on the walking stick. At the sight of it, she cried out and took a quick step backward. The older woman behind her, who was rubbing her hands together nervously, released a long, low moaning sound.

It struck Kate that somehow they seemed to recognize the walking stick. Perhaps they might even know enough about it to show her how to tap its strange power so it could take her home again. She tried to think of some way, any way, to win their trust.

She scanned the camp, racking her brain. Her eyes fell on the fire pit, ashes glowing orange, and an idea flashed into her head. Moving slowly and deliberately, she took off her day pack and removed the thermos. Then, as the three Halamis watched with a mixture of dread and curiosity, she unscrewed the top, poured half a cup of steaming hot chocolate, and drank a sip herself. Then, bending down, she placed the cup of brown liquid on a flat stone near her feet. Backing up a few paces, she pointed to the cup and said, *"Halma-dru."*

Monga scampered over to the cup, sniffed it for a few seconds, then reached his long tongue into the hot chocolate. Lapping it into his mouth, he shook his bushy tail vigorously and barked twice.

With that, Laioni darted out from behind her mother, evading the woman's grasp. Ignoring her worried chattering, Laioni reached for the cup. No sooner did she touch it than she swiftly drew back her hand, yelping as if something had bit her. Turning to her mother, she said in amazement, *"Chu. Chu tkho."*

"Chu," echoed Kate, guessing she had just heard the Halami word for *hot*.

Waving her mother back, Laioni cautiously picked up the cup and sniffed its contents. After a moment of deliberation, she took a small sip. As she swallowed, her face burst into a broad smile. She turned to her mother and said something in an excited voice.

Laioni then carried the cup to her mother, who refused to

try it. After repeated urgings, all of which were rejected, Laioni brought the cup over to the elder woman. With unsteady hands, the old Halami raised the cup, then faltered as Laioni's mother spoke to her harshly. She answered back in a gruff voice, then brought the cup to her face. She inhaled once, chirped in surprise, and took a small taste. Like Laioni before her, the old woman smiled from one high cheekbone to the other. She took another swallow, smiled again, then held the cup out to Laioni's mother.

Hesitantly, the woman took the cup, glanced doubtfully at Kate, then inserted her index finger into the cup. Fear melted into wonder as she felt the liquid, warm without the aid of fire. With another glance at Kate, she brought the cup to her lips and, after smelling its contents, swallowed the remaining hot chocolate. The creases on her forehead relaxed and she nodded at Kate, her eyes still afraid but somewhat accepting.

The rest of the day was spent around the encampment. The two women resumed their work, singing together, pausing only when the infant needed to be nursed or cleaned. The men of this group, Kate learned through Laioni's energetic pantomimes, were away for some time, perhaps on a hunting expedition. Laioni seemed to be concerned for them, almost afraid, though she gave no indication why.

Using her own pantomimes, Kate kept the conversation going, hoping she might eventually learn something useful. She tried to find out whether the Halamis hunted with arrows, with spears, or by digging pits like the one she herself had fallen into. Then she tried to learn whether their prey was elk, deer, rabbit, or squirrel. But she succeeded only in making Laioni laugh.

"So you've never seen a rabbit that looked like that?" Kate asked, giggling herself. "How about like this?" She hopped around the campfire, doing her best imitation of a kangaroo. Laioni laughed again, while the two Halami women glanced worriedly at each other.

Deciding to try another line of questioning, Kate pointed across the lake toward the wall of sheer cliffs surrounding the crater. "Is that where your father went?" she asked Laioni. "Past the cliffs and down into the forest?"

The Halami girl's expression swiftly darkened. She looked toward the cliffs, frowning, as if some grave danger lurked beyond them. She said a few sentences and then kicked angrily at a clump of grass.

Kate did not need to understand her words to know that something was wrong in the forest outside the crater. Yet she had no clue what it might be. Aunt Melanie, she felt sure, would know. But Aunt Melanie was somewhere very, very far away.

Then Laioni gestured toward the walking stick, a look of awe on her face. She asked Kate something in a soft voice, but Kate could not make sense of her words. Yet the impression was clear: Laioni, like her mother, knew something about the stick. With luck, if she waited for the right moment, Kate might learn something from them about its secrets.

Later that afternoon, Laioni showed Kate a simple game of throwing polished sticks at a stake planted in the ground. Since Kate had often played horseshoes with Grandfather, her aim was impressive, though not as good as Laioni's. Whenever Kate missed a throw, Laioni would look at her strangely, as if she thought Kate was not playing as well as she could.

Next, Laioni led her to the confluence of two bubbling rivulets that emptied into the lake not far from camp. Revealing three miniature carved canoes resting in the hollow of a nearby rock, she carried them to the flowing water and placed them in a small whirlpool formed by the meshing currents. The canoes, shaped with pointed bow and box-like stern, were each carved from a single block of wood. They reminded Kate of the dugout canoe she had seen once with Aunt Melanie in a museum close to the airport.

Airport, mused Kate. She had never thought about life without one within an hour's drive. Cars, too, she had taken for granted all her years. She doubted she could ever explain to Laioni that people, ordinary people, would one

day cruise faster than the swiftest deer and fly higher than
the soaring eagle. And she wondered whether Laioni's inti-
mate knowledge of this place, her place, would be possible
in the age of automobiles and airplanes. Motion and speed
were so addictive, crowding out the calmness and focus
needed to know one special place well. Then, with a pang,
she wished she could simply board some time-traveling
airplane that could bring her back to Aunt Melanie.

Laioni took three pebbles from the swirling streams of
water—one buff, one black, one slightly crimson—and
placed one into each of the toy canoes. Released into the
whirlpool, the little boats floated in small circles, sometimes spinning rapidly, sometimes gliding into choppier
waters, where they inevitably capsized.

Kate was soon captivated by the miniature canoes. She
laughed with Laioni whenever one tipped over, dumping
the pebble occupant into the water. By vigorous gestures,
Laioni indicated that the same thing had happened to her
once or twice. Monga, having positioned himself by the
edge, batted at the boats with one of his paws.

What a far cry, Kate reflected, this was from the televi-
sion and high-tech video games of her own world. Not
since she had played Pooh Sticks as a small child down by
the river with Aunt Melanie had she had such a good time
with so few props.

As she bent low to take a drink from one of the rivulets,
Kate viewed the fragmented reflection of Laioni's face in
the water. She watched the Halami girl slowly cock her
head to one side. Strange. For an instant, she saw not
Laioni—but Aunt Melanie. Sitting up with a start, she gazed
at the girl seated next to her and all at once realized why
she had seemed so familiar from the first moment they met.
Laioni's eyes were the eyes of Aunt Melanie, black as
ebony, with a few flecks of hazel green around the edges.
Kate thought about the crumpled photograph she had seen
at the cottage of two youngsters on the Isle of Skye.
The dark-eyed girl in the picture taken fifty years ago (or
four hundred fifty years from now, depending on how one

counted) looked so much like Laioni it was uncanny. Of course, the very notion that they could be related was absurd, yet Kate couldn't banish the feeling entirely.

Abruptly, Kate noticed that Laioni was also staring at her. Not at her face, though: She was examining her green cotton sweatshirt with keen interest. Kate raised her forearm so that Laioni could feel the material. As the Halami girl rubbed the cloth between her thumb and forefinger, her face assumed the wondrous expression of someone encountering silk or satin for the very first time. "Mmmmmmm," she said, closing her eyes.

Kate reached to touch the strips of cedar bark constituting Laioni's skirt, and the Halami girl started to giggle. Kate smiled at her and said, "Pretty different, huh?" Laioni seemed to understand, and giggled again.

At that moment, a strange but lovely smell, almost like almonds roasting, came wafting through the air to them. With the ease of a springing fawn, Laioni jumped to her feet. Monga at once sprinted to her side, his tail swishing expectantly. She pointed to her mouth and patted her abdomen, indicating the time had come for a meal. Kate suddenly observed the slanting light crossing the cliff wall of the crater, and realized that it was late afternoon already. She was hungry, powerfully hungry, having eaten nothing more substantial all day than hot chocolate.

As Kate stood, Laioni plucked the three small boats from the water and returned them to their resting place on the rock. Meanwhile, Kate happened to glance toward the reflectionless blue lake. Beyond the rising mist floated the same sinister island, as unnerving now as it had been the first time she had seen it with Aunt Melanie. Eerie in its utter blackness, it seemed to slide slowly across the surface. With a slight shiver, she turned away.

Laioni led her back to the fire pit, where her mother continued to chant as she worked. At that moment, she was parching some type of seeds on a flat rock next to the hot coals. Kate could not keep herself from investigating the source of the rich aroma. Drawing closer, she watched the woman skillfully moving the seeds around with a wooden stick, taking care to heat each one evenly. It reminded Kate of making popcorn over an open fire, and she felt a sudden sense of loss amidst her swelling hunger. The last time she had made popcorn was with Aunt Melanie.

Just then, the Halami woman put down the stick and directed her daughter to do something. Laioni quickly picked up a round, broad-bottomed basket with straight sides and very tight weave. Taking care to avoid the walking stick that Kate had leaned against a rock, she carried the basket to the nearest rivulet flowing into the lake. Dipping it into the water until its pattern of repeating parallelograms was submerged, she then brought it back to her mother.

Kate turned to see the older woman pounding some seeds into meal on a flat stone between her legs. Every so often she put down her cylindrical pestle and sifted, lightly tapping a shallow basket of meal with her finger to make the finest meal fall into a woven hopper. All the while she watched Kate with a mixture of curiosity and suspicion.

By now, Kate's hunger was almost unbearable. She watched expectantly as Laioni's mother, using wooden tongs, placed two round stones from the fire pit into the water-filled basket. Why is she cooking stones? Kate wondered. Then the woman added a bowl of rootlike tubers to the basket. Methodically, she began removing cooler stones and replacing them with freshly heated ones from the fire pit. Soon the water began to boil, and a new smell overpowered the aroma of the parched seeds. The baby, hungry as well, started to cry.

At last, Laioni's mother nodded to Kate to sit down. She said something to the older woman and to Laioni, and the meal was served. In addition to the freshly cooked tubers, Laioni produced a basket filled with red berries, seeds, and strips of some unknown vegetable. Her mother retrieved from the brush hut a tray of dried fish, as tasty as the smoked salmon Kate had eaten in Scotland once on a trip with Grandfather.

For her own part, Kate contributed what little hot chocolate remained in the thermos, complementing the herbal tea brewing by the fire. Everyone ate ravenously, including Monga, who tore into a generous clump of fish meat by Laioni's side. Lifting her baby from the cradle, Laioni's mother began to nurse the child, who squeaked and squealed like a rusty wheel while drinking.

As they ate together, the sun dropped below the line of cliffs to the west. The air grew a touch colder, though heat from the steaming lake and the fire pit kept them warm. In the distance, a lone owl called *hooo-hooo, hooo-hooo*.

Kate surveyed the various tools and utensils scattered on the ground. They seemed so different here, freshly used and lit by the glow of fire coals, than they would hundreds of years later in some natural history museum or art gallery. Each one was made with such care and grace and pride that it was really a work of art. Yet they were made to be used, not shown. That, she suddenly realized, was the point: In this time, art and life were still the same.

Soon Laioni's mother replaced the now-sleeping baby in the cradle, lacing the strip of deer hide carefully across the tiny body. Kate could see no moon above them, and she shuddered to think that soon they would have no light at all but the campfire. The crater swiftly filled with darkness, the sort of deep impenetrable darkness that always made her feel uneasy. She wondered what might have happened to Jody.

Then the Halami women began to chant, singing to the vanishing light ringing the rim of the crater. Laioni's mother tapped lightly on the bottom of a large basket, while the old woman shook a rattle made from a deer's hoof. Laioni hummed in the background, climbing a scale and then dropping back, joined on occasion by Monga's high whining howl. Kate gazed into the glowing coals and listened, her eyelids growing heavier with each repetition.

Ayah-ho ayah-ho
Tlah hontseh na hoh-ah

Ayah-ho Ayah-ho
Heyowe halma-dru.

Gradually, gradually, her cares melted into the mist and she thought only of the present, of glowing cliffs encircling her, of blue waters gently lapping, of voices strange and sonorous. The night-sky eyes of Laioni saw her nodding off, and she quietly came to guide Kate to her bed of soft grass in the brush hut.

Kate felt like someone both dreaming and waking at once. It seemed almost as if Aunt Melanie had appeared in a younger form to put her to sleep, to tuck her in gently and whisper good-night, just as she had done so often when Kate was a child.

12

the time tunnel

A chain saw buzzed, quite near her head. Kate woke up with a start.

She found herself sandwiched inside the brush hut, with Laioni on one side and the old woman on the other. Laioni's mother was nowhere to be seen. Monga lay curled up outside the entrance. Then the buzzing noise came again, and Kate realized that it was only the elder Halami snoring.

All at once, her worldly concerns came crashing back. She reached for the walking stick, lying at the entrance to the hut, and pulled it to her chest. How stupid to have tried to fetch this stick alone! Aunt Melanie should have warned her, though most likely she didn't know herself of the danger. And now she was here, thrown back five hundred years in time. Worse yet, she had not even a clue how to get home.

She gazed at the indecipherable etchings carved deep into the wooden shaft. The owl's head on the handle gazed back at her, unwilling to reveal its secrets. There must be some way to make it come alive again, Kate told herself. Less for her own sake than for Aunt Melanie's. She needed help, and soon. Kate could feel it, as vividly as she could feel the chain saws about to rip into the trunk of the Ancient One.

Then, like a slap in the face, she realized the true depth of her dilemma. She had traveled back in time inside of the great redwood, whose life reached from this time all the way to her own. If that tree were cut and killed, could she still get back at all? Even if she could solve the riddle of the walking stick's power, if the medium connecting her to the future did not exist anymore, she would be stranded. She struggled to remember the theory about time tunnels. Something about places where living things can grow undisturbed for a very long time . . . So if one of those places is suddenly disturbed, let alone demolished, what happens to the time tunnel?

She lowered the stick, knowing well the answer. Her thoughts then turned again to Jody. Troublesome as he was, he was lost in this strange time just like herself. She pondered what could have happened to him. Perhaps he had somehow wandered off, only to end up at the bottom of some Halami pit. Perhaps he had been removed from the tree by force. There was no way to know.

Stretching, she crawled out of the brush hut onto the stony ground. Although the sun had not yet topped the ridge of cliffs, a diffuse early morning light filled the crater. Across the meadow, birds fluttered and chirped in the branches of the mighty trees. The lake sent up wispy trails of mist, obscuring the black island completely. She heard the sound of footsteps and turned to see Laioni's mother emerging from the forest with a handful of skunk cabbage and a sprig of wild iris, the flower Aunt Melanie liked to call blue flag.

Yesterday's fear still written on her face, the woman glanced nervously at the walking stick, then acknowledged Kate with a nod of her head. Her eyes, not so dark as Laioni's, looked at the purple kerchief tied around Kate's hand, stained with blood from the day before. *"H'ona tuwan teh,"* she said in a low voice.

Kate did not understand, but instinctively pulled her hand to her side. She sat on a nearby rock, watching the woman clean the broad cabbage leaves and the root of the flower in the stream, singing softly as she worked. Then she dangled them over the hot coals of the fire pit for a minute, warming them, before crushing them between two stones. At last, she scraped the moist mass onto her hand and carried it over to Kate.

Keeping an eye on the walking stick, the Halami woman gently lifted Kate's bandaged hand. Ever so delicately, she unwound the kerchief, exposing the tender skin to the air. As Kate winced, she applied the poultice to the spot, chanting some rhythmic words.

Almost instantly, Kate felt a soothing sensation. Despite its pungent smell, the healing substance dulled the pain while sinking into her raw skin. Laioni's mother quickly doused the purple kerchief in the water, then wrapped it again around her hand, weaving the ends together securely. She ceased chanting just as the sun edged above the cliffs.

Laioni emerged from the tent. She eyed Kate mischievously and did an imitation of the old woman's snore before bursting into a giggle. Kate laughed as well, for the moment forgetting her troubles. Monga pranced around the fire pit, bouncing on his scruffy brown legs.

Laioni and her mother then exchanged some sentences, indicating the wounded hand as they spoke. Laioni's mother, clearly concerned about something, tried to ask Kate a question, pointing first to the hand and then to the walking stick. Not comprehending, Kate could only shake her head. More than ever, she longed to return to her own time.

Then Laioni decided to try. She gestured toward the stick, then staggered back a few steps as though she had encountered something of great power. Next she touched her own left hand, wincing as though in pain. She brought the hand nearer to the stick, whereupon her expression changed to satisfaction.

At last, Kate understood. They could not fathom why, possessing the special strength of the walking stick, she had not healed her own hand. How could she explain to them she didn't know how to use it? Then an idea took shape in her mind.

Holding the stick in both hands so they might see the many intricate carvings on the shaft, Kate twirled it slowly in her palms. Finally, she laid it across her lap and began making various faces and gestures designed to show ignorance, confusion, uncertainty. Between each pantomime, she pointed to the stick.

Only bewilderment registered on the Halamis' faces. Determined, Kate tried again, running through any expression she could think of that could possibly convey her problem.

Still there was no communication. Exasperated, Kate pointed to the confused faces of Laioni and her mother, exclaiming, "That's how I feel. Don't you see?"

A light seemed to kindle in Laioni's eyes. She chattered something to her mother, who grew suddenly somber. The woman pointed to the stick, indicating the full length of the shaft, then turned her gaze back to Kate. The look of fear in her face had deepened.

"That's right," blurted Kate, her vision growing misty. "I don't know how to use it." She looked to the sky and raised her hands in despair. "Who can help me?" she cried. "Who can help me?"

The Halami woman stared at her for a long moment. Then she uttered a single word, so softly Kate could barely hear it. *"Azanna,"* she said. *"Azanna."* Then she stepped quickly away to the other side of the fire pit, dragging Laioni by the arm.

Azanna, repeated Kate to herself. The word sounded vaguely familiar. She knew she had heard it before, but where? It doesn't matter, she shrugged sadly. Just another Halami word.

Dejectedly, she lifted herself from the rock. Laioni was arguing with her mother about something, but Kate was not interested. She swung the walking stick angrily. With a sharp crack, its base whacked against the stone.

All at once, she remembered. Kate could hear Aunt Melanie's voice telling her the meaning of *Azanna,* speaking hesitantly in the hollow of the tree. To learn more about the stick, to have even a chance of going home, she knew she must return to the Circle of Stones.

13

the circle of stones

STRIDING around the foggy perimeter of the lake, Kate tightened the knot of the kerchief around her hand. Fear of the deadly green pool rose within her as she stepped over rivulets running down from the cliffs. Aunt Melanie had said that its spell would work only once. Yet Kate now existed in an earlier time, so perhaps the pool's curse would call her still more strongly. She grasped the walking stick tightly, as a climber grasps a safety rope. Almost as dreadful as the green pool, in her mind, were those seven stones themselves. Something about them haunted her, something more than their sheer size. They had seemed eerily aware of her presence, almost as if they were alive.

Before turning to ascend the rocky slope, she stooped to pick up a small piece of pumice and hurled it into the lake. Though fog obscured its landing place, she heard a distant splash. Somewhere across the water was the Halami camp she had left so abruptly, not even staying to have some breakfast. She recalled the faces of Laioni and her mother, one crestfallen to see her go, the other clearly relieved. She picked up another of the light stones and threw it in the same direction. To her surprise, this time there was no splash. All she could hear was the sound of waves lapping against the shore.

She did not linger to learn what had happened. Perhaps it had landed on the island, although that begged the question of why the first stone had hit water instead. Unless the island really could move . . . No, that was impossible. Looking up the slope to her right, she could see the misty outline of the ribbed formation that rose out of the cliff wall behind the Circle of Stones. But the Circle itself remained invisible.

Turning her back to the lake, she started clambering up the rocky incline. As before, she was forced to use her hands to pull herself higher. Suddenly, she heard a clatter of rocks falling not far behind her. She whirled around.

"Laioni!"

The Halami girl struggled up the slope to meet her. Just behind, pouncing from rock to rock, Kate could see a familiar shaggy, brown shape. Stretching below them, a curling cloud rolled across the lake. At length the pair arrived, panting heavily.

Kate shook her head. "You shouldn't come," she said sternly, waving Laioni back.

The girl set her jaw firmly and looked straight at Kate. It was clear she did not want to go back.

"But it's dangerous up there," insisted Kate. "Go back now, while you can."

Laioni didn't budge. Instead, she held out her hand, which was full of dried seeds. She took a mouthful, then offered the rest to Kate.

She not only looks like Aunt Melanie, thought Kate. She's just as stubborn. Frowning, she took a swallow of the seeds but didn't taste them. Then she continued climbing the slope, motioning to Laioni to stay behind her.

As the ground at last began to level off, Kate caught a glimpse of the great boulders. Their cracked and blistered surfaces loomed ominously, half hidden by the swirling mist. They seemed to change constantly as she approached them, like huge faces moving back and forth between light and shadow. Kate eyed the spot, at the base of the smallest of the enormous stones, where she knew she would find the bubbling green pool. Sucking in her breath, she prepared to confront it.

To her astonishment, the pool was bubbling, but not green. Cautiously, Kate drew nearer to see only a natural bowl of boiling water, fed by the same small rivulet where Aunt Melanie had scrubbed her hand so relentlessly. The pool bubbled and splattered like the clearest of hot springs, devoid of any aroma but the faint smell of sulfur. Somehow, the evil spell had vanished. Or, Kate realized all of a sudden, it had not yet arrived.

Straightening herself, she scanned the collection of giant stones. Mist moved slowly over their deeply lined surfaces. Behind the bubbling pool, she saw a narrow passageway between the smallest boulder, which was roughly the size of a pickup truck, and the boulder next to it, which was as broad and bulky as a barn. She knew that the passageway would lead her into the center of the Circle, but she hesitated. *They're watching you,* said the voice of Aunt Melanie in her memory, and the hair on the back of her neck prickled. She stood there, motionless as stone herself, searching for the strength to step into the passageway. Just then, she heard someone breathing beside her.

It was Laioni, her face full of awe to stand before *Azanna,* the Circle of Stones. Without turning from the boulders, she slipped her hand into Kate's. This gesture by the girl with Aunt Melanie's eyes gave Kate an unexpected surge of courage. Yet she also found herself all the more keenly aware that the true Aunt Melanie was far, far away. And, she knew in her bones, Aunt Melanie needed her help.

Side by side and hand in hand, they walked past the pool and between the two great cracked boulders. His head low to the ground, Monga followed at their heels. On their left, the gray wall of the larger boulder rose high above their heads, while on their right, the surface of the smaller boulder was coated with an undulating skin of mist. They spoke not a word, nor did Monga make a sound, as they passed through the channel.

Finally, they emerged and stepped into the middle of the Circle. Standing together, their clothing as unlike as their worlds, Kate and Laioni slowly pivoted as if greeting all seven of the stones. Each of them had a distinct shape, though all shared the same blistered gray texture. The shifting mist swirled thickly around them, making the giant boulders seem like one enormous unbroken ring of rock.

When the visitors had turned a complete circle, they stopped. Not knowing what else to do, Kate let go of Laioni's hand and said aloud, "I am—we are—here, Great Circle. For your help. If you really are watching like my Aunt Melanie said, if you can hear me somehow, then won't you do something to show us? Please. See, you're my only hope."

They waited for several minutes, but no response came. More fog flowed into the ring until all they could see of the boulders were dark shadows hovering behind a cloudy curtain. Kate felt sheepish for trying to communicate with, of all things, rocks. Even gigantic rocks. Things were different here in Lost Crater, but not that different. She shrugged, looking sadly toward Laioni, whose eyes showed only empathy.

Kate started to leave, when her foot tripped on a small stone that had been obscured by the fog. Although she caught herself before falling, the walking stick slipped from her hand and fell with a smack against the ground. As she reached to pick it up, she heard a strange sound, like a faraway echo of the stick's impact.

Slowly, the sound swelled into a distant drumbeat that reverberated around them. Monga whimpered worriedly, and Laioni reached down to stroke his furry back. The sound grew louder, fuller, just the opposite of a normal echo, until it reached the volume of cannons blasting nearby. The cannons erupted faster and faster on all sides until Kate and Laioni both covered their ears with their hands.

The ground beneath them started to shake, clearing the

mist with its vibrations. Kate was knocked to her knees by a powerful tremor, and she feared suddenly that the old volcano had come to life. She and Laioni and Monga would all perish, along with any chance to see Aunt Melanie again. The violent heaving continued, throwing them together in one ungainly heap.

Then, as swiftly as they had begun, the tremors began to fade. The great reverberations slowed and grew quieter by degrees. The mist continued to dissipate, flowing from the Circle like water from a lake whose dam has burst.

Then Kate realized with horror that the giant stones themselves were changing. Before her eyes, as though the fleeting mist were peeling away layers of crusty skin, the boulders began to metamorphose. Laioni let out a little scream and covered her mouth, while Monga crawled quickly into her lap. Kate grabbed the shaft of the walking stick and drew it protectively to herself.

Over the tops and backs of the great boulders grew gnarled and scraggly black hair, thick as tree limbs and curly as uncombed wool. Bent and bulbous noses formed from shafts of protruding rock, some narrow and twisted, others flat and globular. Kate shuddered to see a pair of deep indentations open behind each nose, where burned light as intense as newborn stars. Above these gleaming eyes, heavy ledges of rock transformed into burly brows, sprouting the same unruly hair that now covered most of the surface of the boulders. Wide mouths opened, lined with lips that burgeoned and swelled like streams of lava. Pointed chins jutted almost to the feet of the visitors. Kate suddenly understood that the cracks she had seen covering the boulders were in fact deep lines, wrinkles on the skin of these strange beings.

"You are welcome," an infinitely deep voice rumbled. It came from one of the largest of the stone creatures, directly to Kate's left.

"Yes, welcome," echoed another, smaller one to the right.

"No they are not," objected a third voice, sounding like rocks grinding together. "We don't know them yet."

"T-t-tellll usss whooo youuu arrrre," crackled the biggest of the boulder-beings in a slow, difficult manner.

Kate slowly stood and drew in a deep breath. "I am Kaitlyn Prancer Gordon," she said, her voice unsteady as she scanned the craggy creatures. No arms or legs could be seen beneath the masses of scraggly hair. Only faces, chiseled by time, were visible. And all seven of them were scrutinizing her carefully. "I come from—ah, the future. Blade . . . Blade, Oregon. This is Laioni. She's a Halami, from here, well almost here, and that's her dog, Monga."

After a period of silence, the first creature, whose face bore more wrinkles than any of the others, stirred. "That will do for now. We ourselves have many names, among them *Azanna*, the Ones Beyond Age, although of course we really do age like anything else."

"Speak for yourself," interjected another, less wrinkled creature.

"Silence," thundered the first angrily, as two nearly identical boulders behind Kate started giggling together, making a sound like a couple of bubbling streams. The deeply wrinkled being frowned, then added, "With age, however, comes wisdom."

"So you must be very wise," said the two tittering creatures in unison.

At this, the Circle erupted into a chorus of wheezes, guffaws, and other forms of crude laughter. Only the eldest creature refrained, shifting slightly from side to side with her eyes closed.

At length, the raucous laughter subsided, and the creature's eyes again opened. "You may call us the Stonehags," she said, a trace of disgust in her voice. "We will now tell you our names, in order of seniority. I am Untla, the oldest. I can tell you much, for I have seen many, many years."

"If you don't fall asleep while you're talking," muttered the young Stonehag on her left.

Another chorus of laughter ensued. The two like-shaped creatures rocked so hard in mirth that they bumped into each other with a crash, breaking off some brittle hairs, which tumbled to the ground in a cloud of dust.

Emboldened by these antics, Kate turned back to Untla and asked, "But how do you speak English? I mean, I can understand you perfectly."

"To you I speak English, to your friend I speak Halami, and to the dog I speak Canine," answered the Stonehag. "My sisters and I have the gift of universal communication, which comes from living so long and watching so many different kinds of creatures. Now Gruntla, it's your turn."

The largest of the Stonehags, as big as a brontosaurus, made a low grinding sound as if she were clearing her throat. After a long pause, she said in a voice like an earthquake, "I ammmm Grrruntla. I ammmm the biggggest annd the c-c-closessst to ssstone, ssso heeeed whaaaatever I sssay, lllest I g-get aaangrrry annd—"

"Quit threatening them," chided the smallest Stonehag, seated to the right of Untla. "You should be ashamed, spouting off like that just because they're so tiny." Blinking her deep-set eyes, she continued, "I am Nyla. And I have to put up with this all the time."

Gruntla shook with rage and started to speak again, but Untla gave her a sharp look and commanded, "Enough. Now who's next?"

"I am," grumbled a voice on the other side of the Circle. "But I don't trust these intruders, and I won't tell them my name. Might put a curse on it, they might."

"That's Jbina, trusting everybody as usual," blurted one of the two nearly identical Stonehags. The other one, to her right, started to titter, but she kept right on speaking. "I'm Yogula, twin sister of Bogula."

"And just as stupid," threw in Jbina.

"Now it's my turn," cut in a lighter, thinner voice, belonging to the least wrinkled of the Stonehags. "We always save the best for last, but I hate all the waiting. I am Zletna, the youngest. But tell me," she asked, pushing her pointed chin practically into Kate's chest, "which of us do you think is the most beautiful?"

"Not you, that's for sure," called Jbina.

At that, a raging argument broke out between the two Stonehags. Howling, cursing, squabbling, screeching, and thumping filled the air.

"Wait!" shouted Kate at the top of her lungs. "Stop your fighting." The quarreling Stonehags relented, although Jbina continued to grumble to herself while rocking back and forth. "Please," Kate pleaded. "There isn't time for this."

"What's the hurry?" snapped Jbina. "Our kind of time we count in thousands of years."

"Hear her out," grumbled Nyla.

"Tell us what brought you to us," commanded Untla, her wrinkled face contorting into an enormous yawn.

"I need your help," began Kate. "This stick—it brought me here, but I belong five hundred years from now. And I've got to get back right away."

"Why the rush?" Jbina demanded suspiciously.

"Aunt Melanie's in trouble. And the loggers, they're going to cut down the redwoods any minute now. She'll try to stop them, I know, and anything could happen to her."

Untla, eyes closed, said, "This person is known to us."

Kate's heart skipped a beat. "Aunt Melanie? You know her?"

"Yes," answered Untla. "She has visited us before."

"Yyyyou're wrrrrong," replied Gruntla, speaking in her agonizingly slow manner. "Thaaat waaas annnotherrr p-p-perrrsonnn."

Untla's eyes opened. "No," she declared. "The same. She came with the very walking stick that this girl used just now to summon us."

"That's just it," Kate fretted. "I don't know how to use it. If it called you, that was by accident. I need you to tell me how to make it take me home. Do it for Aunt Melanie's sake, since you know her, not for mine."

"Melanie. Hmmm, I remember her now," said Zletna. "I quite liked her."

"You're such an easy mark," derided Bogula. "You just liked her because she called you 'dear.' "

"So what?" retorted Zletna. "I like being treated with some respect for a change."

"Silence," bellowed Untla. Concentrating her gaze on Kate, she continued, "You indeed have a serious problem, if what you say is true. For there is only one being alive who can tell you how to use that stick, and it is not one of us."

"But who is it?" demanded Kate. "Who can tell me?"

"Wait," interjected Jbina. "How do we know she didn't steal the stick from its rightful owner?" Narrowing her eyes, she added, "None of these two-legged creatures can be trusted. They only arrived here a century or two ago, and they already act like they're the only ones around."

"Some are like that," said Nyla, "but some are not. They're different from each other, just like we are."

"Except for us," piped Yogula, leaning to one side to nudge Bogula, who sniggered noisily.

Stepping nearer to Untla, Kate held the walking stick before her craggy face. "You know I'm telling the truth," she implored.

Untla lifted her knobby nose into the air and looked skyward, deliberating.

"Please," said Kate.

The nose descended. She peered at Kate for a long while, then finally spoke. "The ruler of the Tinnanis. If you want to learn the ways of your stick of power, you must go to him."

Laioni cried out suddenly, startling Kate. With consternation on her face, the Halami girl pointed in the direction of the lake beyond the boulders. She babbled some words Kate could not comprehend.

"What she is telling you," spoke Nyla sympathetically, "is that the Tinnani Chieftain can only be found by voyaging across the blue water to the island called Ho Shantero."

"The black island?" asked Kate in disbelief as a cold shiver slid down her spine.

"Yes," replied the Stonehag. "The one whose name means Island That Moves."

"And the Tinnanis—I thought they were just a myth. Are you sure that's right?"

"The Tinnanis are no myth," answered Untla firmly. "They are merely seldom seen, or are seen only in disguise, like the Stonehags. The stick you carry was made by the Tinnanis many generations ago. It is possible that even the Chieftain does not remember how it can be used."

At that moment, the ancient Untla yawned widely, exposing several rows of blackened teeth. "He is very unpredictable," she continued. "As changeable as the weather, just like his father and grandfather before him. But hear me well: Hold tightly to your stick of power. The world outside this Circle is already fraught with danger, and the power of evil grows steadily stronger."

Kate's mouth went dry and she asked, "Isn't there anything you can tell me about how to get to him safely? That island scares me half to death."

Untla yawned once more, this time making a deep, dull groan, so low in pitch it nearly fell below Kate's range of hearing. "The stick will show you the way, if you pay attention." She then closed her eyes and started immediately to snore, making a sound like a crashing landslide.

Shaking her head, Kate merely stared at the sleeping Stonehag. Then another voice called to her.

It was Nyla, smallest of the Stonehags. "There is one more thing we can tell you," she said in her gentlest rumble. "Show me the walking stick, and I will read you the words carved on its shaft."

Kate lifted the object near to Nyla's wrinkled face. The creature concentrated for a moment, crinkling her bulbous nose. At last, she spoke: "These words are written in the Tinnani Old Tongue, a speech so ancient I have not seen it for many ages. I am not sure I can still remember how to read it."

"Try," pleaded Kate. "It might help."

Nyla's deeply recessed eyes studied the shaft for a long moment. At irregular intervals, she made strange guttural sounds that seemed to indicate puzzlement, discovery, or simply effort. Finally, she spoke again, rumbling with satisfaction: "There. I am not so forgetful as I thought. These words are some sort of prophecy." And she read:

> Fire of greed shall destroy;
> Fire of love shall create.

"But what does it mean?" asked Kate. "What does fire have to do with anything?"

"That," answered the Stonehag, "only you can discover." She furrowed her already wrinkled brow. "But beware. Fire can strengthen and sustain you, but it also can consume you. Your enemies are near, and many. Your path home will be more difficult than you ever imagined." She eyed Kate tenderly for a moment and the edges of her swelling lips lifted slightly. "If you ever make it back to your own time, I want you to come visit me again."

Kate gazed into Nyla's deeply recessed eyes, seeing the bright bowls of light within. "I don't think I'll get the chance."

The Stonehag quivered. "If you can somehow learn the true meaning of the prophecy, then you may find your way home. And, I suspect, you may find something else as well." Nyla heaved a heavy sigh, full of ancient longing. "At least you have a purpose, a calling, something you must do with your life. That is a blessing, a true blessing. Some of us can only wait and watch as life moves past."

"I'll trade you," Kate said flatly, turning to go.

"Wait," commanded the voice of Untla, awake once more. She yawned again, groaning deeply, before continuing. "There is one thing more. We have a gift for you, a gift that might help you on your journey."

Jbina grumbled something to herself, and Nyla glared at her. But Untla paid no heed. The wrinkled being heaved her massive body to one side with a thunderous grunt. Kate drew closer to see what she had uncovered, and discovered a spring of purest water gurgling out of the ground.

"Drink," said Untla.

Kate bent lower when a flash of memory halted her. "There was another pool," she said worriedly, "a poison pool. It was just outside your Circle."

"Then it is no concern of ours," replied Untla. "The water at your feet will enable you, for a time, to share the Stone-hags' gift of communication. You will understand all that you hear, whatever the tongue, and you will answer back and be understood. It is a gift you already possess in part, as does the one you call Aunt Melanie, for you have already shown that you can walk the bridges of time and place."

"I only want to walk back," said Kate quietly as she bent low. Placing her cupped right hand in the water, she drew some out and drank it. The water chilled her teeth, it was so cold. It cascaded down her throat, seeming to linger there for an instant, leaving behind a bracing taste of fresh-ness and purity. She took another drink, then regained her feet.

"You too," said Untla to Laioni. "And also your dog. Drink."

Obediently, Laioni knelt beside the spring. One rope of black hair dropped into the water as she bent down to the bracing fountain. Monga, by her side as always, lapped eagerly, swishing his tail as he drank.

Laioni rose. Before she could even straighten her spine, the distant drumbeat echoed again. Faster and louder it grew, until the sound of booming cannons surrounded them. The earth shook so mightily that Kate kept her feet only with the aid of the walking stick.

Abruptly, the tremors ceased. The Stonehags, enormous boulders once again, sat immobile and ageless as fog flowed into the center of their ring. No more voices rum-bled; no more spring bubbled. The Circle had returned to stone. All that remained of the great beings were their words of warning, still sounding in Kate's ears.

14

fallen brethren

MONGA kept his head low to the ground as he padded behind Laioni and Kate through the channel between the two great boulders. Mist swept across their surfaces, obscuring all but the deepest cracks. The dog nudged Laioni's leg, urging her to go faster, his bushy brown tail curled tightly over his back like the mainspring of a clock.

Kate, preoccupied with thoughts of the sinister island, did not pause to study the massive stones as she passed between them. Already she wondered if the Stonehags were right about the Tinnanis. Maybe they didn't really exist. And even if they did, maybe there was some way to communicate with the Tinnani Chieftain without actually going to the island. Perhaps he or his people came ashore regularly. Surely they must. How else could they have become so deeply ingrained in Halami legend if they didn't appear from time to time?

"It will not be easy to get there," Laioni muttered to herself as they neared the other side of the passageway.

Kate spun around. "I was just thinking the same—" She

caught herself in mid-sentence. "I understood you," she said in wonderment. "I mean, you spoke Halami and I understood you."

The other girl brightened. "And I understood you. It's the gift of the Stonehags."

But Kate had no time for celebration. "The Tinnanis—are they real? Have you ever actually seen one?"

Laioni hesitated. "No one has ever seen one, at least no one I know. But we all know what they look like."

"That's not too convincing," replied Kate. "Well, then, tell me about the island. Is there any safe way to get there?"

Laioni lowered her eyes. "It is bad, very bad. People should not go there at all." She sighed. "The few who have dared to try either have turned up later, wandering aimlessly in the forest with no memory of anything about the island, or have disappeared completely. Some time ago, the son of our eldest, a boy named Toru, dreamed he should go there on a vision quest. I knew him well. We were the same age. We all knew it was too dangerous, and we tried to persuade him to change his mind, but he refused. He left the village—it's by the coast, a day's walk from here—and no one has heard from him since." She pursed her lips angrily. "I think it was the work of Gashra."

"Gashra?" Kate knew she had heard the name, but she couldn't remember where.

"The most evil being alive," replied Laioni venomously. "He lives in the steaming mountain, whose name we never speak lest it increase his power. He can reach into people's minds and twist their thinking in terrible ways. If they are too good to be useful to him, like my friend Toru, he poisons their dreams to make them chase after death. If they are already evil, he draws them into his service, like he did with Sanbu."

"Who is Sanbu?"

"One of my people," Laioni said sadly. "He grew tired of hunting for his food and started stealing from other villages. That was bad enough, but then he joined forces with

Gashra and now no one is safe. His band mutilates animals, trees, and people without care. They've made the forest outside the crater a dangerous place. That is why I am
worried for my father and his hunting party—and for all
the Halamis."

Kate scanned the great gray boulders on either side of
them, then turned back to Laioni. "You don't have to come
with me, you know."

"I know," she answered in a low voice. "I don't even
know exactly why I followed you here to the Circle, except
that something made me feel like—like I was supposed
to help you. Monga felt that too, I could tell, from the
moment you fell into the hunting pit." She surveyed
the carved handle of the walking stick, barely visible in the
dim light between the boulders. "When I was born, it was
foretold that I would make a long and perilous journey for
the sake of my people. And that in that journey, my guide
would be an owl. My name, Laioni, means She Who Follows the Owl."

Raising the carved handle, Kate asked, "And you think
this is the owl?"

"I don't know," whispered Laioni, bending to scratch
the top of Monga's head. "I don't even know the true
meaning of my name, for the owl symbolizes two very different things to my people. To some, it is a symbol of the
forest world that supports us, something to be cherished.
To others, it is a symbol of death, something to be feared."

Kate glanced uncertainly at the walking stick. "That's
another reason not to come with me."

"No," replied Laioni. "By coming with you, I will learn
my true fate. I believe that you did not arrive here when
you did by accident. There must be a reason."

Frowning, Kate lowered the stick. "That's where you're
wrong. It's just bad luck, that's all." She paused, reflecting.
"You don't think I'm some kind of spirit, do you?"

Laioni smiled. "You come through one of the great trees,
you heat tea without a fire, you summon the Stonehags, and
you carry a stick of power. That's enough for me."

"But I'm just a girl, like you."

"Then you wouldn't have feet like that," objected Laioni, pointing to her bright green shoelaces. "They're as green as new leaves."

Shaking her head, Kate repeated, "I'm just a girl."

"Whatever you are, I think you are here to help my people."

Kate bristled. "What do you mean?"

"These are dangerous times, as the Stonehag said. The power of Gashra grows stronger by the day. His mountain has come alive, rumbles with anger, and spouts burning clouds. Sanbu and his warriors steal and waste whatever they want. Parts of the forest where my people have lived for generations are dying, changing from green to brown, rivers are turning to fire, and our brothers and sisters the creatures of the forest are growing scarcer. Even the fish that once were so plentiful we could walk across the streams on their backs are now hard to find. If I am ever going to make a journey for my people, as the prophecy said, it must be soon." She swallowed with some difficulty. "There is something else. That boy, Toru, my friend—he was, he was the one I hoped would father my children someday. I have to find out what happened to him."

"You may be better off looking by yourself."

"I think we're both better off staying together."

"You're an optimist," replied Kate. "Like me. And also like someone else I know, who has eyes just like yours."

"The one you call Aunt Lemony?"

"Aunt Melanie," corrected Kate. "But I think she'd like your way of saying it." Her expression clouded again. "I hope I get to tell her someday."

She turned back to the curling clouds of mist that faced them at the other side of the passageway. The time had come to leave the protection of the boulders, to seek out the Tinnanis, if indeed they existed. She glanced at the smaller boulder to her left that she knew to be Nyla, wishing she could hear again the Stonehag's rumbling voice. But there was no time for that now. Kate started walking again, disregarding the renewed throbbing on the back of her left hand.

At the instant she passed beyond the boulders, she stopped suddenly in her tracks. She blinked her eyes, certain the fog was playing a trick with her vision. Yet she saw what she saw.

Not five paces in front of her, next to the boiling pool of clear liquid that she knew in later times would bear an evil spell, stood an upright figure. His skin, dark green in color, was covered with rows of reptilian scales that rippled as he breathed. Clad with only a brown leather loincloth, two metallic orange bands around each bicep, and another orange band around his forehead to hold his straight black hair in place, the figure stood no higher than Kate's waist. In one hand he held a spear, taller than himself, blade up. His eyes, dull yellow in color, scrutinized her with deep suspicion.

Monga, just out of the channel, barked sharply. Laioni gasped and stood immobile by Kate's side. Just then, the small green figure raised his spear and brought its base down forcefully on the rocks by his feet. The sound reverberated off the cliffs behind the boulders.

At once, Kate was knocked to the ground. Another green warrior, who had leaped onto her back from one of the boulders, tried to pull the walking stick out of her hand. She grappled with him, rolling on the pumice-strewn terrain, amazed to find that his tiny body possessed the strength of someone twice his size.

A new attacker jumped on her back and wrapped his arms around her neck, squeezing hard. She kicked the first attacker in the chest so hard that he released his hold on the stick and fell backward with a thud. But the grip of the second one tightened on her neck and she coughed, sputtering for air.

"Laioni," she croaked desperately.

But Laioni had also been jumped, and was wrestling with one of the green beings at that very moment. Monga, snarling ferociously, bit him on the leg, making him squeal in pain and start beating the dog brutally with his fists. Monga would not let go, however, sinking his teeth deeper into the scaly flesh and shaking his head fiercely from side to side.

Kate fell over backward, landing on the rocks with such force that the warrior groaned and slipped to the side of her neck, loosening his grip just enough to allow her to pull him around her shoulder. With her bandaged hand, she punched him hard in the stomach several times until he finally released his hold. Before she could roll away, though, he kicked her under the chin and sent her sprawling backward.

The walking stick flew out of her grasp and clattered against the ground. Kate lunged for it, but the attacker who had kicked her got there first. He grabbed the stick and, before Kate could stop him, hurled it up to the warrior with the orange arm bands, who had climbed on top of the boulder directly behind the boiling pool—the boulder that only moments before, as Nyla, had warned her: *Beware . . . your enemies are near.*

"The stick!" cried Kate, as she reached for a handhold and started climbing upward. Struggling to ascend, she did not see that the warrior was waiting for her.

Yellow eyes gleaming, he raised his spear above his head. Positioning himself at the extreme edge of the boulder, he prepared to thrust the blade deep into Kate's back. He paused for the barest instant, spear held high, to savor his moment of triumph.

Just then, the boulder shifted underneath him. Merely a slight slip to the side, it was not a major movement like the jolt of an earthquake. Yet it was just enough to throw the warrior off balance. He struggled to stay on his feet, but tumbled headlong over the edge, whizzing over Kate's head to land in the boiling pool below.

Hearing the splash and the blood-curdling scream, Kate pulled herself up to the top of the boulder. There, lying on the cracked gray surface, was the walking stick. She closed her hand around the shaft, just as she heard Laioni cry out below.

She leaped to the ground next to the three other attackers, two of whom were rolling on the rocks with Laioni. Another, splattered with black blood, was trying desperately to pry Monga from his leg. With a flying tackle, she landed on one of Laioni's assailants, pulling him from her side. They rolled to the edge of the boiling pool.

Kate stood and faced the figure vengefully. She could hear the pool bubbling just behind her. His eyes met hers and narrowed to knifelike slits. Then, to her astonishment, he began swiftly to metamorphose. His legs fused together into a single powerful tail covered with green scales, tearing the loincloth to pieces. His arms suddenly shrunk inward and new, stubby legs sprouted from under his hips. Elongating to a point, his head stretched toward his nose, pushing his thin eyes to the sides of his face. The warrior had been transformed into a large green lizard.

Before Kate could move, the creature fell forward onto its belly and began to crawl toward her. She prepared to kick it back, but it swerved around her and crawled to one side. Whirling around, she saw for the first time that the boiling pool had turned green, the same frothing green that had nearly lured her to her death. Her left hand throbbed painfully, but the pool had no power over her. She watched in horror as the giant lizard, captivated by the spell, slithered over the rocks and into the cauldron.

She turned back to the others to see that the two remaining attackers also had changed to reptilian form. They began crawling toward the pool, including one who carried Monga clinging to a torn hind leg. Kate leaped at the dog, grabbed him by the belly, and tore him away from the slithering beast, who continued to crawl undeterred. Holding the dog in one arm, she suddenly saw that Laioni, her eyes wide and entranced, was walking in the direction of the pool.

"Stop!" shouted Kate. "Laioni, stop!"

The Halami girl paid no attention. She continued to stride toward the bubbling pool. Kate threw herself at her, just managing to catch her by the heel with an outstretched hand. She wrenched the foot sideways, pulling Laioni to the ground with a thud.

Laioni sat up, shaking her head in bewilderment. She watched, horrified, as the tail of the last attacker slipped into the frothing pool.

"I—I almost went in there myself," she said weakly.

Kate rose, still clutching the wriggling Monga. With her free hand, she picked up the walking stick. "Let's get out of here," she said. "Are you all right?"

"A little bruised, that's all."

Together, they stumbled down the steep slope. Kate continued to hold Monga tightly, for fear he, too, might be drawn by the deadly spell. Only after descending quite a distance did she finally set the dog free. To her relief, he did not try to run back toward the pool. Instead, he scampered over to a rivulet of water running down from the cliffs and plunged his face into the cold stream.

"He didn't like the taste," said Laioni wryly.

"I don't blame him," answered Kate, with a glance at the Circle of Stones above them. "They almost got the stick. And me, too, if it hadn't been for Nyla."

Then, recalling her first experience with the pool, she thought again of the small red owl that had knocked her aside just in time. Had that been Nyla's doing as well? Turning back to Laioni, she said, "If that's what we have to expect from the Tinnanis, I don't see how we'll ever get any help from their Chieftain."

Laioni grimaced. "Those were not Tinnanis. They were Slimnis, the Tinnanis' fallen brethren. Once they lived freely, like other beings of the forest, but now they serve Gashra. The Tinnanis are their sworn enemy."

Monga lifted his head at last and vigorously shook the water from himself. Watching him, Laioni rubbed her sore right forearm. "It is a bad sign, very bad, that they've entered the crater. This place is the greatest stronghold of the Tinnanis, the very home of their Chieftain. I am glad we defeated them, but I'm afraid more will come after."

"The leader, the one with the arm bands, must have laid

a curse on the pool when he fell in," said Kate. "His way of getting revenge, I guess."

"But he caught only his own warriors," added Laioni.

Kate pulled her bandaged hand close to her chest. "So far."

15

the blue lake

WORDLESSLY, they scrambled down the slippery slope. Kate's legs, whether tugged by gravity alone or by some new inexorable force as well, pulled her downward toward the lake at a rapid clip. Her thigh muscles strained at the steep descent, and several times rocks slid from under her feet, causing her to leap to safety before twisting an ankle or a knee.

At one point she turned to see Laioni, moving down the slope with the ease of mist rolling across the rocks. Though shoeless, she stepped over the jumbled and jagged terrain with confident ease. Monga bounced along behind, stopping every so often to thrust his long nose into a small crevice where some tiny newt or beetle had scurried to safety.

Arriving at the edge of the lake, Kate peered into the fog. No island could be seen, only splotches of shimmering blue through occasional windows in the whirling mist. Bending down, she touched the water with one finger. It felt warm, like a steaming bath. As she stood again, her

vision roamed the shoreline for anything that might con-
ceivably be used as a boat. She really didn't want to cross
the shoreline of this mysterious lake at all, but if she had
to do so, she certainly did not want to swim in its waters
unprotected.

A dark cylindrical shape bobbing near the shore
caught her eye. Moving closer, she saw that it was a log,
perhaps eight feet long, that must have blown down from
the upper reaches of a great fir or cedar and drifted across
the lake. The wood, darkened by dampness, was nearly
black.

Laioni joined her at the water's edge. "Our canoe?"

"I think so," answered Kate as she grabbed one of the
protruding branches and pulled the log closer to shore. "I'd
rather ride in something shaped like your little toys, but we
don't have much choice."

Surveying the reflectionless blue water, Laioni added
doubtfully, "I just hope we can do better than my pebbles."
She cocked her head. "Wait, I have an idea. Would you
give me the little drum you carry? I saw it when you gave
us the sweet brown tea."

Kate slipped off the blue day pack, unzipped it, and
handed the tiny painted drum to Laioni. Immediately, the
Halami girl squatted down on the pumice, placed the drum
between her legs, and closed her eyes for several seconds.
When she opened them, she looked neither at the drum nor
at Kate, but into the mist rising from the lake.

Gently, her fingers began to tap the stretched hide of the
drum, seeking their true rhythm just as Kate had seen Aunt
Melanie do at the mouth of Kahona Falls. She began
slowly to sing, as her hands alternately slid and swished
and pounded. Once again, Kate marveled at the likeness of
Laioni to her own beloved great-aunt. Although her intel-
lect dismissed the possibility of a real connection between
them as ridiculous, as mere fantasy, she remembered what
Grandfather used to say: *Wait long enough, and fantasy
becomes reality.*

Laioni continued to chant, just as Kate had heard in

another time and another place. This time, however, she understood the lilting words:

> Hear me O spirits
> My small walking words:
> All time in the sunrise
> All life in the seed.
>
> Our days may be short
> Our reach may be long
> We touch both our elders
> And children unborn.
>
> My struggles are yours
> Your mystery mine.
> I ask you for guidance
> And know you will say:
>
> Your spirit is one
> With the spirits around you.
> Your spirit is one
> With the spirits around you.

As her last *halma-dru* melted into the mist, Laioni rose silently to her feet. She handed the drum to Kate, who replaced it in the day pack. Together, they waded into the water and straddled the log, positioning themselves between the stubby ends of broken branches that ran its full length. Monga jumped into the water and started paddling vigorously alongside.

Kate, seated in front, pushed off from the shore. The ground beneath her sneakers fell away swiftly; in no more than a yard from the water's edge she could no longer touch bottom. She had no way to measure the depth of this lake, but all her instincts told her it was unfathomably deep.

The log sank slightly under their weight, submerging everything below their hips in the warm water. Fog soon enveloped them, and the cliffs around the rim disappeared from view. Ahead and behind, Kate could see nothing but curls of mist spiraling out of the blue water. She leaned slightly forward and began to paddle, while Laioni did the same. Monga, meanwhile, splashed along beside them. Holding her bandaged hand under the water at one point, Kate noted how clear the water seemed, even as it imbued her forearm, fingers, and kerchief with a vibrant blue color. She had never seen water like this before.

But for the sound of their paddling and the constant lapping of little waves against the log, the lake was still. Gradually, however, Kate grew aware of a slight chill in the air, of a shadow in the mist she could not really see.

Suddenly, the island burst from behind a curtain of fog not fifty yards ahead. Blacker than charcoal, the spindly spires and pinnacles rose like the turrets of an abandoned castle. Then Kate saw what she most dreaded to see: the gleaming black surface of the island seemed to be moving, quivering like living skin. *Like it was crawling or something,* the Forest Service man had said.

At that instant something solid brushed against her foot. She cried out, wrenching up her leg just as Monga started barking furiously. Then the front end of the log rose high out of the water, throwing her backward into Laioni.

With an explosion of spray, the makeshift boat capsized. A great wave lifted and crashed down over the flailing voyagers, drowning their screams in the swell of a powerful whirlpool that dragged them downward.

Soon the eerie stillness returned to the lake. Except for a lone log drifting unattended, nothing but mist moved on the surface.

16

thika the guardian

KATE felt a scratchy tongue licking her face. She sat up with a start.

"Hey, Monga, that's enough," she sputtered, pushing the affectionate dog away. In response, he shook his shaggy body vigorously, splattering her with water.

She looked around to see Laioni and Monga, like herself, dripping wet on a dark stone floor. Though her clothes were drenched, she felt uncomfortably warm. Laioni had lost her woven basketry cap; her twin ropes of black hair were draped, glistening, over her shoulders.

Over their heads swept a great transparent dome. At first Kate thought it had been fashioned from glass or quartz, but then she saw it flex and bend with a gentle undulation, moved by some powerful current. She marveled at the clear membrane, arching above them like an enormous half bubble. Outside, the world was entirely blue, but for the thin shafts of light penetrating from far above and some curious white shapes that encircled the dome. Tall and slender, they waved slowly like great windblown branches. The stone floor was unadorned except for a square silver plank in the center, possibly a trapdoor of some kind.

"Where are we?" asked Laioni, scanning the shifting blue light filtering through the dome.

"Beats me. It's almost like we're under the lake somehow. Everything is so blue up there, except for those big white things. They look almost like trees."

Observing the square plank, Kate said, "I wonder if this is the way out." Crawling nearer, she inspected it closely. Wrought of gleaming silver, with inlaid patterns of interwoven branches, it fit perfectly into the smooth floor. Pulling from her jeans pocket the Swiss army knife she always carried, she tried to pry it open, but with no success. The trapdoor, if indeed it was a trapdoor, would not budge.

"You carry strange tools," said Laioni, staring in wonder at the knife.

"Still doesn't do any good," grumbled Kate. Then she spied something unusual stuck into the slit between the silver door and the floor. Pinching the object between her thumb and forefinger, she pulled it free. "It's a feather," she observed, more mystified than ever. "A pure white feather. An owl maybe?"

"Maybe," answered Laioni in a noncommittal tone.

"But how could an owl get in here? It doesn't—"

Just then a spindly shadow fell across the silver square. Kate jerked her head upward to see one of the white treelike figures moving closer to the dome. It was tall, perhaps ten times as tall as Kate and twice as high as the dome, covered with knuckle-shaped lumps like a branch of coral. As it bent closer to them, it laid a bony appendage on the surface of the dome itself with a sound like fingers rubbing against an inflated balloon. Now Kate could see that the appendage was not pure white as it had appeared from a distance, but rather ribbed with veins of very light yellow. Then, with shock, she realized that the knuckle-shaped lumps each contained a single round, blue eye. Hundreds and hundreds of them covered the knobby skeleton.

"You, hsh-whshhh, dare to enter the realm of Ho Shh-hantero," boomed a watery voice that echoed inside the dome. "What is your name, shwshhh, and your purpose?"

Kate clambered to her feet and attempted to address the many-eyed creature. "Kaitlyn Prancer Gordon is my name, and this is Laioni and Monga. We are here to meet with the Chieftain of the Tinnanis."

"Tell me, shwshhh, why you want to see him," commanded the watery voice, sounding like liquid sloshing through a pipe. "I am Thika, First Guardian of Ho Shh-hantero, and no one may pass beyond here without my permission. Speak quickly, hshh-swshh, for I have very little time."

Kate answered cautiously, "We have something urgent to discuss with him."

Thika's knobby limb moved slightly on the transparent dome. "How do I know, shhhhwshh, you are telling the truth? You might be, hshh, hshh, really an agent of the Wicked One, or just another Halami, shwshhhh, following some deluded dream."

At this, Laioni glanced anxiously at Kate. Monga, sensing her distress, paced around her feet.

"Because I carry this," answered Kate, waving the walking stick.

"That, shhhwsh, is not good enough," gurgled the voice of the Guardian. "I already know you carry a stick of power. Hshhwshhh. That is the only reason I did not banish you immediately, hshhh, through the Tinnanis' tunnels, shhwsh, as I have done with every other intruder who has dared to approach Ho Shhhantero. By now you would be returned to the forest below, ssswhshh, with no memory at all of our meeting. But you could have stolen the stick, hhshh-whhshh, or won it through treachery. No, if you are to pass by me, shhwsh, you must tell me more of your mission."

"All right," Kate said reluctantly. "I need the Chieftain to tell me how to make the stick work, so it can take me back to my own time."

"Shhhwshh," sloshed Thika. "You say, hshhh, you are from another time?"

"Yes."

"Then I, shhhwsh, will let you pass."

Kate and Laioni exchanged relieved glances.

"After," continued Thika, "you have said, shhwwwsh, the password."

"Password?" asked Kate. "But, but—I don't know what you mean."

"Any language, hshhh, will do," declared the coral-like creature, its multiple blue eyes concentrating on Kate. "I am old enough, shhwshh, to remember even the Old Tongue. Now hurry, hurry, hshh-whshh. Choose well your words. For you will have, sshhwsh, only one chance."

A lump expanded in Kate's throat, swelling so much that speaking would have been difficult even if she did know the Guardian's password. She felt a rush of despair, overwhelming her like the waters of the blue lake had overwhelmed her not long before. What could she do now? If she had but one chance as Thika said, then she had already lost it. She would never see the Tinnani Chieftain, never see Aunt Melanie. How could she possibly know some long-forgotten password, as ancient as the Tinnani Old Tongue?

Then, like the subtlest rays of dawn emerging over the horizon, an idea glimmered at the farthest edge of her consciousness. She furrowed her brow in a desperate effort to remember some words she had heard but once, words etched into the shaft of the walking stick, words written in the ancient Old Tongue.

She cleared her throat. Slowly, haltingly, she recited them:

> *Fire of greed shall destroy;*
> *Fire of love shall create.*

With a sudden tearing sound, like the ripping of heavy cloth, the knobby appendage of Thika the Guardian reached through the transparent dome. More supple than it seemed, it wrapped itself around the waists of all three companions, even as they wriggled and kicked to break away.

"Let go!" shouted Kate, fighting in vain to free herself. "You can't send us away."

Thika did not relent. As the appendage tightened around Kate's waist, several of its deep-socketed eyes probed her with curiosity. "You, shhhwhshhh, are an odd creature," it said disapprovingly.

As the Guardian lifted them up through the dome, Kate saw that the transparent membrane instantly sealed itself, like a bubble that could be punctured but not burst. Still struggling to break free, she barely managed to suck in a last breath of air before she was totally submerged in water.

Upward they swam through the omnipresent blue, higher and higher until Kate finally stopped struggling. Below her she saw the shrinking circle of the dome, the silver square clearly visible in the center of its dark floor. Around it stood more than a dozen treelike creatures, each of them studded with eyes identical to Thika's. Above, she saw nothing but a dark shadow growing rapidly larger.

Just at the point she could hold her breath no longer, she heard again the same tearing sound. Air suddenly replaced water, and she could breathe again. The grip around her waist relaxed, and she found herself sprawled on another stone floor, gasping. Beside her lay Laioni and Monga, looking as bewildered as they were drenched.

A smoldering torch, fastened to the wall with a lacy metal band, burned unsteadily above their heads, sputtering as it flickered. It appeared to be consuming some sort of incandescent gas. Dark stone surrounded them. The chamber was featureless but for a single stone stairway beneath the torch leading up into darkness. Kate noticed at once that the perfectly carved steps were very small, half the normal size, just like the ones in the tunnel behind Kahona Falls.

Thika's appendage, rising through a hole in the stone floor that was covered with the same transparent membrane as the dome, studied them with its many round eyes.

"Welcome, hhhsh, to Ho Shhhantero," the now-familiar voice sloshed.

Kate, still grasping the walking stick, leaped to her feet, as did Laioni. "Ho Shantero?" they asked in unison.

"Yessshhwsh," answered the Guardian, twisting and undulating like a snake as it spoke. "You knew the ancient password, shh-wshh, so I have brought you here as I am commanded. Hshhhh. But at times, shwshh, I doubt the wisdom of the commands. You should feel most privileged, hhhshwsh, for you are the only ones of your kind ever to enter here, sshwsh, unaccompanied by a Tinnani."

Reflecting on Thika's words, Kate wondered what humans had ever been admitted here in the company of a Tinnani. And had they ever left? Before she could speak, however, Laioni asked her own version of the same question.

"The boy Toru, one of my people," she began timidly. "He came to the lake as we did, not long ago. What happened to him?"

"I seem, hhhsshhh, to remember him," replied the Guardian, whose movements beneath the torch cast coiling shadows upon the stone walls and floor. "He was driven by a dream, shhwshh, a false dream. It was the work, whhshh, of the Wicked One."

"What did you do with him?" Laioni, water still dripping from her body, stepped a bit closer. "Tell me, please."

"I sent him away, shhhwshh, through the tunnels, whhhshh, escorted by a Tinnani who made him forget all he had seen. Swshhh. He was left in the forest somewhere quite distant, hhhsh-whshh, but he should have returned to your people by now."

Laioni's gaze fell. "He has not."

"It could be, shhwshh, he was captured by the Wicked One," said Thika.

"You mean Ga—" began Kate.

"Hhsssswshh! Never say that name," interrupted the sinuous creature, its blue eyes focused squarely on her. "It is forbidden here. If you must speak of him, hhsh-whhsh, you may call him the Wicked One."

"He's growing stronger, isn't he?" asked Kate in a quiet voice.

The blue eyes scanned her with pained intensity. "By the day, shhwshhh. We measure his strength, hshhwsh, by the warmth of the lake. For as it grows warmer, the Guardians grow weaker. Hhhssshh-swhshh. Already some of our very best have died from the heat, sshwshh, a terrible slow death that saps our strength and turns us whiter than skeletons. Soon the rest of us will follow, hwshhhh, unless something changes."

The many-eyed being made a low gurgling sound, like a dog growling underwater. "But the Wicked One, hwshh, cares not about us, nor about any living thing but himself. He thinks the whole world, shwshh, and everything in it, shw-shh, exists solely for his benefit, to be consumed or destroyed as he chooses. The Guardians he knows only because we stand in the way, hwsswss, of his true desire."

"What is that?"

"To invade Ho Shhhantero and make it his own. Yesshh-hwsh! He does not even care if he destroys it in the process, so long as he controls it at last. Whssshhh, for time beyond memory, since the Great Battle long ago, the cool waters of this lake prevented him and his molten warriors from reaching the floating island, hsh-whshh, for they must stay as hot as their realm underground or perish. And none of his servants above the ground—like the Slimnis—have dared to enter the crater either, hswshh, rightfully fearing the wrath of the Guardians. But those days, whhshhh, are numbered. Hssshhhh. The Guardians are nearly no more."

Kate glanced at Laioni, then addressed Thika. "We saw some of his servants in the crater. The ones you call Slimnis."

Thika's limb lifted with a jerk. "Slimnis? In the crater? Are you sure?"

"I'm sure," answered Kate. She squeezed the knotted kerchief in her left hand, causing more water to drip onto the floor. "We fought them, and we won. But I'm afraid more will follow."

"Those are terrible tidings indeed," replied the Guardian. "Hwhssshh. If the Chieftain ever was going to help you, shhwsh-shhwsh, he will not be in the mood now. He has, hhhswshh, greater problems of his own."

"The waters of the lake are warm in my time, too," said Kate somberly.

"Then, hshwshh, I pity you," spoke the watery voice. The creature straightened itself, observing Kate closely one more time. Then it slipped swiftly down the hole in the stone floor. The sound of ripping fiber rent the air, followed by a distinct pop, followed by silence.

Kate pivoted to face the narrow stairway. The light from the flickering torch danced mysteriously upon the carved steps, making them seem more like water than stone. She stepped closer, drew in a deep breath, and started to climb.

the black island
of ho shantero

LEAVING a trail of water behind her, Kate ascended the darkened stairway, followed by her equally wet companions. She wondered at the skilled hands that had carved these small steps out of the solid rock. Unlike the buff-colored pumice she had seen elsewhere in the crater, this rock was utterly black, perhaps charred in the final fiery gasp of the volcano that created the crater long ago. As in the pumice outside, small holes permeated every surface, lessening the weight of the rock and making it at least conceivable that beings of great intelligence could have somehow caused this island to float. Still, if she had not seen so much to convince her that Ho Shantero did indeed ride upon the waters of the lake, she would never have believed it possible.

The stairway spiraled up, up, and up. At each complete turn of the spiral, another torch flickered, casting its wavering light for several more steps. Beneath each torch, Kate saw the outlines of petroglyphs cut deep into the blackened stone. Faces of all descriptions, winged creatures soaring high above the trees, long-tailed lizards, stick figures that seemed to represent humans, cones and needles, roots and branches, all crowded the dimly lit walls. As she continued to climb, taking the miniature steps three or four at a time, Kate guessed that the petroglyphs told a single connected story. If only the stairway were better lit, its walls would be a continuous mural of Tinnani history, twisting and turning like the cycles of time.

At length, the stairs came to an end. Before them ran a long hallway with a rounded ceiling, itself dimly lit by two of the same sputtering torches. Kate, Laioni, and Monga, ears thrust forward in alert position, started to walk down the hallway, the clattering sound of the walking stick echoing and re-echoing within the walls of stone. Soon they heard a new sound as well: the steady drip-dripping of water not far ahead.

"I wonder where that sound is coming from," said Laioni.

"There, look," observed Kate, pointing to a raised circle in the middle of the floor, barely visible in the dim light. "It looks like a fountain of some kind, except there's so little water."

"And look," added Laioni, leaning close to the tiny spout of water gushing out of a hole in the center of the circle. "This water has colors in it. Can you see?"

As Kate bent lower, she discovered several subtle, shimmering rainbows within the spray. "You're right, but in this light it's hard to tell if it's the torches making those colors or the water itself."

Just then Monga started barking loudly. Kate and Laioni straightened to see—or, more accurately, to sense—they were surrounded by eight or ten nearly invisible beings. A vague white glow hovered in the spot where each of the beings stood, as much a lessening of shadow as a presence of light. Though it was difficult to tell, the figures appeared to be quite compact, no higher than Kate's waist. They were each rather round in shape, and if she wasn't mistaken, Kate thought she glimpsed the barest flash of yellow near the top of each form.

Without a sound, the ring of glowing beings opened in the direction of the hallway, then moved closer to Kate, Laioni, and Monga. They came very near, paused, then as soon as any of the three companions moved down the hallway, moved closer again. Kate realized they were being herded, like sheep, by the vaguely visible creatures.

Monga continued barking until Laioni reached down and stroked his scruffy coat along his neck. "It's all right," she whispered. "They're not going to hurt us."

"What makes you so sure?" asked Kate, her brow furrowed.

"Because," announced Laioni, "they are Tinnanis."

Kate stopped short. "You mean these white glowing shapes? The Tinnanis don't have real bodies?"

At that, a stirring sound filled the hallway, accompanied by a muffled sort of clucking, almost like the stifled laughter of great birds.

"They have bodies," replied Laioni. "Just like the Slimnis can change from their basic lizard forms into manlike shapes, their brothers the Tinnanis can change from their basic forms into invisible puffs of wind. Right now they're not quite invisible so we can see them enough to be herded."

"And what is their basic form, when they're not invisible?"

Laioni did not answer. Her eyes focused on something down the hallway. Kate turned from her to look, and saw that a new and brighter light had come into view. As they drew nearer, the light expanded, until finally it opened into a wide and high room.

As they entered the chamber, Kate thought of the great hall of the grand Scottish castle she had once visited with Grandfather. Glowing balls of white whom she now knew to be Tinnanis lined the walls on both sides. Overhead, a dozen sputtering torches flamed, suspended from a circular chandelier made of heavy metal chains. Though the torches were no brighter than those lining the hallway and the spiraling stairs, because so many of them hung from the chandelier a brighter light filled the room. Darkness still clung to the walls and corners, but at least Kate could see Laioni and Monga more easily.

At the farthest end of the room, Kate spied three grand high-backed thrones. The middle one, tallest of the three, was delicately wrought of white whalebone, studded with stones of all colors and descriptions. Purple amethyst, yellow sulfur, red jasper, green-and-silver agate, and black obsidian rimmed its edges. At the very top, the whalebone curved as if to support something shaped like a sphere, but the cup-shaped space was empty. In a flash of irreverence, Kate imagined that one of her softballs would fit perfectly there. The two thrones on either side, carved from huge transparent crystals of quartz, were identical. They shimmered in the wavering torchlight like two gigantic blocks of ice, clear and cold.

In the central throne, as well as in the transparent seat to its left, round balls of white glimmered. Then, as Kate and Laioni stood transfixed, the two forms started to solidify. The glowing masses grew whiter, even as they grew more defined. Kate glanced to one side to see that the same thing was happening to the rows of Tinnanis lining the walls of the chamber. When she turned back, the true form of the Tinnani Chieftain had nearly materialized.

She gasped, for the owl's head handle of the walking stick had seemingly sprung to life. The Chieftain's eyes, perfectly round and yellow, were those of an owl, but the rest of his face seemed more human. Instead of a beak, a long hooked nose hung low above his small mouth. His eyebrows, made of dozens of tiny feathers, protruded from his forehead like tufts of white cotton. Fluffy white feathers covered his round body, and two great white wings pressed close to his shoulders. Beneath his cloaklike wings, two arms sprouted, now resting across his ample white belly, which was adorned with a wide belt bearing an amethyst crystal in its buckle.

Both legs, like both arms, were covered completely with white feathers. His feet, shaped like those of a man, looked tough and callused. From each of his fingers and toes grew

talons, curved and sharp, though Kate suspected they could
be retracted for everyday uses like walking. He wore a
gleaming silver band around his brow, tilted slightly to one
side. But for his face, hands, and feet, he looked like an
enormous white owl, glowering at both Kate and the walking stick.

To the Tinnani Chieftain's left, another owl-like person
solidified in the crystalline throne. Equally tall but less
rotund, this Tinnani had softer facial features, a shorter nose,
and even larger yellow eyes, which radiated both wisdom
and suffering. In the talons of one hand, she held a long staff
like a scepter, dotted with red rubies. Around her neck was
draped a string of glistening pearls, no less white than her
feathers. Studying the visitors with care, she snapped her
jaws together sharply, making a sharp clicking sound.

The Chieftain stirred impatiently, then called to one of
his aides in a hooting voice much like that of the owl Kate
had heard in the forest. "Oysters!" he commanded. "Bring
me some oysters." Then he added irritably to his wife,
"Will they ever learn to have them ready as soon as I
materialize?"

Her yellow eyes blinked. She hooted softly, "Nobody
knows when you're going to materialize, dear, so it takes
them a moment."

"Well, *I* know when," grumbled the plump Chieftain.
"That ought to be enough." His head turned on his neck a
full one hundred and eighty degrees, and he called to the
scurrying aide: "And get me some pickled mousetails while
you're at it." He smacked his lips and again turned to his
wife. "Don't tell me they're bad for me, I know it already.
But today is a special occasion."

"So was yesterday," she said calmly.

"And so may tomorrow be," thundered the Tinnani from
his throne. "I can eat mousetails anytime I like. It's part of
being Chieftain, about the only part I enjoy. I wish I could
chuck all the rest."

His yellow eyes concentrated on Kate. "Now, as to
you," he hooted, "the one who tells my First Guardian she

comes from the future and calls herself Kaitlyn. How dare you enter Ho Shantero spreading false rumors of warriors and assassins inside the crater? You have already caused me and my council no end of heartburn on the subject. Tell us now, finally and forever, that this rumor is a lie."

Kate started to speak when a Tinnani wearing a wide-brimmed hat made of blue feathers stepped forward. "Begging your pardon, Your Wingedness, but shouldn't we introduce you first?"

The Chieftain ruffled his wings annoyedly. "Formalities, formalities. I know who I am, so what does it matter if they do? Oh, all right, but be quick about it." He sat back, tapping his belt buckle with one sharp talon.

The hatted aide spread his wings wide. From the back of the chamber came a chorus of deep horns, with a slight flourish of flutes at the finish. "I present to you Hockeltock de Notnot, Fourteenth Chieftain of the Tinnanis." Again the horns sounded. "And Chieftess Hufter Blefoninni, who rules at his side." The Tinnani closed his wings, bowed to the enthroned couple, and withdrew.

"Now, your answer," commanded the Chieftain, still tapping his belt buckle.

"The rumor you spoke of," began Kate, speaking as firmly as she could manage, "is not a lie. It is true. We met four of the creatures you call Slimnis near the Circle of Stones. They attacked us and we fought with them." After a pause, she added, "They won't bother anyone again."

"Liar," sputtered the Chieftain, turning to his wife. "Hear how she persists?" The Chieftess sat impassively, following Kate's slightest movement with her wide yellow eyes. "It's enough to give me indigestion," muttered the Chieftain. "Oysters! Where are those oysters?"

At that instant, a pair of Tinnanis wearing long capes of woven grasses flew to the throne from the back of the hall, one bearing a low-rimmed basket piled high with delicacies, the other a narrow container made of shiny purple stone. Laying the bounty on a low table brought by another aide, they bowed and backed slowly away.

"It's about time," snapped the rotund Tinnani, stuffing raw oysters and pickled mousetails into his little mouth. "Mmmmmff, dere id nodding ataw wike ekfewend dafood," he said while chomping.

After swallowing three such mouthfuls, the Chieftain reached for the narrow container, brought it to his mouth, and washed it all down. A brief look of satisfaction, almost mirth, crossed his face, then abruptly turned into a scowl. "Your story is clearly false. What would the Slimnis want with you, two humans and a mangy little dog?"

Monga growled quietly. Laioni reached to him and stroked his head until he grew silent again.

Kate stepped forward, displaying the walking stick. "They attacked us," she declared, "because they wanted this stick."

A fluttering of wings filled the chamber. Several of the Tinnanis drew nearer, hoping to get a better view of the intricately carved object. The Chieftess in particular stretched forward to examine it closely. Then the Chieftain waved them all back with one of his hands and spoke sternly to Kate.

"Do you think you can fool me so easily? That is no stick of power. It is nothing but a fake."

"It is not," objected Kate. "It's the real thing. It brought me here from the future. Through a time tunnel. All I need is for you to tell me how to make it take me back. And soon, before they cut down the Ancient One, or I won't get back at all."

The Chieftain scowled at her. "Even if you speak the truth, why should I help you? All your kind has ever done is torment my people."

Laioni stepped forward. "That's not so, Your Wingedness. The Halamis live with your people and the rest of the forest beings in peace. A few of our number have turned bad, it is true, but most of us take only what we need, honor the land, and cherish its fruits."

"She speaks the truth," spoke the Chieftess gently.

"Oh, she does, does she?" demanded the Tinnani by her

side. Facing Kate, he asked bluntly, "Can you say the same for the humans of your time?"

Kate blanched. "Well, ah, I guess—no, not really. I'm afraid the people in my time have forgotten most of what the Halamis knew." She stiffened her spine. "But some haven't forgotten. Aunt Melanie, the one who—"

"Enough," bellowed the Chieftain, reaching for another handful of mousetails. "We already know what the humans of your time are like. We have even learned to speak their language." He sniffed the delicacy appreciatively. "For we have met one of them."

Kate's heart leaped. "So you know Aunt Melanie?"

The Chieftain leaned forward, dangling the uneaten mousetails from his hand. "I will tell you about the humans of your time. They are thankless, grasping, and unconnected. To themselves, to the land, to their fellow beings. They know no wonderment. Their memory is short and their vision is shorter. They believe the world is nothing more than a bundle of firewood for their use, to be burned and the coals discarded."

"Much like another in our own time," muttered the Chieftess.

"Aunt Melanie's not like that," objected Kate. "And the others—well, they can still learn. They just need help. That's why Aunt Melanie's so important to the future. And she's in big trouble. I know she is. Won't you please help me get back to her?"

"Absolutely not," said the Chieftain. He plunged the mousetails into his mouth, chewed briefly, and swallowed them with a gulp. Then, with a gleam in his yellow eyes, he said, "I will, however, do something better."

He hooted to an aide standing next to the entrance of one of the side tunnels ringing the room. "Bring me the visitor from the future."

Kate gaped at the Chieftain, then at Laioni. "Aunt Melanie? Here?"

They heard a scuffling sound from the side tunnel. Two

Tinnanis emerged escorting someone who alternately kicked and cursed at them.

"Hey, let me go, you stupid owls," shouted the visitor as they entered the great hall. His injured shoulder had been bandaged, and one arm hung in a sling beneath his repaired yellow rain jacket. But his mood was clearly not one of gratitude.

"Jody," said Kate disappointedly.

"Bring him closer," commanded the Chieftain.

As soon as the boy came near, his eyes met Kate's. "You!" he exclaimed angrily. "You're the one who did this. You lousy . . . Where in hell's half acre am I? What did you do with all my friends?"

Kate's eyes narrowed spitefully. "Like the one who dared you to shoot the owl?"

Jody suddenly fell back, as if he had been hit with a two-by-four. He looked at Kate with an expression of real remorse, then suddenly his eyes grew wide with fear. Looking around at the dozens of owl-shaped figures surrounding him, he whispered, "Is this—is this my—my punishment?"

Kate could not help but grin. "Yes, and you'd better behave or they'll do to you what you did to their friend."

The boy shuddered, ran a hand through his red hair. "I've got to be dreaming," he muttered.

The Chieftain spun his head toward Kate. "And you want to go back to people like that?"

Gripping the shaft firmly, she replied, "They're not all like that." Then a question came to her. "Why did you bring him here, since I'm sure you found out what he's like right away? Why didn't you just leave him in the redwood grove?"

"To learn more about the future," snapped the Chieftain, dropping a raw oyster into his mouth. "And we learned more than we wanted to know."

"You could have done that without bringing him here," pressed Kate, "and saved yourself a lot of trouble. I think you had another reason."

The ruler of the Tinnanis did not reply. Then the Chief-tess snapped her jaws and spoke: "You are right. It was the prophecy."

"Prophecy? What prophecy?"

"Silence!" boomed the Chieftain. "I will have no talk of prophecies in front of these unworthies. Now go away, all of you."

"Wait," pleaded Kate. "Won't you tell me anything about this walking stick? I came all this way for your help."

The Chieftess started to speak, but the voice of Hockeltock de Notnot cut her off. "No," he insisted. "We have no more time for strangers. Now, leave. I have other matters to deal with."

Kate could see Laioni's crestfallen face from the corner of her eye, even as her gaze fell to the ground. She thrust her hands sadly into her pockets. Unthinkingly, one hand closed around her Swiss army knife and the other around— something else. Half curious what the small round object could be, she pulled it out to view it. At once, she had an idea.

"Wait," she said, stepping nearer to the throne. "Wait a minute. I have something here you will like." She extended her hand, displaying a single, plastic-wrapped peppermint candy, the one she had found in the tunnel behind Kahona Falls.

The Tinnani ruffled his wings and eyed her suspiciously. "How do I know it's not some kind of poison?"

"It's not. I'll prove it." Kate removed the wrapping and crammed it back into her pocket. Then she took an exagger-ated lick of the peppermint, smiling broadly. "It tastes great."

The aide with the feather hat rushed up, waving his hands excitedly. "Don't do it, Your Wingedness. It's a trick."

"Here," said Kate as she dropped the item into the Chieftain's hand. "I promise it's safe."

Casting an imperial glare at the aide, the enthroned Tinnani turned to his wife. "Does she tell the truth?"

The Chieftess spun her head slowly toward her hus-band, then blinked. "She does."

The Tinnani brought the strange object to his nose and

sniffed. Nothing on his facial expression changed for a long moment. Then all at once, he smiled. "Nothing that smells this good could be poison," he said, plunking the sweet into his mouth.

His eyes widened with pleasure. "Ooooooh," he said giddily. "This is like nothing I've ever tasted before. It is exquisite, fantastic." He leaned forward. "Tell me, where did you get it?"

Kate's eyes twinkled. "It is a great and rare delicacy, Your Wingedness, called peppermint. It is found only in my own time, five hundred years from now."

"Huh?" said Jody, who had been growing increasingly bewildered. Among the various speakers, he could understand only Kate's language. Yet hearing her words did not make them intelligible. "What do you mean, five hundred years from now?"

Kate scowled at him, waving threateningly in his direction the owl's head handle that so resembled the Chieftain. "This is going to get you, if you say another word."

Immediately, the boy stepped back a pace. He stared at her warily.

Kate turned back to the Chieftain, who continued to suck delightedly. "It is an exotic fruit from my time," she said. Then, judging her moment, she added, "If you tell me how to get back there, I promise that if I ever return I'll bring you more."

"How many more?" asked the Tinnani, straightening the silver band on his head.

Kate deliberated. "How many would you like?"

The Chieftain's tufted eyebrows lifted. His voice, cracking with anticipation, replied, "Fifty. A hundred. No, a thousand!"

"A thousand it is," agreed Kate.

"Ten thousand."

"Okay, but that's my limit."

"How soon can you come back?"

"I don't know," she answered cautiously. "But I promise it'll be as soon as I'm able."

Turning to his wife, the Chieftain asked, "Will she keep her word?"

Her yellow eyes scanning Kate as if they could see straight through her, the Chieftess nodded in assent.

Hockeltock de Notnot raised his great wings. "All right then. We will tell you. But I warn you, the answer to your question is easier to say than to do. Go ahead, my Chieftess, tell this human what she needs to know to make the stick of power do her bidding."

And the slender Tinnani by his side raised her scepter, the signal she was about to speak.

18

the tale of the broken touchstone

BENEATH the flickering light from the torches, the assembled Tinnanis drew nearer, embracing their rulers in a wide semicircle. Their eyes, plus all other eyes except Jody's, fell to the feathered creature seated on the crystalline throne. Her gaze, like Jody's, remained on Kate.

The Chieftess stretched herself upward, pressing her plumage close to her body, so that she seemed nearly as tall as her throne. At length, she lowered the scepter. In a deep, gentle voice, she began to speak:

"The walking stick in your possession is indeed a stick of power. And it is old, very old indeed. Its memory stretches far beyond my own, beyond the Chieftain's, beyond that of any living being save the Stonehags, into an earlier time when our world felt not the heat of the Wicked One's breath. Like its makers the Tinnanis, it can render its holder or someone nearby completely invisible." She paused. "I can see by your expression you already know of this power."

Kate, recalling the chase through the muddy streets of Blade, nodded.

"It was given other powers as well," she continued, "many of them long forgotten. It is named the Stick of Fire, and it is said that it will burst into flames when so commanded by its rightful owner. That is not a command to be used lightly, however, for it will destroy the stick and all its powers. Carved on its handle is the likeness of the great-great-grandfather of my husband, the Chieftain Solosing de Notnot. It was he who caused the Stick of Fire to be made and these words to be carved into its shaft:

> *Fire of greed shall destroy;*
> *Fire of love shall create.*

The Stick of Fire possesses other powers, too, but the most important of these by far is the ability to travel through time."

"Yes," said Kate impulsively. "But tell me, how do I make it take me back?"

The yellow eyes of the Chieftess regarded her thoughtfully, with a hint of sadness brewing behind them. "Patience, Kaitlyn, patience. The powers of the stick you carry are more subtle than you think. For in the world that now exists, the Stick of Fire possesses a will of its own, uncontrollable by any creature. Its decisions about who to take through time and when are its own, and there is no predicting what it might do next."

Kate felt suddenly weak in her knees. "You, you mean there's no way to make it take me home?"

"I did not say that," answered the gentle-voiced Tinnani. "There is one possible way to control the power of the Stick of Fire, and only one. That is to do the single deed that would give you even greater power than the stick itself."

"What's that?"

The white wings stirred softly. "Healing the Broken Touchstone."

A muffled chorus of hooting sounds filled the chamber as the Tinnanis whispered among themselves. Again Kate addressed the Chieftess: "What does that mean? Healing the—whatever. Tell me."

"I shall," she replied. "For if you can heal the Broken Touchstone, the Stick of Fire will bend to your will."

The Chieftess paused, closing her round eyes for a long moment. She rotated her round head from side to side, snapping her jaws rhythmically as she did so. Then slowly her eyes reopened, and she began: "The Great One, creator of all that exists, made in the earliest days of this world a single object that would harbor all the glorious powers of creation. It was a single sphere, of purest red obsidian, light as a bubble and powerful as a galaxy of stars. The Great One called it by a simple name: the Touchstone. It was entrusted to the Tinnanis for their safekeeping, and it was installed upon the throne of their Chieftain."

Kate's vision roamed to the empty cup on top of the throne. She noticed that the Chieftain, still sucking on his peppermint, was also gazing at the spot, a look of longing in his eyes.

"For time beyond measure," continued the Chieftess with a slight ruffling of her wings, "the Touchstone rested safely on the throne deep within the walls of Ho Shantero. In exchange for their protection, the Touchstone gave the Tinnanis wonderful powers, and the most important of these was the power to connect living beings of all kinds to one another. So the Tinnanis became friends and stewards to all. They forged connections so that one group's desire did not mean another group's destruction. And because of this, their forest world thrived."

Here she stopped momentarily, squeezing the scepter with her sharp talons. "Then, in the reign of Solosing de Notnot, everything changed. The Wicked One, whose strength had been rising unnoticed for a long time, craved secretly to own the Touchstone, to turn its great power to his own ends. He dared even to enter Ho Shantero itself with the aid of his warriors, mounting a fierce attack. The Tinnanis, peace-loving and trusting, had underestimated his lust for power, and were caught completely unprepared.

Still they managed to beat him back, to win the Great Battle in the end, but only through tapping the Touchstone's own power—and only at enormous cost. Many brave lives were lost in that battle, and one thing more: The Touchstone cracked during the course of the fighting. A fragment of the sphere fell out, and its power decreased dramatically.

"After the battle, the Chieftain Solosing de Notnot decreed that the Broken Touchstone should not be healed, unless at some time in the future its full power was required to nurture the forest lands below—or to save the Tinnanis from total destruction." She lifted her white wings and sighed deeply. "We have reached such a time today. But now, at our moment of greatest need, both pieces of the Touchstone are lost to us."

"Lost?"

"Yes," replied the Chieftess. "As I said, Solosing de Notnot believed it was better for the Tinnanis to live without the Touchstone's full power than to risk its falling into the hands of the Wicked One again. So the sphere was not repaired. The Chieftain replaced the Broken Touchstone on his throne, and he hid the Fragment away in the most distant and difficult place he could find. So much time has now passed that its whereabouts are utterly lost from memory, known only to the spirit of Solosing de Notnot himself. The Wicked One he banished underground forever for his treachery, plus all of his servants with only one exception. To the Slimnis the Chieftain gave a second chance, both because they are the Tinnanis' brothers and because he believed they would never allow themselves to be manipulated again by the Wicked One."

"He was wrong," muttered the Chieftain, bobbing his head angrily. He bit down hard on the remnant of the peppermint.

"Yes," agreed the Tinnani at his side, her eyes increasingly sad. "For a time, the forest thrived again. Living things flourished everywhere and the blue lake cooled to a comfortable temperature. Even with only the partial power of the Broken Touchstone, the world lived in harmony and peace. Then, inexorably, the power of the Wicked One rose once again. He won over the Slimnis, who helped him find further recruits, above the ground. One of them, a man called Sanbu, is the most dangerous of all, for he is both very strong and very clever."

Kate glanced at Laioni. "Is he the same one you told me about?"

The Halami girl grimaced, then said, "The same."

"Gradually the Wicked One developed enough strength to reach into others' minds, even within the very walls of Ho Shantero. One of those minds, sadly, was the Counsellor to the Chieftain, a man named Zinzin. Harshnaga Zinzin."

As she mentioned that name, several Tinnanis screeched angrily in the background. Some scraped their talons against the stone floor. Kate looked at Jody, who stood paralyzed with fear. He clearly believed they were preparing to devour him.

"Zinzin," the Chieftess went on, "heard the whisperings of the Wicked One but lacked the strength to banish him from his mind. The Wicked One promised him wealth beyond measure and power beyond his dreams. One day not long ago came the moment of truth: The Wicked One commanded him to deliver the Broken Touchstone as a gesture of loyalty. He obeyed, and during a holiday feast when no one was watching, he stole the Broken Touchstone and escaped from Ho Shantero. With the help of Sanbu, the traitor delivered it to the Wicked One in his mountain lair. But Sanbu then killed him, perhaps out of jealousy, perhaps thinking his master would reward him for his show of strength. So in the end Zinzin's treachery got him nothing more precious than an early death.

"Since the theft of the Broken Touchstone, our forest has fared poorly. The power of the Wicked One has swollen, and he has tempted many new creatures to join his cause. Sanbu now commands a small but growing band of warriors. Like the Wicked One himself, they see the other beings of the forest not as friends but as adversaries. They use whatever they like with no thought of the future, burning great trees to make bonfires, catching more fish than they can eat and wasting the rest, hunting any animals that get in their way or killing them just for pleasure, fouling the streams with their excrement. The Wicked One has grown so confident that he has climbed steadily upward, almost to the surface, sending fire to the forest below and heat to the waters of our own lake.

The Chieftess raised her wings and gestured toward the assembled Tinnanis. "At the same time, our own power has diminished. No longer can we nurture and strengthen the life of the forest as we have for so long. Without the Touchstone, even our ability to keep the island of Ho Shantero afloat will come to an end, forcing us to abandon our ancestral home before it sinks and is lost forever."

"The island is still floating in my time, five hundred years from now," said Kate hopefully.

The Chieftess remained somber. "Even after we have been forced to leave, the island will stay afloat for a while solely through the lingering enchantment of the Touchstone. So your glimpse of the future tells me nothing about its fate, or ours."

Turning her soulful eyes toward the Chieftain, she concluded her tale with these words: "And amidst all this suffering that we have borne, there is one wound greater than all the rest."

With a wave of her wing she indicated a bench of black stone near the vacant throne. A torch flamed above, illuminating the bench, but Kate could see nothing resting there. Then, by looking slightly askance, she discovered a faint, frail glow of white light upon its seat. The light seemed to pulse, quivering with every breath of some unseen being.

"There," said the Chieftess, "lies our daughter, our only child. Not so many years ago, I held her as a newborn in the curl of my wing, singing her the songs that hold all the history of the Tinnanis. Then, before long, she, too, was singing, in a voice of such beauty that none who heard her could ever forget it. That is why we named her Fanona,

which in the Old Tongue means Song That Never Dies."
She lowered her voice. "It is a bitter irony now."

"It is indeed," agreed the Chieftain, who reached out a
hand to clasp that of his wife.

A heavy silence filled the chamber, and for a long
moment the Chieftess did not move except to blink her yellow eyes several times. Finally, she continued: "When our
little Fanona was born, it was prophesied that in some mysterious way her life would be bound up with the Broken
Touchstone. We took that to mean that somehow, during
her reign far in the future, the missing Fragment would be
found and the Touchstone healed at last. We imagined her
armed with the Touchstone's full power, power she could
use both to nurture the forest and to protect our people
against the Wicked One. Yet when the sphere vanished
from this hall, she grew weaker and frailer by the day, until
she has now not even the strength to show her feathers.
Now we see that the prophecy may have had another
meaning, that she may never rule at all from her throne of
clear crystal. For unless the Broken Touchstone is returned
soon, she surely will die."

She blinked again, then slowly spun her head back
toward Kate. "There is one more prophecy you should
know, though I cannot tell what it might mean for you. It
concerns the lost Fragment:

> *Fragment, object of desire,*
> *Shall be found anew.*
> *One who bears the Stick of Fire*
> *Holds the power true.*

Those are the words of the prophecy, as translated from the
Old Tongue, but hear me well: It could have two quite different meanings. Some believe it means that the Stick of
Fire has the power to find the Fragment. The Wicked One,
as he showed by sending his agents to attack you, believes
that is the true interpretation. He craves nothing more than

the Fragment, for then he could heal the Broken Touchstone and all things would bend to his desires."

"What is the other meaning?"

"That not the stick itself, but the one who bears it, holds the power to find the Fragment. So someone from another time, someone who traveled here through the power of the stick, might be the one to find it."

"Now I understand why you brought him here," said Kate with a nod toward Jody. "You thought maybe he was the person from another time."

"Proof of our desperation," lamented the Chieftain. "Only the prospect of saving both our forest world and our daughter made it worth the effort to bring him to Ho Shantero. We tried to fix his broken arm, but he has deeper injuries beyond our power to repair."

Jody, mustering his courage, stepped forward again. Facing the Chieftain, he declared, "You've got no right to keep me prisoner this way. Even if I did shoot that owl." He turned to Kate. "This has to be a dream, a terrible bad dream. But if it's not, if it's really happening to me, what do I have to do to get out of here?"

"The same thing I have to do," she snapped. "You see this stick? It can take us back to our own time. But only if we can find the Fragment."

"The what?" he asked.

"And also the Broken Touchstone," added Laioni. "You'll need both pieces to heal it."

Kate winced. "That means going—"

"To the lair of the Wicked One," completed the Chieftess, shaking her broad wings. "No task could be more difficult." She glanced at the fragile glow hovering above the bench of stone. "Or more important."

Jody stepped closer to Kate, watching the owl-headed stick warily. "Let me get this right. You're saying that's some kind of magic stick?"

"You could call it that."

"But it won't take us home unless we can find something else?"

Kate nodded. "Two things."

Jody scratched his tangled head of hair. "And finding them means leaving this owls' nest."

"Yes, but it's going to be dangerous."

"I'm coming with you."

"I mean really dangerous," repeated Kate. "You should stay here and wait."

"You just wanna get rid of me! Well, it's not that easy. Where that stick goes, I go." He looked spitefully at the Chieftain. "I won't miss this place one bit."

"The feeling's mutual," said the Chieftain, although to Jody it sounded like nothing more than the hoot of an angry owl.

"What about you?" Kate asked Laioni. "Shouldn't you go back to your people? The chances, they're so slim."

The dark eyes flashed. "What are my chances if I go back? My people are doomed unless the Broken Touchstone is taken back. The Wicked One is destroying our lives, our forest, our home. Unless he is stopped, we will all end up like Toru." She clenched her fists. "If you go to the Wicked One's mountain, then I go too. I am She Who Follows the Owl."

Kate's mind churned. It was likely she would perish in the attempt to find both pieces of the Touchstone, that much was clear. In that case she wouldn't be much use to Aunt Melanie or anybody else, ever again. But if she chose to do nothing, then she and Laioni would be safe, at least for now. Yet that meant she would never even have a chance to help Aunt Melanie in her time of need. Nor would she ever see her again.

She looked for a moment into the yellow eyes of the carved handle. "All right," she announced. "I'm going to try." Casting a harsh glare at Jody, she said, "Why don't you just stay here? You'll only get in the way."

"No way," he replied. "I told you, I go with that stick. If this isn't just a bad dream, I'm not gonna miss my chance."

"He can't stay here," declared the Chieftain. "Gives me heartburn just to look at him."

Kate frowned and faced the ruling couple. "Before we go, then, isn't there anything else you can tell us about where to find the Fragment?"

"Nothing," answered the Chieftess solemnly, spinning her head one way and then the other. "Just remember what you have heard. It may prove useful."

"Then I think," said Kate to Laioni, "we should go first to the lair of the Wicked One. At least we know the Broken Touchstone is there. The Fragment—who knows where it might be? Maybe it doesn't even still exist."

"It exists," declared the Chieftess firmly.

Just then Monga placed his front paws on the table by the Chieftain's side. In one swift gulp, he swallowed all the remaining oysters.

"Monga," exclaimed Laioni in dismay, pulling him away. "Monga, no."

The Chieftain glowered at the dog, who wagged his tail gleefully. Then he turned to Kate. "Make it twenty thousand peppermints."

Kate sighed. "All right, but it's all irrelevant if I get killed trying to get back."

"No getting killed until you deliver the peppermints," commanded the Chieftain. "It is forbidden." Seeing the look of consternation on his wife's face, he quickly proposed, "Now then, let us give you something to sustain you on your journey." Tapping his claws on his belt buckle, he hooted, "Bring me three bags of *minarni.*"

Immediately, one of the grass-caped aides flew to the thrones, bearing three brown leather pouches with long straps meant to be tied around the waist. One he gave to Kate, one to Laioni, and one, reluctantly, to Jody.

Peering into the pouch, Jody lamented, "Bird food! Are we supposed to eat this?"

"Quiet," ordered Kate. "I still haven't decided to let you come."

"You will find it both nourishing and filling," said the Chieftain, adding under his breath, "even if the taste is unremarkable." He stirred his wings. "And before you go, I have one more thing to offer you. It might not be any help, but then again it might." He clapped his hands and spoke a strange word: "Kandeldandel."

From the rear of the crowd of Tinnanis stepped a scrawny-looking figure. His white feathers stuck out unevenly, less orderly even than Monga's fur. In one hand he held a manila-colored wooden flute. His small mouth twisted slightly up to one side, giving the impression of a permanent grin. Upon his left shoulder rested a small, rust-colored owl with large brown eyes. He stepped before the thrones of the Chieftain and Chieftess and bowed awkwardly, nearly losing the creature perched on his shoulder.

Jody's brow furrowed. "I don't like the looks of this one."

"I present to you," announced the Chieftain, "Kandeldandel, third flutist in my orchestra."

"At your service," hooted Kandeldandel in a deep bass voice that seemed permeated with humor, like a cross between a foghorn and a belly laugh.

At that, the small brown-eyed owl flapped his wings and whistled angrily. Kandeldandel cleared his throat and added, "And my friend Arc, Your Wingedness. He is at your service too."

"Mmm, yes," muttered the Chieftain. "I forgot you two go everywhere together." With a note of defensiveness, he continued, "Kandeldandel is one of the few people I can spare right now. When the Broken Touchstone disappeared, he wasn't around to join in the search. Probably off someplace playing his flute—which he does quite well, by the way. Only trouble is, when he plays, it has the unfortunate effect of putting out fires. So he can't play for you at your fire pit. Maybe, though, his music can lighten your hearts while you travel to the Wicked One's mountain." Eyeing the musician, the Chieftain added skeptically, "If he sticks around that long."

The Chieftess nodded in agreement. "It is right that Kandeldandel should go. An excellent choice."

Kandeldandel shifted his weight uncomfortably, dropped his flute with a clatter, bent over to pick it up and dropped

Arc off his shoulder, retrieved the flute, helped the small owl settle back on his perch, then dropped the flute again.

"Gee, thanks," said Kate dismally.

"How do we get out of here?" demanded Jody.

"My, my, he won't like the answer to that question," said the Chieftain to himself. He leaned toward Kate and smacked his lips. "Don't forget your promise, now, if you succeed."

"If I succeed," repeated Kate weakly.

The wise eyes of the Chieftess connected one last time with hers. Raising her wings slightly, she said, "Hold fast to your stick of power. It is your only hope, and ours as well. *Halma-dru* to you all."

It was Laioni who answered. "And to you as well."

The Chieftain clapped his hands three times. Suddenly, Kate heard a fluttering of wings. Before she knew what was happening, a pair of strong talons wrapped around each of her arms, just below the armpit. In an instant, she was airborne, carried vertically as if she were standing on an aerial escalator, rising toward the top of the great room. With a metallic creak, a circular door slid open in the middle of the ceiling, beyond which she saw clouds of white vapor.

She cast a final glance below. White-winged Tinnanis ringed the three thrones, one of which sat empty. The last thing she heard before rising through the door was a voice calling, "Oysters! Bring me more oysters."

19

airborne

As she sailed through the opening, borne by two Tinnanis pumping their broad wings in constant rhythm, Kate saw the island of Ho Shantero from a new vantage point. Blacker than coal it remained, but it seemed somehow less sinister. Water flowed over most of its surface, draining down from the spindly spires to run in broad streams across the island's main bulk. She wondered if this water, pumped to the tops of the spires by some strange mechanism, could be part of the system that kept Ho Shantero afloat.

At once she realized that these very streams, rippling and shifting over the surface, were the source of the impression of movement, of crawling, that had so frightened her. She grinned at her own gullibility, then found herself wishing that some of her fears of Gashra, the Wicked One, might prove to be so unfounded. Yet her heart held little hope.

The island disappeared in a sea of white vapor as the Tinnanis carried the companions ever higher. Kate caught passing glimpses of Laioni, smiling as another pair of white-winged Tinnanis lifted her through the clouds. She saw Jody only once, hoisted by his belt and uninjured arm, his usual downtrodden look replaced with one of sheer amazement. Monga she heard barking through the mist, but never viewed; she imagined the spirited dog was probably enjoying his first taste of flight. Once she spotted Kandeldandel, flute in hand, flying erratically with the small reddish owl by his side.

Kate soon relaxed her body, trusting herself to the hearty creatures whose wings beat so powerfully above her. Their talons squeezed her upper arms tightly, but not hard enough to stop her circulation. She felt the fluffy leggings of their trouser feathers above each of her shoulders, and sometimes the quivering plumage tickled the edges of her ears. To her surprise, she heard virtually no sound as the Tinnanis flew, only the vaguest whoosh of air at the start of each downstroke.

In her mind's eye, Kate tried to fathom what lay below, as if she were drawing her own version of Aunt Melanie's map on the impervious clouds beneath her. She imagined the deep blue lake, two Halami women and a baby in a cradle still camped on its shore. The women sang softly while preparing their next meal, although the younger one regularly lifted her head, listening for a sound she had waited too long to hear. By a field of rushing water at one end of the lake, the green spires of the Hidden Forest rose skyward. Near its center, the great grove of redwood trees towered in stately grace, and in the center of the grove stood the Ancient One. Beyond, toward the ridge of cliffs, a small green pool frothed ominously. Next to it rested a ring of great boulders, silently waiting and watching.

Suddenly the mist melted into trailing wisps that hung in the air like the breath of dragons. Gray sky appeared overhead. The ragged ridge of gray-brown cliffs loomed out of the clouds, encircling the entire crater. From this bird's-eye view, it resembled an enormous bowl of steaming soup. Sunlight scattered in the swirling masses of mist, illuminating their upper reaches. Kate felt suddenly cold, for the first time since crawling through the tunnel behind the waterfall.

Over the rim the Tinnanis carried her, so close she felt she could almost kick the rocks with her feet. No longer protected by the crater, she was buffeted by cold winds. Her teeth started to chatter, and her dangling body swayed within the grip of the talons. Her upper arms and neck began to ache.

Passing across the high cliffs, Kate understood clearly why Lost Crater would remain undisturbed for the next five hundred years. No one, without the aid of wings either natural or man-made, could surmount those steep and slick walls. *The Back of Beyond,* Aunt Melanie had called this place.

As they cleared the rim, the view took her breath away, and for a moment she forgot about the cold. Forest, ancient and sprawling, stretched as far as she could see under the overcast sky. From this height the differences from her own time leaped out boldly: No dusty brown squares splattered the ridges, no mud-filled canyons crawled toward the sea. Not all looked well with the forest, however. Some sections, scorched by fire, still smoldered. Thick, black smoke clung to some of the valleys, and strange clouds of steam rose from the more distant rivers.

Then, on the horizon, Kate spotted an unfamiliar, rounded mountain that was belching steam from its summit. In a flash, she realized it was in the same location as the jagged, fang-shaped peak she had seen from Kahona Falls, the one known in later times as Brimstone Peak. And she knew she was viewing the fortress of Gashra, the Wicked One.

A thunderous, crashing sound filled the air. She looked down to see Kahona Falls, pouring endlessly out of the vertical wall of the crater. The Tinnanis then started to descend, carrying her straight into the billowing spray of the waterfall. As they drew nearer to the trees below, Kate glimpsed a delicate brown rope bridge stretching across the crevasse she had crossed using Aunt Melanie's rickety wooden ladder. Some means of transportation, she thought, had not improved in the last five hundred years.

In seconds, she was dropping into the tops of the trees. The wind died down until it scarcely whispered in her ears. She felt steadily warmer, though not as warm as inside the crater. Burly branches rose around her, and her feet brushed against several lacy canopies. With a whooshing of wings, the two Tinnanis lowered her gently to the forest floor, potent in its fragrance of needles, cones, and resins. Her feet touched down on the spongy ground just as the talons released their grip around her aching arms.

Holding the walking stick in one hand, she craned her stiff neck to see the creatures hovering above her. One of them called good luck in a low hooting voice. Before she could answer, they lifted swiftly toward the sky, white wings beating in unison.

20

call of the owl

SECONDS later, Laioni and Monga joined Kate on the needle-strewn floor of the forest. Tall trees, straight as stalks of corn, pushed skyward on all sides. Their gnarled trunks, though not so covered with moss as their cousins inside the fog-filled crater, rose equally impressively into the air. Delicate fronds of fern sprouted from twisted roots and broken branches, while limbs low to the two girls' heads supported a panoply of birds and squirrels, butter-flies, and beetles. Monga leaped at one squirrel, nipping at the tail almost as bushy as his own.

"How was your ride?" asked Kate, already knowing the answer.

Laioni smiled slowly, still savoring the experience. "For a moment, I had wings."

The aroma of some June blossom, sweet and fresh, wafted to Kate's nose. She listened to the branches swish-ing high above her head. Intermittently, when the wind quieted, she could hear the distant rumbling of Kahona Falls. Then came a loud cracking of twigs.

Jody stepped into view from behind a stately Douglas fir, rubbing the back of his neck with the hand not bound in a sling. "Some ride," he said derisively. "But it was worth it to get away from those owl-people."

"I hope you appreciate what they did for you," said Kate testily.

"What's to appreciate?" he shot back.

"They fixed your shoulder, for one thing."

"And gave you flight," added Laioni sternly.

Jody stared in surprise at the Halami girl, then turned back to Kate. "What did she say?"

"She said you got a chance to fly, and that's something else to appreciate."

Glancing upward, he allowed, "It was pretty amazing, I'll say that. Once you got used to it."

Laioni's expression softened slightly, but she said nothing.

"One thing's for sure," Jody went on, "I don't think I'm dreaming anymore. My neck wouldn't hurt like this if I was dreaming." He contemplated Kate suspiciously. "You just made up all that stuff about their getting revenge for that owl I killed, didn't you?"

Kate merely grinned.

"Hey, how come you understand all these weird languages? You talk to owl-people and Indians, too."

Her hazel eyes narrowed. "Because I listen to people like Aunt Melanie, instead of stealing their mail."

Jody's face reddened. "You're just like her. Think you're the smartest person in the world! Well, you can't fool me. I know you just want to leave me here, wherever this place is. Well, forget about it, because I'm sticking to you like glue till I get home."

"This *is* your home," replied Kate. "Just five centuries earlier."

"You expect me to believe that?"

"I don't care if you do or not. Just keep out of my way. If this walking stick is ever going to get us back, we've got lots of hard work to do."

"No harder than working in the sawmill," said Jody, pushing a scraggly lock of hair off his forehead. "And I've done that for five summers." He scanned the Douglas fir by his side. "Sure are some mothers around here. I couldn't believe it from the air. Never saw anything like it, so many trees. This place would keep the mill busy for years. Got any idea how many houses you could make out of just one tree like this?"

Kate looked at him frostily. "And how many houses would it take to make one of these trees?"

Just then a long, low hooting sound floated through the forest, like the call of an owl but subtler, gentler. It was accompanied by several slightly higher voices from the trees saying *hooo-hooo, hooo-hooo*. The initial owl-like sound grew louder and clearer until a lone Tinnani, flute at his lips, came walking toward them from behind a yew tree. Kandeldandel.

Jody squinted at the Tinnani. "Aw, no. I thought we left all you buzzards behind."

Kandeldandel, whose head reached only as high as the boy's waist, flashed him a vengeful glance. Then he trilled a few high notes on his flute. Immediately, the small red owl Arc swooped down from the branches above. With a loud whistle, the owl veered directly at Jody.

"Hey!" the boy exclaimed, ducking his head just as Arc sailed past. "He tried to dive-bomb me."

Kandeldandel ruffled his feathers and turned his back on him, while Arc whistled again happily and landed on the Tinnani's shoulder. Stepping closer to Kate, Kandeldandel lowered his flute and said in his deep, laughing voice, "Seems your friend doesn't appreciate good music."

Before Kate could respond, Jody picked up a spruce cone and threw it at Arc. It missed by a wide margin, prompting a new round of amused whistles.

"Too bad you're such a lousy shot," Kate lamented.

Jody glared at her. "And what kind of shot are you?"

"Better than you, that's for sure."

He stooped, picked up a cone and tossed it to her. "Let's see."

Kate hefted the cone in her hand. "You see that tree over there leaning to the side?"

Jody's face widened into a grin. "No way you can hit that. Too far away."

"And about ten feet up, you see that white fungus?"

"Give me a break. You're all talk. Besides, you're a—"

"A girl?" Kate's eyes flashed angrily. She turned to the fungus, a white mound not much bigger than a catcher's mitt, sprouting from the side of the trunk. Biting her lip, she concentrated on its position.

"This I've got to see," said Jody derisively.

Rearing back as if she were about to fire one to home plate, she paused, her weight entirely on one foot. Then she flung herself forward as her arm released, snapping like a whip. The cone whizzed through the air, slicing past a heavily laden branch. It glanced off the bottom edge of the fungus, causing a shower of white particles to fall to the forest floor.

The boy gaped in amazement.

Trying to remain nonchalant, Kate resisted the urge to smile. Pointing to the bulldog wielding a baseball bat emblazoned on her sweatshirt, she said simply, "Girls can throw too."

Jody gazed at her with new respect. "Hey, you've got an arm like Luis Aparicio's."

Kate's eyes gleamed. "That's some compliment. He could throw like anything. Made more double plays than any other shortstop in history."

"And stole bases like crazy too."

"Took me two whole years to get his rookie card for my collection."

Jody nodded. "My favorite's Honus Wagner. The Flying Dutchman. Stole seven hundred bases and played every position except catcher for the Pirates."

"But he was best at shortstop," Kate reminded him.

Jody indicated her bright green shoelaces. "Wouldn't even have made the team with laces like that, though," he teased. "They're like a neon sign."

Despite herself, Kate grinned.

Laioni tugged on her sleeve, looking positively bewildered. "I hear your words, but they mean nothing."

"Don't worry," Kate replied, "it's just baseball talk." Her expression hardened again. "Nothing to do with Gashra."

"What's Gashra?" Jody asked.

"He's the one we're up against. He's got the Broken Touchstone, and we'll have to be faster than Honus Wagner to steal it from him. Let's get going."

"We should follow the river to make the best time," said Laioni. "But the canyon is very wide and that will make us easy to spot. Gashra's allies are everywhere."

"Then we should stay more hidden, in the trees. Can you find a way? We'll follow you." Kate suddenly remembered Kandeldandel, who was nowhere in sight. "Where did that Tinnani go?"

"Someplace far away, I hope," muttered Jody. "And his pet owl too."

Just then, an ear-splitting blast as loud as a train whistle sounded right between Jody's feet. He screamed and jumped nearly half his height into the air. Upon landing he whipped around to see what had made the terrifying noise.

Facing him, grinning blithely, stood Kandeldandel. Arc, who had released the whistle, sat innocently upon his shoulder. Kandeldandel bobbed his head in owl-like fashion, then hooted, "Just thought we'd say hello."

Jody could not understand his words, but the mocking tone was clear. He grimaced and lunged at them. Arc lifted off into the branches, while the Tinnani stepped sideways and raised his full-feathered wings. His half grin broadened into a smile. Then, without warning, he brought the wings down and disappeared in a puff of white light. Not even the flute remained visible.

"You scared them," scolded Kate.

"Scared *them?*" blurted Jody. "Didn't you see what they did to me? First they dive-bomb me, then they nearly blast a hole in my backside."

Kate and Laioni exchanged grins before starting to stride into the forest. After a few steps, Kate said, "I guess Kandeldandel can get Arc to do anything."

Laioni cast her a knowing glance. "Tinnanis have a special way with owls. Not only with their close friends like Arc, either. Owls follow them everywhere they go, day or night."

"I thought owls slept all day."

"They do," answered Laioni as she ducked beneath a branch, "unless a Tinnani is around. Tinnanis love to call them into action, hooting just like owls but with deeper voices. Kandeldandel does it with his flute too. So if you ever see an owl in flight during the day, you can be sure it's the work of Tinnanis."

Kate recalled the mysterious owl who had saved her from the spell of the deadly green pool. It even looked a bit like Arc, come to think of it. Could Tinnanis have been responsible for that? No, she told herself. Not possible. Besides, Tinnanis may not even be around in five hundred years—especially if Gashra had his way.

Monga, who was prancing immediately behind them, suddenly turned his head at a sound. Ears alert, he bounded off after some small, scurrying animal. Meanwhile, Jody reluctantly fell in behind, still grumbling to himself about the sneak attacks. He stopped every few steps to check under his legs for any new sign of trouble.

For the next several hours, they trekked through the thick forest. The terrain, hilly and rolling, reminded Kate of the up-and-down trail that ran near her hometown. Of course, there were significant differences: New England had no great trees like this, for one. But what about five hundred years ago? Hadn't her mother once told her that the land in her part of Massachusetts once supported enormous forests of hemlock and chestnut, now replaced with subdivisions and shopping malls? She wondered, and found herself feeling some sympathy for Jody. It wasn't his fault that he happened to grow up in a time and place where the livelihood people thought would continue

forever was finally coming to an end. He was just unlucky
enough to be born at the hardest moment in the history of
his hometown.

Kate spotted an especially juicy clump of huckleberries
and stopped to eat a few. The taste brought back instantly
the tart flavor of Aunt Melanie's homemade pie. Wistfully,
she reached her hand into the pouch provided by the Chieftain. The *minarni* contained some kind of spindly roots
that tasted like burned toast, as well as some reddish leaves,
soaked in sauces and dried, with a flavor like vanilla pud-
ding. As the Chieftain had promised, the food gave an
unexpected surge of strength. Its stiff, chewy texture also
made it seem more filling than its appearance warranted.
She started walking again, then glanced behind at Jody,
wondering whether he had decided to try any. No doubt if
he had, he wouldn't admit it.

Suddenly, she halted in her tracks. A wave of nausea
passed through her. Dozens of deer, including several does
and fawns, lay stacked haphazardly in piles beneath a tall
Douglas fir. Arrows still protruded from some of their
bloody hides. Several decapitated heads hung mutilated
from the tree's lower branches. Many of the carcasses,
their meat rotting and spoiled, bore armies of flies and
squirming brown maggots. Laioni knelt weeping before
the tree, whose bark had been brutally slashed and gouged
by knives. Monga lay beside her, his tail drooping.

Quietly, Kate approached and knelt beside her friend.
She laid her arm across Laioni's bare shoulders and waited
until her sobs eventually ceased. Then she asked simply,
"Who?"

Laioni turned a tearstained face toward her. "Sanbu,"
she whispered.

"But why?"

"Who can tell? Maybe—maybe he just thought it was
fun. Maybe he wanted to get them before anyone else.
Hunters like my father also stalk deer."

Kate shook her head. "But your father would have taken
only what he needed."

"And thanked the deer for the gift," added the Halami girl, staring blankly at the slaughtered animals beneath the tree.

Rising, Kate turned away from the gruesome sight and slowly walked the perimeter of the area. She saw a discarded knife carved from flint embedded in the branches of a bush, but no other sign of Sanbu's band.

Jody joined her. "Who did this?" he asked, surveying the gory scene.

"Sanbu," answered Kate. "One of Gashra's men. Can you believe this mess?"

Jody pushed back a dangling lock of red hair. "Reminds me of a war movie I saw once."

Without looking at him, Kate replied, "Reminds me of a clear-cut I saw once."

Jody stiffened, but said nothing.

Laioni, trailed by Monga, walked up to them. "We should go," she said, her voice hoarse. "Sanbu might still be near."

21

the crossing

OFF they strode into the forest, with Laioni leading the way as before. She took them rapidly higher, ascending the spine of a ridge that they followed for a great distance until it dropped down into a steep-walled valley. The forest grew even thicker, with young trees seeming to sprout from the very roots of their elders. Yet despite the changing landscape and the increasing distance from Sanbu's slaughter, the carnage remained fresh in Kate's mind.

Frequently, they crossed clear pathways through the undergrowth, winding between the towering trees. Animal trails, Kate surmised, though she could not be certain. Some of them Laioni chose to follow for significant distances. Others, perhaps traveled more by people than by four-legged wanderers, she avoided. Kate wished she had studied Aunt Melanie's hand-drawn map more closely. She seemed to recall something near Brimstone Peak, a section of the map that was veiled in darkness. But she could not be sure.

At one point she heard a low whistling above her head.

She looked up to discover Arc descending slowly toward her, his rusty red wings spread wide. The huge brown eyes of the owl studied her intently from the middle of his wide facial disc. For the first time, Kate noticed his little ear tufts and the long white feathers sprouting from both sides of his silvery beak, giving the impression of well-combed whiskers. With a gentle whistle, the diminutive owl settled on her left shoulder.

"So you'd like a ride?" asked Kate, enjoying the feeling of his soft plumage against her cheek.

Arc ruffled his feathers contentedly.

"I wonder where your friend Kandeldandel is," mused Kate.

The owl raised his wings slightly, as if to say, *How should I know?*

"Do you think he'll turn up again?"

Arc merely repeated the gesture.

"Nothing predictable about him," said Kate with a smile.

The owl whistled softly and shook his long whiskers.

Kate realized at that moment how much Arc combined elements of other animals: the wide eyes of a cat, the round shape of a bear, the talons and wings of a hawk. Right now, at rest, he seemed as harmless as a down pillow. Yet in an instant he could become a skillful hunter, sailing sound-lessly through the air in search of prey. A creature of many contrasts, she thought—much like human beings.

They entered an area more verdant than anyplace they had seen since leaving Lost Crater. Walking on the stretches of soft, spongy moss felt like stepping across a mattress. Presently the sound of splashing water reached them. They came upon a narrow canyon with dark rock walls covered with thousands upon thousands of lushly layered ferns. High as houses rose the richly decorated rocks on both sides. Kate counted five small waterfalls streaming down through the ferns, looking like marble columns in a temple of green. Arc moved to the edge of her shoulder and released an ascending whistle that reverberated within the walls. Then he listened to the echo, bobbing his head rhythmically.

Ahead, the canyon opened into a grassy clearing where the water from the waterfalls combined to form a surging stream. As they approached the clearing, the continual rushing of the stream grew louder. Gurgling over rounded rocks, the water cascaded steadily through the wide channel. Monga started barking, and Laioni called to him sharply. Stepping closer, Kate saw the immense form of a black bear standing near the opposite bank, her hind legs submerged in the stream. Nearby two identical cubs rolled on the grass together, wrestling playfully.

Using her forepaws for bats, the bear took several swipes at the stream, spraying water on the bank and her cubs. Finally, she knocked a substantial silver-colored fish out of the water, which lay flapping in the grass for no more than two seconds before the bear cubs reached it. One of them grabbed it and held it between two black paws. Then, like a child eating a Popsicle, the bear sniffed the wriggling fish and took one enormous bite out of the fleshy midsection. The other cub tried to take a bite of his own, causing the fish to fall on the grass. They rolled over each other trying to get it, finally tumbling over the edge of the bank into the rushing water. The mother, meanwhile, ignored them and continued to smack the water in search of more fish.

Suddenly a white-winged creature materialized in the air just above the bear and settled on her massive shoulders. The bear roared and reared up, spinning on her feet like a dancer.

"Kandeldandel!" exclaimed both Kate and Laioni at once. Arc flapped his wings and whistled in greeting.

The playful Tinnani waved to them, flute in hand. He rode the jumping, twisting bear with the moxie of a cowboy riding a bucking bronco. Every time the bear swatted at him, Kandeldandel evaded the blow just in time, losing not so much as a feather. Kate and Laioni were laughing heartily as Jody came up from behind. Seeing the cause of the commotion, the boy merely glowered.

At last Kandeldandel lifted off and landed on the far bank. Grasping the still-flailing fish with his talons, he took flight again just as the bear and both of her cubs came charging at him. He rose barely out of arm's reach as the mother bear swatted and roared angrily. With perfect accuracy, the Tinnani dropped the fish with a splat precisely on her long, black nose. He then flew off into the trees.

"That was some show," said Kate with a smile.

"Too bad the bear didn't get him," grumbled Jody. He eyed the little owl on her shoulder with scorn. "Or his pet owl."

Arc flapped his wings and whistled angrily.

"Kandeldandel's a trickster," Kate replied. "He just likes a good laugh." Turning to Laioni, she added, "I don't know what else he's good for, though. He's here and then he's not here. We sure can't count on him to help us against Gashra."

Laioni indicated Arc with a tilt of her head. "Even his owl friend can't depend on him for a good ride. That's probably why he decided to perch on you for a while."

"At least I'm better than a wild bear," agreed Kate.

"Let's go," said Laioni, giving a pull on one of Monga's ears. "That bear's so mad now she might decide to chase us instead of him."

As Kate started to follow, Arc stretched his wings, then opened his beak wide in a yawn. He gave a long, low whistle, apparently announcing it was time for a nap, before closing his eyes tightly. They hiked along the bank for many miles, climbing successive inclines and declines, wading through stretches of marsh grass, jumping across small side channels and muddy ravines. Throughout, Arc slept peacefully upon his perch.

At last the group entered a valley so pristine that if the allies of Gashra had already entered it, no one could tell. The forest here felt peaceful and harmonious. Although Laioni regularly scanned the bubbling stream and waving branches for any signs of disturbance, Kate grew gradually more relaxed. Danger seemed as distant as Gashra's steaming mountain lair, at least another day's walk away. Even the memory of Sanbu's slain deer began to fade.

At one point, Laioni halted and turned to Kate. "We should cross the stream here." Seeing the sleeping creature on her shoulder, she added, "He looks very comfortable there. I think you've made a new friend."

Kate grinned. "He's kind of cute, don't you think?"

Arc suddenly opened his eyes and bobbed his squat head from side to side, as if he were embarrassed.

"I especially like his whiskers," said Laioni, stepping into the stream.

The small red owl blinked, ruffling his wings proudly. Then, with a chirplike whistle, he lifted off from his perch. His whisker-feathers seemed to flap just as vigorously as his wings as he flew across the stream and vanished into the tall trees.

Kate watched him until he disappeared, then decided to use this opportunity to take a drink. She lowered her head into the rushing water, feeling its coldness cleanse her face. Monga joined her at the water's edge, lapping eagerly. Jody, with some awkwardness due to his sling, bent down to do the same.

"Ahhh," said the boy, raising his face from the stream. "Tastes good." He took another several swallows. "Clear too. I've never seen a stream so clear. You could catch fish here no trouble."

Kate, her face also dripping, lifted herself to her feet. "That bear back there was having some trouble," she said wryly.

"Yeah," answered the boy, raising himself to stand. "Bet she feels the same way I do about pesty owl-people."

Laioni, who had crossed over while they were drinking, called to them from the opposite bank. Monga obediently marched into the stream. Using the walking stick to give her balance in the fast-moving water, Kate followed.

Step by step, she pushed across the channel. About halfway across, she briefly paused to glance back at Jody, who was just entering the stream. Then, without warning, the earth shifted under her feet. She cried out, fighting to keep herself upright.

With a grinding heave, the stream bed lurched to one side, opening a long chasm that snaked from the trees by the far bank over the grassy meadow and into the stream itself. Kate fell into the water, managed to raise herself, then tumbled backward again as the earthquake shook the ground again, this time more intensely. Her lower back struck a pointed rock jutting up from the stream bed and she shouted in pain.

Then fear flooded her veins. The walking stick was gone! Battling to regain her feet, she saw it floating swiftly down the stream. She struggled toward it, but another series of tremors knocked her face first into the churning water.

"The stick!" she sputtered, toiling to stand. But no one could hear her over the thunderous roar that swelled in the air, drowning out any other sound.

At that instant, she felt a shock of heat on her hand. A new, sizzling sound hissed in her ears and she realized that the water just upstream was steaming like a boiling pot. Fiery fingers of orange lava poured out of the chasm and into the water, sending thunderheads of vapor into the sky. Lava rolled along the stream bottom, consuming anything in its path. Through the rising steam Kate saw the oncoming river of orange only a few feet away.

A set of long talons wrapped around her left armpit and lifted her barely out of the water, just as the molten fluid rolled across the spot. Kandeldandel, flapping furiously, carried her over the stream bank, across the grass, and into the shelter of the trees. He dropped her on a tangle of brush with a splintering of broken branches. Laioni and Monga bounded to them.

"The stick!" she exclaimed. "It's in the stream."

Laioni's jaw fell open and she turned downstream.

Kandeldandel hooted, his yellow eyes widening. Not hesitating another second, he flew off into the billowing steam.

Laioni yanked Kate by the arm to help her stand again. They stumbled together along the bank, searching for any sign of the walking stick. Despite the fact that the tremors had grown milder, they could see nothing in the water but sizzling columns of steam, writhing like wrathful spirits.

"It happened so fast," moaned Kate.

"Gashra," said Laioni hatefully. "I should never have taken us back into the open."

"It wasn't your fault," said Kate, wiping the water from her forehead and eyes. "You couldn't have known."

"I should have known. You depended on me and I failed you. And failed my people as well. If the stick is lost—"

"There!" shouted Kate, seeing a winged figure burst forth from the mist with a familiar shape clutched in his talons. As the Tinnani settled on the ground next to them, Kate grasped the walking stick again and hugged Kandeldandel. "Thank you, oh thank you," she said.

"Don't make a fuss, now," he hooted gruffly, pushing her away with his arms. "I just happened to be in the neighborhood."

"I'm still grateful," breathed Kate happily, running her finger along the shaft. "That was too close. Without this we'd be sunk."

Kandeldandel's permanent grin twitched slightly. "You needed a bath, anyway."

"Hey," said Kate. "Where's Jody?"

The grin expanded. "Now comes the fun part."

Spinning his head atop his neck, the Tinnani turned his gaze toward the opposite bank and flapped off into the steaming waterway. Kate and Laioni barely had a chance to look at each other in puzzlement when suddenly he emerged again from the billowing clouds, this time bearing an ungainly package in his talons. Jody, clasped by the back of his belt, was hanging upside down, kicking his legs wildly and cursing the beast who had kidnapped him.

"Put me down," he shouted, his face nearly purple with rage. "Put me down, you big birdbrain."

As soon as they had crossed over the edge of the bank, Kandeldandel obliged. He dropped Jody squarely into a waist-high tangle of skunk cabbage and ferns bordering the stream. With an aerial bow to the boy's flailing feet, he flew off into the trees, playing a rippling tune on his flute.

Kate and Laioni approached, standing with their backs to the forest. They couldn't help snickering as Jody's scraggly red head popped up from amidst the skunk cabbage. He spat out several torn bits of fern. "Bluck. This tastes awful! I'm gonna get even with him yet."

"Don't be too hard on him," said Kate. "He did save me, and also the stick. Now he's just having a few laughs."

"So are we," Laioni whispered in her ear, bringing on another fit of giggles.

Jody tried to stand, but his good arm slid on a mat of slippery stalks and leaves and he tumbled backward in a helpless heap. "Quit laughing and give me a hand, will you?" he pleaded.

Kate laid her walking stick on the grass and stepped forward to help pull him out. Laioni moved in the same direction, when a violent jolt from behind sent her sprawling forward. She crashed into Kate, bowling her over. They both landed on Jody, who fell back again into the mass of greenery.

"What kind of a joke—" Kate's words evaporated as she saw a huge man lifting the walking stick from the grass. "Hey, put that down!"

The man who had plowed into Laioni from behind stood, holding his heavy flint-tipped spear in one hand and the walking stick in the other. His hair, tied on top of his head in a knot skewered by a sharp bone, was as black as Laioni's. Two diagonal slashes of black paint cut across each of his cheeks. But for a simple deerskin loincloth, he wore nothing.

"Sanbu!" shouted Laioni, clambering to her feet.

The muscular man started toward her, when Monga snarled ferociously and charged at his leg. Sanbu whirled around, fury in his eyes, and kicked the dog forcefully in the ribs. Monga flew through the air and landed with a bone-crunching thud on the edge of the stream. Pawing frantically at the loose soil, he slid over the edge and into the still-steaming water.

Laioni screamed, throwing herself in the direction of the yapping dog.

"Put that down," cried Kate, pointing at the walking stick.

The big Halami raised his spear over his head with his other arm, preparing to thrust it into Kate. As he lifted the weapon into the air, a sudden whooshing sound, like concentrated wind, emerged from the forest. Just before he brought it down, six or seven large spotted owls soared out of the trees and directly at him, talons extended.

"Aaaarghh," groaned the warrior as the pack of owls descended on him, screeching angrily.

With amazing agility, Sanbu leaped to one side and swung both the spear and the walking stick wildly over his head, causing the owls to change course and dodge him. They soared past without inflicting any harm. Spear still held high, the warrior took aim once again at Kate. He leaned back, gathering his strength for the kill.

Just then a lone rust-colored owl, much smaller than the others, came sailing out of the woods, whistling wrathfully. It was Arc. His brown eyes, disproportionately large for his small body, focused on Sanbu and sized up the situation. With all the speed he could muster, Arc lowered his head and flew straight into Sanbu's chest.

Sanbu cried out in surprise as the small missile made contact. The force of the impact knocked him back a step and caused him to drop the spear, while Arc fell to the ground, momentarily stunned. Before his fellow creatures could regroup for another attack, Sanbu whipped the walking stick around and brought its heavy handle down with all his might on the helpless owl, crushing the bird's feathery chest.

"Arc!" screamed Kate, eyeing the lifeless owl as she rose to her feet.

She dove at Sanbu, trying to grab the stick. Simultaneously, Jody leaped onto Sanbu's back, wrapping his good arm around the warrior's neck.

Sanbu shrieked and snapped forward at the waist, sending Jody hurtling to the ground. He then easily twisted free of Kate's grip. Stepping back, he swung the stick at her viciously.

Kate ducked as the shaft whizzed just over her head. As Sanbu raised it for another attempt, the screeching pack of owls descended again. This time they circled close, talons scraping and scratching him wherever possible, trying to get near his head.

As one talon gouged deeply into the flesh of his forehead, Sanbu cried out in pain. He spun around and retreated into the forest, with the owls in close pursuit. Kate watched him vanish into the dense growth, her stomach clenching. For in his hand he held the Stick of Fire.

22

the burial

A somber rain began to fall as the bedraggled group moved away from the exposed stream bank to find protection under the tall trees. Wordlessly, they gathered at the base of a mighty Douglas fir. From somewhere out of sight, Kandeldandel played long, low notes of mourning on his flute, notes that sounded vaguely like the call of an owl, but mellower, deeper. The slow lament filtered through the trees, one note following the next like a funeral procession.

Kate, feeling drained of hope, stood leaning against the trunk of the tree. Her right hand felt strangely naked now with no shaft to grasp. Moving stiffly, Jody sat down on a root near her feet.

"You all right?" he asked, looking up at her. "I mean, are you hurt?"

Kate shook her head and managed to say, "I wish I'd picked up his spear when he dropped it. We'll never get another chance like that." She glanced at him, adding, "Thanks for trying to help."

Jody frowned. "I wasn't really helping you. I was just trying to get the stick back."

Laioni approached them, followed by Monga, who was limping slightly. In her hands, she carried the body of the dead owl. Carefully, she laid it in the fold between two wet roots. Arc's reddish feathers, still fluffy and soft, nestled easily within the wooden cavity.

As Laioni knelt by the owl's side, Kandeldandel's music ceased. The final flair of his flute melted into the continual patter of rain on the branches. With sagging wings, he emerged from the forest and strode solemnly to the grave of his friend. His crooked mouth twisted lopsidedly, no longer seeming to smile.

"I'm going to miss that little guy," said Kate.

"He's been on my shoulder since he was just an owlet," said Kandeldandel, the laughter gone out of his voice. "His whistling wasn't like real talking, but I never mistook his meaning. He was always there whenever I needed him. But the one time he needed me—where was I? Off playing my flute."

Kate nodded despondently.

The rain grew heavier, splattering the earth with large droplets, as though the air of the forest itself had condensed into tears. Then Kandeldandel lifted his deep bass voice in gentle song. Lost in her own thoughts, Kate did not listen carefully to his words of mourning, but heard only one small part:

> *Farewell old friend*
> *I will miss your song*
> *Your laughing voice*
> *Is now so still*
> *As quiet as I feel*
> *As quiet as death.*

In time the song came to an end. Kandeldandel bent low and ran his finger slowly over the length of the fallen owl's whisker feathers. Finally he stood up again, rigid as a tree. He remained there, motionless, eyes fixed upon the grave.

Meanwhile, Laioni rose and walked purposefully toward a cedar nearby. A few minutes later, she returned with a handful of green needles, which she rubbed briskly between her palms until they gave off a strong scent of cedar. She spread the crushed needles over Arc's plumage, taking care to distribute them evenly.

Laioni then stroked the feathers of the owl's chest, lightly and lovingly—once, twice, three times. Lifting a large section of moss from the earth at the base of the fir, she laid it gently over the body like a blanket.

Jody gave a muffled gasp, and Kate turned to see him watching the ceremony intently. He seemed deeply moved, touched by this ritual whose ancient origins made it feel no less familiar. His mind, Kate knew, bore the image of another fallen owl.

Spotting a few stems of maidenhair fern, Laioni walked over and bowed her head in gratitude to the plant. Then she picked some shafts and carried them over to the tangle of roots next to Jody. Positioning herself on one of the larger roots, she plucked off the fronds and began to bite along the full length of each stem, moving each one methodically through her mouth. When the stems were pliable she laid them lengthwise beside her.

Monga approached, limping. He watched her working with melancholy eyes, then curled into a compressed brown ball by her feet. Kate followed her motions absently, as did Jody. Meanwhile, Kandeldandel paid no attention to her, continuing to gaze at the final resting place of his friend.

Carefully, Laioni ran her fingernail along each black stem. The pressure flattened the fibers and created a slit running the full length. She separated the sections, then began to twine them together, using her teeth as well as her fingers to hold them in position.

Kate, watching her work, grew gradually more curious. "What are you making?" she asked at last.

Laioni answered without raising her head. "Something for Arc."

Before long, the object took enough shape that Kate recognized it: a miniature version of the round basketry cap that Laioni had been wearing when they first met. Biting off the uneven ends, Laioni held the small woven circle in the palm of one hand. She examined the little black moon thoughtfully. Then she carried it to the owl's resting place and laid the gift gently on top of the blanket of moss.

The rain slackened, falling more as mist than as droplets. Laioni stepped again to the cedar and reached for one of the burly branches protruding from its trunk. From the underside of the branch she pulled a small section of fibrous bark and stretched it apart until it was a mass of thin threads in her hands. Then she snapped two sticks, one thinner than the other, from a dead limb overhead. Swiftly, using her fingernails, she peeled the bark from the thicker stick. When she tried to do the same with the thinner one, however, she caught a sharp sliver under her fingernail.

"Eh!" she cried, shaking her hand.

"Here, I'll do that," said Jody, taking the stick from her. Pulling a small knife out of his pocket, he opened the blade and sliced off the bark in a few swift strokes.

"That is a beautiful tool," said Laioni gratefully as she took back the stick.

"What did she say?" Jody asked.

"She said she likes your knife."

Jody closed it and replaced it in his pocket. "It's my granddad's. He let me borrow it." He wrinkled his brow. "Hope I get to give it back someday." Glancing at Laioni, he asked, "What's she doing now?"

"Making a fire, I think."

"Good idea," he replied. "I'd sure like to warm my hands."

"I'd like to warm my everything," said Kate. "This rain is making me really cold."

"You took a swim too," added Jody.

Laioni, having bitten a small notch in the thicker stick, placed it on top of the shredded cedar bark. Bending over to keep the rain off, she placed one end of the thinner stick in the notch and started rapidly rolling it between her palms. As the stick twirled, glowing hot dust fell onto the cedar bark tinder.

As Kate and Jody watched expectantly, a thin trail of smoke started to rise from the shredded bark. Laioni then ceased twirling the stick and lifted the tinder, blowing on it gently. Nothing happened. She replaced the pieces and resumed the operation until the tinder again began to smoke. Once more, she blew lightly across it until, at length, it burst into flames. She dropped it to the ground and placed a few small dry twigs on top.

"I'll get some bigger sticks," said Jody.

As he moved away, Kate whispered to Laioni, "Guess he's not as bad as I thought."

"I feel pain in him," she replied. "Great pain."

Blowing over the growing flames, Kate tried to recall what Aunt Melanie had said about his past. Something about losing his parents . . . and about Frank, his grandfather. Before long, the fire crackled vigorously on the forest floor, and she stood up to warm herself.

"Come over here," she said to Kandeldandel, still standing dejectedly beside Arc's grave. "Come on," she repeated with a wave of her hand. "It feels good to get warm."

Monga, who had already shifted his location to be nearer the fire, sighed contentedly.

"Good idea," said Jody, emerging from the trees with as many dry sticks as his one arm could hold.

As he dropped the pile of sticks, Kate reached for a downed limb nearby. She snapped it in two and tossed both halves into the flames.

Kandeldandel approached, ruffling his wings, and settled himself by the fire next to Kate. Jody stepped warily aside but the Tinnani did not even look at him. Lifting his wooden flute to his lips, he began to play a slow and simple melody, permeated with sadness.

Eyeing the winged creature cautiously, Jody stretched his free hand toward the fire. Suddenly, the flames extinguished, dying out completely. Only a few smoldering coals remained where an instant before fire had burned strongly.

"What the heck happened?" the boy moaned. "I didn't even get near enough to feel it."

"I don't know," answered Kate. "There wasn't any wind."

Kandeldandel's eyes widened, and he quickly put down his flute. The music ended in mid-note, but the fire instantly burst back to life.

Laioni smiled. "That was a clever trick."

"Not so clever," lamented Kandeldandel. "Happens to me all the time, whenever I play near a fire."

Jody, who could not comprehend any of the Tinnani's words, said, "Don't be surprised if my being here puts it out again. I'm just a jinx."

"Why do you say that?" asked Kate.

The boy shook his head dismally. "Because every time I start feeling a little comfortable—not even happy, really, just comfortable—something always happens to spoil it."

Kate sighed heavily. "Same thing happens to me."

Jody glanced at her skeptically.

"What do you mean?" asked Laioni.

Kate gazed for a while into the orange flames before responding. "Every time," she started, then swallowed her words. "Every time I get close to somebody, anybody—I lose them. Anybody important to me. First it happened to Grandfather, and now it's happened to Aunt Melanie too. I'll never see her again, or Mom and Dad either." She turned toward Laioni as tears began to cloud her vision. "Just when Aunt Melanie needs me most, we get separated."

Laioni reached for Kate's unbandaged hand and brought it to the leather bib covering her chest. Placing the hand over her heart, she said quietly, "You won't lose me. I promise."

Kate studied her, then replied, "I hope you're right."

Releasing her hand, Laioni added, "You're not the only one who has lost someone you love."

Kate glanced toward Kandeldandel, whose yellow eyes merely stared at her blankly. Turning back to Laioni, she said, "You mean your friend Toru. Do you really think he's dead?"

Laioni's gaze fell. "I don't know."

"The hardest part for me is not even saying good-bye," said Kate.

"I know what you mean," agreed Jody. He shook his dangling locks. "My folks just went out for an errand. Back in two hours, they said. Ha. Some joke."

Kate felt a surge of empathy. "That's the worst, no warning at all. At least when I lost Grandfather, I knew it was coming."

"The same with Toru," said Laioni.

"How did you know?" asked Kate.

"Monga told me." Laioni turned to the dog peacefully curled up by the fire. "He spoke to me."

"You mean the way he acted?"

"No," she answered firmly. "I mean he spoke to me." She looked again at Kate. "My people know that when an animal speaks with a human voice, then someone's death is near. Just before Toru left our village to follow his dream, Monga barked—but instead of a barking sound, he spoke words. Real words. I was standing right beside him, so I know. No one else heard him, so as hard as I tried I couldn't persuade Toru to stay."

"What did Monga say?"

"He said, *It is time.*" Laioni threw another chunk of wood on the fire, sending sparks into the air. She motioned to Jody. "The boy, did he say he lost both his parents at once?"

"Yes," replied Kate.

Laioni moved to Jody's side. "I am sorry for you," she said, her voice so filled with sympathy that he seemed to understand. He looked at her for a moment with both sadness and gratitude, then turned away, embarrassed.

As the fire continued to warm the companions, Kate lifted her head to scan the trees rising like steeples on every side. The rain had stopped. Gray sky above the treetops glowed dusky peach with hints of purple. The forest, darkening toward the end of the day, creaked and stirred with new sounds. She saw the shadowy shape of a small animal scooting between two massive trunks, beginning its evening prowlings. Monga must have caught its scent, for he suddenly raised his head, ears alert, sniffing.

"What do we do now?" asked Kate, not sure whether she was speaking to anyone in particular. "Maybe there's nothing left to do, now that the stick is gone."

"You mean we're stuck here for good?" questioned Jody.

"Looks that way."

"I have an idea," said Laioni softly. "It won't return the ones we have lost, and it won't bring back the Stick of Fire, but it might help somehow."

Stooping low, she retrieved a broken cedar bough from the ground, its needles wet from rain. Carefully, she placed it on the fire, creating a thick column of smoke that smelled of cedar. She cocked her head, then said, "I need just one more thing."

"What?"

Slowly, Laioni's head swung toward Kandeldandel, still holding his flute. "A feather."

"Now, hold on," protested the musician, covering his chest with his wings as he backed away. "Just because I put out your fire doesn't mean you can pluck one of my feathers."

"I wasn't going to pluck one," she replied. "I thought you might have one that's ready to drop."

Kandeldandel's fluffy brows came together. "Oh, all right," he hooted. "But you should face it, you're finished. Whatever chance you had to find the Touchstone, let alone the missing piece, it's gone now. And without Arc . . . well, all the fun's gone for me. So I'm leaving." He pulled a white feather from under one of his wings, twirled it once, then handed it to Laioni. Spinning his head toward Kate, he added, "This is the last you'll ever see of me. Good-bye."

He vanished in a puff of white light.

Kate gazed sadly at the spot. "Just when I thought he was maybe going to stay with us for a while, he disappears."

"Count your blessings," muttered Jody.

Laioni raised the feather, as big as her hand, high above her head. Then she lowered it to the flaming cedar bough and said, "Cedar, rain, and feather. Earth, water, air. Join with our fire to call the four directions."

She waved a puff of scented smoke toward the stream. In a low voice, she chanted, *"North, origin of weather, color of white, we ask you for wisdom."* Again she swept the feather through the rising smoke, this time toward the forest, singing as she did, *"South, birthplace of new life, color of green, we ask you for wonder."* Then, waving in another direction, *"West, source of our dreams, color of blue, we ask you for vision."* And, last of all, to the opposite side, *"East, home of the sun, color of yellow, we ask you for strength."*

As her words hung above the crackling fire, mixing with the aromatic smoke, Laioni lifted the feather and drew a large circle above her head. Then, lowering her arm, she waved it gracefully at Kate, then at Jody, then at Monga, sending each the power of the four directions. She then dropped the feather into the flames.

After a long silence, Kate said, "That was beautiful." She studied her empty right hand. "Too bad it won't help us get the stick back."

"Maybe we could help ourselves," suggested Jody meekly.

Kate turned to him. "What do you mean?"

"I mean," said the red-haired boy, speaking a little louder this time, "maybe it's still worth a try to get it back."

"Sanbu's halfway to the mountain by now," Kate replied dismissively. Then, facing Laioni, she asked, "He'll take it straight to Gashra, won't he?"

The Halami girl contemplated for a moment before answering. "Sanbu's camp is on the way to the mountain. It's too far to go the whole way before nightfall, so he'll probably stay at his camp tonight, celebrating with his men, then leave for the mountain in the morning."

"What did she say?" questioned Jody.

"That he'll probably stay at his camp tonight and deliver the stick in the morning."

"Then why don't we go after him now?" he suggested.

"Are you crazy? Track him through the night?"

"At least then we'd have a chance to get the stick back," urged Jody. "A surprise attack."

Kate muttered, "I don't know. For one thing, how could we find his camp at night? For another, do you think we could stand even half a chance against his band of warriors?"

Jody stepped closer. "If we don't get the stick back, we're stuck here forever. Right?"

Kate said nothing.

"So we've got nothing to lose. At least it's worth a try."

"I know where his camp is supposed to be hidden," offered Laioni. Then, regarding Kate thoughtfully, she added, "There's something else, isn't there?"

"Why do you say that?"

The Halami girl studied her tenderly. "What is it?"

"Well, it's—it's," she stammered, "it's just that, well, I really don't—don't like the dark."

Jody started to smirk, then caught himself. "That's okay," he said. "I used to hate being out in the woods at night too. Especially with big trees like this around. But now I know it's no big deal."

Kate drew in a deep breath. She scanned the swiftly darkening boughs above them. "I don't know."

"Hey," said Jody. "You remember that story about Babe Ruth, the one where he stands at home plate after two strikes and points to the stands?"

"Sure," grumbled Kate. "Everybody knows that one. He pointed to the center-field bleachers, then hit a homer right there. What's that have to do with anything?"

"Well, you see," began Jody, "I never thought the best part about that story was the homer. Lots of guys hit homers. Even I've hit two or three. The best part was he had the guts to stand up there and say he was gonna try. To take a risk. In front of everybody. That took real courage."

Kate looked into the flickering fire. She heard again the words of the Chieftess: *Hold fast to your stick of power. It is your only hope, and ours as well.* The fire coals crackled, and she saw deep within the flames the remains of Kandeldandel's feather. Now nothing but a burnt shaft, it still held itself as straight as the stick she once had carried.

"All right," she said at last. "Let's give it a try."

PART THREE

Into the Tree

23

night vision

BEFORE starting off, Kate and Jody separated the burning sticks, threw dirt over them, and stamped out the remaining flames. Seeing Laioni watching them with fascination, Kate realized that it must never have occurred to her to put out a fire with one's foot. Kate smiled to herself, appreciating anew the advantages of sneakers—even ones with bright green laces.

As the last lick of flame withdrew from the embers, Kate's eyes fell to the cradle of roots holding the small bundle of feathers that once was Arc. How similar they were, cold embers and lifeless body, both deprived of the fire that made them something so utterly different.

Laioni squeezed her arm gently. "We should go now."

"Where exactly do we have to go?" asked Kate, feeling the same queasiness she always felt when no light burned nearby.

"We will stay in this part of the forest for several more hours," answered Laioni. "I know this area well, so even without any moon, we should not lose our way." She hesitated before going on. "Then we will descend into a valley that is always dark, even in the daytime. No Halami goes there, not even my father when he is hunting, because there the power of Gashra is very strong."

Kate squirmed. "Isn't there another way?"

"No," Laioni replied. "Not if we want to reach Sanbu's camp before dawn. The Dark Valley lies between us and Gashra's steaming mountain. We must cross the Dark Valley, then climb the ridge until we are above the trees, to reach Sanbu's camp."

"I really don't like this idea."

"Neither do I," said Laioni. "I have never set foot in the Dark Valley. But going that way is our only hope to catch him before he delivers the stick to Gashra, if he hasn't already."

At that moment, Monga passed close to Laioni's legs, brushing his tail against her. She reached down and rubbed his head, whispering, "I know you'll be with me." The dog then nuzzled against Kate's jeans. Grinning, Laioni added, "And with Kate too."

Laioni then turned and started into the forest. Jody tramped along stiffly behind her. Monga hung back, waiting for Kate to start walking. When at last she did, the dog stayed just ahead of her, still limping slightly.

As they entered the deep woods, darkness pressed still closer. Kate could barely see the shadowy shapes of trunks and fallen branches in the swiftly departing light, and with every step the forest grew thicker and darker. Unseen branches stretched out long arms to scratch her face and poke her chest, sudden puddles of water swallowed up her sneakers without warning, slippery logs tripped her more than once. She could tell by the crashes and cursing ahead that Jody was doing little better. By contrast, Laioni seemed to move through the trees with the ease of a strutting deer.

Each time Kate stumbled or bumped into something, Monga trotted to her side within seconds. He seemed genuinely concerned for her well-being, whimpering sympathetically or tugging on her pant leg with his teeth to help

her find a better route. Kate began to feel like a toddler trying to walk, constantly thwarted by too-little legs that buckled without mercy. Frustration and anger swelled inside
her, shoving aside fear, and even Monga's concern started
to irritate her.

"Leave me alone," she grumbled, pushing the dog away
as he tried to lick her neck after she walked into a mossy
boulder. "I can do just f—Ohh!"

In her impatience to back away, she thrust her head
directly into a jagged limb. Laioni, hearing her shout,
strode back and quickly joined her.

"Are you all right?"

"Fine," snapped Kate, rubbing the back of her head.
"Except that I'm stuck in the wrong time and stumbling
around like a two-year-old in the middle of the night." She
studied the outline of Laioni, whose black hair and eyes
blended thoroughly into the background, and added quietly, "It's hopeless. I can't keep on like this."

"I have an idea," said the other girl. "It might help."

Without a sound, she knelt beside Kate's feet and began
fumbling with the tops of her sneakers. At first Kate stepped
backward in surprise. Then, weighed down by a growing
sense of despair, she merely stood passively, certain that
whatever wild idea Laioni had would make no difference
anyway. After quite a bit of tugging, pulling, and twisting,
Laioni removed Kate's green-laced sneakers and her socks
as well.

"What are you doing?" Kate demanded.

Laioni rose, pushing the socks and sneakers at Kate.
"Put these in the basket on your back. I want you to try
walking without them."

"What?" exclaimed Kate. "Are you kidding? It'll be ten
times worse."

"Try it."

"All right, but it's stupid." She slipped her arms out of
the day pack, unzipped it, and threw in the footgear. "Totally
stupid."

"The ground is soft, even though your feet are like my

baby brother's. Touching the earth with your feet will help you see."

"That's ridiculous," grumbled Kate. "How can my feet help me see?"

"Try it," repeated Laioni.

She stepped away, picking her route with special care through the growing blackness of the woods. Monga, tail held high, padded close behind. Awkwardly, Kate started to trudge after them.

Immediately, the newly barefoot girl felt a flood of sensations from her feet. Protected as they had been for most of their existence, they seemed more aware to touch than her fingertips. Kate's amazement at their sensitivity did not last long, however, soon giving way to an overwhelming sense of discomfort. Sticks and roots jabbed into her arches, slimy puddle water seeped between her toes, and unidentified insects wriggled across the tops of her feet. Still, trying to be brave, she stifled her groans and pushed slowly ahead.

To her dismay, the forest grew steadily darker with each passing minute. As the last lingering remnant of light faded from the cloudy sky above, the towering trees and mounting mist seemed to soak up any stray sources of illumination. No moon shone through the darkening boughs; no stars glittered overhead. Night had come to the ancient forest, and with night came true and total darkness.

Then, to Kate's astonishment, a subtle change began to occur. Perhaps because there was now no light left to trick her vision, perhaps because she was forced to rely only on her other senses, she began to feel gradually more secure in her movements. Her feet pained her less, though they remained uncomfortably sensitive. Stepping somewhat more easily on the spongy turf, she seemed to have sprouted special antennae that could perceive the shadowy shapes surrounding her, at first only barely, but with time more and more fully. She could almost reach out with this new sense, or combination of senses, to touch and see in ways that required neither hands nor eyes.

With slightly more confidence, Kate moved through the lightless forest. Soon she grew comfortable enough to close her eyes for a brief moment, just to feel whether it would slow her down. It did, but much less than she expected. She somehow *knew* where a low branch loomed or a log rose out of the earth. Her senses were saturated by the subtle slopes and contours of the forest floor underfoot and the swishing sound of Monga's tail brushing ferns and flowers just ahead. She understood that to her five senses a new one had been added, one that she had never known before: a kind of quiet hearing, a vision of the night.

Just then, a bat flew quite close to her face, brushing her cheek with its wing. She froze, cowering, as several more bats swooped near. All at once, her momentary calm disappeared. She dreaded again the dangers lurking in this place.

She recalled a description by Aunt Melanie of a night stroll she had once taken, in woods far removed not in distance but in time from the woods where Kate now walked. Aunt Melanie described proceeding through a dark and moonless forest, a prospect that made Kate shiver at the time, only to discover a strange beam of light cutting across her path. It seemed shockingly bright to Aunt Melanie, utterly out of place in the deep darkness. The beam sliced through the thick web of snags and branches to fall like a spotlight on a large brown-winged moth resting on the trunk of an aging fir. The light, Aunt Melanie said, hung in the air like an incandescent rope reaching from one end of the forest to the other. She wondered what could possibly cause such a thing, when all at once she discovered its source: It was the light of the rising moon.

Kate sighed, wishing the moon might send a shaft of bright light into this forest on this night. What she would give to see its silvery sphere swim into view above the treetops! Now that she had experienced night vision, she desired the moon's light less for guidance than for comfort. More bats swished past her head. The darkness of this place felt increasingly menacing. Yet no moon appeared. Instead, the forest seemed to grow ever blacker, ever more perilous.

The ground sloped downward, and Kate knew that they were descending into some kind of valley. She wondered whether this could be the Dark Valley that Laioni had described. She stepped on a stick that suddenly hissed and slithered out from under her foot. With a start, she jumped back. Her intelligence told her it was only a snake, yet that did little to calm the rapid beating of her heart.

Trees creaked and groaned on all sides as she moved past. The air smelled smoky here, as if the earth had been singed by fire not long ago. Perhaps because of the smoke, Kate's eyes started to sting, causing her to blink frequently. Bushes and ferns held more and more gleaming eyes, some of them round and black, some slanted and yellow. Most frightening of all, however, was the darkness itself. As she dropped deeper into the valley, the darkness grew thicker and heavier, submerging everything around her in impenetrable ink.

Something heavy stepped on her toe. She gasped and quickly backed away, then jabbed her neck on the broken branch of a tree. As she cried out in pain, Monga pawed her leg, whimpering.

"Who's there?" she asked.

"It's me," answered the voice of Jody. "I walked— walked right into this tree. Almost knocked me flat on my can."

"You klutz, you really scared me. Can you believe how dark it is? I'm getting the jitters about this place."

A scream pierced the night. It came from not far away. Monga barked, then dashed into the darkness.

"Laioni," exclaimed Kate. "That's her voice, I know it." She tried calling her name, but no answer came.

The crunch of needles told her Jody had stepped nearer. "This doesn't feel like regular night." He crunched still closer. "And all this smoke in the air . . . Makes it hard to breathe."

"Jody, I'm really worried." She cupped her hands to her mouth and called again: "Laaaiooo-ni."

Still no answer.

Then, from the blackness, they heard a strange, heavy breathing. It was accompanied by a new crunching sound, coming closer. Yet this crunching did not sound like feet, at least not like human feet. It sounded more like a body sliding, dragging, over the ground. Kate stood utterly still, while Jody moved so close that his shoulder rubbed against hers. The breathing and crunching grew steadily louder.

Suddenly a hand grabbed Kate's ankle. "Hey," she cried, yanking her leg free. "Let go!"

"Don't be frightened," whispered a voice by her knees.

"Laioni! What are you doing down there?"

"I'm crawling," she replied weakly. "Feeling my way. Here, help me up."

Both Kate and Jody bent low to pull the Halami girl upright. She struggled to stand, as if she were dazed, then leaned against Kate for support. Monga whimpered, moving around them in a slow circle.

"What happened?" asked Kate as she wrapped her arm around Laioni's shoulder. Feeling something wet against her hand, she exclaimed, "Hey, you're bleeding."

"It's all right, just a scrape," Laioni said, her voice still barely audible.

"Why didn't you answer when I called?"

"I couldn't," came the whispered reply. "Something strange happened to my voice. I can't—can't talk any louder than this." She rubbed her neck. "But I'm lucky to be here at all. A hunting pit, over there somewhere. I almost fell in. Only saved myself by grabbing onto a root."

"Like the one I fell into," said Kate.

"Yes, but you'd probably never have found me. This smoke, it's so thick." She coughed, sounding not much different from the grating and rasping of the branches overhead. From faraway, some unseen animal shrieked in a long, high-pitched wail. Then, with chilling certainty, Laioni added, "There's something more than smoke here."

"The Dark Valley," said Kate, her own voice feeling weak.

"The whole place feels haunted," whispered Jody.

"How are we ever going to find Sanbu's camp if we keep bumping into trees and falling into pits?" Kate's eyes, already watery from the pervasive smoke, brimmed still more. "Now we're never going to get the stick back."

"Ask your Indian friend if she can lead us out of here," said Jody.

"She's already cut up from trying," answered Kate. "She can't see any better than we can."

Laioni whispered somberly, "I've never felt like this before in the forest. I don't know where to go, don't know what's ahead. The trees do not speak to me. Even Monga doesn't know what to do." A distant screeching sound rose up like raucous laughter. "It is the work of the Wicked One."

"But what do we do now? How do we get out of here?"

Laioni gave no answer. Instinctively, the three voyagers moved closer together, standing like three small islands in a swirling sea of darkness. Monga, too, drew nearer, his tail curled tightly over his back. They listened to the gnashing and scraping limbs, the creaking and groaning trunks, the howling and screaming of invisible beings surrounding them.

Then, from the dark reaches of the forest, a new sound joined the others. It was warmer, fuller, flowing out of the trees like a sweet fragrance. A low, continuous sound. Like the call of an owl, but mellower, deeper.

"Kandeldandel," said all three at once. Monga barked excitedly.

"It's his flute, for sure," cried Kate. "Maybe it can lead us out of here."

"Let's find him," whispered Laioni.

As Kate started forward, Jody grabbed her by the arm. "Wait. Are you sure this isn't just one of his tricks? He could be leading us over a cliff for all we know."

"We'll have to take the chance," replied Kate. "It's our only way out of here. Let's go, before he stops playing."

With Laioni in front, the three proceeded cautiously into the forest. Though the mysterious groanings of trees and beasts continued, the call of Kandeldandel's flute filtered through to them. Whenever they seemed to be approaching its source, the music moved farther away, leading them onward.

Soon the terrain began to change. Instead of going down, they were climbing upward. Gradually, the smoky smell began to dissipate, and Kate began to see the shadowy outlines of trees and branches once again. Though no moon shone, the sky radiated a diffuse light, perhaps from the stars shining behind the curtain of clouds overhead. As they pushed higher, not pausing even to catch their breath, the gentle illumination from the sky grew stronger. She noticed that the trees were getting sparser, their trunks thinner.

She paused to study one of the spindly shapes, her eyes no longer irritated by smoke. "The trees," she panted, "they're getting shorter."

"We're climbing above the tree line," huffed Jody. "Pretty soon there won't be any trees at all."

"Hush," urged Laioni, her voice returning. "I think I know where we are now, and we must be quiet."

Higher, ever higher, the hooting flute led them. Before long the needle-strewn ground evolved into broken bits of moss-covered rock. Large round boulders appeared more frequently, dotting the terrain. Forest noises no longer permeated the night air. As small shrubs and grasses replaced the gnarled and twisted trees, Kate's vision improved still more and she began to perceive even subtle shapes like Monga's pointed ears.

As the terrain grew more rocky, she leaned her back against a boulder and put her socks and sneakers on again. Jody looked at her in amazement as he passed by, realizing for the first time that she had been walking barefoot in the forest.

The music beckoned to them, drawing them still farther up the slope. This time, however, the flute did not seem to depart as they came near. As Kate stepped over the increasingly stony surface, she saw Laioni stop at a large boulder

at the crest of the ridge no more than twenty yards ahead.
As the owl-like music swelled in volume, she moved swiftly
up the incline, reaching the boulder at the same time as
Jody.

There, leaning casually against the opposite side of the
boulder, was the Tinnani. His enormous round eyes flickered in Kate's direction as she topped the rise, but otherwise he gave no sign of noticing that he had company. He
trilled a few lilting notes on the flute, then lowered it from
his half-grinning lips.

"Thank you," said Laioni very softly.

Kandeldandel swiveled his head in her direction.
"Thank you for what?" he asked, also in a quiet voice.

"For leading us out of that valley," whispered Kate.

"Valley? What valley? I was just playing my flute, that's
all."

"Come on," replied Kate. "You know what you did."

"Still don't know what you're talking about," hooted
Kandeldandel quietly. "I just happened to be in the neighborhood again."

"And we just happen to be glad you were," said Kate,
smiling.

The Tinnani's yellow eyes met hers, connecting for an
instant. Kate saw in them an unmistakable gleam of satisfaction, and she suspected, despite the protestations, that
he was pleased.

Jody stepped forward and nudged Kate's elbow. "Man,
am I glad to get out of there." Then he added, without looking at Kandeldandel, "Since you know how to talk to him,
why don't you tell him thanks from me too?"

The Tinnani lifted his tufted brows. "His manners are
improving."

"In a big way," answered Kate.

"Too bad," replied the flute player, sounding disap-
pointed. "He was much more fun the other way."

At that moment, Laioni gasped. Kate turned to see her
staring at a ridge that ran parallel to their own, slightly
higher and to the left. Like theirs, it climbed ever more

steeply into the clouds, ultimately to join the massive shoulder of a mountain summit. Mountain, Kate realized with a jolt. This must be Gashra's mountain.

Then she saw what Laioni had seen. Near the top of the visible flank of the ridge burned a single campfire. Three or four figures, dimly lit by the golden glow, danced slowly in front of the flames. Listening very carefully, she caught the barest hint of human voices chanting in unison.

"Sanbu's camp?" she whispered.

Laioni viewed her gravely. "That is where we will find our hope—or meet our death."

At that moment, Monga stepped deliberately between the two of them. He shook himself once vigorously, as if he had just emerged from a swim. Then, turning toward Kate, he barked. But instead of a dog's bark, he spoke three unmistakable words.

"It is time," said the dog.

24

attack

KATE'S anxious eyes met Laioni's. "Did you hear that?"

"I heard it."

"But who—"

"We will know soon enough," the Halami girl whispered. "Let's go. Sunrise is near, and it will take some time to get up there."

Then Jody spoke, his gaze fixed on the distant campfire. "They must have some guards around here someplace. But where?"

"No way to tell from here," said Kate.

"We can't just walk right into them," countered Jody.

"Do you have a better idea?" Kate demanded, trying hard not to raise her voice.

Before the boy could reply, Kandeldandel took off with a flapping of his wide wings. Flute clutched in one hand, he rose into the air and glided into a billowing bank of clouds.

"Guess that's the last we're gonna see of him," said Jody.

Kate followed the white-winged figure until it disappeared from sight. "Don't be so sure."

"We should go," said Laioni, glancing at each of the others.

"I wish we had stopped Sanbu when he was alone," said Kate.

Jody shook his head. "It's not like we didn't try. This time, though, we have surprise on our side."

"Hope we have some luck too," added Kate.

Monga pawed the ground uneasily. Then, suddenly, he lifted his head with a jerk.

Above them, a familiar white figure emerged from the gray clouds. Down Kandeldandel plummeted like a meteor. Then at the last possible instant, he veered up before landing on top of the boulder. He folded his wings behind his back and said simply, "There is only one guard."

"What did he say?" asked Jody.

"One guard," answered Kate. "He must have checked it out from above." Then, facing the Tinnani, she asked, "Where is he?"

"Never mind," said Kandeldandel. "I'll take care of him." He considered the idea briefly, then added with a smirk, "It will be a pleasure."

"Don't take any chances," warned Laioni. "Someone is going to die before this is over."

"It won't be me," replied Kandeldandel briskly. Then his permanent grin faded. "I have a score to settle with Sanbu."

"A score?" Kate scrutinized him. "You mean what he did to Arc?"

The Tinnani fiddled with his flute for a moment. "That, and something else. Something big enough that I want to do a lot more than just put out his fire." He faced Kate squarely. "You see," he said slowly, "my full name is Kandeldandel Zinzin."

"Zinzin . . ." Kate furrowed her brow. "Wasn't that the name of—"

"The traitor who stole the Broken Touchstone," finished the Tinnani. "The one who was murdered by Sanbu." His round yellow eyes narrowed. "He was my father."

"I understand," said Kate.

"No you don't," retorted Kandeldandel. "How could you? How could anyone? But it doesn't matter, as long as the lowly musician who happens to be his son can avenge his death, and Arc's too. And maybe restore a tiny bit of honor to an old family name in the process."

"All right," declared Kate. "You can take the guard if that's what you want. But let's get one thing straight, here and now. You're more than just some lowly musician. You're one of us."

Kandeldandel fluttered his wings uncomfortably. "Fine," he said, "but just don't try to depend on me. That's the one thing I can't stand, someone depending on me."

"Okay, then. We won't depend on you to nail that guard. We'll just hope like the dickens you do it."

The Tinnani nodded. "That's better."

"Hey, check this out," said Jody, forgetting to keep his voice quiet.

"Shhhhh," admonished Kate. Then she saw what he had discovered: a long flint-tipped spear resting on the ground by the boulder. "That looks like Sanbu's," she whispered in surprise.

"It is," hooted Kandeldandel. "I brought it with me, just in case."

Jody hefted the heavy spear, struggling to hold it with his one good arm. But it clearly required two hands—or one the size of Sanbu's—to carry it.

"That won't work," said Kate. "Let me take it."

"Well, all right," agreed the boy reluctantly. "Guess I'll have to stick with my knife."

"We must go," whispered Laioni in earnest. "The sun will rise soon."

Kate gripped the spear firmly, hoping she might once again hold the Stick of Fire. "Let's go."

At that the Tinnani took flight, rising silently and swiftly into the clouds. Kate, Jody, and Laioni, Monga at her heels, began to traverse the rugged, rock-littered terrain to the parallel ridge. They descended into a steep-walled canyon carved by successive rock slides from the higher elevations. Crammed with broken boulders, the canyon required jumping from rock to rock, always gauging one's weight carefully to avoid slipping. Even without his limp, the usually sure-footed Monga would have found the crossing difficult.

Finally they left the boulder field and started to scale the neighboring ridge. The terrain was steep, but at least they could walk again. They pushed upward, panting from exertion, even as the eastern sky began to lighten above them. Kate felt the temperature drop noticeably as they ascended, drawing closer to the lumbering clouds that obscured the sky. Then, for no apparent reason, her bandaged hand began to ache.

Suddenly, a triangular green head lifted above a large boulder not far ahead. Two thin yellow eyes focused directly on Kate. Then the lizardlike being reared up on his hind legs. He raised his hands to his mouth and readied to call out a warning.

Kate seized Laioni's arm and pointed at the Slimni. Just then, a winged figure rocketed down from the clouds, talons extended. As the Slimni started to shout, Kandeldandel attacked from behind, digging his talons deep into the green scales of the creature's back. With a squeal of pain, the Slimni dropped his hands and twisted violently to free himself. Kandeldandel rolled sideways off the boulder, pulling the reptile with him. They fell out of sight.

The group clambered as fast as they could up to the boulder. Monga, first to arrive, froze at the spot. He stood still, growling barely audibly, until the others joined him.

There, standing over the body of the slain Slimni, stood Kandeldandel. Black blood was splattered on his talons and once-white abdominal feathers. The lizardlike being, though nearly decapitated, still grasped one of his legs. Finally the Tinnani succeeded in pulling free, then said in a low voice to Monga, "You can stop growling now." Spinning his head toward Kate, he added, "One down, five to go."

"That's how many you saw?" questioned Kate, placing her throbbing left hand protectively under her right armpit.

Kandeldandel, still clutching his flute, tried to shake the black blood from his leg feathers. "That's all. There might have been more inside one of the huts, but I don't think so. They were celebrating, and no scoundrel likes to miss a party."

"We're in luck, then," whispered Laioni. "The rest must be off hunting."

"Or pillaging," threw in Kandeldandel.

"Is Sanbu there?" asked Kate.

"He is."

"Did you see the walking stick?"

The Tinnani's gaze fell. "No. Either he's already given it to the Wicked One, or it's in one of the huts. My eyesight is good enough I'm sure I didn't miss it."

"Pretty good spying for a lowly musician," said Kate, tossing her braid over her shoulder. "I sure hope they still have it. Otherwise all this is for nothing." She paused. "Hey, listen."

From far up the ridge came the chanting of husky voices, wafting on the wind. A single drum pounded relentlessly in the background.

"A victory chant," observed Laioni.

"Come on," said Kate. "Let's spoil their party."

Stealthily, the attackers crept forward across the rocks. Monga led the way, though still hobbled from his last encounter with Sanbu. The brave dog pushed himself to go first, for he, too, had some business to settle at the camp. Laioni followed him closely, hunching her back to keep low. Next came Kate, carrying the spear parallel to the ground so it would not be seen by Sanbu or his men. Just behind came Kandeldandel and Jody, allies for the moment at least.

As they advanced, the chanting voices grew gradually louder. Finally, Monga stopped at the side of a large boulder covered with orange lichen, wagging his prodigious tail. As Kate and the others joined him, crouching behind the boulder, they could see the camp just ahead. Five men, one larger than the rest, sat on stones beside the flames, poking the fire with sticks and singing. All wore deerskin loincloths and black streaks painted across their cheekbones. The warriors seemed unprepared for battle, their black hair falling loose to their shoulders.

In contrast to the encampment of Laioni's mother, no tools decorated the ground. Instead, Kate saw three spears, all with the same gray head as Sanbu's, a stone hatchet, several knives, a large pile of firewood, and a bow with two flint-tipped arrows leaning against a stone nearby. The half-eaten carcass of a mutilated deer lay discarded near the fire, covered with flies.

The larger man turned to say something to one of the others, who laughed boisterously in response. As the big man rose to his feet, Kate sucked in her breath, for she could see he was indeed Sanbu. He stepped over to the other warrior and pushed him backward off his stone. The smaller man sprung to his feet and said something in an angry voice, whereupon Sanbu struck him in the jaw with a brutal blow. The warrior fell backward onto the rocky terrain, groaning as he rolled to one side.

Sanbu strutted back to his place and sat down again. He grabbed a slice of dried meat from the man seated next to him, then uttered a command. The warriors resumed their chanting. One of them pounded heavily on a drum of stretched deerskin. Sanbu's victim rejoined the group, rubbing his tender jaw. Meanwhile, the first reddish rays of sunrise struck the camp, bathing the men and their two brush huts with rubescent light.

"If Monga could jump one of them, that would distract the others," Kate whispered to Laioni. "Then we could search the huts for the stick."

Laioni whispered into Monga's ear, which stood rigid and alert on his head. The bushy tail swished from side to side until she had finished. For an instant his dark eyes connected with Laioni's, then he bounded off toward the campfire.

Suddenly, he halted, sniffing the air. Laioni turned to Kate and said anxiously, "Something's wrong."

Monga abruptly changed his course. Instead of pouncing on one of the men seated by the fire, he veered sharply to the side and bolted for one of the brush huts. At that instant, a shaggy brown dog, a full head taller than Monga, emerged from the entrance. With a ferocious bark, the dog sprang at Monga, who met him in midair just outside the hut. They dropped to the ground, rolling over each other and snarling viciously.

Kate, Laioni, and Jody dashed into the camp, as Kandeldandel took flight. The five warriors leaped to their feet, reaching for their weapons. Sanbu saw Kate running toward him, carrying his own spear, and he let loose an earsplitting cry of vengeance. The powerful Halami picked up a spear, reared back, and hurled it at Kate.

Just as Sanbu released it, something knocked against his arm, throwing his aim askew. The spear clattered against the rocks as Kandeldandel, talons extended, descended on top of him. Screeching like twenty owls, the Tinnani swiped across his shoulder, cutting deep into the flesh. Sanbu whirled around, grabbing one feathered leg with both of his burly hands. He threw Kandeldandel to the ground and bent to grab the stone hatchet.

At that instant, Kate plowed into his side with the spear, throwing all her weight into the charge. Sanbu roared in pain, dropped the hatchet, and staggered backward. He tripped over one of the sitting stones and fell into the fire. With a shriek, he rolled out of the coals and struggled to pull the spear from his ribs.

At the sight of Sanbu tumbling into the fire, the man he had struck only a few moments before cried out in fear and ran down the ridge as fast as he could. Meanwhile, Laioni and Jody battled together against another warrior, their three arms against his two, wrestling with him on the rocky terrain. Kandeldandel, having regained his feet, danced just out of reach of a stocky, muscular man who now wielded the hatchet. Nearby, Monga fought desperately with the bigger dog. They rolled across the ground in a snarling tangle of brown fur.

Kate seized the opportunity to search for the walking stick. She turned toward one of the two brush huts and dashed to the entrance. Kneeling, she peered inside the dimly lit enclosure, searching for the Stick of Fire.

As she knelt down, another warrior appeared from his hiding place behind a lichen-streaked boulder. He raised his bow, drew back the string, and shot an arrow directly at Kate's back. His aim was good, and the arrow whizzed straight toward the unsuspecting target. It plunged into the blue day pack and smacked against the metal thermos still within, knocking Kate on her face with the force.

Saved by the thermos, she rose unharmed. She pulled the arrow out of the pack and stared at it, aghast. Silently, she thanked Aunt Melanie for packing the hot chocolate. She peered out the entrance, but could not see the marksman.

Mustering her courage, she darted over to the other brush hut. This time she threw herself inside before anyone could attack from behind. Scanning the interior, she spied a familiar shape in the shadows. She lunged for it, grasping the shaft in her hand— only to discover it was just another spear. She threw it aside, heart pounding like the warrior's drum. Where is that stick? She hoped it was not already in Gashra's hands.

In a gesture of hopelessness, she threw back her head and took a deep breath. Two yellow dots gleamed at her from the ceiling of the hut. The walking stick! Hidden in the brush above her head, it was nearly invisible but for the carved owl's head handle. Kate reached upward and yanked it free, just as a powerful hand grasped her ankle and dragged her violently out of the hut.

The warrior whose arrow had missed its mark stood above her, glowering. Now brandishing a knife instead of a bow, he suddenly kicked hard at her head. Kate dodged the blow and jumped to her feet, still holding the walking stick. As the man spun around to face her, she swung the stick with all the force of a home run hitter, connecting with a thud on his left eye. The blow sent him reeling backward.

But before Kate could recover her balance, another hand grasped the shaft.

"Sanbu!" she cried, as the warrior's angry eyes, roiling with rage, met her own.

He tried to jerk the stick away, but Kate held fast. Then she did the only thing she could think of doing: She bit, and hard. Sinking her teeth into Sanbu's sweaty wrist, she closed her jaw with all her strength.

"Eeaaaah!" he shouted, smashing his fist against Kate's shoulder.

Pain seared her upper back, but still she hung on. Again Sanbu struck, this time on the back of her neck. She bit with all her energy, translating her pain into force.

Sanbu suddenly abandoned his grip on the shaft and pulled back his hand, wrenching her neck sideways. As Kate toppled to the ground, he reached to pick up a spear, blood streaming from the wound in his side. Lifting the spear high, he screamed vengefully as he prepared to end her life.

Just then, Laioni hurled herself directly into his chest. "Run!" she cried to Kate. "Escape while you can."

Sanbu threw Laioni to the ground and stabbed fiercely at her with his spear. Before Kate could even rise to her feet, he sliced into Laioni's thigh, cutting her deeply. Again he raised the spear, cursing wrathfully at this Halami girl who dared to challenge him.

At that moment, Monga released his death grip on the throat of the large dog. He backed away, staggered, and fell, then lifted himself weakly. One ear hung badly torn, while his right front leg dragged useless along the ground. Seeing Laioni's peril, he forced himself to bound across the camp. Just as Sanbu was about to drive the spear into her chest, he leaped at the warrior with his last particle of strength.

As Sanbu shrieked, Monga clamped his jaws around the man's neck. Sanbu fell backward, struggling to pull the dog away. But Monga held firm.

Kate glanced in the direction where she had last seen Jody and Kandeldandel, but saw no sign of them. She

stepped to Laioni's side and helped her to stand, though
her leg bled profusely. Together, they stumbled away from
the camp, climbing higher on the ridge. Using the walking
stick as it was meant to be used, she steadied herself against
the increasing weight of Laioni's body.

"Leave me," rasped Laioni. "Leave me or they'll catch
us. I'm too weak to go on."

"I'm not leaving you," declared Kate, leaning her against
an angular boulder. Ripping the purple kerchief from her
hand, she wrapped it tightly around the slashed leg to slow
the bleeding.

Laioni whispered, "Go on, please. They'll kill you too."

"You're not going to die," retorted Kate. Gazing at the
camp below, she saw Sanbu and Monga still rolling on
the ground, locked in deadly combat. Yet she could see no
one else. Where were Jody and Kandeldandel? And the
other warriors?

All at once, the pale early-morning light swiftly dimmed.
Kate turned toward the sky to see legions of dark clouds
gathering overhead. A stiff breeze, cold as ice on her face,
swept across the ridge. The few shrubs and grasses sprouting from between the scattered rocks bent savagely under
the weight of the wind. Then came the first rumble of thunder, echoing ominously over the face of the mountain.

Laioni suddenly started to slump forward. Barely catching her before she fell, Kate draped the unconscious body
across her own shoulders, grabbed Laioni's dangling arm,
and lifted her in a fireman's carry. She straightened up with
difficulty, feeling the weight in her knees and lower back.
But where to go? She could not carry such a burden very
far. She only knew she needed to find some sort of shelter,
away from the oncoming storm and any of Sanbu's men
who might try to track them.

Straining to see in the limited light, Kate's eyes roamed
past the camp, across the rocky scree, and into the high
reaches of the forest. There the shrunken and twisted trees,
though deformed by endless winds, might offer some protection. Farther down the slope stretched the forest itself,

visible now only as a sweeping sea of deep green, but for one nearby valley that was utterly dark. Beyond the forest, she could barely make out the towering cliffs of Lost Crater.

A blast of lightning sizzled across the sky. In the momentary light, Kate glimpsed two men, one carrying a spear, standing amidst the boulders just above the camp. They surveyed the ridge, searching for something.

Immediately, Kate turned to climb. Height was now her only hope for escape. Even with the help of the walking stick, Laioni's weight made progress very difficult. Yet she forced herself, laboring mightily, to ascend the rocky ridge. It did not occur to her that every step brought her closer to the lair of the Wicked One.

25

the sacrifice

HIGHER Kate climbed, step by arduous step. Laioni's body sagged heavily on her shoulders, causing her to stop regularly to catch her breath. After resting only a few seconds, she continued up the slope, panting in the thin air.

She constantly craned her neck, scanning the ridge for any sort of hiding place that might shield them from the sharp eyes of Sanbu's warriors, let alone Sanbu himself if he survived Monga's attack. Yet she saw no sign of shelter, only an increasingly jagged jumble of gray granite and white quartz. Even the shriveled shrubs grew fewer and fewer, requiring something more receptive than solid stone to sink their roots.

A clap of thunder exploded, and with it came the first splattering of sleet upon the rocks. Kate positioned herself on a flat, oblong stone and swung around to view the camp below. But heavy gray clouds now rolled across the ridge, and she could see nothing beyond the approaching storm.

As she turned back toward the high shoulders of the mountain, a sudden flash of lightning burst against the boulders just to her right. She leaped instinctively to the side and, in doing so, lost her footing. She tumbled with Laioni onto the rocks, her shout overwhelmed by a new pounding of thunder.

As she rolled to her knees, the dark clouds opened fully, showering the slope with a freezing downpour of sleet and hail. By the time she could crawl to Laioni's side, hail-stones dotted her twin ropes of black hair. It took all of Kate's strength to lift her again. Standing unsteadily, she straightened her back against the frigid gusts of wind.

Another simultaneous blast of lightning and thunder crashed across the slope, nearly knocking her down again. In the wavering light she spied a shallow overhang of rock nearby. It looked barely big enough to cover the two of them, but she knew there was no other choice. Tottering across the slippery slope with the help of the walking stick, she carried Laioni to the overhang. Kneeling, she wedged Laioni into the deepest recess under the gray stone slab and slid herself, exhausted, beside her.

The hail gathered swiftly on the stones outside their shelter. Soon the rocky expanse of the ridge was transformed into a sheet of white ice. The air grew bitter cold, and Kate realized that she could see the puffs of her own breath. Laioni's breathing, though, she could not see at all. Placing her hand against the Halami girl's mouth, she felt just the barest hint of warmth, and that only at irregular intervals.

"Laioni," she cried, shaking her friend by the shoulders. "Laioni, don't die. Please don't die."

She laid her hand against Laioni's leather bib, on the same spot where she felt a heart beating strongly not long before. "You promised," she pleaded. "Remember? You promised."

Tears brimmed in Kate's eyes, even as she started to shiver from the cold. Feeling her fingers going numb, she thrust them under her armpits for warmth. Her neck and shoulders ached, both from Sanbu's blows and from the weight of the burden they had carried so far up the rocky

ridge. She examined the blood-soaked kerchief tied around
Laioni's thigh. The bleeding had halted at last, but that
meant nothing if now she died from exposure to the
elements.

Kate touched Laioni's pale cheek with two throbbing
fingers. To her shock, she discovered that the cheek felt
even colder. As the wind whipped across the slope, driving
the hail into wavelike drifts, she pulled off the day pack
and removed her sweatshirt. Frantically, she tried to wrap
it like a blanket around Laioni. Yet she knew it would do
little to slow the deadly process. She remembered Aunt
Melanie telling her the tragic story of a young couple, mar-
ried not yet one week, who froze to death in a sudden
storm on Brimstone Peak. Rescuers found them several
days later, huddled together, inseparable in death as in life.

Laioni shivered all at once as if having a seizure, which
caused her head to fall forward. Kate, herself shivering in
her T-shirt, raised the heavy head again. She noticed once
more how much this girl from another time looked like
Aunt Melanie, even with her eyes closed. Was this how
Laioni's life would end? Frozen to death on the side of a
mountain?

Kate bit her lip at the thought. *It's so cold—cold. She's
going to d-die unless I can do something. Sh-she's going to
d-d-die.*

The storm swirled across the ridge with increasing fury.
Kate listened in vain for some slackening in the wintry
wind. But the wind howled incessantly, stealing what flickering flame of life remained in the girl by her side.

Monga knew, thought Kate. He knew that someone's
death was near. But did he know it was Laioni's? She
struck her knee angrily with her fist. It's too soon for her to
die. Too soon!

She observed Laioni's face, now frosted with hundreds
of tiny hairs of ice. Her lips looked like gray-blue granite,
her skin like shadowy storm clouds. *If only I could build a
fire. Then at least she'd have a chance.* Glancing at her
own sneakers, Kate wondered whether they might burn.

No, too wet. And besides, she had no matches. She didn't even have a pair of sticks to rub together, as Laioni had done in the forest.

Another series of shivers rattled Laioni. Kate moved still closer to her chilled body, enveloping her with her own bare arms. Her eyes, blurring with tears of pain and help-lessness, fell to the walking stick. Frost partially covered the shaft, obscuring the symbols carved into the wood. The eyes of the handle stared icily back at her. So this is Laioni's fate, she said to herself bitterly. This is what hap-pens to She Who Follows the Owl. She wanted to learn the true meaning of her name, and it is Death. *If only I could make a fire. If only . . .*

She blinked, focusing again on the stick. The Stick of Fire. What was it the Chieftess believed? Something to do with the name. Then she remembered: *It will burst into flames when so commanded by its rightful owner.*

No, she told herself. Forget it. Forget the whole idea. Besides, the rightful owner was Aunt Melanie, and she was as far away as ever. Even if Kate herself were the rightful owner, burning the stick would throw away her sole chance of ever seeing her great-aunt again.

Yet, could it be that some small part of Aunt Melanie might reside right here in this Halami girl? Whether or not a traceable connection between them existed, Kate knew that wasn't the point. She had begun to feel that all living things are linked, often in ways impossible to see. Perhaps in some mysterious way she herself was more connected than she could ever know to Laioni, somehow tied to an unknown people from an unremembered time.

She reached for the walking stick, then caught herself. *Hold fast to your stick of power,* the Chieftess said at their parting. *It is your only hope, and ours as well.* Her only hope of returning to her own time. Her only hope of helping Aunt Melanie. Her only hope of saving the Ancient One.

Filled with uncertainty, she touched the stick with the tip of one finger. *Do not do this lightly,* rang the voice of the Chieftess, *for it will destroy the stick and all its powers.*

Again Laioni's frame convulsed in a sudden shiver.

Kate seized the stick and brought it close to her face. "Burn," she said in a low voice. "Burn if you can, Stick of Fire."

Nothing happened. The icy wind screamed across the frigid ridge, mocking her act of desperation. Kate listened, then realizing the futility of her attempt, threw the stick to the ground. It clattered on the hail-coated rocks by her feet.

Then, so slowly as to be almost imperceptible, the yellow eyes of the handle began to glow strangely. A thin plume of smoke started to curl upward from the middle of the shaft, and the hailstones beneath the stick hissed in contact with some new source of heat. Soon, an ellipse of melting ice formed around the walking stick, while water dripped along the edges of the stones.

Kate watched with a mixture of hope and grief as the Stick of Fire ignited. With growing intensity, strange white flames flickered along its length, licking the wood eagerly, burning away the ancient images of the Tinnani Old Tongue. As fiercely as the blizzard blew beyond the overhang, it could not snuff out this crackling fire.

The walking stick burned vigorously, swelling in strength, until Kate's feet and legs began to feel progressively warmer. She leaned Laioni closer, so that she would be warmed but not singed by the heat. So brilliant were the flames, as if their source were not a stick but a star, she could not look directly into them without scalding her eyes.

Gently, very gently, she lay Laioni's head upon her shoulder so that she might hear her breathe above the continual wailing of the wind. And then she waited.

26

dying flames

FOR several hours, the tempest raged. Hail and sleet surged across the mountainside. But for the circle of bare rock surrounding the overhang where a small fire burned brightly, the entire ridge wore a cloak of white ice. Kate, exhausted from the long trek and fierce battle, basked in the warmth of the flaming stick until at last she dropped off into a fitful sleep.

She woke with a start. Laioni's head now lay on her lap, the Stick of Fire still burning at their feet. Her heart leaped to see the ruddiness returned to Laioni's complexion. Touching her cheek gently, Kate felt again the warmth and life of her loyal friend. Amidst all that she had lost, all that she had left behind, at least this one thing had been saved.

She's alive. Kate savored the words, leaning her head back against the rock. *Laioni is alive.*

Yes, her sober inner voice replied, but what good will it do? Laioni would survive the storm, and even now slumbered peacefully on her lap. Yet the powers of Gashra continued undiminished. Aided by the Broken Touchstone, he would surely press ahead with his plans to devour the forest and destroy any creatures who dared to stand in his way. Her sacrifice, quite probably, was in vain. Most likely Laioni was spared only to fall some other day.

At least, Kate assured herself, there was this silver lining: The Stick of Fire will not fall into the hands of Gashra. He can never use it to find the missing Fragment. He can never heal the Broken Touchstone, augmenting his already terrible power. That much, at least, Kate had denied him, even if she had denied herself in the process.

Looking into the dancing white flames, Kate marveled at how evenly and strongly the stick blazed, yet with only a tiny trace of smoke. Never had she seen any light so intense, except perhaps in the eyes of Nyla, smallest of the Stonehags. Even in its final act of self-destruction the stick displayed deep power. Although the shaft lay largely disintegrated, the coals burned on with vigor. She knew they would continue to flame for some time. The carved handle, though completely charred, burned more slowly than the rest, so that the head of Chieftain Solosing de Notnot, creator of the Stick of Fire, remained recognizable. That's appropriate, thought Kate. The Chieftain's image will be the last part of the stick reduced to cinders, his yellow eyes aglow to the very last.

She sighed, remembering the warm glow from the fireplace in Aunt Melanie's living room. She would never know the comfortable feeling of that room again, its damp cedar smell, its many hideaways for Atha, its stockpile of quilts. She recognized that she would spend the rest of her days imagining but not tasting Aunt Melanie's homemade spice tea. With everything else from her own time that she would miss—Mom and Dad, Cumberland, her favorite shortstop glove, baseball cards, extra-thick mocha shakes—nothing exceeded the longing she felt to see again the old cottage and the elflike woman who lived there. Most of all, she hoped that Aunt Melanie was safe, though doubt loomed larger than hope in her heart.

She surveyed the landscape beyond the overhang. The

storm, its anger finally spent, was at last beginning to disperse. Scattered shafts of sunlight broke through the parting clouds and swept across the ridge, illuminating patches of ice-crusted rocks. The wind slackened, and she could now make out most of the mighty shoulder of the mountain, although the summit remained hidden by clouds.

Then she remembered. This was Gashra's mountain. Somewhere up there beyond the vapors encircling the summit lay the very lair of the Wicked One. She glanced again at Laioni, sleeping deeply in the healing warmth of the Stick of Fire. Soon she would wake to find the stick destroyed, along with her people's last hope of halting the growth of Gashra's power. Perhaps she would resent Kate for valuing her life above everything else.

Whatever she might think, the deed was done. It could not be reversed. While the stick continued to burn vigorously, it moved inexorably closer to becoming nothing more than a heap of ashes, its power consumed, spent, used up.

The same could be said, Kate realized sadly, about her own brief life. With no hope left of returning to her own time, there was nothing left for her to do but to live out the rest of her days with the Halamis, waiting for the inevitable time when Gashra would crush them completely. In losing the walking stick she had lost any chance to do something significant in the struggle against him. Saving Laioni was the last act of real worth she would ever accomplish. And though it might not mean much in the grand scheme of things, she knew that she could not have done differently.

Feeling the aching stiffness in her back, Kate decided to stand. Carefully, she slid her legs out from under Laioni, laying her head gently upon the flat stone. The girl snorted and her arm twitched as if she were about to wake up, but soon she drifted back into slumber.

Slowly, Kate rose to her feet. She stepped around the crackling fire and away from the overhanging rock that had shielded them from the storm. Out of reach from the heat of the fire, she felt the brush of brisk wind against her chest. She grabbed her green sweatshirt, which now lay on the rocks by Laioni's side, and pulled it on. Then, cautiously, she crept around the side of the rock and peered at Sanbu's camp a few hundred feet below. She saw no sign of any life there.

Questions tugged at her mind. Had Monga survived the attack? His bravery was so much bigger than his body, yet courage alone was no match for Sanbu's strength. If indeed he lived, did that mean Sanbu did not? That the little dog had not followed her trail, had not found his way to Laioni's side during the storm, worried Kate deeply. She wondered for the first time whether the death he had foreseen was in fact his own. And what of Jody? Despite himself, the boy from her own time had begun to win her grudging respect, if not her friendship. And Kandeldandel? What she would give right now to hear the soothing strains of his owl-like flute, or to see that mischievous grin again. She dreaded the thought that he might have been injured or that he was now, like Arc, a lifeless bundle of feathers.

Sadly, her eyes roamed across the great forest world stretching endlessly before her. In very little time all of it, including the sheer volcanic cone she could see rising in the distance, would fall under the domination of the Wicked One. And she had seen enough of his work to know that he would destroy whatever was not useful to him and devour the rest. Not only did that mean many individuals would die, from Laioni to her mother, from a certain Tinnani flute player to Fanona, stricken daughter of the Chieftain and Chieftess, it also meant that the forest itself, the living, breathing community that Kate was only beginning to comprehend, would ultimately perish. What that might mean for Lost Crater, and for the Hidden Forest deep within its walls, she shuddered to think. And the Ancient One: If Gashra had his way, it would not be there for Aunt Melanie to encounter five hundred years from now. The loggers' work would have been accomplished long before their time.

She bent down to touch her toes, stretching the sore muscles of her legs and back. Then she straightened herself, again scanning Sanbu's camp below. Gradually, a new feeling of resolve took hold. Maybe her own usefulness was not yet exhausted after all. If Sanbu lurked down there somewhere, perhaps she could use whatever energy she had left to inflict a small but painful sting in his, and therefore Gashra's, hide. There was no reason left to be cautious. Her days were numbered just as surely as Fanona's.

Yet she knew deep inside herself that such thinking was folly. What could she possibly do to harm Sanbu, let alone Gashra? At the first opportunity they would finish her off. Only the storm had granted her any protection, and its fury had now passed. She possessed no weapons, no warriors, no chance. Nothing would be stupider than to walk into a waiting ambush at Sanbu's camp, except perhaps strolling unarmed into Gashra's own lair. Even a ruse was impossible, for she had no way to fool them. She didn't even have the one thing they still thought she had: the Stick of Fire.

Regretfully, she watched the white flames consuming the remains of the stick. *The one thing they still thought she had . . .*

Suddenly an idea dawned. Possibly, just possibly, she could use Gashra's desire to find the Fragment to trick him into giving up the Broken Touchstone. Such a plan, she realized, was more than risky. It was impossible. Almost certainly it would spell her own death. Yet if she had to die in this strange time and place, perhaps it would be better to die in pursuit of something important. Rather than wait passively for the enemy to strike her down, she would take the battle to the enemy. Her stomach churned uneasily, for she knew this meant searching not for Sanbu, nor for any other agents of Gashra—but for Gashra himself.

Kate swung her eyes toward the cloud-covered summit. Knowing she faced certain defeat somehow liberated her deepest reserves of courage. If through some miracle she could lure Gashra into parting with the Broken Touchstone, his power to damage the forest and all its inhabitants would shrink drastically. If she failed, they would be no worse off for her effort. Either way, she would not die without having lived with some purpose. For if she could not protect Aunt

Melanie herself, at least she could try to protect the Halami girl who shared with her great-aunt more than just eye color. And if she could not save the Ancient One from destruction in her own time, at least she could try to save it in another.

She cast one more glance toward the sleeping form by the blazing coals. Laioni was safe for now, at least. Kate swallowed, knowing she would almost certainly never see her friend again. Then, from somewhere in her memory, she heard the words of the Stonehag Nyla: *At least you have a purpose, a calling, something you must do with your life. That is a blessing, a true blessing.*

Grabbing her blue day pack, she slipped her arms through the straps. Then she stepped away from the overhang onto the icy rocks of the ridge, starting for the summit. She did not know whether she would succeed in her quest, but only that, like Babe Ruth, she would try.

27

alone

STRUGGLING to ascend the frosted ridge, Kate nearly slipped several times, tottering momentarily on the edge of an icy rock before regaining her balance. Even when her sneakers seemed firmly planted, they were dangerously unstable. Pausing once to catch her breath, she turned to discover a distinct trail of her own footprints across the whitened slope. If Sanbu or his warriors wanted to pursue her, they now would have no trouble. She pushed on, wishing she could simply rise into the air with a few beats of her wings like Kandeldandel, avoiding the laborious climb.

Gradually, she crossed beyond the reach of the hailstorm. The rocks, while still wet, no longer glistened with ice. Stepping more confidently, Kate continued to climb higher, stopping intermittently to check to the rear for any followers. As she gained altitude, the sweeping wind swelled steadily in volume. Soon it sounded as loud as Kahona Falls, roaring ceaselessly. At the same time, fog swirled about her again. She felt increasingly warm, though she assumed this feeling came from her own exertion.

Then, all at once, she discovered the source of both the sound and the heat. Scores of deep cracks ran down the ridge from the summit, reaching toward her like elongated fingers, shooting walls of steam skyward. A city of geysers confronted her, hissing incessantly. She halted, staring in amazement at this inferno. Reaching the summit meant finding a path between the roaring plumes of steam, if such a path even existed.

Biting her lip, she strode forward into a narrow channel between two of the long cracks. The rushing of steam filled her ears, just as the billowing clouds of white vapor filled the air above her head. On either side, dozens of fumaroles rose from the ground, painted brilliant shades of orange, rust, yellow, and blue. Acidic gases sputtered from small craters beside the steam vents, while murky pools bubbled and churned.

Perspiring from the heat, Kate started to run through this gauntlet of steaming crevasses. The deep cracks drew nearer together, and steam clouds smothered her completely. The air reeked of foul-smelling sulfur, burning her throat and scalding her eyes. She choked, gasping for air.

Stumbling forward, she finally reached what seemed to be a gap between the crevasses, a narrow space less than an arm's length wide. She hesitated for an instant, not knowing what lay on the other side. Then she threw herself across the gap and fell to her knees on the rocks.

Panting, she drank in the cooler air, wiping her streaming eyes on her sweatshirt. Fog no longer swirled around her and she could see the darkening late-afternoon sky above the ridge. Behind, curling columns of seething gases poured out of the crevasses. Ahead, the summit loomed starkly, ringed with craggy cliffs and cinder cones.

The wind whipped across the desolate mountaintop, bitter cold against her face. No one but Gashra could feel at home in this tormented landscape. Everywhere, rocks bore the scars of excessive heat and force, whether singed until they turned black or baked until they burst apart. The ridge resembled the inside of a cauldron whose contents had long since boiled away, leaving behind a residue of incinerated rubble.

Rising to her feet, Kate spotted a small pool of clear water not far away. Unlike the other pools on the summit, it did not froth and bubble darkly. Instead, it stood perfectly still, clear as a crystal. Something about this pool called to Kate, beckoned to her softly and compellingly. She was too weak to resist its pull, too tired to remember the attraction of another enchanted pool, near the Circle of Stones.

How strange, she thought, to find a place of such beauty and purity amidst such devastation. If the rest of the mountaintop was designed to frighten away intruders, this transparent pool seemed a stunning exception. It sparkled invitingly, reflecting the slanting light of the setting sun.

She bent lower to examine the lovely little pool. The roaring steam vents still sounded in her ears, but she felt a renewed peacefulness gazing into this water. Although she hadn't expected to see her reflection, her own face looked up at her, tinged with gold from the sunset. So clear and still was the water that she could even see the hazel green hue of her eyes. She turned her head, and the mirrorlike surface revealed the loose, haphazard knotting of her braid, as well as the caked dirt on her neck and lower jaw.

Captivated by the perfect image, Kate smiled in satisfaction. As she did, she watched her own lips part to reveal a row of pearly white teeth. Then, unaccountably, the teeth in the reflection started to darken, to take on the color of her tongue, until finally they disappeared. Her mouth, oddly misshapen, grew redder and redder, as if it overflowed with her own blood. Her eyes sank drastically inward and her cheekbones suddenly hollowed, stretching her face into ghoulish proportions. At the same time, all her hair fell away, while her nose hooked cruelly downward. A deep gash appeared, slashing across her face.

She cried out, putting her hands to her cheeks. Though she felt the living skin still there, she staggered backward, almost falling into the steaming crevasse behind her. She caught herself just before tumbling into the scalding gases.

Then she ran past the clear pool, up the rock-strewn slope toward the summit. Like a terrified animal fleeing from a deadly predator, she ran without sense or direction, trying only to get as far away as possible.

At length, she leaned against a charred boulder twice her own height, panting for breath, her heart beating rapidly from both exertion and fright. So this was how Gashra welcomed his guests, she told herself, still seeing the haunted image. She shook her head, trying to dispel it forever. Throwing her braid over her shoulder, she drew herself up straight. *Well, he can't scare me so easily. No way. I won't let him.*

Even as she felt that sudden surge of resolve, the sun dropped below the shoulder of the mountain. The sky grew instantly darker. Her confidence departed as well, dissolving into the starless night.

In the last lingering light, she noticed some deep indentations in the surface of the boulder. Backing away, she could see the design more clearly. It was a face, an enlarged version of the Halami warning stone in the Hidden Forest. The carved face glared at her, mouth open wide, exuding panic. Despite herself, Kate shivered at the sight.

Then, as the light grew still dimmer, the mouth began to move. At first the lips quivered ever so slightly. Then they drew closer together, before suddenly stretching apart in an effort to shout.

"You will die!" screamed the face on the rock. "You will die!"

Kate lurched backward, then tripped over a jagged rock just behind her. She fell on her back with a thud, then rolled to one side. Fighting to keep some semblance of calm in the deepening darkness, she crawled quickly away from the boulder. Glancing back at the carved face, she could no longer discern its outline, nor even see the boulder against the night sky. Nothing but blackness filled her eyes; nothing but wailing wind filled her ears. She held her breath, paralyzed, half expecting the very rocks beneath her hands to come alive.

Then she saw three rounded rocks beginning to gleam with a vague reddish light. Instinctively, she jumped to her feet, but some hypnotic power within the light forced her to halt and sit down again. The glow within the rocks deepened, turning them into pulsing points of luminous red. All at once a spindly column of wavering light started to rise slowly out of each. The three glowing red columns swayed and twirled, growing taller all the time, until they condensed into the shapes of thin, wispy women. Halami women. They wore loose stringy skirts, chest bibs, and hair tied into twin ropes by their shoulders, though they were no more solid than shredded clouds. Silently, the ghostly trio turned to face Kate, red eyes gleaming wrathfully. They released a chorus of ear-splitting screams that made her cover her ears and bury her head between her knees.

At length the screams ceased and she raised her head again. At that moment the three ghostly figures began dancing around her, baying and howling, encircling her in a ring of shimmering red light. As though reliving the agony of their own tortured deaths, the spirits wailed hideously, flailing their arms and tossing their heads wildly from side to side.

"Stop," Kate cried in desperation. "Leave me alone!"

But the spirit-women did not stop. Long into the night, for hours that weighed on Kate like centuries, they wove their shrieking circle ever more tightly around her. At one point she picked up a rock and hurled it at one of them. It passed harmlessly through the vaporous head, landing in the darkened distance.

As the deathly dance wore on, Kate's eyelids drooped heavily. She fought to keep them open, knowing she must remain alert, despite her exhaustion. Anything could happen if she fell asleep. She slapped herself on the cheek so hard it hurt. Then she continued to watch the writhing spirits, waiting for the dawn she feared might never come.

28

in the lair
of the wicked one

THE ground suddenly shook violently, jolting Kate awake. Rocks leaped into the air around her, and she could hear nothing but a deafening roar welling up from deep inside the mountain. She tried to stand, bracing herself against an oblong rock, but the terrible tremors knocked her back to her knees.

Then, with one final heave, the earth ceased shaking. Kate pushed herself slowly to her feet. She stood there, watching the first rays of dawn's light touch the crest of the peak. Far away, she heard the rumble of a distant rock slide set off by the earthquake. She knew that Gashra must be preparing a great onslaught against those who resisted his control. And she also knew that, somehow, she had survived the night alone on his haunted mountain.

Feeling hungry, she thrust her hand into the leather pouch still tied around her waist. Cramming the remainder of the *minarni* into her mouth, she tasted again the deep history and knowledge of the Tinnanis, whose very existence now hung in the balance. The food, dry and chewy, renewed her strength, even though she wished she could find some water to wash it down. She was not about to drink from any of the pools on this mountainside.

Slowly, she started trudging up the slope. The entrance to Gashra's lair had to be somewhere near, although she could only guess what it might look like. Then, sensing something following her, she whirled around, heart pounding. She saw nothing but the clouds of steam rising from the crevasses below and the blackened debris of the rocky ridge. She shivered involuntarily, recalling the ghostly apparitions of the past night. Perhaps they were still stalking her, even in daylight.

She felt the entrance before she saw it. A powerful gust of heated air, like a blast from an open furnace, struck her face. Turning toward the heat, she spotted a triangular cave among the charred boulders, descending into the dark depths of the mountain. Two pools of lava bubbled and steamed at either side of the entrance, casting a wavering orange light into the mouth of the cave.

As she stepped closer, the heated air blew more strongly in her face, smelling like sulfur, drying her eyes and forcing her to squint. Then the hot wind slackened, only to resume a few moments later, as if the mountain itself were breathing through this passageway. The large scab on the back of her left hand began to throb again, just as it had before whenever Slimnis lurked nearby. She swallowed, certain that this was the entrance to the lair of the Wicked One.

She scanned the dimly lit cave. What chance could she possibly have to outwit Gashra, to steal the Broken Touchstone? Next to none, probably. But she knew the odds against her were no worse than those against Aunt Melanie, five hundred years later, struggling to save a cherished stand of redwoods.

Waiting until the fiery breath slackened, Kate entered the mouth of the cave. Long rows of lava pools lined the passageway like torches, throwing their eerie light upon the rock walls. As she walked, her sneakers sometimes slid across slick puddles of mud or crunched on crumbling bits of pumice. Her elbow brushed against a knifelike protrusion, ripping her sleeve and gashing her skin.

At that instant she heard a loud hiss, followed by the sound of slithering bodies ahead of her in the cave. She froze, until the sounds melted into the steady gurgling of the pots of lava. She placed her aching left hand protectively under her sweatshirt, but the throbbing pain only grew more intense. Then, feeling something moving behind her, she turned to the rear. But she saw nothing except the dimly lit cave.

Creeping forward again, she began to notice the varieties of colors and formations sprouting from the rock walls. Hundreds of lavender crystals, spun fine as hairs, drooped down like scraggly beards. One formation puffed outward like a cluster of silver balloons, expanding and contracting with the underground wind. From the ceiling hung mineralized tendrils and jagged stalactites, sometimes merging into columns with the sharp stalagmites thrusting upward from the floor.

The passageway wound downward, descending into the abdomen of the mountain. With every step, the air grew warmer. Kate frequently mopped her dripping brow with the sleeve of her sweatshirt, but perspiration continued to sting her eyes.

Then, mysteriously, the chain of lava pools came abruptly to an end. Inching ahead, she perceived in the darkness before her the slightest glimmer of orange light. As she drew closer, the glimmer brightened into a strong glow, while the floor of the cave sloped much more steeply downward. Soon the drop became so sharp that she could not help but run, across loose rocks and broken bits of crystal, toward the source of the light.

Suddenly she found herself standing in a mammoth chamber. Frothing orange lava filled most of its floor. Only the polished shelf of stone on which she stood and a steeple-shaped island of black rock rising out of the bubbling lake of lava were not submerged. High above her head, giant red stalactites hung down like pointed fangs, casting fearsome shadows on the ceiling.

At that moment the surface of the lake began to swirl in a powerful whirlpool. Slowly, accompanied by a clamorous slurping sound, a colossal figure started to emerge out of the froth. Dripping in superheated lava, the creature rose out of the lake as if riding on an invisible escalator, then strode onto the wide stone ledge only a few yards from Kate.

A towering red beast, with the head and body of a *Tyrannosaurus rex* and the enlarged arms and legs of a human, glowered down at her. Standing more than twenty feet tall, the creature swished his massive tail angrily on the stone floor, spraying lava globules around the room. Armorlike red scales covered his entire body, though often obscured by the layers of caked lava. Only the bulbous black eyes, each one the size of Kate's whole head, and the deep purple lips that ran the length of his teeth-studded jaws did not carry scales. As the beast raised one of his huge arms, she could see a row of fleshy suction cups embedded in the scales underneath, running from the armpit all the way down to the palm of his hand. A foot-long slab of meat, all that remained of some unfortunate being, dangled from the center of one suction cup near his wrist.

Part dinosaur, part man, and part octopus, the great carnivorous creature snorted furiously, sending from his nostrils a poisonous cloud of red vapor. As he did so, dozens of gemstones and skulls and glittering baubles hanging from bands around his neck jiggled and clattered. Simultaneously, several lizardlike Slimnis emerged from the shadows at the edge of the floor and slithered toward darkened tunnels in the rock near the cave entrance. With lightning speed, a long arm lashed out and slapped its suction cups across the back of one escaping Slimni. Roaring thunderously, the red beast lifted the squirming creature into the air and took a single dinosaur-size bite out of the midsection, then snapped up the green head and tail with another enormous swallow.

A thousand-tooth grin spread across his face, and he bellowed, "Hmmmmm, breakfast." With that, he released a single titanic belch that rattled the great stalactites on the ceiling. Lowering his gigantic head toward Kate, the monster then rumbled, "What, you come to Gashra with no offerings?" His swollen eyes scanned her closely. "Hmmmmm . . . What is hidden in your sack?"

Feeling the heat from his body as well as his sulfurous breath, Kate backed away. Slipping one arm out of the day pack, she unzipped it and pulled out the small painted drum. She held it in front of herself with both hands and said nervously, "An offering. For you."

"Rubbish," roared the gigantic beast, swatting the drum with a swipe of his huge hand. It skidded across the stone floor and landed beside a vast hoard of accumulated treasures, including piles of sparkling jewels, spears, knives, Halami baskets, assorted tools, carved statuettes of Gashra himself, and several large red stones twisted into strange shapes. "But," he added, "I'll keep it anyway." He bent closer. "Hmmmmm . . . what else do you have?"

Kate reached into the pack and retrieved the last of its contents: Aunt Melanie's metal thermos. Slinging the now-empty sack over her shoulder again, she displayed the thermos to Gashra, more uncertain than ever about her goal. It would be difficult enough even to learn the location of the Broken Touchstone, let alone steal it. She needed to stall for time. But how? He clearly didn't like the drum, and was even less likely to appreciate a beaten-up old thermos.

To her surprise, another many-toothed grin wrapped around the face of the Wicked One. He slapped the thermos with the palm of one hand, attaching it to a suction cup. Bringing it closer to his jaws, he bit ferociously into the middle. "Hmmmmm," he said, emitting a sound like gurgling lava that could only be a laugh. "Good ore."

Clapping his hands together, he bent the thermos in half. Then, with a distinct air of self-satisfaction, he slung it over one of his necklaces and pinched the two ends together to affix its position. Eyeing Kate again, he rumbled,

"Nice. Very nice." His eyes suddenly narrowed and he thundered, "But it doesn't make up for all the trouble you've caused me."

Kate cleared her throat. "What trouble do you mean?"

Gashra glared at her. "You killed my servant Sanbu."

The news hit Kate like a bucket of cold water. If Sanbu was really dead, then maybe Monga . . .

"I will miss him," continued Gashra, gnashing his teeth savagely. "He was, hmmmmm, useful to me. Very useful."

Planting her feet firmly on the stone floor, Kate declared, "He tried to steal the Stick of Fire from me."

"Did he?" growled the beast, feigning surprise. "Hmmmmm, how clumsy of him." Then Gashra bent low and said in his most soothing voice, "The last thing I would want is for a servant of mine to cause you any harm! Oh, no. You are far too important. I wouldn't want you getting hurt. Not even a little bit bruised." The purple lips stretched into a gargantuan smile. "By the way, where is the stick now? Hmmmmm?"

Kate, perspiring from more than the heat of the chamber, answered, "I destroyed it."

The Wicked One reared up and waved his tentacle-like arms. "You *what?*" he roared, so forcefully that one giant stalactite broke loose from the ceiling and plunged into the frothing lake of lava. "Don't you know that stick is the only way to find the Fragment? Hmmmmm?"

"I know," answered Kate, maintaining her calm. Then she added, trying her best to sound truthful, "I already found it."

The oversized eyes of Gashra swelled still larger. "You did? You have it?" His tail waved excitedly. "Show it to me."

"It's hidden," she replied. "Why should I show it to you?"

Gashra snorted angrily, releasing a cloud of red vapor. "Because," he snarled, "I will kill you if you don't."

Forcing herself to remain stationary, Kate declared, "Then you'll never find the Fragment."

Gashra paced back and forth, contemplating. "Hmmmmm. I hope it's not too hot in here for you," he said, again using his most soothing voice. "Like all underground beings, I require a certain amount of heat." He flashed a few dozen teeth, adding, "But not for long. With every minute, my power is building, thanks to the Broken Touchstone. Soon I will be strong enough to stride freely on the surface. And a great moment that will be! But now, back to you. Tell me your name. Your short name, the one your friends call you."

"Kate."

"Kate," repeated Gashra. "Such a nice name, hmmmmm. Yes, very nice. Now, Kate, consider this thought. Have you ever imagined what we could accomplish together?" He waved his tail again. "If you help me, your greatest dreams will come true. Just think of it! We will control everything, you and I. The whole world will be ours. Every last needle on every last tree, every last feather on every last wing. Nothing can stop us."

Kate fidgeted. Then, judging her moment, she asked, "How do I know you really have the Broken Touchstone?"

"I have it," rumbled Gashra cautiously.

"Where?"

The bulbous eyes surveyed her with suspicion. "Somewhere."

"Then how do I know you really have it?"

"How do I know you have the Fragment?"

"I wouldn't be foolish enough to come here unless I did," answered Kate.

Gashra lifted his long arm and licked the row of suction cups. "If you don't cooperate, I could boil you in lava. You'd end up like the rest of my souvenirs." He waved a hand toward his hoard of treasures.

Kate gasped, for she suddenly recognized the origin of the twisted red stones scattered throughout the jumbled pile. Bodies. Bodies of all kinds of animals: deer, owls, Slimnis, serpents, squirrels, and at least one Tinnani that she could see.

Powered by renewed rage, Kate turned back to Gashra, who continued to lick his suction cups with evident pleasure.

"You can't threaten me," she said firmly. "I know how much you want that Fragment."

Gashra lowered his arm and examined her thoughtfully. "It's a pity, hmmmmm. You look like such a tasty little morsel. But you're right. I do want that Fragment. And I will grant you your deepest wish if you will just give it to me."

Taken aback, Kate asked, "What wish?"

The dinosaur's eyes closed for a moment, then reopened. "I will reunite you with the one you call Aunt Melanie."

Kate shuddered. "How did—how did you know that?"

"The forest has many ears loyal to me," rumbled the reply. "Even if you don't really have the Fragment, for I can feel a great capacity for treachery in you, I think you could still help me find it. Hmmmmm, yes, I'm sure that's right. After all, the Stick of Fire chose you for a reason. Here is my promise to you: If you help me find it, I will send you back to your Aunt Melanie."

Her resolve disintegrating, Kate asked hesitantly, "You would really do that?"

"Of course," roared the Wicked One. "In a flash." He scooped up a handful of lava in his hand from the lake, then rubbed the hot liquid against the back of his neck. "Good for the skin," he explained, grinning broadly. "Unless of course you're made of mere flesh."

At once Kate remembered her scalded left hand. She cringed at the memory of the deadly green pool, of Aunt Melanie scrubbing the hand so furiously in the rivulet. In her mind's eye she followed that small stream as it flowed down over the rocks of the crater and into the depths of the Hidden Forest, ultimately to empty into the blue lake and finally to join the crashing cascade of Kahona Falls. She wanted to see Aunt Melanie again more than anything else in the world.

"If I'm going to join with you," she said slowly, "you've first got to tell me your plan."

"My plan is to conquer," bellowed the beast. "To own everything I can, hmmmmm, and destroy whatever I cannot. And my first great assault is only minutes away." He shrugged his head toward the bubbling lake of lava. "Even without the whole Touchstone, my power is swelling rapidly. Soon it will be great enough to drown most of the forest in a sea of fire. That will take care of those miserable Tinnanis, and their friends the Halamis, for good. Ha! They'll regret ever trying to stop me. In just a few minutes, the pressure of this lava will be so great that it will burst free at last, blasting away the top of this mountain and everything else in its path."

Kate then noticed that the level of the frothing lake had risen steadily since she first arrived. Now it slopped over the edge of the stone floor, consuming more of the ledge every second, nearing the dark tunnels through which the Slimnis had escaped. Lava lapped still higher on the steeple-shaped island, while Gashra's tail now swam in the scalding fluid.

"Are you with me or not?" roared the Wicked One.

Stepping back from the rising lava, Kate found herself standing near the entrance to the cave through which she had fallen. Looking down at her feet, she kicked a loose rock into the orange liquid. It hissed as it was swallowed by lava. "All right," she said at last. "I'm with you. But first show me the Broken Touchstone."

"Hmmmmm, gladly," gurgled Gashra triumphantly, as he opened his massive jaws to the widest. He reached inside his mouth and removed from under his tongue a glowing red sphere no bigger than a softball. Holding the sphere high above his head, Gashra savored its deep radiance for a moment. "Here," he announced proudly, "is the Broken Touchstone."

"I still can't see it," said Kate. "I want to see the place where the Fragment fits."

Hesitating for a moment, Gashra lowered his hand to the level of Kate's head, keeping it just beyond her reach. Resting comfortably between two of his enormous fingers sat the ruby red sphere.

She looked at the glittering stone, captivated by its inner luminescence. A jagged crack cut diagonally across its surface, leaving a gap no more than three inches long and half an inch wide. Perhaps, she thought, by joining forces with Gashra, she could possibly tame him, moderating his greed enough that all the beings of the forest could again live together in peace. After all, anything was possible with the restored Touchstone. Yet, even as she nursed this idea, it felt strangely foreign somehow, almost as if it came from outside of herself rather than from within. Again her thoughts turned to Aunt Melanie. Kate could see her face, even hear her voice. But the words sounded blurred; she could not quite make out what her great-aunt was saying.

At that moment the mountain shook violently. The walls of the chamber swayed and buckled as if made from mere paper. Several of the huge stalactites on the ceiling broke loose and came crashing down into the lava in a series of splashes. Large stones tumbled from the island, as the lake surrounding it bubbled with new ferocity. Molten rock surged higher, lapping against the base of the treasure hoard and reaching almost to Kate's feet. She struggled to keep her balance so that she would not fall into the lava, but she felt its heat singe the hairs of her legs under her jeans.

Gashra, waving his tail with anticipation, turned his head away from Kate to see the frothing lake just behind him. At that instant, a small globule of lava flew off his tail and landed with a loud hiss on Kate's right sneaker. She jumped back, her foot sizzling with pain.

Shaking the orange substance from her sneaker, she saw the charred remains of her once bright green laces, now black as charcoal. *Like new green leaves on the first day of spring,* Aunt Melanie had said of them. *As green as new leaves,* in Laioni's words. How would new leaves fare under Gashra's domination? She tried to imagine the next first day of spring in this land, and saw nothing. She listened for the call of an owl in the forest, and heard nothing.

Just then, her eyes fell upon one especially contorted red stone that lay at the very top of the treasure hoard. It was larger than the others, twisted almost beyond recognition. Yet Kate knew instantaneously that this was the body of a young human being. A boy or a girl—perhaps even Laioni's lost friend Toru—had joined the Wicked One's list of victims, a list that would soon grow much longer.

Seizing the moment before Gashra turned around, she lunged for the Broken Touchstone resting lightly on his fingers. Grasping it in one hand, she started to scramble up the pile of rocks leading to the cave. In an instant she was within a few feet of the entrance. Struggling to reach it, she could see the flickering light of the lava torches just ahead.

Then, with a thunderous blow, Gashra's tail smashed against the wall of the chamber right above the entrance. Rocks and dust and stalactites tumbled down, blocking the cave and sealing it forever. Kate tumbled backward and rolled down the rocky slope, dropping the sphere. She stretched out her arm, reaching to retrieve it, but Gashra moved more quickly. He scooped up the sphere, breathing heavily as if the few seconds out of its contact had weakened him significantly.

"How dare you?" he roared, his full strength returning along with the fiery color of his scales. "Treacherous human! I should never have listened to you."

Bruised and scraped, Kate rose to her feet and declared, "I will never help you. Never."

"Then you shall die, like all the other forest creatures," raged Gashra. "I already have enough power to rule the world from here to the ocean. Hmmmmm! I don't need you or the Fragment to destroy my enemies once and for all."

Squeezing the glowing sphere in his enormous hand, Gashra waded into the lava lake. Whipping his massive tail back and forth so rapidly it propelled him across the churning surface, he stepped onto the steeple-shaped island. With three great bounds, he ascended the black rocks and stood atop the pinnacle. There he stood, laughing, looking down upon Kate.

Holding the Broken Touchstone in his outstretched hand, Gashra leaned back his head and cried, "The time has come, O mountain of wrath. Break your bonds, free your power. Explode in triumph!"

Again the mountain rumbled and shook, though this time it vibrated down to its deepest roots. The lava lake seethed with new energy, spitting fire high into the air, as hot winds swept around the chamber. Powerful explosions under the earth rocked the walls arching overhead, drowning out every sound but the gurgling laughter of Gashra.

In that instant, Kate did the only thing left to do. She picked up a fist-size stone. There was no time to take proper aim. Her legs wobbled from the vibrations and her eyes stung from perspiration, but she knew she would never make a more important throw. Rearing back like a practiced shortstop, she hurled the stone at the small sphere resting on Gashra's hand. She watched expectantly as it sailed through the air, straight at its target.

But it missed. The stone passed just above the Broken Touchstone, striking a giant stalactite hanging down from the ceiling. With a plop, the stone fell harmlessly into the bubbling lake of lava.

Seeing this, Gashra laughed still louder. Kate was crestfallen. She knew that she had lost her last chance to separate the sphere from its greedy master. Then, as she backed nearer to the rock wall to escape the surging lava, she saw the stalactite swaying precariously.

Dislodged by her stone, the huge formation broke loose from the ceiling with an ear-piercing crack. Gashra looked up just as the stalactite crashed down onto his outstretched arm, knocking the sphere from his hand. It fell, bounced off the rocks at the base of the island, and landed in the frothing lake. With a shriek of terror, he leaped down from the pinnacle and swung his long arm toward the precious object.

Suddenly, from the shadows behind the treasure hoard a white-winged creature appeared. Soaring like an arrow, it flew toward the floating sphere, clasping it in its talons only an instant before Gashra's hand reached the spot.

"Kandeldandel!" cried Kate, her voice mingling with the violent rumbling of the mountain.

"Take it," called the Tinnani as he flew over her head and dropped the Broken Touchstone into her hands. He then landed on the narrow ledge beside her and pulled on her arm. "Follow me," he cried, ducking into one of the dark tunnels.

Kate darted after him, even as the volcano erupted with a deafening roar.

29

torrent of fire

GUIDED by Kandeldandel's wide owl eyes, which could sense contour and shadow where Kate saw only blackness, the pair hurried through the lightless tunnel. Knowing that Kate could not run in such darkness, the Tinnani walked as briskly as he could without leaving her behind. Staying no more than a few steps behind him, she clasped the sphere in both hands, aware of nothing but her desire to escape and the insistent throbbing of her left hand. Kandeldandel hooted frequently, perhaps to keep her aware of his exact location, perhaps to frighten any Slimnis lurking ahead in the dark passage.

The tunnel, narrower than the cave by which she had entered Gashra's lair, sloped gradually downward. Soon Kate discovered a smooth trail running along the middle of the tunnel floor, scraped away by countless Slimnis slithering over the rocks. Feeling more confident, Kate accelerated her pace, keeping her feet within the bounds of the smooth trail, so that she was striding almost on Kandeldandel's heels.

A powerful tremor rocked the mountain, knocking loose some rocks from the roof of the tunnel. One of them grazed Kandeldandel's wing, causing him to step suddenly to the side. Kate, following closely, moved likewise. Her foot caught on something protruding from the floor and she fell forward, plowing into the rock wall.

"Uhhh," she exclaimed, sprawling on the tunnel floor. "The Touchstone! I dropped it."

"I don't see it anywhere," panted Kandeldandel, scanning the darkness for any sign of the sphere. "It can't be lost."

"All I feel are rocks," said Kate as she groped with both hands in the debris. "Where is it?"

At that moment, a dim illumination began to fill the tunnel. From somewhere behind them, a gentle glow expanded, casting a few flickering rays of light on the pair and their surroundings. Kandeldandel stood bolt upright, facing the source of the strange light, but before he could speak Kate spied a familiar round object hidden behind a rectangular rock.

"There," she cried, seizing the Broken Touchstone once again. She lifted it into the air to show Kandeldandel, but his attention was focused on the tunnel behind them.

"Lava," declared the Tinnani, his yellow eyes swelling. He grabbed Kate's shoulder with the talons of one hand and jerked hard to make her stand. "Let's get out of here."

They dashed through the tunnel with all the speed they could muster. Darkness posed no problem now, since the orange glow behind them grew stronger and stronger. Hurtling down the jagged-walled corridor, they started to hear the sizzling of lava pressing closer, destroying anything it touched. Even as she ran, Kate noticed that the back of her neck felt increasingly warm.

"The way out," hooted Kandeldandel, pointing to a pinpoint of gray light far ahead.

Running still faster, the pair practically flew down the tunnel, leaping over dislodged rocks every few steps. Kate held tightly to the sphere, while the gurgling and hissing behind her grew steadily louder. She huffed for breath, her throat burning from the caustic taste of sulfur.

Just as he reached the narrow crack in the rocks that was the exit, Kandeldandel stopped suddenly and whirled around. Kate bumped squarely into his feathery chest. Then, seeing the bright illumination on his face, she turned around herself. What she saw made her gasp and nearly drop the sphere. Not ten feet away flowed a thick tongue of incandescent lava, filling the entire tunnel with sizzling igneous fluid, bearing down on them fast.

"Let's go," cried Kate, pushing the Tinnani toward the opening.

Kandeldandel slid through the narrow exit, his fluffy plumage pressing close to his body. "Come on," he shouted from the other side.

"I'm coming," answered Kate, glancing back at the moving wall of fire.

She ducked her head, since the opening had not been made with humans in mind, and turned sideways to pass through more easily. Sliding into the crack, she felt the scorching heat of approaching lava on the hand that held the Broken Touchstone. Even the rocks around her were growing warmer, reflecting the volcanic heat.

The passage was narrower than she thought. Squirming, she edged still deeper, but the rocks pressed ever more tightly upon her chest and back. She dug in her feet and pushed as hard as she could, succeeding only in wedging herself more firmly. She pushed again. No motion. She tried to back up, but could not move. Her heart pounded and perspiration rolled down her brow and stung her eyes. But she could not lift her arm to wipe her sweaty face.

She was stuck.

"Come on," called Kandeldandel. "What's taking you so long?"

"I'm stuck," moaned Kate. "Can't move! And the lava— it's like fire. Help me!"

The wall of molten rock moved steadily closer. All she could see was the orange light dancing on the rocks next to her face. She drew in her legs as far as possible, but the simmering lava advanced irresistibly. Hotter than a blazing furnace, the fluid flowed nearer. In another few seconds it would incinerate her, drowning her quest forever in a river of fire.

Then, above the lava's spitting and crackling, Kate heard a new sound. Low, mellifluous notes flowed into the opening, like the call of an owl but somehow mellower. She recognized it at once.

"Hey," she cried to Kandeldandel, "are you crazy? I need your help, not your music!" The leading edge of the lava advanced toward her sneakers, and the treads on her soles started to melt. "Please," she pleaded, feeling the heat on the bottoms of her feet. "Help me."

The Tinnani merely continued to play on his flute, filling the air with cheerful song.

"Kandeldandel," gasped Kate. "This is no time for games. I'm going to die!"

All at once the orange light around Kate faded. The heat of the rocks swiftly diminished, while the treads of her sneakers stopped burning. The lava in the tunnel grew quickly colder and harder, congealing within seconds into solid rock.

"What—what happened?" she asked, her heart still racing.

Kandeldandel, having lowered his flute, replied, "I never thought my little flute could come in so handy."

"You did that?"

"Guess so," the Tinnani answered in his laughing voice. "You gave me the idea when you said the lava was like fire."

"I'm still stuck, though. Even your magic flute isn't going to pry me out of this crack."

"Try this," suggested Kandeldandel. "Take as deep a breath as you can, then when I say, blow out all the air. And hurry, before the lava heats up again."

Inhaling as instructed, Kate waited for the command, then exhaled completely. At that instant, powerful talons clutched her forward arm and pulled. She felt herself move, but only slightly. Again Kandeldandel tugged, budging her only a fraction of an inch. The rocks around her face and hands grew steadily warmer, reflecting the first flickers of orange light. Just as she was about to gasp for air, the Tinnani pulled a third time. She slid forward and tumbled out of the opening, landing right on top of him.

"You did it!" she shouted, hugging Kandeldandel no less tightly than she clutched the sphere of red obsidian in her hand.

"Owww," he screeched, pushing her away. "You hurt my wing."

"Sorry," said Kate, rolling away. She sat on the rock-strewn ridge, drinking in the cool mountain air. "I never thought I'd be glad to see this place again, but I sure am."

"I'm not," answered Kandeldandel, struggling to his feet. He tried to move his left wing, then winced in pain. "I think something's broken."

"Gosh, I'm—"

A loud rumbling filled the air, cutting short Kate's apology. She looked up, noticing for the first time the heavy black clouds darkening the sky above them. Yet she knew they were not clouds of rain or snow, just as the rumbling was not thunder. Turning toward the summit, she realized they had exited below the hissing steam vents, still pouring clouds of hot vapor into the air. Beyond the steaming crevasses she saw a gargantuan pillar of smoking, smoldering ash rising out of the top of the peak, lifting its billowing burden skyward.

The rumbling expanded to an ear-splitting roar. Suddenly the mountain shook with an explosion so violent it knocked both Kate and Kandeldandel to the ground. Struggling to regain their feet, they saw the entire summit above the steam vents rip itself apart in a catastrophic burst of orange flame. Bubbling lava surged out of the gaping crater, while incandescent globs rained down on the ridge like a torrent of fire.

"Let's get out of here," cried Kate.

Hurtling down the slope as fast as they could, the pair raced to outrun the lava flowing out of the seething summit. Disregarding the danger of slipping on the jagged and slippery stones, they ran with one thought and one thought only: to escape. More explosions rocked the mountainside above them, flinging lava high into the darkened sky, fueling the outpouring of molten rock.

They dashed ahead of the all-consuming avalanche, but it gained on them rapidly. The ridge line began to level out, and soon they reached the upper edge of the forest. Kate scanned the twisted trees, survivors of countless brutal storms, knowing that in no time they would perish in a flood of fire. As they continued downward, the jumbled rocks of the ridge were replaced by a soft mat of mosses and ferns. Before long, mighty trees towered over their heads, their branches laden with nests and cones and needles.

The air grew thick and smoky, and Kate realized they were entering the Dark Valley. Though her step faltered for an instant, she quickly picked up speed again. She had no choice.

The ground shook again, as the rumbling to the rear grew ever louder. Kate glanced over her shoulder to see a tidal wave of superheated lava descending on the forest, snapping tall trees like toothpicks, instantly cremating trunks and branches. In a matter of seconds, the wave would be upon them. She held the Broken Touchstone close to her chest, consoling herself that at least she had robbed Gashra of his greatest prize.

Just ahead, Kandeldandel halted at the base of an especially grand fir tree. He moved close to the trunk, whose girth almost equaled that of the Ancient One, and laid the hand that held his flute against its gnarled bark. Kate ran over to him, sensing that the Tinnani had chosen this tree as his place to die.

He turned a solemn face toward her and reached out his other hand. Kate took it wordlessly, stepping close to his side. They stood together by the trunk of the great tree, their feet upon its massive roots, as the hot wind of the onrushing lava blew against their faces. Trees cracked and swayed and burst into flames all around them.

Kandeldandel released a long, low hooting sound. The earth under them started to quiver and quake. Closing her eyes, Kate whispered some words of good-bye to Aunt Melanie, hoping that somehow, some way, she might one day hear them. As she started to say the same parting words to Laioni, the roots of the tree suddenly buckled and spread apart.

30

torchlight

THEY dropped swiftly down, landing with an echoing thud on the earthen floor of an underground cavern. Gnarled roots lined the walls around them. Kate looked up just in time to see the fir tree consumed by a rolling wave of flames, barely an instant before the roots above her head closed tight again. She turned to Kandeldandel, sitting beside her on the dirt floor, his face illuminated by the light of a torch affixed to the wall. The playful half grin had returned.

"Thought I'd keep you in suspense," he hooted casually.

"You did that all right," declared Kate. "Where in the world are we?"

"Can't you guess?"

As she scanned the hollow cavern around them, Kate's first thought was that this was yet another underground tunnel leading to the mountain. But if that were so, why wasn't it already filled with lava? No orange glow in here. The only light came from the slender torch suspended high above them.

Then Kate peered directly at the torch itself. It seemed

familiar in some way. It burned some sort of incandescent gas, but bore no markings at all except the lacy metal band that held it to the wall. Suddenly she remembered where she had seen torches like this before.

"Ho Shantero!" she exclaimed. "This must be one of your Tinnani tunnels."

"Indeed," answered Kandeldandel. "If you hadn't broken my wing back there, I could have taken you back by an easier route."

"You mean by the seat of my pants, like you did Jody."

The half grin broadened into a smile. "With you, I thought I could hoist you by your braid."

"No way." Kate beamed. "I'd pluck out all your feathers first."

The Tinnani's round eyes widened. "You wouldn't dare."

"Don't tempt me."

"Don't worry, I won't." Kandeldandel waved a hand toward the gleaming sphere. "Anybody who could get that away from the Wicked One is too much for just one little Tinnani."

Gazing into the luminous Touchstone, Kate hefted it in her hand. It felt remarkably light for an object of such unfathomable power. She caught Kandeldandel's eye. "Nobody's more surprised than me," she confessed. "Besides, I couldn't have done it without you." Nudging his leg, she added, "Guess I'll let you keep your feathers. For now, anyway."

Kandeldandel hooted happily.

Then Kate furrowed her brow. "What do you think happened to Gashra? Is he dead?"

"I doubt it," answered her friend. "He's been defeated before, only to rise again later. His plans are ruined, and he'll need some time to regain his strength, but he'll be back someday. You can count on it."

Kate, thinking of a time far in the future, nodded sadly. "Then let's go back to Ho Shantero. At least the Broken Touchstone can help your people repair the forest after the eruption."

Kandeldandel bobbed his head thoughtfully. "I hope

there's some forest left to repair." He indicated the sphere, and his voice brightened. "Don't get me wrong, though. There will be plenty of happy people when you march in with that little item in your hand."

"Especially the Chieftess—if, like she said, the Touchstone will make her daughter well again."

"That's right," agreed Kandeldandel. "Just to hear Fanona sing again . . . Believe me, that would be worth all our trouble."

"So what are we waiting for?" asked Kate, jumping to her feet.

Kandeldandel, wincing slightly from his injured wing, followed suit. "Let's go," he said, his deep voice echoing inside the cavern.

Since the tunnel had been designed to accommodate many Tinannis, both in flight and on foot, Kate could easily stand with ample headroom. Holding the sphere in the palm of her right hand, she passed beneath the glimmering torch. Suddenly, it flamed much stronger and brighter than before. Seeing this, Kandeldandel half grinned at her.

Kate returned the favor. "For someone who calls himself 'just one little Tinnani,' you sure managed to do your part for your old family name back there."

For an instant, the half grin disappeared and Kandeldandel regarded her intently. "You really think so?"

"Absolutely," replied Kate as she passed beneath another torch. It too swelled in strength, illuminating them both. They continued walking side by side, listening only to the reverberations of their footsteps in the tunnel. At length, Kate asked, "By the way, how did you ever get inside the mountain?"

"Same way you did. I just followed you, after turning invisible of course. Those Slimnis were so eager to avoid getting eaten, they didn't even notice."

"I thought something was following me back there in the cave. I'm glad it was you and not one of those ghosts." She stared ahead into the long tunnel, lit by a series of identically wrought torches. "How far is it to Ho Shantero, anyway?"

The Tinnani ruffled his feathers. "A good day's walk, I'm afraid. It's quicker than going overland, but not as fast as flying."

Kate teased, "At least with your broken wing I know you'll stick around for a while."

"Sad but true," answered Kandeldandel.

Suddenly Kate remembered Jody's injured arm. "What about the others?" she asked. "Jody and Monga—and Laioni. Are they all right?"

Kandeldandel fiddled nervously with his flute as he walked. "Jody's fine. He was fighting for his life, and doing pretty well for having only one arm. But then he got into some big trouble. He'd have been killed for sure if I hadn't carried him off."

"So that's why I couldn't find either of you when Laioni and I were escaping."

"And when I returned, you were gone." He clucked with satisfaction. "But I got back in time to help Monga finish off Sanbu."

"So he's really dead."

"Really."

Kate pulled on Kandeldandel's feathered arm, slowing him to a stop. "You're not telling me something."

The yellow eyes lowered. "Monga's dead too. Died with his jaws clamped around Sanbu's neck. The little fighter, he gave it everything he had."

"And more," added Kate somberly.

The Tinnani sighed. "He had more courage than a whole army of Slimnis."

Leaning toward him, Kate said, "Like another little fighter I remember."

Kandeldandel raised his eyes to meet hers. "I can't believe Arc is gone."

They started walking again, neither wanting to speak. Only after several minutes did Kate raise her voice again. "Do you think you might find yourself another owl someday? That spot on your shoulder looks kind of bare."

The Tinnani spun his head halfway around, then back again. "Haven't thought about it."

Kate reflected for a moment. "Thanks to that little owl, I'm here today."

"And thanks to you, Laioni is too. She told us what you did."

"You found her?" asked Kate as another torch sprang to life above her head.

"It took a little looking, but finally I saw the circle of melted ice from the air. When Jody and I got there, Laioni was just trying to make herself walk so she could follow you. But she couldn't have gone more than a few paces, she was so weak. She told us everything, though she didn't have to. The burned stick said it all. Jody stayed to help her get down off the mountain while I left to find you."

"I'm glad she's alive," said Kate quietly. "Even though the stick was my only chance to get back, I really had no choice."

"You had a choice," replied Kandeldandel. Then he added lightly, "Besides, your way of starting a fire was a lot easier than her way."

Kate nodded. "But now I know why Aunt Melanie always likes to pack matches." She shifted the blue day pack on her back. "It's hard to believe I'll never see her again."

Kandeldandel lifted his good wing and stretched it toward her. "You've made some other friends, though. Friends you will see again."

Together they strode down the tunnel. Many miles lay between them and the floating island of Ho Shantero, but they had much to discuss. Kandeldandel was particularly keen to learn the rules of modern baseball, though he soon proved himself a forgetful student. Kate, for her part, received her first instruction in how to hoot like an owl. As they moved past each successive torch, its power would instantly increase, flooding the tunnel in new and potent light.

31

the fire of love

ALTHOUGH they passed dozens of intersecting tunnels along the way, Kandeldandel guided them effortlessly through each and every turn. At last, they approached a circular terminus illuminated by a ring of torches. As the Tinnani indicated the ceiling, Kate lifted her eyes to see a small square of silver embedded in the stone high above them.

"The trapdoor," she said. "We must be under the lake."

Kandeldandel hooted lightheartedly, then suddenly stopped. "I forgot about something."

"What?"

"These tunnels—we made them without stairs so that no intruders could pass out of them if they somehow got inside. The only way to go through that silver door is to fly." He hunched his injured wing. "And that's impossible."

Kate looked from him to the trapdoor and back to him again. "This is terrible," she moaned. "We come all this way, and now we can't get through the front door."

"It could be weeks before anybody comes along to give us a lift," muttered the Tinnani.

Kate squeezed the Broken Touchstone in frustration. "This is one of those times I wish I could fly."

At that, an infinitesimal glimmer of light flashed deep within the sphere. Before Kate could take another breath, she found herself rising slowly into the air. Too amazed to utter a sound, she rose to a height of approximately three feet off the ground, then drifted to one side until she hung suspended directly above Kandeldandel's head.

"Guess it's my chance to give you a ride," she said in amazement. "Grab onto my feet."

The astonished Tinnani did as he was instructed. With no effort whatsoever, Kate lifted him straight up into the air above the torches. Upon reaching the silver door, she pushed on its surface and felt it swing open with unexpected ease. She passed through the hole, carrying her passenger as well. After setting him down safely on the dark stone floor, she landed by his side and closed the trapdoor.

A sudden tearing sound ripped the air. A tall, treelike figure studded with knobby blue eyes reached through the transparent dome above them. As the appendage approached, Kate noticed that sunny yellow now replaced its former bone white color.

"Thika," said Kate, gazing into as many of the round blue eyes as she could.

"Kaitlyn," the watery voice replied. "This time, hssshwhshhh, I have no need to ask you for the password."

"You sound stronger than before."

"Indeed I am," sloshed the many-eyed creature. "As are the other Guardians. Though we are told much of the forest land outside the crater has been destroyed, shwshhh, the Wicked One's power is spent. Already our lake grows cooler. And all this, whhshhh, thanks to you." Thika swayed back and forth with a series of quick undulations. "I only wish the temperature would never rise again."

"Yes, I know," answered Kate solemnly. "I can't do anything about that now."

"You have already done, hhsssh, more than you know," gurgled the Guardian. "For by saving our world in this time you have given the creatures of that later time a chance to save themselves. Hsh-whshh. Let us hope they are wise enough to do it."

Kate made no reply.

"Hey," piped up Kandeldandel, tapping his flute impatiently on his leg. "Can't you talk some other time? We have some important business up there."

"Whshhh, I see doing battle has not cured you of cheekiness," said Thika sharply. "But this time you are forgiven. I see you are injured, shhhwhsh, and the Chieftain and Chieftess await."

"And besides," added Kandeldandel, "I'm hungry."

The knobby appendage wrapped itself around the waists of the two travelers, avoiding the Tinnani's drooping wing. Instinctively, Kate pulled the sphere close to her chest. She barely had a chance to inhale before she was being transported through the deep blue waters of the lake. Upward Thika carried them, until the dome seemed nothing more than a distant bubble below them surrounded by several gangling yellow creatures.

She heard the tearing sound once more, then suddenly she could breathe again. As she turned to Kandeldandel, sitting in a puddle beside her own at the base of the narrow stone stairway, Thika the Guardian bent low before her in what could only be a bow.

"Thank you, shhwsh," the familiar voice sloshed. "Though you have only two eyes, hssshhwsh, you are now an honorary Guardian."

"You're welcome," said Kate, electing to take the words as a compliment.

With a rip and a pop, the many eyes of Thika disappeared down the hole in the middle of the stone floor. As Kate, dripping wet, rose to her feet, the torch lighting the stairway immediately swelled in luminosity. Kandeldandel stood and shook his feathers like a wet dog, then gestured to Kate to lead the way.

Up the spiraling stairs she climbed, Kandeldandel on her heels. He began to hum a playful tune, no less melodious than that of a meadowlark but with the deeper resonance of an owl. As the ascending torches flamed more brightly, Kate could see the enormously detailed carvings in the black stone of the stairwell. A pictorial history of the Tinnanis since the beginning of time unfolded before her eyes, a tale of mountains rising and forests blooming, of creatures birthing and living and dying, of struggle and harmony, of great migrations, of simple homes under the roots of trees, of loyalty and betrayal, of season following season time and time again.

Nearing the top of the stairs, she heard a faint tapping sound. As she rounded the final spiral, it grew steadily louder, until with a start she discovered its source. A lone Tinnani, shorter and plumper than Kandeldandel, was at work carving a new scene into the stone. He stood upon wooden scaffolding, one chisel in each hand and a sharp-tipped implement held between his teeth. Turning briefly to Kate he grunted in greeting before returning to his painstaking labor.

Peering over his folded wings, Kate examined the new petroglyph. She saw a huge mountain exploding, with the unmistakable image of Gashra raising his arms wrathfully deep inside the volcano. Animals, birds, and people fled from the fiery outpouring of lava, while towering trees collapsed and burned all around. Then, to her surprise, she spotted a small human figure, joined by a flute-bearing Tinnani, scurrying to escape the cataclysm. In the human figure's hands rested a radiant sphere, drawn larger than life, bearing a jagged crack across its surface.

"Can't you make me taller?" asked Kandeldandel, scrutinizing the scene from below the scaffolding.

The craftsman scowled at him, then went back to work. Kate grinned at Kandeldandel before continuing up the last few stairs. As she topped the stairway she confronted the entrance to the great chamber. She realized instantly how little of it she had seen on her first visit.

Lit by powerful torches, the rounded ceiling revealed an intricate engraving of a single majestic tree, whose many

branches bore fruits and flowers of all sizes and descriptions. Its stature reminded Kate of the Ancient One,
although she had never heard of any tree bearing such
a wide variety of fruits. Then at once, she understood.
Instead of bearing the normal fruits of the forest, this gargantuan tree supported all the living beings ever found in
this world. Thousands upon thousands of creatures, from a
tiny ant to a great woolly mammoth rested upon the
branches. Elk and spider, butterfly and bear, mushroom and
hornet, fern and salmon, Tinnani and human, each held a
particular place in the pattern. Each stood as a separate
individual, each stood as a member of the whole. The num-
berless branches of this tree wove back and forth in a complex interlocking design, bristling with energy and vitality.
For this was the Tree of Life.

As she proceeded toward the chamber, she walked beside
the circular stone fountain in the center of the floor.
Its meager trickle instantly shot skyward in the form of an
energetic geyser. Instead of clear water, however, the
splashing fountain radiated a spectrum of intense colors.
Flashing prismatic hues in every droplet, it shimmered like
a cascade of liquid light.

"The Rainbow Fountain is restored," said Kandeldandel
approvingly.

Kate nodded, but already her attention was caught by the
assemblage of white-feathered figures she could see through
the nearby archway of inlaid yellow and black stone. Passing beneath the archway, she entered a high-ceilinged
chamber whose walls displayed a repeating motif of tall
trees tended by soaring Tinnanis. As she entered, the flickering torches suspended from the chandelier flamed strongly,
revealing the careful craftsmanship of the walls as well as
the recessed stone ceiling, a vaulting dome of glittering
concentric circles. After long absence, bright light again
graced the central chamber of Ho Shantero.

Tinnanis filled the chamber, many more than the last
time Kate stood within its walls. Some wore streaks of
gray or red on their white plumage, some stood slightly

taller than the rest of the crowd, some carried infants not much bigger than Arc upon their shoulders. All of them hushed with a brief fluttering of feathers when Kate stepped into the room. Kandeldandel, strutting behind her, puffed out his chest and held his head high. Watching the pair with wide owl eyes, the Tinnanis parted as they approached, clearing a pathway that led to the three carved thrones at the far end of the room.

The rounded body of the Chieftain filled the central throne of white whalebone, while the more slender Chieftess sat erect in the transparent throne to his left. The crystalline seat to the right remained empty, but next to it a frail white form lay on the bench of polished black stone.

As Kate drew nearer, the reclining form seemed to solidify, to harden before her eyes. Fanona. She was tall, like the Chieftess, with the same large, knowing eyes, and two small silvery tufts protruding from the top of her head. The Chieftess glanced in the direction of her daughter, whereupon a slow smile crossed her face.

Kate stood before the Chieftain and Chieftess, bowed slightly, then held in her outstretched arms the glowing red sphere. The Chieftain, dangling several mousetails from his mouth, reached his own hands toward it, quivering with anticipation.

"The Broken Touchstone," announced Kate.

"Dewiffud mby Kootwyn, mmmff, da Conquawa, mmmff," replied the Chieftain.

"It's best not to make pronouncements with your mouth full, dear," chided the Chieftess gently.

Glancing at her sharply, the Chieftain swallowed with all the subtlety of a croaking bullfrog. Then he wriggled in his throne and repeated, "Delivered by Kaitlyn the Conqueror."

"Call me Kate, please," she said as she handed him the sphere.

The Chieftain took it carefully in his hands, talons retracted so as not to scratch its surface, and studied it momentarily. Then he lifted it into position at the top of his throne. As it came into contact with the cup-shaped pedestal, the Broken Touchstone flashed brilliantly, causing the assembled Tinnanis in the chamber to cluck and hoot in admiration.

"Guests," bellowed the Chieftain. "Bring in the guests." Pausing for a second, he added, "And bring some more oysters while you're at it." Turning to Kate, he said, "We are most grateful to you."

"And to you," declared the Chieftess, looking straight at Kandeldandel.

At her words, Kandeldandel shifted nervously, dropping his flute with a clatter on the stone floor. Seeing this, the Chieftain closed his eyes and shook his white head in dismay.

At length he peered again at Kate. "You have saved our realm from destruction," he continued. "The Wicked One is defeated, the Touchstone is returned, and most precious of all," he said with a wave toward the black stone bench, "our daughter Fanona is nearly revived." Shifting his gaze to Kandeldandel, he studied the musician for a moment, his face showing both amazement and pride. Then he declared, "And you, Kandeldandel Zinzin, have brought honor both to yourself and your proud family."

The musician straightened his back and stood as tall as he could manage. This time he did not drop the flute. He bowed to the enthroned Tinnanis and hooted softly, "I was glad to be of service, Your Wingedness."

The chamber instantly echoed with a loud chorus of cheers, hoots, and hurrahs that shook the chandelier. Tinnanis bellowed and screeched, celebrating their great victory. They danced together in small circles, tossing loose feathers into the air. Then the Chieftess, who had been pensively fingering the string of gleaming pearls around her neck, snapped her jaw and raised her ruby-studded scepter. Silence descended.

"We are joyous," said the Chieftess in her clear, ringing voice, "for all the reasons you have heard. Yet we cannot forget that our joy is also mixed with sadness." She gazed again about the room, with the expression of someone who knows both triumph and tragedy. "While we cherish our victory, it came only at great cost. Much of the lowland forest beyond the walls of our crater is now lost, buried beneath a blanket of molten stone. Regeneration will require many lifetimes, and our friends who died cannot ever be returned. Many of our favorite places are wiped away forever."

She sighed, as her round eyes scanned the many faces filling the room. "And we have also lost something else. None of you, not even the youngest, will ever live to see the final healing of the Touchstone. The missing Fragment will never be found, for the only clues to its whereabouts were destroyed with the Stick of Fire."

The Chieftess focused on Kate, who averted her eyes. "Your sacrifice was great, but it was even greater than you know. For with the loss of the Fragment, the Touchstone must remain forever diminished. Though our daughter Fanona grows stronger by the minute, and will one day assume her place on the throne, she will never nurture the forest with the power that was prophesied."

She glanced toward the Touchstone. "But saddest of all is the glimpse of the future that I have seen in my dreams. Though the Halamis who survived will leave, seeking new lands to the south, other humans will eventually arrive. They will exist here, yet not live here. The forest to them will be only a tool, a meal to be consumed. They will not know it as a friend."

Ruffling her white wings, the Chieftess turned once again to Kate. "As the people without wonder arrive, I am afraid that the Tinnanis will be forced to leave. For, just like the trees, we cannot survive very long in such a world. Though I do not know with certainty that we will need to depart, my heart has little hope that we can stay.

"All that will remain are a few tokens of our past, such as this island, which will stay afloat for a while after we have abandoned it. Yet when the power of the Wicked One rises again several centuries from now, do not expect to find any Tinnanis residing in the realm of Ho Shantero." She hooted once softly. "Though I have lived now for many thousands of years, I never have known a time of such grief."

Kate, along with the rest of the room, stood in stony silence. A grass-caped Tinnani flew to the throne of the Chieftain bearing a tray of raw oysters. Uncharacteristically, he pushed them aside, grumbling something about indigestion. At that moment, two familiar faces appeared in the crowd, pushing their way toward the front.

"Laioni!" Kate cried, reaching to hug her friend tightly.

"You're safe," bubbled Laioni. "I thought I'd never see you again."

Kate looked deep into her smiling eyes, then at the bandage around her thigh. "I thought I'd never see *you* again."

"You should not have burned the stick."

"I did what I did," answered Kate.

Then the joy in Laioni's face evaporated, and she pulled back from the embrace. "Most of my people, you know, were killed in the eruption."

"And your mother?"

Laioni's eyes grew misty. "My mother too. And my grandmother and baby brother. They should have stayed here in the crater instead of trying to return to the village. My father, they say, has survived, but he is busy organizing the few others who lived so we can find a new home. Almost everyone I knew is gone."

Kate said softly, "They have joined Toru."

The Halami girl stiffened. "Did you see him?"

"I—I don't know, for sure."

"Then," said Laioni, "I will keep hoping he is alive. Perhaps we will find each other again, even if it's a long time from now."

Kate viewed her lovingly. "I guess anything is possible."

Laioni's head drooped. "It's not possible to bring Monga back to life. I wish he didn't have to die."

Hugging her again, Kate could only say, "I know."

"He loved me not like a dog, but like a brother."

"Or," whispered Kate, "like a sister."

Though her vision was clouded, Kate then caught sight of Jody, standing uncomfortably in a sea of Tinnanis. He no longer wore an arm sling, but his face was lined with pain. Without letting go of Laioni, she said, "You were great up there."

The boy shrugged, pushing the stray locks of red hair off his forehead. "A whole lot of good it did. Without that stick of yours, we'll never get back to where we belong. Now we're stuck forever in this crazy owls' nest."

The Chieftain glared at him.

"Sorry," said Kate, tugged herself by the thought of home.

Jody, seeing her consternation, said, "Look, don't be too hard on yourself, okay? You did it to save somebody's life, and that's important. More important than anything Honus Wagner ever did."

Kate almost smiled. She released Laioni and stepped toward him. "Thanks," she said quietly.

"Sure," he replied, his eyes fixed on hers.

Feeling a sudden surge of gratitude, Kate gave him an awkward hug. "You're a real friend," she said, then backed away again.

"Oh, I don't know." Blushing, he thrust his hands into the pockets of his jeans. "Oh, yeah," he said, clearly hoping to change the subject. "I thought you might want this." He pulled out a charred, jagged object. "It was all that was left of the stick when the fire went out. From inside the handle, I think. Thought you might want to keep it, though I'm not sure why."

As she took the object in her hand, Kate noticed a tiny glint of red beneath its blackened exterior. She rubbed it against her sweatshirt, revealing more of the true color. Suddenly, she gasped, closing her hand around it. Rushing toward the Chieftain's throne, she darted to its base and reached for the Broken Touchstone.

"What in the world?" sputtered the Chieftain. "Put that back!"

"Just a minute," answered Kate. Holding the Touchstone in one hand and the charred remains of the handle in the other, she brought them together, fitting the object into the crack in the sphere's surface. It slid inside perfectly.

A burst of bright red light and the sound of a distant explosion filled the chamber as the two pieces fused into one. Lifting the sphere above her head for all to see, Kate declared, "The Touchstone is healed."

A simultaneous exclamation of awe arose from the Tinnanis, like the breath of a unified being. Then from somewhere at the back of the room, several deep horns blew triumphantly. "The Touchstone is healed," chanted many voices at once. "The Touchstone is healed."

As Kate replaced the glowing sphere atop the throne, her eyes met those of the Chieftess, whose countenance now bore a new lightness. "So it was in the stick all the time," said the Tinnani in wonderment. Softly, she recited the words of the ancient prophecy:

> Fragment, object of desire,
> Shall be found anew.
> One who bears the Stick of Fire
> Holds the power true.

"This is a day to remember," announced the Chieftain. "Let there be a feast! A feast like none ever seen before in the history of my people." Above the cheers from the crowd, he commanded, "Break out my entire storehouse of delicacies!"

"Yes, Your Wingedness," replied the Tinnani wearing a long cape, before flying off toward one of the side tunnels.

Yet despite the rising tide of joy around her, Kate stood alone and detached. For although this place and time now bathed in the light of the unified Touchstone, her longing for her own place and time only increased.

Laioni, perceiving her sadness, came closer. "We have lost many, you and I." Then, taking Kate's hand in her own, she suggested, "Come with me, as one of my people. Join the Halamis—the few that are left—and help us find our new home."

Kate looked at her soulfully. "I will come with you," she said at last. "But my home will never be here, now. My true home I'll never see again."

"It is a pity," spoke the Chieftess, who had been listening. "The very act which found the Fragment, lost for so many ages, is the same act which denies you the ability to return to your own time. For when you destroyed the Stick of Fire, you destroyed its power to travel through time. There is no other way."

"No," declared another voice, resonant and melodic. "There is another way."

Kate turned to see Fanona, her strength now fully restored, standing atop the bench of black stone. She spread her wings to their fullest, her feathers gleaming whiter than purest quartz. The two silvery tufts atop her head made her height, already considerable for a Tinnani, even more dramatic. Her wide yellow eyes, deeply thoughtful, roamed from her mother to her father to the Touchstone and finally to Kate.

"You are right," said Fanona, "to say that the Stick of Fire is no more. Yet because it was destroyed in an act of love, new power has been created. As the words carved into its shaft foretold:

> *Fire of greed shall destroy;*
> *Fire of love shall create."*

She lowered her wings. "The power that once resided in the stick now dwells in the Touchstone itself."

"Really?" asked Kate. "You mean I can go home?"

"You can?" demanded Jody. "How? When?"

"The Touchstone," answered Kate, indicating the luminous sphere. "She says it has the power."

"And she is right," declared the Chieftess, looking proudly

at her daughter. "Yes, just as the prophecy at her birth was right. She saw what I failed to see, that the fire of love can create."

"How do we get back?" asked Jody.

The Chieftain, eyeing the boy with disdain, raised his voice. "Tell us now, Fanona, how can the Touchstone send these people home?"

Fanona emitted a flowing, rippling sound, more like the gurgle of a brook than the call of an owl. "All it requires is the help of one being whose life stretches unbroken from this time into the future." She contemplated for a moment, then asked Kate, "Do you know any such being?"

"The Ancient One," she replied. "The redwood tree that brought us here."

"And so shall it take you home," declared Fanona.

Suddenly remembering the tree's imminent peril, Kate blurted, "But what if it's cut—killed, before we get back?"

"Then you will be stranded in a timeless prison, a shadow land cut off from time as you know it." Fanona concentrated her round eyes on Kate. "It is a serious risk. Are you sure you are willing to take it?"

"Stay here," whispered Laioni. "Stay here with me."

Kate shook her head. "I can't, Laioni. I want to go back, and I'll take my chances."

"Me too," said Jody.

"Then let us fly to the redwoods," urged Fanona. "There is no time to waste."

32

Iaioni's promise

LAST to arrive at the redwood grove was the Chieftain. Flapping his white wings vigorously, he landed beside the small bonfire built by some of his attendants, who had already started roasting a variety of delicacies over the hot coals.

"Don't forget the chives," he ordered as he folded his wings and straightened the silver band on his head. Then, facing his wife, he said, "Sorry to keep you waiting. Had to check on the preparations for tonight's feast."

"You're forgiven," replied the Chieftess. "Never let it be said that Chieftain Hockeltock de Notnot ever neglected his culinary duties."

Kate detected a note of resignation in her remark, but the Chieftain did not seem to notice. He stepped over to Fanona, who was seated on one of the burly roots of the Ancient One, gazing into the radiant Touchstone.

"It is good to see you well again," he hooted softly.

Fanona looked up and smiled at him. "It is good to be well, even though I do not yet have enough strength to bear the thought of leaving Ho Shantero."

"Don't trouble yourself with such thoughts now," answered the Chieftain. "You won't have to do that for a while yet."

"It is still too soon," said Fanona, ruffling her white wings. "I can only hope that the new people, the ones in my mother's dreams, might somehow come to change their ways. Then perhaps we will not have to leave at all."

Turning to Kate, the Chieftain asked, "Well? Are you ready to begin your voyage?"

"I'm ready," she declared. Then she faced Jody, who stood listlessly by the trunk of the great redwood, and called, "Are you set to go?"

He nodded his head, but did not look at her.

"He is going, isn't he?" asked the Chieftain.

"He's going," said Kate. "Something's bugging him, though."

"Perhaps he wishes he could stay for the feast," chuckled the Chieftain, tapping his belt buckle with his finger talons.

"Sorry we'll have to miss it. I'm sure it'll be great."

"That's all right," replied the plump Tinnani. "Leaves more food for the rest of us."

"I'm afraid I won't be bringing you any more peppermints," Kate said. "I mean, without the stick, I'm not going to be doing much time traveling."

The Chieftain frowned. "I hadn't thought about that."

"You might be surprised," said the Chieftess, stepping closer to Kate. "You might find another way to visit us. There is more than one way to travel through time. In any case, if you should ever return, you know you are always welcome."

"With peppermints, of course," added her husband hopefully.

Kate turned to face Kandeldandel, whose injured wing was thoroughly wrapped in bandages. "I wish you could come with me. You'd love some of the flute music that gets written in the next few centuries."

The half grin broadened slightly. "I'm sure. But I wish

you didn't have to go at all. I mean, what happens when I start to forget all those baseball rules you explained while we were walking in the tunnel?"

"That's another reason to find a new little owl for your shoulder," answered Kate. "He'll help you remember." She paused. "And when I forget how to make those owl calls you taught me, what do I do then?"

"That's easy," Kandeldandel answered. "Just practice them. The way I practice my flute."

He lifted his flute to his lips and started to play a sweet, prancing melody. Without any warning, a loud commotion arose from the Chieftain's attendants preparing the roasted delicacies. Kandeldandel, oblivious to any sounds other than his own music, continued to play jauntily.

Then the voice of one of the attendant Tinnanis rose above the clamor: "But how could the fire go out? There isn't even any wind!"

Kandeldandel's eyes widened and he shot a remorseful glance at Kate. He quickly lowered his flute, and the bonfire sprang to life once again. Cries of amazement came from the attendants.

"What luck," said the musician disgustedly.

Laughing, Kate whispered to him, "Don't worry. The Chieftain will get enough to eat tonight."

Kandeldandel grinned at her, bobbing his head from side to side. Then he stopped, his expression suddenly serious. "I'm going to miss you," he said. "Never thought I'd feel this way about, of all things, a human being. And it looks like this is our last conversation. Even though I hope to still be around in five hundred years, all the Tinnanis will probably have left the crater by then."

"Maybe you can sign up for some sort of special duty that would keep you here after everyone else," she suggested, trying to maintain a lighthearted tone.

"Doubtful," answered Kandeldandel. He moved nearer, then touched her arm lightly with his good wing. "No hugs, now," he cautioned sternly. "You're likely to break my other wing."

Kate, unable to find any words, merely ran a finger over the soft feathers of his shoulder.

At that, Kandeldandel turned and walked over to Jody, still standing off to the side. The Tinnani extended a hand, saying in his bass voice, "You did all right."

To Jody, his words sounded only like deep hooting. Yet the boy lifted his head and studied Kandeldandel thoughtfully. Slowly, reluctantly, he, too, extended a hand. They clasped, boy and Tinnani, and shook briefly.

Kate joined them as their hands separated. She looked quizzically at Jody. "Something's on your mind, I can tell."

Pushing back the loose locks of red hair, Jody said, "I just, well, I just . . ."

"Yes?"

"I just want you to know something."

"What's that?"

"I know you're gonna try to stop them from cutting down these redwoods."

"If they're still standing," Kate replied.

"Well," continued Jody, "I just hope you don't expect me to help."

"No, I don't expect that. All I ask is that you stay out of my way."

Jody gazed down at his feet, saying nothing.

"We'd better get going," said Kate. "If the Ancient One gets cut before we get back, the time tunnel will shut and this whole conversation's pointless."

"Before you go," spoke a familiar voice, "I want to say good-bye."

Kate spun around to face a dark-eyed Halami girl. They studied each other for a long moment. Finally, Kate reached into her pocket and pulled out her well-worn Swiss army knife. "Here. This is for you. It might come in handy."

Laioni hesitated, but when Kate pushed the knife toward her, she finally accepted it. "Your special tool," she said gratefully. Then, in a hopeful voice, she added, "Perhaps you can use the one carried by Aunt Lemony."

Kate smiled, choosing not to correct her.

"I have no gift for you," Laioni said somberly. "Only a promise."

"A promise?"

Laioni's features hardened with determination. "I promise to teach all the Halami ways I know to any children who survived the eruption. They will learn our songs, our stories, and our blessings. They will teach their own children, who will teach their children, forever into the future. That way, perhaps, in your world many, many years from now, there might be a few small reminders of the Halamis left to greet you."

"I won't need any reminders," said Kate. "But I know you'll do as you say. And I'll think of you often, even though I'll never get to see you again."

Laioni cocked her head to one side. She gazed intently at Kate for several seconds. "You cannot be certain of that."

At that moment, a lilting song filled the air. Its source was Fanona, still seated upon a massive root. As she lifted her resonant voice, all conversation ceased. Even the wind seemed to hold its breath, listening to the young Tinnani whose name meant Song That Never Dies.

> *The feather falls*
> *drifting down through the clouds*
> *hoping to fly*
> *Away . . . under moon under sun*
>
> *Touching the boughs*
> *reaching upward like arms*
> *seeking to fly*
> *Afar . . . over trees over peaks*
>
> *To find the ground*
> *landing soft as a seed*
> *again to fly*
> *Above . . . beyond years beyond stars.*

As her last note melted away, Fanona gracefully rose from her seat. Bearing the glowing Touchstone in her hands, she positioned herself just outside the hollow of the Ancient One. "It is time," she declared.

Then Kate heard a chorus of gentle hooting above her head. She looked up to see a dozen or more owls, of several different sizes and colorings, resting in the lower branches of the great redwood. Some of the owls ruffled their wings and bobbed their heads, while others sat motionless on their perches. All of them watched the scene below with wide, understanding eyes.

She turned for the last time to Laioni. "Good-bye," she said, her voice barely audible above the calls of the assembled owls.

"Halma-dru," came the reply.

Kate stepped to the base of the massive tree. As she passed in front of the Chieftain, he tugged her sleeve and whispered, "Don't forget what to bring, if you ever come back."

Nodding, she ducked into the hollow. She sat there, smelling once again the tree's moist resins, as Jody entered. He glanced at her doubtfully before squeezing in beside her. She paid no attention, concentrating instead on her echoing memory of Laioni's final word.

The owls' hooting abruptly ceased. A sudden flash of red light filled the hollow. Kate felt herself whirling, whirling impossibly fast, before she lost consciousness.

33

deep roots

KATE awoke, yet her body slept on. Her conscious mind swelled with strange new sensations, alert and aware, while her skin and bones and muscles felt numb, or worse than numb. Her body felt nothing at all, not even the absence of feeling. It was detached. Departed. Gone.

"Where am I?" she cried, and her words rang emptily in the airy darkness.

"What happened?" she called again.

No answer came. She felt as if she were floating somehow. Blackness surrounded her. She could see nothing, hear nothing, feel nothing. Not even the pulse of her own heartbeat broke the omnipresent silence.

Then, a scent. Barely present, neither far away nor near at hand. Elusive. Subtle. Tingling her, tickling her. Fresh and potent, fragrant as crushed pine needles. A moist smell, ripe with resins. Flowing through and around her, holding her essence like water in a cup. The scent of the forest, so strong that it seemed alive.

"Where am I?"

Still no answer. No sound at all.

And then, echoing out of the fragrant air itself, she heard a voice. Deeper than the deepest double bass, the voice vibrated from both above and below.

"I hold you, small friend. I hold you and protect you."

It was the voice of the Ancient One.

Kate's consciousness whirled. Could it be true? Was her mind, or whatever was left of her mind, just playing tricks?

"Tell me your wish," reverberated the voice. The smell of moist resins grew stronger.

"I—I want to go home," she answered. "To my own time. To the twenty-first century."

The air around her shuddered, as if a powerful wind had shaken the redwood down to the roots. "Are you certain? That is a time of great sadness, great pain."

"It's my time," she answered, "and I want to go there."

Silence ensued, tense and uneasy, until the Ancient One spoke again. "Not all creatures who stand upright and vertical know they are connected to everything else. Some of your kind know only their loneliness. They have lost their own roots, drifting aimlessly as fireweed seeds. They are angry, and might hurt you if you go there."

"I know," she answered. "But they might hurt Aunt Melanie, too, and I've got to stop them. I've got to." She felt a piercing, knifelike pain slice through her being. "And they'll hurt you too. They'll try to cut you down! You've got to take me back. Now. Before it's too late."

The tree seemed to sigh deeply, and she could almost feel lacelike branches stirring around her. "Perhaps. Perhaps. But first you must go deeper within me. You must understand things you never understood before. It will be hard for you, very hard. For you are of a race that has forgotten how to stand still. To stop all running, all racing, all searching—and instead to sink your roots in a single place, to watch the seasons roll past by the thousands. And to stand tall and straight, anchored equally in earth and sky, to bend with the wind but not to break, to bear your own weight gladly."

As she listened to the low, richly toned voice, Kate began to hear something else, something even deeper than the voice itself. It was a rushing, coursing sound, like the surging of several rivers. She realized with a start that this was the sound of resins moving through the trunk and limbs of the tree. And, strangely, through her own self as well.

Then she heard something more. With all her concentration, she listened to a distant gurgling sound. It came from far below her, rising from the deepest roots of the tree. They were drinking, drawing sustenance from the soil.

Another sound joined with the rest, completing the pattern. Like an intricate fugue, it ran from the tips of the remotest needles all the way down the massive column of heartwood and into the roots of the redwood. Back and forth, in and out, always changing, always the same. This was the sound, Kate realized at last, of the tree itself breathing. The sound of air being cleansed for all the creatures of the forest. The sound of life being exchanged for life, breath for breath.

"Great tree," said Kate in wonder "I feel so young, and you are so very, very old."

A full, resonant laughter filled the air, stirring even the sturdiest branches. "I am not so young as you, perhaps, but old I surely am not. The mountains, they are old. The oceans, they are old. The sun is older still, as are the stars. And how old is the cloud, whose body is made from the vapors of an earlier cloud that once watered the soil, then flowed to the river, then rose again into the sky? I am part of the very first seed, planted in the light of the earliest dawn. And so are you. So perhaps we are neither older nor younger, but truly the same age."

As she listened to the rhythmic breathing of the tree, Kate felt herself beginning to breathe in unison. A sense of her body was slowly returning, a body that bent and swayed with the fragrant wind. Every element of her being stretched upward and downward, pulling taller and straighter without end. Her arms became supple, sinewy limbs; her feet drove deeply into the soil and anchored there. She felt tall and strong, centered and surrounded, sturdy and whole— content beyond human experience.

A sweep of time swirled past, seconds into hours, days into seasons, years into centuries. Spring: azaleas blossoming and pink sorrel flowering. Summer: bright light scattering through the morning mist, scents of wild ginger and licorice fern. Autumn: harsh winds shaking branches, gentle winds bearing geese. Winter: ceaseless rains, frosty gales, more rains brewing. Again and again, again and again. Seasons without end, years beyond count.

Fire! Flames scar her outer bark, charring even her heartwood. But she survives, standing tall, saddened by the loss of a few less sturdy friends. Winds, powerful winds. Healing the scar, she grows new girth above the burn to balance better her colossal weight. Near to the ground, a radial crack develops, very small at first, becoming a home for generations of insects and a restaurant for generations of birds. Young redwoods sprout at her base, yearning for life, full of green vitality.

White rot infects her, stinging with pain, lasting many cycles of seasons. Winds and rain. Winds and rain. Hail as big as spruce cones. Internal stresses creep into the body of a large lower branch until, with the next wild wind, it splinters and breaks apart, rocking her very roots. *Hooo-hooo, hooo-hooo.* Fire again! This time much more is lost—bark, sapwood, heartwood. Some of the old fire scar is obliterated by the new. Healing, waiting, balancing in the shifting soil, standing sturdy throughout. Winter, spring, summer, autumn. New growth works its way across the scar.

A lone Tinnani stands beneath her boughs, spreads his white wings in awe. Welcome, Little One. The creature lowers his head sadly, departs from the grove. Gale winds, broken branches. Mist, mist, mist. An earthquake shatters the stillness one winter morning. As the earth trembles, the great roots grip tightly, feeling the strain, yet hold firm. *Hooo-hooo, hooo-hooo.* Rhododendrons, azaleas, salmonberry, huckleberry.

Five-finger fern takes root at her base, mingling with the maidenhair. On a peaceful day, the mist spirals gracefully skyward. A doe and her spotted fawn step serenely into the glade, nibbling at the ferns.

Then, suddenly: A sound unlike any other sound ever heard fills the forest. Piercing, screeching, banishing forever the centuries of stillness. A shudder, a scream of pain erupts from her whole being. *Stop! Stop, please. Go away, leave in peace.*

But the pain only deepens. The sound grows louder.

It is the sound of chain saws.

34

new light
in the forest

DAZEDLY, Kate shook her head. The ridge of hard wood pushing against her back told her she possessed a human body again. Instinctively, she reached to touch her long braid, feeling the strands of hair between her fingers. In the dim light she could see Jody seated across from her, looking rather dazed himself.

The hollow. They were once again in the hollow. The gargantuan trunk of the Ancient One embraced them both. She could still feel the watery breathing of the redwood pulsing through her veins. She could, even now, hear the rumble of its deep voice echoing in her ears.

Then she heard something else. A whining, screeching, screaming sound.

"No!" she cried, leaping to her feet and springing out of the hollow.

Billy, wearing his weather-beaten hard hat, held his chain saw firmly as it tore into the flesh of the Ancient One. His red T-shirt, wet with perspiration, hung untucked around his waist. He leaned into the saw, spraying chips of bark and sawdust into the air.

Even as her eyes adjusted to the light outside the hollow, Kate instantly perceived the plight of the great tree. A huge notch had already been cut in the trunk, opposite the side where Billy now worked. Yet she hesitated, feeling helpless to stop the big man. Looking around desperately for anyone or anything that might help, she could see no more than a few half-melted hailstones on the ground, evidence that the storm had passed some time ago. But she saw no one else in the grove. No sign of Aunt Melanie, nor even another logger.

"Stop!" she cried at the top of her lungs, trying to attract Billy's attention. "Please, stop."

But he could not hear her over the roar of the chain saw. Sawdust continued to fly, as he ripped ever deeper into the trunk of the redwood.

Then she spotted a two-gallon can of gasoline, resting on an exposed root a few feet behind Billy. She lunged for it. Lifting the can with both hands, she raised it over her head. Stepping as close to Billy as she dared, she threw it at his broad back.

"Oww," cried the surprised logger. He straightened up, yanked the saw out of the tree trunk, cut the engine, and whirled around. Seeing the gasoline can at his feet, his eyes flashed with anger and immediately focused on Kate.

"What do you think you're doing?" he demanded.

"Stop cutting," pleaded Kate. "You can't cut down this tree."

"I can cut anything I want," retorted Billy. "Now get out of my way. It's dangerous this close, and you're gonna get hurt."

As he placed his heavy boot on the engine housing, preparing to start the saw again, Kate stepped closer. "Please stop. Please."

"Out of my way," the man growled. "I've got work to do. I'd still have help, too, if that old aunt of yours hadn't talked Frank into convincing the other guys to quit." He grasped the handle of the starter cord. "Never saw such a bunch of chicken hearts in my life. Those that weren't scared off by the storm—just because Harry got too close to some lightning bolt—were scared off by Frank's baloney. Can't believe they bought that line about not doing anybody any good. Even Sly fell for it." He shook his head in dismay. "Well, that leaves me, and I'm gonna get at least a few of these mothers before the day is out. Already close to finishing off this big one here."

"But—"

"Get away!" commanded Billy.

Kate stood immobile.

"I said, get away." Billy dropped the starter cord and pulled her by the arm to the other side of the grove. "Now stay here."

"I'll watch her for you," said someone walking toward them.

"Jody!" exclaimed Kate. "He's going to—"

"Shut up," said the boy with a scowl. Turning to Billy, he declared, "I'll make sure she won't bother you."

"All right," grumbled the logger. "But don't mess it up like you did last time."

Jody's face reddened. "I won't." Then, as Billy turned to go, Jody caught his arm. "But first, can I start your saw for you? I always liked that big model, and my granddad never lets me start his."

"Oh, all right," replied Billy, striding back to the tree. "Just make it quick."

"But Jody," cried Kate. "You can't!"

"Wanna bet?" replied Jody, sprinting over to the chain saw. He placed his boot against the housing for support. Then, leaving one hand in his pocket, he grabbed the handle with the other hand and started to extend the cord.

"No, don't," cried Kate, running several paces closer. Billy then turned toward her, eyeing her sternly, and she froze. Glowering at Jody, she muttered, "I should have known."

Testing the tension on the cord, Jody stretched it slowly away from the housing. Six, twelve, eighteen inches.

"C'mon, hurry," said Billy impatiently.

"Don't," Kate shouted in desperation.

At that instant Jody pulled his other hand from his pocket, clasping his pocket knife. He quickly pulled open the blade. Then, with a swift downward swipe, he slashed the starter rope in two. The cut cord snapped back into the housing.

"Hey," exclaimed Billy, staring in disbelief at the now-inoperable saw. "What the hell are you doing?"

"Just helping out," replied the red-haired boy, smirking as he stuffed the handle and most of the starter cord into his pocket.

Furious, Billy started after him. Jody leaped over a fallen branch and dashed as fast as he could into the forest with the big man on his heels.

Kate felt like cheering. Before she could utter a sound, however, Billy halted his pursuit after just a few steps. He spun to his right, stooped over, and lifted from the bushes another chain saw, evidently left behind by another logger fleeing from the storm. Cursing to himself, he stepped on the housing, yanked the starter cord, and immediately gunned the engine. Without even glancing at Kate, he strode purposefully back to the Ancient One and plunged the chain saw deep into its trunk.

As the blade tore into the body of the tree, Kate suddenly felt a searing pain in her side. Gasping, she saw that Billy had pierced the innermost core of the trunk. As he drove his saw deeper, her pain intensified, as if a serrated knife had sliced into her ribs, pulling back and forth, ripping at her abdomen. She stumbled, then tripped on a rock just behind her, twisting her knee badly as she fell.

"Ehhh," she moaned, rolling to one side. She tried to stand, but her leg buckled underneath her. "Aunt Melanie," she wailed, as the pain in both her knee and her torso grew worse. "Help me." But her words were lost in the din of the chain saw.

Oblivious to her agony, Billy pushed the saw blade farther into the heart of the tree. Sawdust spewed in all directions. The towering redwood leaned slightly in the direction of the notch in its trunk—and in the direction of Kate.

Meanwhile the pain in her abdomen swelled steadily. Writhing on the ground, she thought she would pass out. Then, all of a sudden, the pain ceased. She lay on her back, breathing heavily, utterly exhausted. But for the ongoing throbbing in her knee, she was hardly sure she was still alive. Above her she saw the majestic boughs that still felt like limbs of her own, supported by the massive trunk that linked earth to sky, past to present. With all her heart she hoped that the tree might survive this assault, just as it had survived the assaults of so many fires, storms, and earthquakes in the past. She tried to sit up, but was still too weak to move.

Slowly, the redwood began swaying from side to side. With a tremble that reached from its roots to its tallest canopy, it tottered on its base, wobbling precariously. The bulging roots, coated with sawdust, held the soil as firmly as ever, but could no longer support the weight of the great tree. Yet still it stood. This tree would not go down easily.

At last Billy pulled out his saw, cut the engine, and backed quickly away from the trunk. Only a thin shaft of hinge wood remained of the once-sturdy column. Although Kate was now much nearer to the tree than himself, he could not see her from his new position. He watched with satisfaction as the redwood tilted still farther to one side. Holding itself high to the very last, it seemed to stand suspended by the sky alone for a long and perilous moment.

Then, in slow motion, the Ancient One leaned, leaned some more, leaned even more. Billy stepped sideways to get a better view, when suddenly he caught sight of Kate, doing her best to crawl clumsily away from the tree.

"Move!" he shouted.

"I'm trying," she panted, dragging herself across the ground.

Without pausing to think, Billy ran toward her, even as the hinge wood finally shattered with an ear-splitting *crack,* as unforgiving as a backbone snapping in two. Grabbing her by the waist, he carried her out of the way just before the tree toppled to the ground with a thunderous crash. Cones and small branches rained down on them, and the entire forest shook from floor to ceiling.

Panting heavily, Billy dropped Kate on a bed of moss-covered sticks and tumbled to the ground beside her. He wiped the perspiration from his eyes with his T-shirt, then glared at the ungainly heap at his side.

"Of all the damn fool things," he said angrily. "You could've gotten us both killed."

Kate pushed herself slowly to a sitting position, wincing as she leaned against her injured knee. Her eyes met Billy's briefly, then looked past him to the fallen form in the center of the grove. She could not believe that a being so magnificent as the Ancient One was now destined to be reduced to an assortment of patio chairs, redwood decks, and hot tub sidings. More than a millennium of life— destroyed in no time at all by a single chain saw. Her gaze lifted to the gaping hole against the sky where the tree had once stood. Despite the new light now reaching the forest floor, she felt submerged in darkness.

"Don't you even say thanks?" fumed Billy. "I saved your life, for Pete's sake."

Sadly, she swung her face toward him, her eyes brimming with tears. "Thanks," she whispered, then turned away again.

For a long moment, Billy looked at her. Then, with a disgusted grunt, he rose to his feet. He stepped over to the chain saw, started to bend down to retrieve it, then caught himself. He straightened, glancing again at the mournful girl seated at the edge of the grove. A frown crossed his face and he said something under his breath. Then he turned and walked off sullenly into the forest.

A few moments later, a diminutive figure stole quietly out of the trees to Kate's side. Feeling herself suddenly embraced, she faced the person kneeling next to her. Blinking to see more clearly, she found herself looking straight into a pair of warm, ebony-colored eyes.

"Aunt Melanie," she said weakly. "It's you."

"It's me, dear," answered the white-haired woman, hugging her. At last she drew back, her shell earrings clinking softly as she moved. "I'm so glad you're all right. The walking stick kept you safe, didn't it?"

Kate could only nod.

The dark eyes studied her knowingly. "I wish I could have been with you."

"You were," answered Kate. Then she blurted, "The Ancient One. Billy—"

"I know, I know." She brushed a hand through her white curls. "But he's stopped now. Frank and I saw him heading for his truck as we were coming back here to try to find you."

"How—how could he?" Tears again filled her eyes.

Aunt Melanie looked to the ground. As she started to speak, she noticed Kate's swollen knee. "Your leg!" she exclaimed. "We should get you to the doctor."

"It hurts," sobbed Kate. "It hurts so much."

Aunt Melanie nodded, knowing full well that Kate did not mean the pain in her leg.

Just then a pair of heavy leather boots crunched toward them on the needles. A gaunt-looking man bent down to them. "Is she hurt?"

"Her knee, Frank."

"Let's take her back to town. Doc Harris can put anything back together."

Aunt Melanie glanced toward the fallen redwood. "Almost anything," she whispered.

afterword

FOR Kate, the next year flew past with the speed of a fast pitch. Her knee healed rapidly, and the Bulldogs' first-string shortstop was soon back on the field. But in contrast to prior years, softball was not Kate's sole diversion from classes. The school play, the Language Club, and the Time Travel Book Club (which she co-founded) also required lots of attention. She barely had any time to toss sticks with Cumberland in the yard, or even to write an occasional letter to Aunt Melanie.

Not that she didn't often wonder about Lost Crater, about Laioni and Kandeldandel, about the new park Aunt Melanie's letters described, about Jody and Frank and Billy. Sometimes, too, she woke up in the middle of the night, frightened by a dream about a giant tree crashing down on top of her. Yet just as often, she was overwhelmed with a craving for fresh huckleberry pie and spice tea. So it was with genuine enthusiasm that she accepted Aunt Melanie's invitation to visit her again during June. She did not need her parents' encouragement to say yes, as she had last year. This time, however, she packed her waterproof boots.

Once she arrived, she felt almost as if she had never left. The days were filled with fresh oatmeal cookies on top of homemade pie, the moist fragrance of spruce trees outside the cottage, the familiar musty smell within, the feeling of snuggling inside a soft quilt before the fire, laughter at Aunt Melanie's mischievous jokes, and of course the occasional peppermint candy. One evening Frank and Jody came by for supper, and Frank was coaxed to play his harmonica late into the night. After they left, Aunt Melanie read a poem that Jody had written about the pain of losing loved ones, a poem that Kate felt she could have written herself.

Kate and her great-aunt took walks together. They played Pooh Sticks on the bridge. They ate and ate, and ate some more. They talked freely, about the town's changes, about cooking with local herbs, about times good and bad.

And they talked about Kate's adventure. About Laioni, about Kandeldandel, about Gashra. The Touchstone. Fanona, whose voice Kate could still hear in her memory. The floating island of Ho Shantero. The Chieftain and Chieftess. Parching seeds the Halami way. The Stick of Fire. The Dark Valley. Sanbu. Monga. Nyla and her six Stonehag sisters. Whether Tinnanis still inhabited Lost Crater. The Slimnis. Arc. Thika. The Ancient One. And so much more. Although Aunt Melanie listened closely to each of Kate's descriptions, she seemed to pay special attention to any details regarding Laioni.

"You would have liked her," said Kate before slurping noisily from her mug of hot chocolate.

The white-haired woman smiled mysteriously. "I'm sure."

"I couldn't believe how much she was like you."

"We're all cut from the same cloth, you know," said Aunt Melanie. "Makes no difference whether we were born five years ago or five hundred years ago, whether we live on this side of the ocean or another." She scrutinized

Kate thoughtfully. "I imagine the same thing even holds true for tree spirits."

Suddenly Aunt Melanie tossed aside her quilt, rudely awakening Atha, who was curled up by her side. "That reminds me. I almost forgot. There's something you left behind last time you visited."

She darted out of the living room, trailed by Atha padding softly behind her. Soon the sound of boxes and furniture being slid around, plus a few angry grumbles, filled the cottage. Finally she returned, bearing two dilapidated sneakers, ragged and torn. One of them sported luminous green laces, while the other's laces were burned as black as charcoal.

"My sneakers!" exclaimed Kate. "I thought I'd lost them. I can't believe you kept them for a whole year."

"Just thought you might like to see them again." She added with a grin, "Though for the life of me I'll never understand how you could have let those nice green shoelaces get ruined."

"It's amazing, really. That the thing that brought me to my senses when Gashra was doing his best to trick me— was those stupid laces."

The elder nodded. "Now that's an impressive connection across time and space. Your grandfather would have loved to hear about it."

Kate laughed out loud. "That's for sure."

"By the way, how did your hand heal?"

"Just fine, except for this little scar."

Aunt Melanie took a peppermint from the abalone shell, popped it into her mouth, and offered one to her guest. "Here. Have one for the road."

"The road? Are we going someplace?"

She crunched down on the peppermint, then swallowed. "Yes, dear. We're going up to Lost Crater."

"Really? Is there still time today?"

"Just enough. The road's been paved. Of course, if you'd rather use the old ladder again, we could wait until tomorrow and go in that way."

Kate rolled her eyes. "Let's take the road."

Aunt Melanie smiled. "Somehow, that's what I thought you'd say. Let's go, then. There's something in the redwood grove I want you to see. A surprise." She gave Kate's hand a squeeze. "And don't worry. This time I'll remember to bring matches."

SOON Kate found herself walking with Aunt Melanie along a newly completed trail that started at the hole blasted one year ago in the wall of the crater, descended over the rocky slope and through the swamp, then wound its way deep into the Hidden Forest. Not so hidden anymore, Kate reflected, thinking of the large asphalt parking lot where Trusty sat next to a dozen other cars. Presently they came to a large painted sign saying:

Welcome to Cronon's Crater Park, containing the northernmost stand of ancient redwood trees in existence. Please remain on the trail. Exploration of other parts of the crater is strictly prohibited until scientific studies are completed.

As they moved down the trail, Kate drank in the rich aromas, abundant sounds, and lush green growth of this forest. Mist curled through the branches above; needles padded the ground below. With every step deeper into the virgin woods, she felt embraced by the vibrant array of life around her. Embraced, it almost seemed, by friends. Yet she also felt queasy, even a little bit frightened, to confront the sawed-off tombstone of the great redwood.

At one point she heard a soft laughter beside her and turned to Aunt Melanie. "What's so funny?"

"Oh," she replied, "I was just thinking about that silly Chieftain. Imagine thinking peppermints are such a great delicacy."

"I knew you'd get a kick out of that."

Aunt Melanie nodded. "Almost as much of a kick as I

get from owning a pack with a genuine arrow hole in it."
She swiveled slightly to reveal the prominent stitches in
the material of the blue day pack. "Awfully glad it wasn't
you instead."

"So am I," Kate replied.

Abruptly Kate halted. She stood again at the edge of
the clearing, facing the towering grove of redwood trees.
Upward they climbed, like columns supporting the dome
of the sky. A rush of reverence filled her, along with a
whisper of peace she had not felt for a year. And something
more, something strange, almost like a sense of gratitude
lingering among the boughs.

Then, in the center of the grove, she saw the stump. The
rest of the massive tree had been removed, so that its
remains jutted out of the ground with unnatural severity.
As Kate moved closer, she saw several small signs affixed
to the stump. One of them, positioned to face the trail,
read: *Height: 363 feet. Circumference: 27 feet. Weight:
513 tons. Age: 1,423 years.* On the face of the stump, signs
marked particular tree rings on the cambium or heartwood.
Said one: *Charlemagne crowned Emperor, 800 A.D.* Said
another: *Norman conquest of England, 1066 A.D.* Then,
moving outward toward the bark: *Eruption of Brimstone
Peak, 1452 A.D.; Fire scar, 1583 A.D.; Declaration of
Independence signed, 1776 A.D.; Severe fire scar, 1810
A.D.; Earthquake damage, 1847 A.D.* Last of all, at the
outer edge of the trunk, was this sign: *Felled by loggers,
1992 A.D.*

Turning to face Aunt Melanie, Kate asked, "Is this what
you meant by a surprise? These signs?"

The white head moved slowly from side to side. "Look
again."

Scrutinizing the stump once more, Kate noted the intricately drawn rings, some so close together they could
barely be distinguished. She scanned the thick band of
ridged bark encircling the wood, the burly roots at the
base. Yet she could not find anything that could have
prompted Aunt Melanie's interest.

Suddenly she noticed something else. At the far edge of the stump, lifting its tiny head skyward, sprouted a single young seedling. It stood barely a foot tall, yet its branches were lined with new-growth needles, no less green than a pair of shoelaces she had once worn.

She glanced at Aunt Melanie, who smiled at her gently. Then she stepped over to the seedling and bent lower to touch it. Running her finger down its length, all the way to the delicate, hairlike roots, she could feel both sturdiness and suppleness in its fibers. The young redwood held itself with unmistakable dignity, seemingly aware of what had stood before on the same spot.

As she straightened up, Kate caught sight of a small, rust-colored owl resting on the lowest branch of a neighboring tree. He studied her with wide brown eyes above flowing whisker-feathers, looking for all the world like a great-great-great grandson of Arc. The owl fluttered his wings slightly.

Then, from another direction, Kate heard the sound of an owl hooting deeply, richly. It hung eerily in the air, like the call of a distant flute.